retromancer

retromancer

Robert Rankin

RETROMANCER

GOLLANCZ
London

Copyright © Robert Rankin 2009

The right of Robert Rankin to be identified as the author of this
work has been asserted by him in accordance with the
Copyright, Designs and Patents Act 1988.

First published in Great Britain in 2009 by Gollancz
An imprint of the Orion Publishing Group
Orion House, 5 Upper St Martin's Lane, London WC2H 9EA
An Hachette UK company

A CIP catalogue record for this book is
available from the British Library

ISBN 978 0 575 07872 7 (Cased)
ISBN 978 0 575 08497 1 (Export Trade Paperback)

1 3 5 7 9 10 8 6 4 2

Typeset at The Spartan Press Ltd,
Lymington, Hants

Printed and bound in the UK by
CPI Mackays, Chatham ME5 8TD

The Orion Publishing Group's policy is to use papers that
are natural, renewable and recyclable products and made
from wood grown in sustainable forests. The logging and
manufacturing processes are expected to conform to the
environmental regulations of the country of origin.

www.thegoldensprout.com

www.orionbooks.co.uk

FOR MY GOOD FRIEND

NEIL GARDNER

WITH MANY MANY
MANY THANKS

He named me Rizla, and for one extraordinary year I was his acolyte, his assistant and his amanuensis.

And also too, I would like to think, his friend.

His name was Hugo Artemis Solon Saturnicus Reginald Arthur Rune and I have no qualms in stating that he was without a doubt the most remarkable personage I have ever encountered.

An adventurer and world traveller – 'of *this* and many others', he assured me. One-time circus strongman, prizefighter, expert swords-man and Master of Dimac. Gourmet, connoisseur of fine wines and finer women, mystic, guru to gurus, reinventor of the ocarina, private detective and Best-Dressed Man of Nineteen Thirty-Three. Mr Rune had been there, done that *and* invented the T-shirt.

Many and marvellous were the claims of this singular individual. That he had once jogged alone to the South Pole, clad in naught but his brogues and shooting-tweeds and sporting upon his head a copy of *The Times* newspaper that he had fashioned into a hat. This perilous journey he had undertaken to 'tickle the fancy of a most bewitching lady' – Scott of the Antarctic's less famous sister, Dot.*

Everest too – 'a walk in the park' – he had conquered, again in his tweeds, although this time with the encumbrance of George Bernard Shaw, to whom he gave a piggyback.

'I asked Shaw whether he might care to come along for the ride as it were and the buffoon literally took me at my word.'

I confess that it felt natural to me to doubt such extravagant and outlandish claims. But each time I did, some independent piece of

---

* Dot of the Antarctic was the founder of TSFTFSOTF, the unpronounceable and instantly forgettable acronym of The Society for the Forgotten Sisters of the Famous. In its heyday TSFTFSOTF numbered amongst its members not only Florence of Arabia, Fay Guevara and Sharon Munchausen, but also Jordon of Khartoum and Julia Caesar. Today the society is, alas, all but forgotten.

corroborative evidence would appear to confer legitimacy upon all that Mr Rune averred.

His was *the* extravagant shadow, cast in the fashionable places of his day. *He* was the Man of the Moment, prepared to give his all in the Fight for Right. And his knack for always being in the right place at the right time when history was being made was nothing less than uncanny.

But as is often the case with those whose lives transcend the everyday, Mr Rune was not without his foibles and eccentricities. An inveterate diner-out at swank eateries, he harboured an all but pathological aversion to actually paying for the inordinate quantities of gourmet food and vintage wine that he consumed.

'I offer the world my genius,' he often said. 'All I ask in return is that the world cover my expenses.'

And the brutality he meted out to cabbies, who he would smite with his stout stick upon the flimsiest of pretexts and with next to no provocation, is well recorded.

'I have no comment to make at this time, your honour.'

Such matters as these might well be viewed as smudges upon his otherwise besmirchless record of public service, but considering the scale of his achievements, they should best be forgiven and forgotten.

During the twelve months that I spent in his exalted company, I aided him in the solution of twelve Cosmic Conundra. The very fabric of human existence hung upon the success of our adventures together and Mr Rune being Mr Rune came through and saved the day.

I chronicled these adventures in a book entitled *The Brightonomicon*, which later became an award-winning radio series starring that distinguished Shakespearian actor David Warner in the part of Mr Rune.

The Brightonomicon, or Brighton Zodiac as it was also called, consisted of twelve new zodiac signs discovered by Mr Rune. Carriageway constellations, formed from the layout of roads and streets in Brighton.

Each zodiac sign represented one of the Cosmic Conundra that we had to solve in order that the fabric of human existence should remain unfrayed. And each in turn led us closer to our ultimate Mankind-saving goal of acquiring the Chronovision.

The Chronovision was a 'window upon time', a fantastic device created by a Benedictine monk named Father Ernetti. It resembled a nineteen-fifties-style Bakelite television set, but there all connection with normalcy ended. Because upon its screen could be viewed events that had occurred in the past. Events that had taken place long before the invention of television.

I myself can vouch for its authenticity because I had the chilling experience of watching the actual crucifixion of Christ on the Chronovision. Something that moved me beyond words and which I will never forget.

Twelve Cosmic Conundra, each a case to be solved, we solved together, and at last secured the Chronovision.

At times I felt that the route we took was somewhat circuitous and availed Mr Rune of my opinions regarding this. But he always put me straight upon the matter.

'There are always twelve cases,' he told me, 'and all are always to do with time. It is what I do and what I am. This is how it has always been and how it must always be. Twelve Cosmic Conundra, twelve cases to be solved, all leading as one to a final solution.'

And who was I to doubt him? Because in the end we succeeded and I felt that I played my part. And what times we had. Fraught with peril and danger, but filled with excitement. What thrills.

The cases were outré and their outcome unpredictable (although Mr Rune would perhaps argue otherwise regarding the unpredict-ability). Peopled with extraordinary personalities. Bartholomew the Bog Troll Buccaneer, Chief Whitehawk, Fangio the ever-present barlord. Not to mention Norris Styver, the demonic driver of a phan-tom Morris Minor that circumnavigates the one-way system of Lewes for ever and ever. And indeed Mr Rune's arch-enemy, the Moriarty to his Holmes. The most evil man who ever lived, Count Otto Black.

How vividly I recall these cases, involving as they did an atomic-powered subterranean ark, space crabs from another galaxy, a statue of Queen Victoria that wept tears of Earl Grey, a killer robot from the past, numerous pirates, sundry supernatural entities, witches, weirdos and countless tiny spaniels. And, I must add, it was with considerable awe that I came to meet Lord Tobes, the many-times great-grandson of Jesus Christ.

It was indeed a very big adventure.

And when it was all over, I returned to the world of the everyday. Conveyed back into it by Mr Rune in such a fashion that although a year had passed for me, but a single day had passed for those in that everyday world.

And I returned to my life, my everyday life, as an unemployed teenager in a West London suburb called Brentford. And I must confess that in doing so I came to feel a certain lack. For after the wonders I had seen and the dangers and thrills I had encountered, this everyday world now held little charm for me. And I wondered whether I would ever see Mr Hugo Rune again. And indeed whether Mr Hugo Rune had actually existed, and whether my adventures in the company of that astonishing individual were nothing more than Far-Fetched Fiction. And had it not been for certain tangible items that remained in my possession to assure me of the reality of my adventures, these conclusions may well have been drawn by me, as they were by others to whom I revealed them.

Ah, yes, for a single year I had inhabited a world of wonder. But I now knew that it was over and so I must apply myself to that terrible something which inspires horror and disgust within the minds of all right-thinking teenagers.

That the awful blight that must inevitably fall upon them must also fall upon me.

That I must embrace and engage with the real and the everyday and take on the . . . *Regular Employment.*

1

But before that, let me record but briefly. Regarding myself, my name is James Arbuthnot Pooley and I was born, educated and live in Brentford, which is acknowledged by many to be London's most beautiful borough. It lies to the west of the capital, lovingly cradled in an aqueous elbow of old Mother Thames. It is home.

For the most part Brentford has escaped the monstrous excesses and wanton vandalism of the town planning department, retaining its period charm, with notable historic vistas that bring joy to all who behold them. Blessed indeed are the fine folk of Brentford and proud am I to be one of them.

My parents I do not remember. The precise circumstances of their demise have never been made known to me. An accident, I have been given to understand. A family tragedy. And although I have asked many times I have as yet to receive a satisfactory reply.

Both mother and father to me has been my Aunt Edna. A cheery soul, who bustles about in an abundance of gingham, doing all that she can to school me in the ways of the world and teach me 'values'. *Noble* values these – friendship, chivalry, trustworthiness, compassion and the rest. To be virtuous, to be decent, and I do try to be good.

And so it is with some regret that I must begin this tale in a more fragile state than would normally be my wont. For I confess that the previous night I had engaged most liberally in the pleasures of the pump room.

I had downed much beer, in celebration of my return from my year-long adventure, and I had done this in the company of my bestest friend, John Vincent Omally.

John is Irish born and Brentford bred. A lad of my own age, if perhaps lacking for my natural sophistication. A rough diamond, but a mucker, a mate, my chum.

We had drunk and we had ambled home, the borough bathed by moonlight of the fullest. Such beauty as to make a fellow sigh.

But now to awake in suddenness.

And shock. Upon this February morning.

The sunlight pierced the gap between my curtains, striped the laundered linen of my pillow, worried at my eyelids, warmed upon my chin. And I did yawnings of the mouth and awoke as the world went wild.

'*Achtung! Achtung! And a guten Morgen.*' Or so it sounded to me. And it came loudly to my ears and I liked not its sounding.

This din came from the electric alarm clock wireless set, which had been a present to me from my Aunt Edna. That its rantings should encourage me from bed each morning and urge me off on my way to work.

Work being something that my aunt spoke seriously and often about to me. For she was keen that I get to it.

For myself, well—

'*Achtung! Achtung!*' went that voice once more. And I knew well that voice. It was the voice of Mickey Nicholson, or Lad Nicholson as he preferred to be called. Or the Voice of Free Radio Brentford, as he was widely known in the borough.

Free Radio Brentford was our local pirate station. It operated from the interior of a commandeered Post Office van, which the Lad kept on the move to avoid detection by the authorities.

Its transmitter had been cobbled together from an extraordinary collection of bits and bobs and a great deal of Meccano by Norman Hartnel (not to be confused with the other Norman Hartnel). Norman was a good friend of mine, whose daddy owned the corner shop on the Ealing Road.

'*Achtung! Achtung! Achtung!*'

'What is all this *achtunging*?' I dragged myself from the desecrated comfort of my cosy bed and sought to tear the wireless set's plug from the socket. A task I did of a morning. If I had neglected to do it of a night before. And here I encountered an anomaly. Today there was no plug to be found; the cable simply vanished into the wall.

'Most unsporting, Aunt Edna,' I said. And I shook the alarm clock wireless set affair about. There did not appear to be an on/off switch on it either.

Lad Nicholson was now prattling on about what a great day today was for the workers and how if we all just pulled together that little bit harder, then an assured future of peace and prosperity awaited us.

This I found somewhat odd. This was hardly his usual style. The Lad's usual style was somewhat more laid-back, prettily coloured by the heroic quantities of recreational drugs he was known to consume. This being the swinging sixties and everything. So what all this *achtunging* was about was anyone's guess, but not mine, I concluded.

I smothered the alarm clock wireless set jobbie beneath my pillow, dragging my sheet and blanket over it too to staunch the sonic assault on my person.

And then I sat down on the lot of it.

'*Achtung!*' I said. 'What next?'

My Aunt Edna was of that order of sensible beings who understand the value of a hearty breakfast. That it is the most important meal of the day. The very foundation upon which all that lies ahead might be built. Oh yes.

And I was determined that I would tackle same, whilst giving thoughtful contemplation to the matter of regular employment, and so I dressed, vacated my bedroom and took myself down to the kitchen.

To confront another anomaly.

'What is this?' I so enquired, as I viewed the plate before me. The gas-ring goddess smiled down at my person between her bounteous bosoms.

And said the word, 'Bratwurst.'

'Bratwurst?' I queried.

'Bratwurst,' she confirmed. 'The very Führer of the sausage world. Pork and veal, with salt and pepper, nutmeg, parsley, marjoram, celery seed and ginger.'

'That sounds appalling,' was my opinion. 'Whatever happened to the usual bacon and eggs? And English sausages? And black pudding? And the fried slice? And—'

Aunt Edna took to laughing to the busting of her bust. She placed her hands upon her hips, rocked to and fro and scuffed her blakeys on the tiled floor. Which caused static electricity to crackle between the knees of her surgical stockings.

'You'll be the death of me,' she managed, breathlessly, between great gustos of hilarity. 'Whatever next, as I live and breathe, oh mercy, mercy me.'

And then, still chuckling and sparking about the knee regions, she took herself off to the Krupps to brew coffee.

The Krupps? I took in this intelligence. A Krupps cooker? Here in *our* house? 'What is *this*?' I now asked of my aunt. 'A Krupps cooker? Surely this is new. What happened to the old grey enamel jobbie that you always assured me would see you out, if not the returned Messiah in?'

Aunt Edna laughed some more, then said, 'The young,' in a manner that I considered a tad dismissive.

'And *coffee*?' I added. 'Not tea?'

'And there you go again.' And Aunt Edna clutched at her chest. 'You *will* be the death of me and there's a sad fact for us all.'

And would not you know it, or would not you not, I did not get breakfast at all. I pushed aside my Bratwurst in a pointed manner which I hoped she would see the point of and informed my aunt that I would take my breakfast elsewhere that morning.

'Before seeking work?'

'A long time before *that*, yes.'

'And will you need money for the bus?'

'For the bus and breakfast too.'

My aunt took herself off to her purse and returned in the company of paper money, which she pushed into my outstretched hand. I smiled up upon my aunt and she smiled down at me.

'You are a good boy, James,' she said as she smiled. 'I know that if your dear mother was here you would try to make her proud. But as she is not, do you think that you might try to make *me* proud instead?'

'I will certainly try,' I said.

'So I can expect that you will return later on with the good news that you have secured employment?'

'I can guarantee at least fifty per cent of that,' I said. 'I will certainly return later on.'

'But you will go to the Hall of Labour, won't you?' asked my aunt.

'The *what*?' I asked in return.

'Enough of your tomfoolery,' said she, and she hoisted me from my chair and propelled me from the kitchen and into the hall.

And from there through the open front doorway.

'You will find yourself regular employment,' she told me. 'Today,' she told me. 'At all costs,' she told me. 'Or I will be forced to inform upon you.'

This she told me too.
'You will do *what*?' I now asked of her.
But she slammed the door upon me.

2

It is funny at times what sticks in your mind and what apparently does not. I had lived for all of my life thus far in this Brentford backstreet named Mafeking Avenue, but I had never noticed before that the street sign was bilingual – English below, and above that, in the distinctive Gothic font that says 'German', what I took to be the German equivalent.

I viewed this with some surprise. How had a thing like that managed to slip by me for all these years? Or was it perhaps new? I stood and I viewed and considered that, no, it was not.

I shrugged and considered my hangover. And as it did not seem to be worthy of consideration, I dismissed it from my mind. What I needed now was breakfast. A brisk walk, then a bellyful.

Upon the rooftops and up in the trees, sparrows sang the songs their mothers had taught them. And as I breezed along in the unfailingly cheerful manner that is natural to me, I joined these jolly birdies in their choruses.

And as I breezed along a-whistling, a thought came unto me regarding the smoking of cigarettes. I had for some time been thinking about taking up the smoking. The smoking was a manly thing; so much was clear from the shop window advertisements that extolled the virtues of the smoking. Men admired and ladies loved a smoker. A man without a smoke was not quite a man.

The most famous brand known unto me was Wild Woodbine. Then at the very peak of its popularity, Sir Edmund Hillary had brought fame to the Wild Woodbine a decade before when he smoked them as he conquered Everest (some twenty years after Hugo Rune, it should be noted, and Mr Rune smoked his Woodbines in an ivory cigarette holder on the way up).

Ah yes, the Wild Woodbine.

I paused on the corner of Mafeking Avenue and considered the brief twenty paces to the Ealing Road and the corner confectioner's, tobacconist's and newsagent's that was Old Mr Hartnel's shop. Old Mr Hartnel always went angling down at the Grand Union Canal on Monday mornings with his best friend Far-Fetched Frank. And left the shop in the care of his son Norman. My friend Norman. My friend Norman who would surely sell me some cigarettes, even though I was underage.

Hm.

I did bobbings of the head. If I was to make an attempt at securing regular employment today, then surely my chances of securing it would be greatly enhanced if I turned up for the interview with a Wild Woodbine sticking out of my face. Of course it would.

So, Wild Woodbine first and then the full English.

Sorted.

Old Mr Hartnel did not hold with modernity. His corner shop had hardly changed at all during the preceding thirty years. It was all indeed what the past had been, but right here in the present, and I loved it.

I pushed upon the shop door and the shop bell rang. A clarion clanger announcing that one had entered from the outside world into this world where all time stood still and the past was ever-present.

And you can smell the past, you really can. The past smells like the interiors of old wardrobes. And the lavender bags that perfume the drawers of your aunty's dressing table. And mothballs and musty tweeds and cigarette smoke on net curtains, and wax furniture polish and Brasso and sometimes baking bread.

And as the shop door closed behind me, I stood in the uncertain light that struggled to gain entry through rarely washed upper windowpanes and I breathed in that smell of the past and said—

'What is that terrible pong?'

And behind the ancient counter Norman grinned. He stood and he grinned before those shelves that held those jars with their nostalgic-looking labels and their humbugs and sherbet lemons and rhubarbs and custards and hundreds and thousands and Google's Gob Gums.

And all the other wonderful sweets within this wonderful shop.

Norman wore an old-fashioned shopkeeper's coat. This had been a present from his father for his sixteenth birthday. As Norman had outgrown the one his father had given him for his tenth birthday. And Norman wore this and grinned a bit more and then he said, 'Hello.'

'Hello to yourself,' I said to the grinner. 'And once more, what is that terrible pong?'

'It is sulphur,' said Norman. 'Or brimstone, if you prefer.'

'I exhibit no preference,' I replied. 'I simply abhor its pestilential pehuverance. Could you not open a window? Or something?'

'I tried *something*,' said Norman. 'I tried opening my mouth. But it hasn't helped. And I'm not allowed to open the windows. My daddy says that the ambience might escape if I do.'

'Your daddy will not take kindly to you poisoning his ambience with brimstone,' I suggested.

'You're right,' agreed Norman. 'Which is why I shall not be mentioning it to him.'

I opened *my* mouth to give voice to the obvious, but instead asked, 'Wherefrom comes this pungent pong?'

'From the Bottomless Pit,' replied Norman. 'I have discovered its entrance upon upping some tiles in the kitchenette. Just as predicted, I hasten to say.'

'By whom?' I enquired.

'By me. Through a fastidious study of the Book of Revelation with the aid of a pocket calculator that I built from Meccano and more judgement than luck, in a nutshell.'

'Right,' I said. And I nodded my head. Not fast, but somewhat sagely.

'Doubting Thomas,' said Norman.

'Not a bit of it,' said I. 'Conduct me to the kitchenette and I will cast a glance at this pit.'

'Regrettably, no,' said Norman. 'I am not allowed to leave the shop unattended. Perhaps some other time.'

'Perhaps.'

'When I have completed my experiments, which are presently ongoing. I have tipped all manner of toot into that pit and as yet I have not heard one thing strike its bottom.'

'Which does not necessarily mean that it does not have one,' I said to Norman. 'It might well have one a good way down that is soft and absorbs sound. Have you considered that?'

'Naturally,' said Norman, and he drummed his fingers upon the countertop to the tune of Hubert Parry and William Blake's

'Jerusalem'. 'It is the real McClooty. The biblical Bottomless Pit, wherein lurk the demonic beasties that frequent those unholy and unfathomable regions.'

'I frankly have misgivings regarding this,' I now said. 'I fear that catastrophe awaits you, should you not cover up this pit hole post-haste. Beasties and unfathomable regions notwithstanding, yourself, or your daddy, might step or trip unwarily and—' And I mimed the tumbling down and down.

'Nice miming,' said Norman. 'And point well taken. But considering the benefits to Mankind that my discovery will bring, I can hardly just cover it up again, can I?'

I did shruggings of the shoulders and set free the hint of a sigh. 'Do pardon me,' I said, politely, 'but what, *precisely*, might these benefits be?'

'Oh, do wake up,' Norman said. And he tapped at his left temple with the forefinger of his left hand. 'It is the *Bottomless* Pit. Which means that anything you dump into it will keep falling for ever and ever and never hit the bottom.'

I shrugged once more.

'Which means,' Norman continued, 'that it could become the most valuable resource on the planet. How ironic, eh? That something deemed so evil can have the potential to do so much good.'

'I am perplexed,' said I.

And, 'Rubbish,' said Norman.

'No, I really *am*.'

'Not *you* talking rubbish, although you so often do. I mean all the rubbish of Mankind, all the detritus and junk, the toxic waste, the contaminated muck. The whole damn kit and caboodle.'

And Norman mimed tumbling down and down.

'All flushed down the Bottomless Pit,' he said. 'Naturally I will make a small charge for each dumping. I feel that the pecuniary benefits might be substantial. And—' and he buffed his fingernails upon his lapel '—I would not be at all surprised if I was awarded a Nobel Prize for my services to Humankind.' And Norman grinned some more.

And I said, 'No. No. No. No, no, no upon so many levels. That is *not* a good idea, Norman. Not a good idea at all. I fear that the beasties will take umbrage and also the good people of Brentford, who might not take too kindly to you turning the borough into the waste disposal capital of the world.'

Norman made a thoughtful face. 'You might have a point,' he conceded. 'What if they brought the waste around to the back? And at night?'

'And the beasties?'

'We'll cross that bridge when we come to it.'

'Carefully,' said I and tapped at my nose. 'Most carefully indeed.'

And Norman grinned and then he said, 'So how might I help you, sir?'

'I would like five Wild Woodbines, please, my good man,' I said.

And Norman, still grinning, shook his head. 'You're underage,' he said to me. 'Now please get out of the shop.'

3

He parted with those Wild Woodbines, did Norman. And with a box of Swan Vestas. And he did not charge me for either. Because, as I told him, if he did not hand over same I would find myself forced to mention to his daddy that the shop now smelled of brimstone, which quite spoiled its period ambience.

I tucked both cigarettes and matches into my pockets and prepared to take my leave, warning Norman just the once more that he should give the Bottomless Pit business a severe good thinking about. And that although I could see the sound foundations for financial opportunity, the probability of cataclysmic repercussions, of an apocalyptic or Armageddon End Times nature, tainted these considerably. And then I asked, 'What are those?'

And Norman said, 'What do you mean?'

And I pointed at what I meant and asked once more as to what it was that I was pointing at.

'Why, Champagne truffles, of course,' said Norman. 'Whatever did you think they were?'

'I did not think anything. Which was why I asked.'

'They're everyone's favourite,' said Norman. 'We can't get enough of them to satisfy demand.'

'That is evidentially untrue.'

'It's a figure of speech, or term of endearment or suchlike. But they are *very* popular and have been for as long as I can remember.'

'Then how come I have never heard of them?'

Norman shrugged his shopkeeper's shoulders. 'I've no idea. You'll be telling me next that you've never heard of *Kirschwasser* truffles.' And Norman did lip-smackings and rubbed at his belly. 'Or *Mandel Splitters*. Or *Mandel Krokant Karos*. Or *Alex Vierecks*. Or—'

'No,' I said, shaking my head with vigour. 'You are making up all these names.'

'I'm not,' said Norman. 'They're up on the shelves. In the old sweetie jars. The ones with the nostalgic-looking labels.'

And I looked on and I beheld. And it was as Norman had said. There amongst the sweeties that I knew and loved were others that I knew not of.

'For such is printed on the nostalgic-looking labels,' said Norman. 'So such must they be QED.'

'I like not this conversation,' I said, 'and I know not of these confections. Surely this is some kind of elaborate hoax.'

'It is no such thing,' said Norman, a-shaking of his head. 'But isn't it interesting how hoaxes are always "elaborate"? I'd have thought that a quite simple hoax would be sufficient to fool most people. Wouldn't you?'

'Indeed,' I agreed. And I viewed once more the anomalous sweetie jars. 'Well, I am away now,' I said. 'Off for breakfast and then possibly to search for regular employment.'

'What?' And Norman made gagging, choking sounds. 'Regular employment? *You?* Oh, wait, I see. Your Aunt Edna is prodding you in that direction, isn't she? I'll bet she's threatening to inform upon you if you don't take a job and soon.'

'Well—' I said.

'Then best take yourself and your ill-won spoils off to the Hall of Labour at the hurry-up. The bounties that the Party offers to informers nowadays make the prospect of informing, even upon one's own, a tempting proposition.'

'What?' I now said to Norman. 'What are you talking about? Your words are strange to me and if there is meaning hidden within them, then this meaning surpasseth my understanding.'

'Sometimes you have a lovely way with words.' Norman pointed towards the door. 'Why not take yourself off somewhere and hide and have a nice smoke, or something.'

'All right,' I said. 'And I will pay you for the fags and the matches. I am not quite feeling myself today, it must be something I ate last night. Or something.'

'Something you *drank*,' said Norman. 'Something you *drank* last night. I was with you, don't you recall? You got in that big argument with the landlord about the beer.'

'I did?' And then I recalled that I had. And how Norman had been with John and me the previous night. 'I had forgotten that business about the beer,' I said to Norman.

'Well, I haven't. How embarrassing was *that*? "I want English beer," you went, "I want a pint of Large." They haven't served beer like that since the Second World War, you nutter.'

'Oh dear,' I said and I felt somewhat giddy.

And I paid Norman for both ciggies and matches, because I felt bad about blackmailing him out of them, and I wished him well for the balance of the day. And then I took my leave.

I had now reached a state of no small confusion. I did recall, although blurrily, that I had argued with the landlord about English ale. I had wanted it and the landlord had told me not to be absurd and that fine Rhineland lagers were good enough for any Party Member and that I should keep my dissenting opinions to myself because walls had ears.

And there had been some unpleasantness and I had been ejected from the establishment. John and Norman hard upon my tumbling heels.

'Oh dear,' I said once more, although this time only to myself. 'I do not think that I am altogether the full shilling. Perhaps with a hearty breakfast inside me all will fall into place.'

And so I took myself off to the Wife's Legs Café.

The Wife's Legs Café lacked not for its share of nostalgia. It had been fitted out in the middle years of the rockin' fifties, with much chrome work and a frothy-coffee machine and had since remained untouched.

I entered with a stepping that was not quite so breezy as it had formerly been, but still had a smidgen of spring left in it. Behind the counter stood the wife, as lovely as a bonnet that lacked for a bee (as the poet will have it) and a-stirring at something in a great big pot.

Chairs and tables spoke eloquently of a decade past and supported, respectively, the bottoms and breakfasts of the Wife's Legs' patrons. Well-knit working men were these, with mighty bottom cleavage (or artisan's cleft, as they preferred to call it), a-tucking into their tucker. There were ladies of the night-time also, dining before heading home. A dwarf or two, as the circus was in town. And one or two fellows in sharp black uniforms of a type that I could not readily identify. These gazed morosely around and about and conversed in muted

Neanderthal tones. I shrugged a shrug, rubbed palm upon palm and took me up to the counter.

'Good morning to you, the wife,' said I to the proprietress.

'Good morning to you, Jim,' replied this lady. 'John not with you this morning?'

'I suspect that he is probably having a lie-in. He imbibed somewhat freely last evening and lacks for my hardy disposition.'

Certain sounds issued from the mouth of the wife. Tinkling fairy-like sounds, not unlike those of stifled laughter.

'Quite so,' she said, when she had done with this. 'You certainly are a regular little storm trooper and no mistake.'

'This term is strange to me, sweet lady,' said I. 'But if it is meant as the compliment that I take it to be, then so shall I take it as such.'

'You do that very thing,' said the wife. And fairy-tinklings followed.

'So,' I said, 'I am planning to pursue certain career opportunities today and will therefore require suitable sustenance of the breakfast persuasion. All found, fried, with double bangers and toast.'

'Bratwurst?' said the wife.

'Not even close.' And I raised my eyebrows.

'Then—' And then she spoke, naming other victuals.

Victuals of a Germanic nature, whose names, I supposed, should they be printed, would be also in that distinctive Gothic font.

'I will have to stop you there,' I told her. 'I want the full *English*.'

And would not you know it, or would not you not, at the exact moment that I voiced the word *English*, all conversation momentarily ceased within the Wife's Legs Café, which made the word sound terribly loud within so very much silence.

And heads turned towards me and people took to staring.

'What?' I said. '*What?* I want a full English. Where is the problem with this?' And I stared from face to face of them and they stared back at me.

In the corner by the door sat octogenarian Old Pete, with his half-spaniel Chips. And Old Pete crossed at himself and I swear that his dog did likewise.

'English,' I reiterated. '*The Full English Breakfast.* I want one and I want it now.'

And, 'Out of my cafe!' bawled the wife. 'We'll have no such sedition here. Go back to Russia, you communist swine.'

'To *Russia*?' I said. 'For an *English*?'

But now the wife raised her stirring spoon and menaced me with it. And I heard someone say, as in a stage whisper, 'Here's one to be informed upon, there's bound to be a good bounty.'

And then I saw the morose-looking fellows in the black uniforms rising from their seats and reaching towards gun-holsters on their hips.

And I knew then it was time to leave.

Indeed, and time to run also.

And run I did, at speed. And any traces of former breeziness and jollity were no longer to be discerned in the style of my urgent perambulation. Out of the door ran I and right off down the street.

And behind me I heard shoutings. And these in the German tongue. *Schnell! Schnell!* And *Handy-Hok*, or so it seemed to me. And these foreign shoutings were not music to my ears and I ran on and on.

I evaded my pursuers somewhere down near the Memorial Park and settled myself into a hideaway in the midst of a large clump of bushes. This had in childhood days gone by been a camp for John and myself. And I now gnawed at my knuckles and did rockings to and fro. Everything was wrong wrong wrong. All about me it was wrong, yet I seemed the only one to be aware of it.

I tried to calm down and take stock. It had all begun with Lad Nicholson's *achtungings*. And my Aunt Edna offering me Bratwurst and speaking of the Hall of Labour and informing. And then there had been the bilingual street signs and the German sweeties at Old Mr Hartnel's. And more talk of informing from Norman and then all that at the Wife's Legs Café.

What did it all mean?

And then I had a revelation. As one does. Sometimes.

German. German. German. And those men in the black uniforms. They were Gestapo. Something terrible had happened. Overnight. Brentford had been invaded. By latter-day Nazis. And not only invaded. The people of Brentford had been brainwashed, perhaps with some top-secret mind-altering drug – brainwashed into believing that everything was all right. As it should be. As it always had been.

And I was the only one who knew otherwise. Knew the truth – because . . .

Well, why?

Because of some special mutant gene in my DNA that made me immune to the mind-altering drugs, perhaps—

Or more likely—

Yes, more likely it was because I had been away for a year – a year that Mr Rune had turned into a day. And all of this had gone on while I was away.

That had to be it. That all made sense.

'Well,' I whispered to myself, 'that has to be it. It all falls into place. And—' and I brightened somewhat at this '—I will tell you what it also means.' And I took out one of my Wild Woodbines. 'It means that whatever I do today, it *will not* be seeking employment!'

4

And so I smoked my first Wild Woodbine.

It drew not the admiring glances of my fellows, nor caused the ladies' hearts to flutter. It made me gag and cough and croak, but such is the way with the smoking.

I did fannings at the air. I had no wish to be discovered by raising any smoke signals. Nor did I wish for some Nazi officer with a thing about Moses taking an interest in what might appear to be a burning bush.

I coughed some more, but quietly. Smoking was good for the nerves, I had heard. Far better indeed than the cup of tea that my Aunt Edna considered a universal panacea. But my nerves, alas, were all a-jangle and the Wild Woodbine searing my throat and convulsing my lungs did not seem to be helping much at all. Perhaps I was smoking it wrong.

I took tiny little sippings of smoke and settled back against a bush trunk that had my own initials carved upon it. This indeed was a fine kettle of fish and things had come to a pretty pass and I was deep in doggy-do which was no fun at all.

Because, hide as I might now, I would sooner or later have to go home. And it was anybody's guess, although a reasonably sound one, as to what would be awaiting me there.

Germans in black uniforms!

Because this *was* Brentford and almost everyone knew where I lived. And there were apparently big rewards for informers.

I took to flapping my hands just a little. Flapping my hands quite a lot and turning around in small circles has always been a habit of mine when I find myself in severe peril. It helps me to concentrate. To focus. And should in no way be confused with a display of terror and blind panic. Certainly not.

I took deep breaths. I needed a plan.

And then I thought of Mr Rune.

What would Hugo do?

He would bluff and bluster it out, I supposed, then triumph and end the day with a slap-up meal at the Gestapo's expense. But Mr Rune was not here and so I was going to have to deal with this all on my ownsome. The prospect held no charm.

I could, of course, make a run for it. Have it away on my toes to parts distant. That would indeed be a plan. Supposing, of course, that this Nazi mind-control-invasion business was a localised affair. Which surely it had to be. The entire country could not be infected by this madness, surely. Across the river to Kew, that would be the best bet, regroup, as it were, and then return. With what? With a liberating army of manly hard-nosed Woodbine-smoking warriors. That would be what's what.

'Kew it is, then,' I whispered to myself. And would not you know it, or would not you not, my voice, it seemed, had dropped by an octave. And I had only been smoking for two minutes. *Result!*

'Kew it is, then,' I said once more in a gruff voice and manly fashion. And climbing to my feet, I straightened up my shoulders and thrust out my chest. I was on a noble mission here and I *was* up to the challenge. I slotted the ciggie into the corner of my mouth and stepped from the cover of the bushes.

And then I skulked away towards the High Street.

The High Street had undergone sufficient subtle changes for all trace of subtlety to be thoroughly erased.

Bunting hung across the street. Red bunting with white circular centrepieces on which were displayed the dreaded swastika. And I could hear the distinctive sounds of brass-band music issuing from this open shop doorway and that one too. And there was much in the way of German-manufactured odds and soddery to be seen in each shop window and a selection of German sausages in the butcher's that was nothing less than a cliché.

'This will not be going on in Kew,' I whispered hoarsely to myself. 'The posh folk of Kew will be unaffected by this Aryan taint. All will be well in Kew.'

I turned up the collar of my jacket, despite the clemency of the weather, hunched my shoulders and hurried up my steppings.

'Jim,' I heard a voice call out. And then I took to running.

'Jim – stop, you buffoon. Hold on there, Jim.'

And I knew that voice, so I stopped and I turned. And there was John Omally. My good friend John. My bestest friend. A friend in need, indeed.

'John,' I said. And I took a deep breath.

'You have a fag,' said John Omally. 'Give us a puff of that fag.'

'Have it, my friend,' I said. And I would have plucked it from my mouth's corner, where it was firmly lodged, despite all run and talk, had Omally not beaten me to it.

'A Wild Woodbine,' he declared. And he took a great toke upon it. And then he took to violent coughing, which cheered me not a little.

'Why were you running away?' he asked, once he had been able to draw a decent breath and wipe the tears from his eyes.

'The Gestapo are after me,' I told him.

'Your Aunt Edna has at last informed upon you?'

I looked hard at Omally. 'You too,' I said, in scarce but a whisper.

'Me too what?' himself replied.

'This Nazi thing,' I said. 'The Nazis, here in Brentford.'

'What about them?' Omally asked.

'Well, they should not be here, should they?'

'Well, of course they shouldn't. Which is why you and me will be joining the Resistance. As soon as we're old enough.'

'The Resistance?' I said. 'Oh yes,' I also said.

'They have to be beaten,' said Omally. 'Otherwise you and I are going to have to take to the Work. And I for one of us am not keen at all on that scenario.'

'No,' said I. 'Nor me. But I must speak to you of these things and I am all confused. Let us go somewhere and talk.'

'The Wife's Legs Café?'

'Not there.'

'Then down to Cider Island.'

Cider Island is a tiny parcel of land that lies for the most part hidden behind tall walls of corrugated iron, down beside the weir. Which is down beside the Thames, which is down at the bottom of Horseferry Lane.

Where the bushes in the Memorial Park had been our 'camp' when we were young, Cider Island had been our 'hideout'.

It had not been called Cider Island then, but only later when the local homeless drunkards, having been ejected from their former location, Sherry Plateau, moved in.

Cider Island slept in the sunlight, as might a fat tomcat in a window box, or a well-loved wife on a Saturday morn. Comfortably. Cosily. Contentedly too. As well they all might.

John swung aside the sheet of corrugated iron that masked the secret entrance and we two slipped onto Cider Island.

The drunkards there all snoozed as they might and I followed John down to a ruined barge that lay half-in and half-out of the ancient dock. We boarded this and slipped inside and settled down in the gloom.

This crumbling hulk did not smell too much of nostalgia, more of dog droppings and drunken man's wee-wee. It was not an agreeable or healthsome combination, but I was in no mood to be picky.

'I just do not understand it,' I told John. 'How it happened. How no one but me seems to know that it is all wrong.'

'We all know it's wrong,' said John. 'All Brentonians. All right-thinking Britishers. As to how it happened, well, that's just history, isn't it? We did that at school.'

'We certainly did *not*,' I said.

'I do believe that you are drunk,' said John. 'Do you have a small bottle about yourself that you are keeping from me?'

'I have no bottle, John. Nor do I have a recollection of any history at school that involved the Germans invading England.' And then I sighed. Deeply. 'So Kew is German-occupied too?' I said.

'All these sceptred isles, except for Scotland. They fought off the Romans and the Germans too. Bravo those kilted lads, say I.'

'And me also. But tell me how it happened, John. Tell me what you say we were taught at school. I cannot remember any of it. I am beginning to think that there might be something wrong with my brain box.'

'More so than usual, eh?' Omally chuckled. 'Give us another fag.'

And I had one too. And we sat and we drew upon them and we coughed in unison and Omally spoke to me.

'Just in case you have only temporarily lost all your ball bearings, I'll give you a quick rundown. If your memory suddenly returns then tell me and we'll talk about something else.'

'Go ahead then,' I said. And Omally did so.

'As far as I remember this,' he said, 'and frankly I never did pay too much attention to it at school, because it *was* history. And who's interested in history? As far as I remember it, it was getting to the end of the Second World War. And there'd been the D-Day Landings and the British and American troops were pushing across Europe towards Berlin, when everything went arse-up'ards, as it were. Mr Hitler unleashed the ultimate terror weapon and that was that!'

And he took another toke upon his cigarette and took once more to coughing.

'That, I regret, is insufficient information,' I sufficiently informed him.

'The bomb,' said Omally.

'As in *atomic* bomb?' I said.

'That would be the lad, yes.'

'The Americans dropped two,' I said. 'One on Hiroshima, one on Nagasaki. The bombs were called "Little Boy" and "Fat Man", the aeroplane that dropped "Little Boy" was called the *Enola Gay*.'

'You have a vivid imagination, I'll say that for you,' said Omally. 'But no, that didn't happen. The Germans invented the atom bomb first. Wotan invented it for them. And they bombed America with it. Wiped out America. A nuclear desert, it is.'

'A *what*?' I went. And I coughed a-plenty. 'It is a *what*, did you say?'

'America?' said John. 'Destroyed,' he continued. 'All gone. And with it the war. We put our hands up. Gave in. The war was lost. England was invaded and a German Government installed. And we grew up under this Government, you and me. Don't you remember anything, Jim? We played at war in this very barge. This was our HQ hideout. Our bunker. In our war against the Russians.'

'We are at war with the Russians?' My head was now spinning. This was all too much.

'No, we're not *at war* with them. But they are the enemy. Commies are the enemy. We were certainly taught *that* at school. Every damn day, if I recall correctly. And I do. Very much so.'

'America destroyed,' I said. 'I cannot believe it. It is too awful.'

'Could have been worse,' said John.

'Could have been *worse*?' I said.

'Could have been *us*,' said John. 'They could have nuked England as an encore, or instead.'

And I shook my head. 'And I do not remember any of this, not one jot.'

Omally shook his head a bit also. 'Well, Jim,' he said, and he said it slowly, 'you're not exactly yourself, are you? You went down to Brighton for a St Valentine's weekend, got thrown into the sea and ambulanced back the next day. And what did you tell me? That you had spent an entire year away, saving the world in the company of a Mr Hugo Ruin.'

'*Rune*,' I said. 'Hugo Rune. The Most Amazing Man Who Ever Lived.'

'But you *were* only gone for a single day. I can attest to this. *And* Norman. *And* your Aunt Edna. The odds are somewhat stacked against you, Jim. You would appear to be a group of one.'

'Do you think I have gone mad, John?'

'You were in the Special Ward of the Cottage Hospital, Jim. That is where they put the, er, *troubled people*.'

'I am not mad, John. I have never felt less mad. Never more scared. But never less mad.'

'Whatever you say, my friend. You are my friend, after all, and I'll stick by you come what may. But you are wrong on this one, you really are. So let's both hope you get better.'

And I shrugged my shoulders. 'Get better?' I said. 'Yes, I suppose "get better" will do. I cannot see how things can get any worse.'

And would not you know it?

Or would not you not—

'*Achtung! Achtung!* Come out with your hands held high,' came an amplified bullhorn sort of a voice. 'Come out at once, or we'll send in the hounds.'

5

'As your memory appears to be somewhat sounder than my own,' I said to Omally, 'can you recall whether we had a secret escape route from this childhood hideout of ours?'

'Not as I recall,' said himself.

'Unfortunate,' I said.

'Perhaps, though, all is not lost.'

'Then speak words of comfort and solicitation to me, sweet friend,' I said.

'Well,' said John, 'just because all is lost for you, that does not mean all is lost for *us*. So to speak. How would it be if, as you clearly have no way of escaping from this, how shall I put it, *death trap* – what if I was to play the part of citizen's arrestor, bop you on the head and then turn you over to the powers that be?'

'And how would this benefit me?' I asked.

'It would mean that you'd be carried away unconscious, rather than shot upon some flimsy pretext, as often happens.'

'It does?' I said. 'Does it?'

'Frequently. Although not to the same person, of course. One man, one bullet, as it were.'

I made groaning sounds—

'That kind of thing, yes,' said Omally. 'So if you were unconscious, or even feigning unconsciousness, it would be well for you.'

'It would?'

'And myself also because I could claim the reward which must surely be currently on your head. You being a commie sympathiser and everything.'

'What?'

And Omally took a swing at my head.

But I dodged it nimbly. Or at least as nimbly as I could, considering the confined surroundings. And I did snatch up a length of useful-looking timber from amongst the unspeakable litter that lay all around and about us. And with this timber I did administer a mighty blow to the topknot of my bestest friend.

Who sank in a heap to said litter.

Which, I considered, was jolly decent of me, as now the chances of him being caught in some kind of crossfire when I 'resisted arrest' were considerably lessened.

'He will thank me for that later,' I told myself, as John was now in no fit state to hear it. 'And so on my toes and away.'

And I prepared to take flight.

Dive off the water side of the barge and swim to Kew.

It seemed like a likely solution.

And although I had never actually learned how to swim, I felt that there could not be much to it once you got yourself started.

I peeped out of a porthole. There were at least half a dozen fellows in black uniforms out there. And they all carried guns. And two of them not only carried guns, but also strained against the leashes of some rather fierce-looking dogs. It did not look at all to be a hopeful situation. In fact it looked to be a terrible situation and, struck dumb with terror, I sank down to my knees and chewed upon my knuckles.

More stern words were flung in my direction through the electric megaphone jobbie, ordering me to exit the barge immediately with my hands in the upwards position. Compliance with these instructions was not optional, I was given to understand.

I took deep breaths, struggled to my feet and took myself over to the water side of the barge. The porthole there hung open; it would take but a minute or two to squirm through, drop into the water and swim to freedom. Compliance to this ideal, I considered, was not optional.

Although.

And I dithered.

And then they turned the dogs loose.

And then I awoke.

Yes, *awoke*, that is what happened next. Exactly what happened before this was unknown to me. One minute there were dogs barking loudly. Then nothing—

And then I awoke.

To find—

That I was *not* in Kew.

Although it might have been Kew. But then it might have been anywhere. They are all very much the same, or so I have since been told. No matter what city, or town, or part of the world. All very much the same. They look very much the same and they smell very much the same—

Torture chambers.

And even though I had never been in one before in my life, I recognised this one to be what it was, almost on the instant.

As I awoke. Naked. Strapped into the iron chair and surrounded on all visible sides by instruments of torment.

A very bright light shone down upon me and a very bad smell engulfed me. And I could not move my hands to my nose and I became very afeared.

And—

Slap!

Someone caught me a massive wallop across my mouthparts that shook my brains and loosened my teeth. And *slap!* it went once again.

'Ooh!' I cried, 'stop hitting me. Mercy. Please stop.'

And a fellow appeared in my line of vision and grinned into my face.

'So,' he said. And it sounded like *Zo*. 'Zo, our little communist awakes. Did you sleep well after your swim?'

'My swim?' I said. And I shivered as I said it.

'Ill-advised to leap into rivers when you cannot swim. If we hadn't pulled you out, you might well have come to harm.'

'Well, thank you very much,' I said. 'Very kind of you. Sorry to have taken up your valuable time. If you would just give me my clothes, I will be off about my business.'

'Business. Yes.' And this fellow grinned some more. Although rather too close for my liking and in a manner that I felt lacked for a certain warmth. 'You have work, yes?'

'Oh yes,' I said. 'And I will be late back from my lunch.'

'Right.' And now the fellow's head bobbed from side to side and he straightened up and away from me. I got a better look at him then, although I did not exactly take to what I saw.

He was small and somewhat slender, with shaven head, broken nose, monocle and duelling scar. His all-black uniform looked very expensive and made to measure. And was ornamented here and there by silver fixtures and fittings beset with eagle and death's-head motifs. This I assumed to be a high-ranking fellow. And one with whom playing 'silly buggers' would not be best advised.

Not that I was in any mood to play 'silly buggers'. I was so scared that I almost—

'I need the toilet,' I said. 'Sorry, sir, but I do.'

'Time enough,' said he, 'when you have answered all of my questions.'

'Anything, sir,' I said. 'You ask, I answer. Anything at all.'

'Is good,' he said. And now he drew a chair into my line of vision. A rather comfy-looking chair, with a nice cushion on it and everything. And he dropped into this chair, carefully pulling up the knees of his trousers and straightening the creases.

'Very nice riding boots,' I observed. As I tried, without success, to cross my legs. 'I really do need the toilet. Oh dear.'

From an upper pocket the fellow took a notebook and silver pen. It was a biro, and he clicked it with his thumb.

'Name?' said he. And I told him my name.

'Address?' And I told him that too.

'Occupation?' I paused.

'Occupation?'

'Well . . .' And I paused once again.

'Well?' said the fellow. 'What is "well"? Is it "well" as in "well-poisoner", perhaps?'

'Oh no,' I said. 'It is not *that*.'

'No.' And the fellow leaned forwards, raised his biro, examined its tip and then drove it down with a fearsome force right into my right kneecap.

And the pain! And I howled! And I howled and I howled and I wept. And I begged too, I will tell you.

'Stop,' I begged and I wept as I begged. 'Please stop. Oh my God, that hurts, pull it out, please pull it out.'

But he ground it around before he *slowly* pulled it out.

'Unemployed,' said the fellow, as he wiped my blood from his biro onto my leg, then shook his head and tutted.

And I shook from top to toe, and then I peed myself.

The fellow asked me many things on that terrible afternoon and I must have told him many things, although most of them were probably gibberish, because I would have told him anything at all in order that he stop inflicting pain upon me.

But he did not stop and the things that he did to me got worse and worse and worse.

And then it became apparent to me that I was not going to leave this awful room alive. I was going to die there in agony. That was all that was left for me.

And I do recall the electrical apparatus. The electrodes that he pressed to my person. And then the flash and the horrible explosion.

And that was that for me.

6

'And now *awake*!'

And I awoke, in terror and confusion.

'And get stuck into your breakfast, or I will be forced to relieve you of at least one of those splendid pork sausages.'

And I did awakenings and focusings of the eyes and then I made free with a very startled squawk and fainted dead away.

To be awoken once more, by the application of a smelling-bottle to my nasal parts. Which caused more squawkings from my oral parts and cries to desist and leave off.

'Aha, young Rizla. You are with us once more.'

And I beheld and lo it was Hugo Rune.

And I did great blinkings of the eyes and gaggings of the mouth as I gazed all around and about and recognised my surroundings. I was surely once more in the rooms that we had inhabited together during the year of my adventures with him. The rooms at 49 Grand Parade, Brighton.

'Oh,' I went. And, 'Bless my soul.' And, 'Thank the Lord.' And things of that nature generally.

And then a terrible thought struck me and I ceased with such joyous ejaculations and became all downcast and glum.

'What ails you, young Rizla?' asked Mr Rune. 'I have delivered you from your tormentor and awoken you to a hero's breakfast. Why the long face and deeply furrowed brow?'

'Because it is all a falsehood,' I declared and I glared as I declared this. 'The contents of this room were destroyed in a fire last year. This is some kind of evil trick. The mind-altering chemicals, is that the game?'

But Mr Rune munched toast. He reached forwards and dunked his toast into the fried egg on my plate and then he munched some more.

And then he said, 'Mind-altering chemicals, did I hear you say?'

And I said, yes, he had. And that this was all a fake and that I was not going to fall for it, not at all, no. And to add weight to my words I shook my head. Which hurt quite a bit, because I seemed to have something of a headache.

But Hugo Rune just smiled upon me. And then he helped himself to one of my sausages.

'Leave that alone,' I told him. And I reached out and snatched it back.

'You will find it preferable to Bratwurst, I'm thinking,' said the guru's guru, and he winked at me.

I took breaths of the deepest kind and tried to steady my crumpled-up mind. And I looked all around and about and all looked real to me.

I sat at the breakfasting table at which Mr Rune and I had taken many a breakfast. Our chairs were of the Victorian persuasion, as were indeed the greater part of the furnishings within this wonderful room. Upon mahogany shelves the leather spines of Mr Rune's vast collection of thaumaturgical books glowed with a rich patina. As indeed did everything, it seemed. The cases of stuffed creatures, many, I recalled, of an apparently mythical nature. The polished brass of the intricate machines, whose purposes I had never fathomed. The curiosities that Mr Rune had gathered during his world travellings. The magical items that were the gifts from grateful monarchs and society figures for whom Mr Rune had rendered certain discreet services.

All was as I remembered it.

But all, I knew, had been destroyed by fire.

'It is somehow fake,' I said and I popped the sausage into my mouth and chewed with vigour upon it. 'I do not know how it has been done, or why it has been done. But neither at this moment do I care.' And then I forked up bacon and conveyed it speedily into my mouth.

'Would you care for coffee?' asked Hugo Rune. 'It is ersatz, of course, but then it would be, wouldn't it?'

I shrugged my shoulders and got stuck into my breakfast.

'I'll wager you'd care for an explanation,' said Hugo Rune. But I just shrugged once more and stuck further into the sticking in.

But I viewed him over my breakfasting fork and took in his striking presence. It *was* him, of this there could be no doubt. This was Hugo Rune, the *real* Hugo Rune. No substitute could ever there be. Tall and imposing, even when seated. The heavy brows and shaven head, with its pentagram tattoo. The quilted velvet smoking jacket, the high-collared shirt with cravat.

And those eyes. Those mischievous twinkling eyes. That held such wisdom. Held such power.

Then Hugo Rune poured coffee from a proper coffee pot.

'It is you,' said I, between sweet mastications. 'It is you and this is the room that we shared. But how?'

Smiling, Hugo Rune raised his coffee cup as if in toast to me. 'The contents of the room you know and recognise, young Rizla. But we are not in Brighton, we are in Brentford, in my home on the famous Butts Estate.'

I did groanings of the voice at this, and shudderings of the shoulders. 'Then my joy at our reunion, for joy indeed it is, will be brief,' I said, 'for I am a wanted man.'

'Wanted by the Gestapo?' said Himself.

And I nodded in response and said that regrettably this was so. And I took the opportunity to now do the right thing and to thank Mr Rune for saving me from the merciless hands of my tormentor. I rubbed at my wounded parts and found to my surprise that they appeared no longer wounded.

So I thanked Mr Rune for this also. As I had no doubt in my mind that it was he who had healed me.

'My pleasure,' he said, and he drained his coffee cup.

'And I will tell you this,' I said, taking up *my* coffee cup and tossing coffee down my throat. 'That— Wahh!' And I spat coffee the full length of the table.

'Oh sorry, sorry,' I went, 'but what was *that*?'

Gagging, I clutched at my throat and I pointed with my free hand to the coffee pot.

'Ersatz coffee,' said Mr Rune, dabbing flecks of same from his velvet lapels. 'I did warn you. After all, there *is* a war on, you know.'

'A war?' I said. And hope, as Bing Crosby might say, sprang eternal. 'So the plain people of Brentford are fighting back against the mind-altering neo-Nazis?'

'Not as such.' Mr Rune did shakings of his proud and noble head. 'It will be necessary for me to explain matters to you, Rizla—'

At this I opened my mouth to offer my real name. But then I thought much better of it and so did not. If Mr Rune chose to call me Rizla, then that was the name I would happily go by in his company.

Being myself and going by my real name had not proved of late to be a particularly viable proposition.

'To explain matters,' said Mr Rune once more, 'things have become somewhat complicated. Therefore I wish to call again upon your services to aid me in expediting matters. If not speedily, then at least with a view to ultimate success.' Hugo Rune smiled once more upon me.

'An explanation would be nice at this time,' I told him. 'But please let me thank you once more for saving my life. Also let me say that I should away from these premises with alacrity – I am after all a most wanted man and I would not want you to suffer on my behalf.'

'Ah, the noble Rizla. It is a joy to work with you once again.'

'Work?' I said, and I made the face of one who has just popped doggy-doo into his mouth, thinking it to be a chocolate toffee. 'As in *regular employment?*'

Mr Hugo Rune laughed. In a big basso profundo with gusto and with vigour. 'Regular employment?' quoth he. 'Why, Rizla, how well do you know me?'

'In truth I would say hardly at all,' I replied. 'You are a riddle, wrapped in an enigma, sealed with gaffer tape and posted through the wrong letterbox by a postman with an eye for the ladies and a nose for a car-boot-sale bargain.'

Hugo Rune made so-so gestures with a mighty hand. 'That is all as may be,' he declared, 'but Hugo Rune does *not* offer regular employment.'

I smiled and said, 'Splendid. That is a relief.'

'Hugo Rune offers *irregular employment.*'

'What does it pay?' I asked him.

And Mr Rune changed the subject.

'Will you be wanting all those baked beans?' he asked me.

And I assured him that I would.

'And the black pudding?'

'*And* the black pudding. But certainly no more coffee.'

'I agree that it's terrible stuff,' said Mr Rune. 'Made from acorns, I believe.'

'Hardly up to your exacting standards. Have Harrods closed your account due to non-payment?'

'Now now, Rizla,' said Mr Rune. 'You know my views regarding the matter of *payments*. Payments are for little people. And Hugo Rune is not one of the little people.'

'Indeed not,' I agreed. 'Would you be so kind as to pass me that last piece of toast?'

'Of course not. More coffee?'

'No thanks.'

And so we ate what was left of the breakfast. For the most part in silence, but for the necessary sounds of mastication and the occasional satisfied belch. And when we were done we repaired to fireside chairs and Mr Rune offered me a cigar.

'I am having a crack at cigarettes,' I told him. 'The Wild Wood-bine. I do not suppose that you managed to save my clothes when you saved me, as it were?'

'The blue jeans and the T-shirt?' Hugo Rune did pinchings of the nostrils. 'Absolutely not. But surely you approve of your present duds.' And he gestured unto myself and I became cognisant, really for the first time, as to what now clothed my body parts.

For it was a suit of the finest Boleskine tweed. With a cotton shirt and a knitted tie. And smart brown brogues on my feet.

'Very nice,' I said. 'And thank you very much indeed. But—' And here I hesitated.

And Mr Rune punctuated my hesitation by the application of the word, 'What?'

'These tweeds,' I said, 'and please do not think me ungrateful, but the flight-deck shoulders and double-breasted jacket front, not to mention the Oxford bags, which surely I will *not* – they do look somewhat old-fashioned.'

'On the contrary.' Mr Rune brought a lighted taper from the fire and put it to his cigar. 'That suit is quite the latest thing.'

'Ah,' I said. 'The nineteen-forties retro look. I see.'

'You don't,' said Mr Rune. 'But never mind.'

I stared into the crackling flames and many thoughts passed through my head. At length I asked, 'Are we going to return to Brighton?'

Mr Rune shook his head.

'Are we going somewhere, anywhere other than here?'

Mr Rune shook his head once more and sucked daintily upon his cigar. 'Are you sure that I can't tempt you to one of these, Rizla? They are the genuine article, somewhat rare in this very day and age.'

I now grew somewhat edgy. 'I will have to leave soon,' I told Mr

Rune. 'Someone probably saw you bring me here. Nothing much ever slips by Brentonians. I really must away.'

'You really mustn't. Calm yourself, Rizla, do.'

'I am afeared,' I said. 'And rightly too. The Gestapo tortured me. They will be after me for sure.'

'They are not after you, I can assure you of that.'

'You can?'

'Absolutely. You trust Hugo Rune, do you not?'

'I do,' I said. 'Unreservedly. Although my acquaintanceship with you has been somewhat fraught with danger.'

'But you loved every minute of it.'

'Well, most of them, anyway.'

'And you will love them once more. We have a new quest, Rizla. A new set of challenges. A new set of Cosmic Conundra to solve. And once more we shall do this in the service of Mankind. Twelve new cases await us.'

'They do?' And I perked up considerably at this. 'You have a new zodiac?' I asked. 'Like the Brightonomicon? Is it the Brentfordomicon this time?'

'Don't be absurd, Rizla, please.'

'Then what?'

'That is up to you.'

'Please explain.'

'It is for you and me to set things right, young Rizla.'

'Form a Resistance movement, beat the Nazi invaders?'

'Not as such, no.' And Hugo Rune sucked more at his cigar.

'You have a plan, do you not?' I said.

'Naturally. Twelve cases and we win the war.'

'Twelve cases, I see.' And I did. Well, sort of.

'It is always twelve cases, as I have told you before. It is always to do with time and it always involves the solving of twelve Cosmic Conundra. It is what I do and what I am.'

'And I will be proud to aid you,' I said.

'And aid me you will. And together we will win the war.'

'And drive the evil Nazis out of Brentford,' I said.

'On the contrary, Rizla, we will see to it that they never invade.'

'Ah,' I said. 'Now that might not be too easy. Seeing how they already have.'

'Oh no they haven't.'

'Oh yes they have.'

'Oh no they haven't.'

'They have.'

'*They have not!*' And Hugo Rune stamped a great foot, causing everything in the room to jump. Including me.

'I think you will find that they have,' I said. In a tiny whispery voice.

But Hugo Rune shook his head. 'Rizla,' he said, 'do you hear *that*?' And he cupped his hand to his ear.

I listened and then I said, 'Your letterbox, by the sound of it.'

'The paperboy,' said Mr Rune. 'Would you kindly fetch the paper?'

And so I did. I left the wonderful room, traipsed along a wonderful hall, its walls made even more wonderful by the hangings of what I took to be the Rune family's ancestral portraits. To a doormat that had yet to wear out its welcome. From where I took up the morning's paper.

I rolled it and tapped it against my thigh and returned to Mr Rune.

'And?' said he.

'And what?'

'The paper, Rizla, the paper.'

'What about the paper?' I asked.

Hugo Rune made exasperated gaspings. 'Just look at the paper,' said he. 'Just view the front page. And then you will know why the Gestapo are not after you and why the furnishings in this room are all intact and have not been destroyed by fire. Why the tweeds you are wearing seem so old-fashioned. And why we must win the war together and stop Brentford from ever being invaded.'

And I sighed deeply and unrolled the paper and I perused the front page.

And then I looked up at Mr Rune and said, 'No.'

And Mr Rune nodded his head and said, 'Yes.'

And then I said, 'But it—'

And he said, 'It can and it is.'

And I said, 'No,' once again.

And he likewise said, 'Yes.'

And then I said, 'But this means—'

And Mr Rune nodded once more. 'It means, young Rizla, that you and I are no longer in nineteen sixty-seven. You and I are now in nineteen forty-four.'

7

I did *not* faint this time. I felt that it would have been such a cliché to do so, and so I did not. I just stared at Mr Rune and asked, 'How?'

'The "how" need not concern you, Rizla. Only know that I brought these circumstances about. A great wrong has been done and we are the ones who must right this wrong. The Nazis must *not* win the Second World War. America must *not* be destroyed by an atomic holocaust. England must *not* be invaded. Are you with me on this?'

'I am,' I said. And I was. 'But please tell me how you transported us through time. Do you have a time machine, or a police telephone box, or something?'

Hugo Rune did enigmatic tappings of the nose. 'The magician never divulges how his magic is accomplished,' said he. 'But know that you and I are now in nineteen forty-four. This house, my manse, is a safe haven – we inhabited it in nineteen sixty-seven, therefore it does not get bombed in the time we now inhabit. But out there—' and Mr Rune waved his hands towards the world beyond his home '—there is great danger, Rizla. A war wages. We must be ever upon our guard.'

'One question,' I said. 'Although countless spring readily to mind. One question, please. This is your house and has been for many years, am I correct?' And Mr Rune nodded. 'So you owned this house during the Second World War?' He nodded again. 'And did you live in it then?'

'Aha,' said Hugo Rune. 'You are thinking to yourself, where is the Hugo Rune of nineteen forty-four? Will I bump into my former self and cause some cosmic paradox to occur that might rend the fabric of time and bring about the destruction of the universe. Yes?'

'No,' I said. 'I just did not fancy the prospect of having two of you nicking my breakfast.'

Oh how we laughed.

Then we stopped.

'Twelve Cosmic Conundra,' said Mr Rune. 'Twelve cases that we must solve in order to defeat the Nazi peril, save America, save Mankind, secure a future for England that is free and liberated.'

'I am for all of that,' I said and I raised an imaginary glass.

'And so it falls to you, Rizla. Through your choice, or at least through you, shall the cases be chosen.'

'How?' I asked. And not without reason, I think.

'Through these.' And Mr Rune produced from his pocket a small leather box.

'A cigarette case,' I said, 'containing Wild Woodbines, I hope.'

'A card case,' said Mr Rune, 'containing a set of tarot cards, designed by myself and illustrated by a delightful creature by the name of Lady Frieda Harris. Tarot cards, young Rizla. Tarot cards.'

'Then you intend to read my fortune?'

'No!' Hugo Rune did once more the stamping of his foot. And once more everything jumped.

'I wish you would not do that,' I told him. 'It fair puts the wind up me.'

'Then pay attention. This is my personal tarot deck. Each card is symbolic. Heavily symbolic. Each represents a potential Cosmic Conundrum. *You* will shuffle the pack and *you* will deal out twelve cards. The future of Mankind depends upon this.'

'Oh my,' I said. And, 'Oh dear. I do believe that this would be a responsibility well beyond myself. Please do the shuffling and dealing out, Mr Rune. You know so much and I know nothing. It would be better if you did the dealing out. Yes?'

'No!' And there almost came another stamp. But not quite. Mr Rune's foot hovered airwards and I took the card case from his hands.

'Now take yourself over to the breakfasting table, which you will notice has been cleared of its breakfasting paraphernalia by an agency of my commission—'

'A demon?' I said. 'A calling?'

'My butler, Gammon.'

'Ah.'

'Deal twelve cards. Go on, now.'

And so it came to pass. I took the card case and returned to the breakfasting table. I took the cards from the case and slowly, but thoroughly, shuffled them. They were beautiful cards, each unique, gorgeously wrought, magical and mystical, and I was quite entranced.

'Shuffle them up and then deal out twelve.'

And so *that* came to pass.

I shuffled the beautiful cards and then I dealt twelve. Onto the linen tablecloth, twelve cards, in a circle, as if they were the numbers on a clock face.

And I stared down upon the cards that I had dealt.

And Mr Rune came forwards and peered over my shoulder. And then he called out the numbers and the names that were written upon those twelve cards.

0 THE FOOL
1 THE MAGICIAN
2 THE HIGH PRIESTESS
7 THE CHARIOT
9 THE HERMIT
10 THE WHEEL OF FORTUNE
11 JUSTICE
12 THE HANGÈD MAN
13 DEATH
16 THE TOWER
18 THE MOON
19 THE SUN

And then Mr Rune said, 'Well done, Rizla. Now choose one, from anywhere, choose one.'

I pointed and I said, 'THE HERMIT.'

And Mr Rune said, 'What an excellent choice. That will be our first case.'

THE HERMIT

8

THE HERMIT

So there I was in nineteen forty-four.

I was eager to get out and about. I was also filled with questions. How had Mr Rune conveyed us through time? How had history changed so drastically as to require this miraculous conveyancing? But more than anything, I *did* want to get out and about. Have a shufti, as it were, see what lay beyond the walls of Mr Rune's marvellous manse. See what the Brentford of nineteen forty-four looked like. A little perambulation about the borough could surely do no harm at all.

But Mr Rune said no.

He seemed genuinely concerned for my safety and impressed upon me again that dire consequences might well come to pass from my wanderings.

'You must understand, Rizla,' said he to me. Over breakfast it was, I recall. 'We are strangers in this particular portion of time. We should not really be here. A wrong move on our part could easily result in some future calamity. We are here in the past to alter the future, after all. But to alter it *correctly*, as it were. We tread a fine line; care must be our watchword.'

'I will not break anything,' I said. 'I just want to have a look around Brentford. You can understand this, surely.'

'I understand *all*,' said Hugo Rune. 'Trust me, I am an avatar.'

'Then you must know that I will not cause any harm.'

And perhaps he did, or knew to the contrary, but he forbade me to leave the house, so I just sat and sulked.

'You'll turn the powdered milk sour,' said Mr Rune. 'Perk up and read from the paper. You are au fait with my method of doing things. Seek us out a case.'

The daily paper in question was the borough's organ, the *Brentford*

Mercury. This venerable news-sheet, founded by the legendary Victorian newspaper magnate Sir Cecil Doveston in eighteen seventy-five, had hardly changed its basic format since that time. Indeed, but for the date, and the general contents, the copy I held in my hand seemed all but identical to any one that I might have held, or *did* hold, or *would* hold, in nineteen sixty-seven. Some things were just built to last and a classic never dates.

I read aloud the banner headline.

BRENTFORD ALLOTMENTEERS
DIG FOR VICTORY

The *Brentford Mercury* always led with local news, no matter the nature or importance of ongoing world events. I recall that on the day after Kennedy's assassination it ran a front-page article about the local electrical shop stocking a new make of battery.

'Thrilling stuff,' I said, and I made a certain face.

'It's an improvement on the sulky one,' said the breakfasting avatar, 'but not much. Dig into the inside pages, worm us out a little nugget on which to hang our first case. Let *us* do some digging for victory.'

I shrugged and said, 'I will never understand the logic in your method of doing things.'

'And I trust that you never will. Now dig.'

And so I turned pages and dug.

'A woman in Chiswick has given birth to a child the shape of a vacuum cleaner,' I said.

'Dig further.'

'Brentford Football Club have beaten Manchester United four–nil,' I said. And I whistled as I said it, and after I had said it too.

'And that is something they will do again. But a long way into the future and in quite another story altogether.'*

'Aha,' I said. 'Perhaps this is it. "SCIENTIST VANISHES". Is that the kind of thing you are looking for?'

'What do *you* think?' Mr Rune asked, as his hand snaked out towards my bacon.

'Yes,' I said. 'I think that it is. I recall that the first Brightonomicon case we took on involved a lost dog. I think the case of a missing

* And a good one, too: *Knees Up Mother Earth*.

scientist might be a suitable one with which to begin our new quest. Would you care for me to go and take a stroll around the borough and see if I can find him by myself?'

Mr Rune did shakings of his head and swallowings too of my bacon. 'From where did this scientist go missing?' he enquired, once he had swallowed.

I skimmed through the article and read aloud from it.

Professor James Stigmata Campbell, a particle physicist working for the Ministry of Home Affairs, vanished from his laboratory in mysterious circumstances. His cellar laboratory was locked from the inside and his clothes were found strewn upon the floor. Professor Campbell had most recently announced a significant breakthrough in his field of endeavour, which he had been expected to deliver in a paper to a meeting of the Fellows of the Royal Society tonight. Police are baffled.

'Perfect,' said Hugo Rune. 'And now go and answer the telephone.'

'But the telephone is not ringing.'

Mr Rune cupped a hand to his ear, counted three and the telephone rang.

I rose, a-shaking of my head, put down the newspaper and went off to answer the phone.

A fussy-voiced fellow in a state of considerable agitation demanded to speak to 'that scoundrel Rune'. I asked him his name and he said it was Mr McMurdo. I placed my hand over the receiver and conveyed this intelligence to Mr Rune.

He mouthed the word 'perfect' once again. Said, 'Tell him I will be right with him,' then settled down for a nap.

I did as Mr Rune had told me, then put down the receiver and returned to my newspaper.

Some time later Hugo Rune rose and took up the phone.

Words were exchanged and then Mr Rune said, 'You may consider the case of your missing scientist Professor Campbell as good as solved.'

He then replaced the telephone receiver, announced that now all was as it should be and counselled me to put on my socks and brogues as we were going out. And then he gave me a little box affair on a strap and told me that I must wear it over my shoulder at all times. I asked exactly what it might be and Mr Rune said that it was a gas mask.

'But the Germans never used gas in the Second World War,' I said. 'Everyone knows that.'

'And they never used the atom bomb either. According to what everyone thought they knew.'

'Good point,' I said. 'Whatever it means.' And I accepted my gas mask. 'Will you be wanting me to hail a taxi?' I asked, with justifiable trepidation, recalling as I did Mr Rune's brutality towards cab drivers.

'I think not, Rizla,' said the guru's guru, shrugging on a magnificent ulster coat. 'Have you ever travelled on a tram?'

And I had not. As a child I had travelled on trolley buses and I remembered those well. But trams I had only seen in the Transport Museum, and the prospect of travelling upon one held considerable charm.

'Top deck,' said Mr Hugo Rune. 'Then you will see wartime London.'

And so we travelled by tram. They ran the length of Brentford High Street – for in these times you could travel from Hounslow to the City of London by tram. And oh what a noise they made. And what a smell too. That electrical ozone smell that you generally associate only with bumper cars. And oh what sights I saw from the top deck of that tram. And oh how they saddened me greatly.

London was in ruins. I had never imagined the scale of the damage. Yes, I had seen *The World at War** on television and I knew about the Blitz. But it seemed that hardly a house or a shop or a church or a public building had escaped some kind of damage. The destruction was heartbreaking; civilisation was literally being torn to pieces.

I must have made a very glum face at this, and I know that a tear or two took shape in my eyes. Mr Rune could see my distress and he told me to brighten up and offered me a fag.

'A Capstan Full Strength,' said he. 'If you are intending to smoke,

---

* Before some astute reader takes me to task regarding the year that the first broadcast of *The World At War* took place (1973), let me clarify that this is not a mistake on my part; it is caused by the Chevalier Effect (see *The Brightonomicon* for details of this phenomenon).

then do it as you would do any other thing – by fearlessly jumping in at the deep end. The poodle of perspicacity must bow its furry knee before the spaniel of spontaneity.'

And who was I to doubt him?

I had noticed, due to the fug and general stench, that the upper deck of the tram was the haunt of smokers and so I accepted Mr Rune's offer and took to the ruining of my health as I viewed more ruination.

And sick at heart I felt as we travelled on that tram. I watched the gallant lads of the Auxiliary Fire Service dousing smouldering remains and members of the Ambulance Corps loading shrouded bodies into their canvas-cloaked lorries. I also saw members of the Home Guard coming and going and it looked for all the world to me as if it was some great film set for a wartime movie.

But I knew that it was none of this. It was real. The destruction and death. The sorrow and desperation. And I realised that *I* was now part of *it*. That Mr Rune and I were on a quest upon the outcome of which clung the lives of millions. This was no laughing matter.

Not that I felt like laughing. My unfailing cheerfulness had now failed me. I could not imagine that I would ever be happy again. That anyone who had experienced any of this could ever be happy again.

Although.

Well, my Aunt Edna had been through the Blitz. She had served in the Fire Brigade. And throughout my childhood, she had always been cheery enough. She had got over the horror. And so it seemed had most people of that generation. They had struggled through. And if they had survived intact they had been grateful for it and struggled on.

And I *had* heard about the Blitz Spirit.

Although I could not really see any evidence of that right here and now.

'Perhaps we should have taken the Underground,' said Hugo Rune. 'This must be difficult for you.'

'I will survive,' I said. 'But it is terrible. Awful. I had no idea that it would be as dreadful as this.'

'And it could get so very much worse. Which is why we are here to put things aright. Are you enjoying that Capstan?'

I put on what I considered to be a brave face. Although, I feared, one tinged with grey. I was now having considerable trouble keeping my breakfast down.

My brave face was spied out by a rather shabby-looking individual sporting the traditional cloth cap that marked him out as one of the working class of this particular period, poor but honest and given to a cockney singalong at the drop of his, or anyone else's, hat.

'Gawd smother my loins in liniment,' said he, 'but that's a brave face you're putting on there, guv'nor. And you a toff by the look of your right-royal raiments.'

I glanced at Mr Rune, wondering whether this fellow's banter might cause the Perfect Master to bring his stout stick into play. But Mr Rune now appeared to be snoozing, so I just smiled at the fellow.

'You couldn't see your way clear to sparing us three 'a'pence for a pint of porter, could you, your Lordship? I've been bombed out of me 'ouse and 'ome an' 'ave naught but the rags I stand up in.'

'I am sorry,' I said, 'but I am a bit like Twiggy at present – flat busted.' And then I realised that I had made a joke, if naught but a feeble one. And certainly a feeble one that would have meant absolutely nothing to a fellow in nineteen forty-four. 'I have no cash,' I explained. In order to put the matter clearly.

'A puff on your posh cigarette, then?'

'Gladly so.' And I parted with my Capstan.

The fellow snatched it to his mouth and took great drags upon it.

'So you were bombed out,' I said to him. 'Where are you living now?'

'Right 'ere,' he said in return. 'Right 'ere on the top of this 'ere tram.'

'And the tram company allows this?'

'I won't tell 'em if you don't.' And he winked a bleary eye at me.

'Right.' I watched him as he smoked my cigarette. And I wondered who he was. And, oddly, when he would die. He looked rather old and ill, which probably meant that he would not last until nineteen sixty-seven. So I would not be able to go and look him up, should I be lucky enough to return intact to that time. So in a way it was as if his days were numbered. And I somehow was doing the numbering.

'That's a queer thing you're musing upon, guv'nor,' said he, between great breathings-in of my Capstan Full Strength. 'When or when not a man's time it is to die is between that man and the God what made 'im, so it is.'

'Oh,' I said. And I was shocked by this. 'Did you just read my thoughts? I do not understand.'

The fellow tapped at his shabby nose with an even shabbier finger. And then he beckoned me with it and I leaned over the belly of Mr Rune to hear what this wretch had to say.

'Step very carefully, young Rizla,' he whispered into my ear. And I felt his warm breath on me and smelled that breath as well. 'Much depends upon you. And there are those who will seek to destroy you. You must take care, young Rizla, you really must. And when you see that number twenty-seven, don't think, just run.'

'But how?' I said in much wonder and confusion. 'And what do you mean? And who are you?'

'You may know me as Diogenes. Now take care.'

And he handed me back what remained of my cigarette and he tipped his cap to me. And I straightened up in my seat and then I went suddenly, 'Wahh!'

And I jumped considerably and Hugo Rune laughed.

'What?' I went. And, 'Where?' And, 'Ow!' And I looked down at the fingers of my right hand, which hurt. Considerably.

'You nodded off,' said Hugo Rune, 'with a lit cigarette between your fingers. You must take care, young Rizla. You really must.'

I opened my mouth, but had nothing to say.

And so I closed it again.

9

We disembarked from the tram at Mornington Crescent.

And approached the Underground station.

I was feeling a tad wobbly about the knees of me. Something odd had happened on that tram and although 'odd' was the currency in which Mr Rune dealt, it still had the ability to throw me off my balance and out of my kilter.

What had I experienced upon that top deck? A dream, a vision? Had I actually met Mr Diogenes? Had he imparted important information to me? The business regarding the number twenty-seven and the running that must be done upon the seeing of this number? I was dazed and roundly confused and this clearly showed on my face.

'Perk up, young Rizla,' said Mr Rune. 'A treat awaits you within.' And he gestured with his stick towards the entrance to the Underground. 'We are going below.'

'I have travelled on the Tube before,' I said. 'I will find little of the treat in that.'

'We are *not* going a-travelling. We have arrived. At the Ministry of Serendipity.'

Now Mr Rune had spoken to me before of this mysterious Ministry and there had been at least two cases in *The Brightonomicon* in which their involvement had been apparent. What knowledge regarding this Ministry that I had gleaned from Hugo Rune was that it was 'the power behind many thrones'. That 'those who control the controllers of our nation' were to be found within. Precisely what Mr Rune's relationship with this literally underground organisation was, I had not been told. And so I asked to be now.

'They are presently covering my expenses,' was the reply. And Mr Rune tapped his stout stick on the pavement. 'They require my skills and knowledge. I am engaged, as it were, in furthering the War Effort.'

'We are clearly here because of the phone call you received,' I said. 'The tarot card I picked is therefore surely irrelevant.'

Mr Rune composed his eyebrows into a Gothic arch. 'Shame on you, Rizla,' he said. 'The Ministry might pay my bills, but I work for a greater good. I will say this to you. It is the Ministry of Serendipity that controls the waging of the war against Germany. When Mr McMurdo sneezes, Winston Churchill offers his handkerchief. But Rune is immune to such snifflings. Rune is above and beyond. Now pacy-pacy and follow me. The squamulose square-rigger squats not for squaw-man, squash nor squirrel-fish. Especially not for the latter!'

'There is no doubting *that*,' I said and I followed Mr Rune.

We passed by the ticket window and entered the lift.

It was a Magnathy and Pericule front-lattice cage-lift, with brass quadroon-filibasters and wibbly-wobbly faybill tremblers. Rather posh by anyone's standards.

Mr Rune did not press a floor button; rather he fished into his tweedy waistcoat and drew out a key that was affixed to his watch fob by a golden chain. He flipped aside one of the floor buttons, inserted the key and gave it a little twist.

'Hold on tightly,' said Hugo Rune.

'Hold on tightly? Why?'

But that was altogether a foolish question upon my part, as the lift now gathered speed and plunged in the downwards direction.

I went, 'Ooooh!' as my ears went 'pop' and my bladder nearly went 'wee'. And down and down and down we went.

And down and down some more.

Although greatly afeared and clinging desperately to a curlicue stanchion double-racked handrail, I watched Mr Rune as we descended at break-your-neck speed surely down into the very bowels of the Earth. The guru's guru stood at the centre of the plummeting lift, his brogued feet four-square upon the floor, his stout stick going *tap-tap-tap*. And a great big smile on his face.

And then the lift just suddenly stopped.

And I all but sank in anguish to my knees.

And Hugo Rune said, 'Didn't you just love that bit?'

And I said, 'No, I did not.'

Hugo Rune flung the lift doors open and we found ourselves in what looked for all the wide world to me to be the entrance hall of a stately home.

It was richly floored in the Churrigueresque fashion, but with sufficient renderings of Chuvash chyle-coloured chryoprase as to engender surprise. The ceiling was arched in that style known as Orphean-retro, so appropriate to the atmosphere of this chthonian scene. Framed portraits, framed I should add after the manner of Dalbatto, hung the length of this hall, each illuminated by an electric *torchère*.

I paused to admire an Annibale Carracci.

But Mr Rune urged me on. 'Not one of his finest canvasses,' he said, sniffily. 'I feel that his best work is to be found in the stateroom of the Palazzo Farnese in Rome.'

'I'm sure you are right,' I said. 'But then I would not know a José de Churriguera from a Constantin Meunier.'

Mr Rune raised his stout stick to me. But he heartily grinned as he did so. 'Ah,' said he. 'We are here at last.' And he rapped on a big brass door.

For big and brassy *was* this door, from its top to its very bottom, and well buffed and polished and burnished as gold with many a brazen rivet.

'Why is this door all made out of brass?' I asked, as the door swung open. But then suddenly I no longer craved an answer to this question, but felt another, far more urgent, forming in my mind and eager to take shape at my lips.

Because before us, on the threshold of the room that lay beyond, there stood a man. A well-turned-out and dapperly done-up fellow this, in an impeccable pinstriped suit. A veritable poem in praise of understated dandification.

> His shoes were black and shone like silk,
> As did his Brylcreemed napper.
> And pince-nez specs clung to his nose
> With a 'tache below, well dapper.
>
> His eyes were blue,
> His tie was too,
> His schmutter
> Was utterly
> Dash-cutter-do!

But it was not the sartorial elegance of this fellow that caused an urgent question to come springing to my mouth.

It was his height and overall dimensions.

For he was a tiny man. No dwarf or midget was this man, being much smaller indeed than either. He could surely not have been more than eighteen inches in height, yet he was perfectly formed and carried himself in a manner that was aloof and pompous and very very angry.

'What time do you call *this*?' he bawled up at Mr Rune, who towered above him in every sense of the word.

'Time for a gin and tonic, methinks.' And Mr Rune stepped *over* this man and entered the room beyond.

The tiny man coughed and spluttered with rage. 'And who do you think *you* are?' he asked me.

'I am with Mr Rune,' I said, as I too entered the room. And if I had been impressed by the entrance hall, and I *had*, then I was more than impressed by this room. It was all a-glitter and a-twinkle with nautical fol-de-rollery, its fixtures and furnishings redolent of quinque-remes (of Nineveh, obviously), brigantines, schooners, feluccas and gallivants.

> Corsairs and showboats,
> Galleons, rowboats,
> Three-masted barques
> With mainsails and spankers,
> Clippers and crumsters
> With outboards and anchors
> And so forth . . .

Mr Rune stood before a cocktail cabinet that resembled the prow of a Pomeranian galliot, pouring gin into a cut-crystal tumbler. 'Same for you, Rizla?' he called out to me. 'And what about you, McMurdo?'

The little man huffed and puffed in fury and grew most red in the face.

'Oh, come come,' said Mr Rune. 'The sun is over the yardarm and the cabin boys are restless. A drink will calm those nerves of yours. Would you care for a *short*?'

'A *short*?' The little man, now purple in the face, jumped up and down. 'I blame you for this,' he cried.

'For *what*?' asked Hugo Rune.

'For *what*? For *what*?' The small man all but fainted dead away.

Hugo Rune smiled and passed me a G & T. And then he took himself over to one of several comfy-looking chairs which had much of the quilted tramp steamer about them and settled himself into it.

The tiny man threw up his hands, stalked to the cocktail cabinet, swarmed up it in an appropriately sailor-up-the-rigging manner and struggled with a whisky bottle all but as tall as himself.

I just stood and sipped at my drink. I did not know what to say.

'Formal introductions are in order,' said Mr Hugo Rune. 'Norris McMurdo, *High* Honcho to the Ministry of Serendipity, be up-standing for Rizla, my trusted acolyte, assistant and amanuensis. I can personally vouch for his honesty, dedication and loyalty to King and country. All that you might say to me, you might say to him.'

'Pleased to meet you, Mr McMurdo,' *I* managed to say. 'Could I give you a hand with that bottle?'

'I can manage. I can manage.' And the diddy fellow wrestled with the bottle cap.

'You are probably wondering something, aren't you, Rizla?' asked Mr Rune.

'Wondering something? Me?' I did toothy grinnings. Clearly the relationship between Mr Rune and Mr McMurdo was not one of mutual support and admiration. And this man, diminutive as he was, was apparently one of the most powerful men in the world. So I really did not want to get on his wrong side by asking embarrassing questions regarding his height.

'I am surprised,' said Hugo Rune. 'I thought you might have some questions regarding short-arse here.'

'*What did you say?*' shrieked Mr McMurdo, giving up the unequal battle against the whisky-bottle top. 'What did you call me, you rotter?'

'I asked my companion whether he might have some questions regarding the *shot-glass* here,' said Mr Rune, and he raised his glass to his foreshortened employer. And toasted him with it.

'I know what you said . . . you . . . you—'

'Come come,' said Mr Rune. 'Enough of this, please. I am doing everything I can to rectify the situation. Why, only this morning when you telephoned, I was in the middle of subtle chemical experimentation seeking to formulate a restorative to return you to your former dimensions.'

'Another restorative, is it?' Mr McMurdo did a kind of manic dance upon the cocktail cabinet that sent glasses tumbling and cocktail stirrers tinkling to the carpet. 'Of the nature of the one you formulated for me last week that had me rushing to the toilet all night long?'

Last week? I thought to myself. Had Mr Rune been here in this time, last week, which was to say— But I soon gave it up as far too confusing and supped at my gin instead. And very nice gin it was too.

'We will speak further of these matters anon,' said Mr Rune. 'But for now there are more pressing causes for concern – the disappearance of Professor James Stigmata Campbell, for one. What have you to tell me of this?'

'I'm telling you to find him!' Mr McMurdo ceased his dance and knotted his doll-like fists. 'And find him today. He must deliver his paper tonight. Our future depends on it.'

'Our *future*?' And Mr Rune nodded at me.

And I nodded back to him.

'Tell me then,' said he to Mr McMurdo, 'all that you are authorised to tell me. Omit nothing. Speak your piece. And kindly couch your words in such a manner that they might be understood by my acolyte here. His help in solving this case, and indeed finding a solution to the curse that presently afflicts your person, will, I promise, prove invaluable.'

And Mr Rune nodded once more at me.

So I nodded once more at him.

And Mr McMurdo took in as deep a breath as his miniature frame allowed, sat wearily down upon the top of the cocktail cabinet and regarded Mr Rune with a most bitter expression.

And then he told a curious tale that fair put the wind up me.

10

'You must know,' said Mr McMurdo, addressing, it seemed, his words to myself, 'that the Ministry of Serendipity is at the very spearhead of the War Effort. It is here that plans are formulated and campaigns organised. And these are not wholly of a military nature. There is great evil abroad upon the face of the planet and it is the Ministry's duty to stamp out the malignant pestilence and restore peace and decency and Britishness.'

'Here here,' said Hugo Rune. 'I'll drink to that.' And he rose from his chair, took himself over to where Mr McMurdo sat and poured himself another drink. And if not necessarily out of kindness, but rather perhaps decency and Britishness, he uncapped the whisky bottle and splashed spirit into a vacant glass for Mr McMurdo.

'Mine too for a top-up,' I put in. For I had no idea how long Mr McMurdo's talk might last and I had already developed a taste for his gin.

When all was done in the drinks department and Mr Rune reseated, Mr McMurdo continued. 'We at the Ministry have studied the rise of Germany's National Socialist Workers' Party. Hitler did not ascend to his lofty position, which is one of almost messianic proportions, through opportunism and corrupt dealings alone. Although these did play their part.

'He became the right man in the right place at the right time through the exercise of occult power. The Nazi Party is founded upon the principles of the blackest of the black arts. Ancient magic has been reactivated, ancient symbols brought once more into prominence. Dark forces revived. Let me make it clear, I am not talking about Satanism. Mr Hitler does not worship the devil of Christian theology. His master predates this. The Nazi hierarchy consider themselves to be true Aryans, the present-day heirs to the Teutonic heritage of Odinism.

'The swastika is the symbol of Thor. Hitler believes the swastika to be a sacred Aryan symbol derived from the *Feuerquirl*. Literally, the protean fire-whisk with which the universe was created by the Supreme God of Germanic mythology. Hitler's God is Wotan.

'The revival of such ancient magic, I regret to say, has caught the West somewhat on the hop. There are few in this country with sufficient knowledge of the esoteric arts to counter such a situation. The knowledge has mostly been lost to us.'

Mr Rune did clearings of his throat.

'Present company excepted,' said Mr McMurdo, in a grudging yet resigned tone of voice.

'Please continue,' said Mr Hugo Rune.

'Mr Rune is presently employed by the Ministry of Serendipity to aid us in our countermeasures against whatever occult weaponry the enemy might aim towards us. And also to formulate such weaponry that we might use against them. *Which brings me once more to the matter of—*' And Mr McMurdo rose once more to his feet and took once more to some demented jigging about.

'A regrettable circumstance,' said Hugo Rune. 'Had the spell in question achieved the desired effect – that of creating a temporary cloak of invisibility – I would no doubt be kneeling now before a grateful monarch to receive yet another knighthood. Have sympathy for my disappointment also in this matter, please.'

Mr McMurdo huffed and puffed some more. 'You wrought this calamity upon me, Rune.'

'You volunteered,' said the Perfect Master, as he perfectly mastered his G & T towards his mouth. 'How anxious you were to volunteer, I recall.'

'Out of my loyalty to King and country.'

'Really?' said Mr Rune. 'And yet I also recall that I overheard you speaking to one of your minions, in confidence of course, words to the effect that "my first pleasure as the Invisible Man will be to kick the bum of that pompous buffoon Hugo Rune".'

'I did no such thing . . . I—' And Mr McMurdo huffed and puffed some more.

And certain thoughts entered my head regarding the spell that Mr Rune had seemingly cast with such 'unexpected' results. But I dismissed these thoughts from my mind and asked Mr McMurdo whether, having now explained to me the noble motivations of those who toiled away in the Ministry of Serendipity, he might now care to avail Mr Rune and I of the facts in the case concerning the missing scientist, Professor James Stigmata Campbell. As time was now passing by at a goodly rate and he had seemed anxious that the case be solved by this very evening. Which was why Mr Rune and I were here.

'Quite,' said Mr McMurdo, as Hugo Rune sought, with little success, to disguise another beaming grin. 'The facts in the case are these. We have a number of deep-cover operatives in Germany, brave chaps all who risk their lives to supply us with information regarding the Nazis' scope of operations and current areas of scientific research. There is a fine line between science and magic, as is evidenced by the enemy's present endeavours.'

I supped at my drink and Mr Rune did likewise.

And Mr McMurdo continued with the telling of his tale.

'Particle physics,' he said. 'Which is to say the study of forces and matter upon an atomic and subatomic level. It is a study of the very fabric of existence. We know that Nazi scientists are engaged in this and we have scientists of our own similarly engaged. Professor Campbell is the leading light in this field of research.'

'Might I ask,' I asked, 'precisely what Professor Campbell was engaged in?'

'The nature of his experiments is top secret. I cannot divulge that information to you.'

'You might divulge the theory behind them,' Mr Rune suggested, 'without compromising security.'

'Then it is this way. Many theories exist regarding how the universe was brought into being. Some believe that the universe has always existed; it might expand and contract, it might do all manner of things, but essentially it has always been here. Others subscribe to the belief that everything that we understand to be the universe began with a Big Bang, and that our universe is now expanding from this point of cosmic detonation. And a third faction retains the earliest belief of Mankind – that it was God who created the universe. I can only say that I have every reason to believe that Professor Campbell uncovered the truth.'

'Golly gosh,' I said. 'So which one is it?'

'That I cannot say.'

Hugo Rune took out his pocket watch and perused its face. 'Lunchtime is upon us,' said he. 'I require only Professor Campbell's address. I assume that he conducted his research and experimentation within his own home.'

'That is correct.' Mr McMurdo plucked a tiny stylus from an inner pocket of his immaculate suit, took up a paper napkin and wrote an address upon it. 'You told me on the telephone that the case was as good as solved,' he said to Mr Rune, as the guru's guru approached him and took the napkin from his delicate hand. 'Be so good as to honour your word upon this occasion.'

'Your servant, sir,' said Hugo Rune. And he clicked his heels together in a martial manner and twirled his stout stick upon his fingers. 'Be seeing you.'

And he led me from the room.

11

We took our luncheon at The Ritz.

'Taking tea there is so passé,' Mr Rune informed me, 'but they do a passable lunchtime nosebag.'

I was entranced by the décor, the frescoed domes of ceilings, the chandeliers and marble columns, the gilded furniture and all over Louis XVI-ness all around and about. And as I took it all in, each wondrous detail and facet, I knew in my heart of hearts that *this* was the life. And that this place definitely had the edge on the Wife's Legs Café in Brentford.

The head waiter seemed genuinely pleased to see Mr Rune and wrung him warmly by the hand, this causing me to conclude that either (a) Mr Rune had not dined here before, or (b) that he *had* and his restaurant bills were presently being covered by the Ministry of Serendipity. It proved, indeed, to be the latter.

'Your favourite table, monsieur,' said the head waiter, guiding Mr Rune towards it. 'Neither too near to the band nor the Gents, but less than a stone's throw from the kitchen.'

'Splendid, splendid, splendid,' said Himself, settling into his favourite chair and gesturing for me to seat myself.

I surveyed the line of various knives and forks before me with some trepidation. I *do* know how to handle myself in the company of High Society. But there were an awful lot of knives and forks.

Mr Rune ordered a bottle of something exquisite and expensive, without the need of consulting the wine list, and we sat and awaited its arrival.

'What does this fork do?' I asked, out of idle conversation.

'That's a seven-pronged soufflé dipper. I trust that you will shortly be bringing it into play. Shall we dip ourselves into the menus?'

I replaced my seven-pronged soufflé dipper and rubbed my palms together.

'Why do you hate Mr McMurdo so?' I asked as I rubbed.

'I do not hate him, particularly,' Mr Rune replied. 'It is what he represents that I hold in contempt. He is a bureaucrat and a bully. He'd see me at a rope's end if he had half a chance.'

I nodded as the light of understanding dawned. 'Which is why you saw to it that he *accidentally* became reduced in size.'

'I am a Magus,' said Hugo Rune. 'I will not prostitute the High Arts to serve some self-seeking, jumped-up little—'

'Would monsieur care to sample the wine?' A wine waiter, clad in the distinctive livery of the establishment – powdered purple periwig, pink pinafore and pantaloons, peg-heeled pumps and pristine puttees – prettily proffered us plonk.

'Splash it in,' said Hugo Rune, 'and I'll run it round my gums.'

The wine was clearly to his liking, as the Magus gestured for his glass to be filled at the hurry-up. The wine waiter left the bottle on the table and I had to pour my own.

'So what is it all about?' I asked of Hugo Rune.

'Love, and the pursuit of happiness,' he replied. 'Drink up, Rizla – this 1787 Château d'Yquem Sauternes is exceptionally fine.'

I supped at the wine and found it pleasing. But then I would have found most things pleasing, and indeed did so. Which was mostly down to the quantity of gin I had consumed in Mr McMurdo's office.

'I was thinking more about the particle physics business,' I said. 'I do not really see how it can help the war effort.'

'Have you ever heard of the atomic bomb?' asked Hugo Rune.

'Well, of course I have. It is why we are here, is it not? The Germans getting the bomb before the Allies. And destroying America and winning the war.'

'It is all to do with splitting the atom.'

'And this is what Professor Campbell has done, is it?'

'No,' said Hugo Rune. 'I think not. I think his researches took him into a different sphere altogether. But that cannot be confirmed until after luncheon, when we visit his house.'

'So we will be taking a light luncheon then, will we?' I made an encouraging face.

Hugo Rune just shook his head. 'An army marches on its stomach,' he replied. 'Hugo Rune strolls sedately upon a full tum.'

We ordered and then consumed some of the most marvellous

food I have ever tasted. I recall each course we had and each delicious mouthful.

❧ ❧ ❧ ❧ ❧

FIRST COURSES
Gamut of Wrap-Rascal, in scallywag double-de-clutch
Veritable bi-polar launderette (Liberty horse)
Soup of the day. Flying Dutchman pyjamas
Grilled Velocity

ENTRÉES
Paget's Disease in trumped-up-charges. Cockle
One-up-jump-up-long-shot-kick-de-bucket (choice of vegetables)
Three of spades, five and dime. Fly past
Haddock rock lollipop jamboree

DESSERTS
Off your trolley

❧ ❧ ❧ ❧ ❧

As far as I can remember, although French was never my first language.

We were into the Palaeocene niceties from the trolley when I broached once more the topic of particle physics.

'How do you think the universe began?' I asked Hugo Rune.

'I have my personal convictions,' replied the guru's guru. 'I expect them to be confirmed this very afternoon.'

'And are you really expecting to find the missing scientist today?'

'I am expecting to solve the case today, yes.'

'I do not think that is the answer to my question. Would you be so kind as to pass that plate of Rosary Ink-Blot?'

'Absolutely not.' And Mr Rune drew the plate closer to himself. 'But let me tell you this, Rizla, as it will save time later and might give you an insight into the case. I know precisely what field of endeavour Professor Campbell is working upon, because it was *I* who suggested it to him.'

And I now made groaning noises. Although not so loud as to draw unwanted attention to myself from the other diners. 'I really should have guessed something of the sort. You always have a tendency towards *inside knowledge*, in regard to each case that we get involved in.'

'Whatever are you suggesting, Rizla?' And Hugo Rune reached over and snaffled away the last of my Paddock of Gonfalon.

'Well, the reason that I rarely, if ever, am able to help you with your cases is that you always have some secret information regarding them that you neglect to mention.'

'Outrageous,' said Hugo Rune. 'But there is perhaps an element of truth to it. Do you want that last piece of Dry Dock?'

'Yes, I do,' I said, and I snatched up same and rammed it into my mouth.

'You greedy boy. But listen. I will give you a fair chance to solve this case. You know as much as I. The professor vanished from his cellar laboratory. The door was locked from the inside, his clothes were found strewn on the floor. He was to deliver an important paper to the Fellows of the Royal Society tonight, one that is clearly important to the War Effort. This much we know, do you agree?'

I nodded. But did not speak with my mouth full, because to have done so would have been rude.

'Then let me tell you what I know and you do not. Regarding Professor Campbell's line of research. The one that *I* suggested to him. In words of one or more syllables, the professor was searching for the God Particle.'

As I had swallowed, I now said, 'The what?' in a voice laced with surprise.

'It is, in its way, a simple matter,' said Mr Rune. 'Although scientists always seek to overcomplicate, in order to make themselves seem clever and important. If God created the universe, Rizla, then what did he create it from?'

'That is a question well beyond my mental means to answer,' I replied.

'But not mine. Because the answer is simplicity itself. If in the beginning there was God, then there was *nothing but* God. Because if *in the beginning* there was God and *something else*, then you really don't need God at all because you have the beginnings of a universe in the *something else*. Are you following me here?'

'I am,' I said. 'So far.'

'Then bear with me on this, then. If in the beginning there was only God and God created the universe, He created it out of material that was available to Himself. And the only material that was available to Him was *Him*. God created the universe out of Himself.'

'Assuming that you believe in the existence of God,' I said.

'Precisely,' said Hugo Rune. 'But even if you do not, if God *did* create the universe, it follows that there must be some scientific way of checking whether He did or not.'

'And hence you had Professor Campbell seek the God Particle.'

'Precisely once more. If, as the old line goes, "God is everywhere", He is everywhere, because He is everything. He is inside everything. Inside on a subatomic level. The Particle within the particle within the particle. Now what do you think of *that*?'

'I do not believe in God,' I said, 'so personally I do not think that Professor Campbell found this God Particle.'

'So why did he vanish on the eve of reading his paper?'

'Aha,' I said. 'Because he ran away rather than confess that he had failed in his quest.'

'As an argument, that is not without its merits. But you are incorrect. However, we shall see what we shall see. Brandy and cigars now, do you think?'

I felt somewhat woolly at the edges. 'I fear that I will fall asleep if we do,' I said. 'Perhaps I should take a little nap while you go on without me. You clearly have the case solved in your own mind, and I do not really think you will need me around.'

'On the contrary, my dear Rizla. I wouldn't want you to miss all the excitement.'

'Oh,' I said, 'there is going to be some excitement, is there? So far it has mostly been eating and drinking and talking.'

'Rizla,' said Hugo Rune, in an admonitory fashion, 'you had an exciting ride down in a lift to a secret subterranean Ministry, where you met one of the most powerful men in the world, who, I might add, has been reduced to doll-like proportions through the application of High Magick. And you are presently dining in one of the world's top eateries. And yet you complain that the case so far lacks for excitement?'

'Sorry,' I said. 'I suppose I have just got used to having my life put in danger every time I go out on a case with you.'

And then I heard a terrible sound.

'And what is that terrible sound?' I enquired.

'That is the air-raid siren,' said Hugo Rune, 'which means that we are under attack from the skies. Does *that* suit you well for excitement?'

12

The Underground stations served as air-raid shelters during the Second World War. They were never intended to, but so many people flocked into them that the authorities simply turned a blind eye.

Down we went on the escalator into the bowels of Piccadilly. I had something of a shake going on. I fancied a bit of excitement, truly, but not getting blown up by a bomb.

'How long do air raids generally last?' I asked Hugo Rune as we descended on the escalator.

'That depends very much on whether they are real air raids or not,' he said.

'You mean sometimes they are false alarms?'

'I mean no such thing. Sometimes the Ministry of Serendipity wants the streets cleared for reasons of its own.'

'What kind of reasons might these be?'

Mr Rune did tappings at his nose and pointed to a poster that read WALLS HAVE EARS.

That phrase rang a terrible bell, from my recent experiences in enemy-occupied Brentford. But I asked Mr Rune what it meant.

'Spies,' he whispered into my ear. 'Fifth Columnists. Quizlings and beings of that nature, generally.'

'There are German spies here?' I whispered back and then did glancings all around.

Hugo Rune nodded and whispered some more. 'Regarding air raids. When the air-raid siren sounds, all non-London-serving military personnel, essential services, ARP, Home Guard, police, ambulance services, firefighters and so on, must adjourn to the shelters *at once*. This is the law. Martial law. Anyone caught on the streets can be shot as a looter.'

'That is never true,' I said.

'Oh yes it is,' the Perfect Master whispered. 'There is much that history does not record about this war. The Fire Service Secret Priority List, for instance.' And he went on in whispered words to explain just what that was. 'When the bombs start to drop and the calls come in to the fire stations, the gallant lads are expected to respond to these calls in order of priority – hospitals, Government buildings, food supply depots and suchlike. Now recall that the streets are deserted and there is no one to watch in which direction the appliances travel. The Secret Priority List in the station house does not list the Government-approved priority targets for fire extinguishing. On the contrary, it lists pubs, jewellery shops, furriers, high-class tailors and sweet shops. You may draw your own conclusions as to why.'

'That is the most cynical thing I have ever heard you say,' I said to Hugo Rune. 'Those firemen are heroes. I have been told that my own father was a fireman here in London during the Blitz.' And that made me think about my father. About meeting him. Because he *was* here, somewhere in London, right here and now. Alive.

Hugo Rune could tell what I was thinking and he mouthed 'no' towards me. 'You must understand this, Rizla,' he went on, 'war brings out the best in people, the noble virtues. But it also brings out the worst. And the fear that the next minute may be your last does not always engender a charitable disposition.'

'I am disgusted by your words,' I said. 'And also,' and I fanned at my nose, 'by this pong. The London populace that shelters here from the bombings is of a somewhat unwashed persuasion, I am thinking.'

'Indeed.' And Hugo Rune applied a nosegay to his sniffer. 'But if your love is for a cockney singalong about getting your knees up and eating jellied eels, then this is *the place* to be.'

'We are losing time here,' I said. 'If you wish to solve this case by the end of the day we have to get out of here at the hurry-up.'

'And so we will, Rizla. Now follow me.'

And I followed Hugo Rune, down onto the platform of Piccadilly Underground Station, through the hurly-burly and hustle and bustle of cockney costermongers, pearly kings and queens, chimney-sweeping lads and a whole host of colourful period characters who surely should have peopled a Victorian music hall rather than a nineteen-forties Underground station.

'Style never dates,' said Hugo Rune, as if in answer to my unasked question. 'Now follow me further.'

And we left the platform's edge and stepped down onto the track.

'Oh no!' I cried. 'We shall surely be electrocuted or run over by a train. This is not a good idea at all.'

'Be not so timid, Rizla,' called Himself, striding away with vigour. 'The power is switched off during air raids. We have a good twenty minutes. Hurry now, the fun-fur-collared anorak of dread masks not the tattooed shoulder of Talula the hula-hula girl from Kealakekua, Hawaii. No siree. By golly.'

And so I shrugged and followed Mr Rune.

I am still uncertain as to how he created the light which shone ahead of us along the darkness of the tunnel. It appeared to flow from the pommel of his stout stick, but as to how I do not know, because I did not ask.

'Where are we heading to?' I did ask, tripping for the umpteenth time and stumbling about.

'Only to Whitechapel.'

'What?' I replied. 'That is miles away, surely.'

'Naught but a brisk stroll. Are you tooled-up?'

And I had to ask just what he meant.

'Are you armed, Rizla? As my good friend Mr Sherlock Holmes used to say, "Always carry a firearm east of Aldwych".'

'You never knew—' But I did not bother to finish. I stumbled and bumbled along behind Mr Rune, who, it seemed to me, although I might well have been mistaken, took some pleasure in my stumblings and bumblings. By his unstifled laughter.

'It is not funny, me falling down,' I told him.

'Nearly there, Rizla,' he replied. And then he chuckled some more.

And eventually we reached Whitechapel Station. I now had very grazed knees and was not at the peak of my general unfailing cheerfulness. 'You can be a thoroughgoing rotter at times,' I told Hugo Rune. 'On this matter I agree with little Mr McMurdo.'

We hustled and bustled through many more cockneys and climbed over the turnstiles when no station staff were watching and reached daylight in time to hear the 'all clear'.

Which somehow seemed so convenient.

I looked up at Hugo Rune.

And then I shook my head.

'Well, you wanted excitement,' he said. 'Now let's press on.' And press on so we did.

I had never been to this area of London before and I must say that it had taken a terrible pounding. But apparently not today, as I saw no signs of smoke, nor gallant firemen with pockets full of diamonds and guts all full of liberated beer.

'This is Jack the Ripper territory,' I said to Hugo Rune.

And the great man smiled and said, 'Don't get me going on him.' And then he pointed with his cane and said, 'That way, down the Radcliffe Highway.'

At length we reached a rather delightful house. It had blooming wisteria all about its door, which considering the month of the year it really should not have. And it had flowering chrysanthemums and hollyhocks and tulips, roses and *Rafflesia arnoldii* in its neat little trimmed front garden. The house was constructed of London Stock, beneath a roof of Northampton Slate. And there was something altogether musical about it. The front door was of Henry wood and the windows, Philip glass.

I noted also a doorstop of Sly stone and that the afternoon sun angling down gave the front garden the look of a dusty spring field.

'Stop that as soon as you like!' said Mr Rune, and he rapped with his stout stick on the door.

The lady who answered his rappings was beauteous to behold. Her hair was simply red and her coat was deacon blue. It seemed we had just caught her as she was on her way out, and her face was flushed and pink.

Mr Rune made faces at me and introduced himself.

'I know who you are,' I told him.

'I am introducing myself to this lady,' he said.

'I am sorry. I got confused.' I scuffed my heels upon the doorstop and noticed that my brogues where Arthur brown.

The beauteous lady bade us enter with many urgent gestures and we followed her inside.

Mr Rune got straight down to business. 'Show us to the cellar,' he said. 'There is no time to waste.'

We were directed to a door beneath the stairs. 'Down there,' said the lady. 'I will not join you, if you don't mind. I find the professor's laboratory an uncomfortable place to be.'

'The ceiling is very low?' I suggested.

'Its ambience,' said the lady and she shivered. 'And now I have to go, I am in a terrible hurry. Please make sure the front door is secure when you leave.'

'Farewell, then. My companion and I will go down without you,' said Mr Rune. 'Rizla, you first, I think.'

'Hold on,' I said. 'Why me?'

But Mr Rune had opened the door and thrust me through the opening. There was a string that hung down in my face and I gave that string a pull. A narrow staircase was illuminated and I stepped cautiously down it.

'This is not quite what I expected,' I said to Mr Rune. 'I thought that a professor working on a project of national importance would probably live in a big Georgian house with a laboratory that looked a bit like your sitting room, but with more test tubes.'

'You did?'

'And retorts.'

'You did?'

'And Bunsen burners too. Oh, and litmus paper. I have always loved litmus paper. The blue, you understand, never the pink.'

'Quite so, never the pink.'

And then we came to a door. A very sturdy door and a brass one also. This door had clearly been jemmied open and its lock was all broken in.

Mr Rune pushed past me, pushed upon the door, found a light switch, flicked it on.

A most curious room came into view and one with a very low ceiling. It certainly did not resemble my idea of a scientist's laboratory. There were no test tubes, nor retorts, nor Bunsen burners, nor litmus paper of any colour or hue. There was a desk and there were books. And there were more books and there were papers too. And there were more papers and even more papers and, from what I could see of these papers, they all appeared to be covered in mathematical calculations.

'He made a lot of notes,' I observed. 'He was clearly seeking to see if things added up.' And I did a kind of foolish titter. And for my pains received a light cuff to the forehead.

'Ouch,' I said.

'Buffoon,' said Hugo Rune.

'Oh look,' I said. 'His clothes, they are still laid out on the floor.'

Hugo Rune gazed down at the clothes and said, 'That is most suggestive.'

'Perhaps to you,' I said, 'but men's clothes do not really do it for me.'

'Rizla, you are acting the giddy goat, will you please smarten up.'

'I am sorry,' I said. 'Perhaps I am drunk. What would you say the hue of that paper is? Barry white, do you think?'

'I think you need to sit down.'

And indeed I did.

Mr Rune sat me down upon the only chair, which stood behind the book- and paper-smothered desk. I drummed my fingers upon that desk and grinned foolishly. I really did feel rather strange.

Mr Rune did *not* do all those things that detectives are expected to do. He did not throw himself onto the floor and search about for clues. Nor did he pace up and down, deep in thought, before exclaiming, 'I have it.'

Instead he simply took out his cigar case and selected a smoke.

'You are, I believe, my good Rizla, in a somewhat heightened state of mind. Whilst in this state would you care to make free with your observations?'

'I am thinking that I would like some cheese,' I said. 'Which I find puzzling, as I am no real lover of cheese.'

'Anything else?'

'Can this be relevant?'

'Please indulge me, do.'

'I am feeling, and this is really weird, I am feeling that we are not the only ones present in this room. There is someone else here, but I cannot see who it is.'

'Splendid, Rizla, splendid. Then perhaps I can assist you.'

'I really do not understand.'

'But you will.' And Hugo Rune lit up his fine cigar and did great puffings upon it. 'This might surprise you, Rizla,' he said as he puffed. 'Indeed it might frighten you. But you need not be afeared for I am here to protect you.'

'I will take comfort in your words,' I said. 'Whatever they mean.'

'Then in that case, Rizla, let me introduce you to Professor James Stigmata Campbell, would-be discoverer of the God Particle.'

And Mr Rune took great lungfuls of smoke and blew them out through his mouth. And the smoke billowed into the low-ceilinged room and much to my surprise and indeed shock it wafted all around and about the shape of a man. An invisible man, so it seemed, who stood stock still in the centre room, frozen in an attitude of terror.

I could make out for a moment the expression on his face as the smoke brought his features into visibility. And that expression was one of horror. His arms were flung up as if to protect himself from the onrush of some hideous force. His knees were bent, his shoulders stooped and he was all over naked.

Hugo Rune blew further smoke, but I had seen enough. I jumped from that chair and fled from that room and ran with great speed up the stairs.

13

I bent over in that flowery garden, my hands upon my knees, feeling all sick and woozy and no good to man nor to beast.

Mr Rune joined me there, still puffing on his cigar.

'You are a villain,' I said, drawing myself into the vertical plane. 'You are a scoundrel and a rotter. Of course you could solve this case. Because you are the cause of the horror. You did that to that poor man. Turned him invisible with your magic, as you turned Mr McMurdo into a garden gnome.'

'A garden gnome?' And Mr Rune chuckled. 'I rather like that. But no, Rizla, once more you have it wrong. I did *not* do that to Professor Campbell. Rather it would seem that he did it to himself.'

'Are you serious?' I asked. 'Are you telling me the truth? This is all too weird for me. Is Professor Campbell dead? Can he be brought back to life?'

'Questions, questions, questions.' Hugo Rune took a further suck at his cigar and blew out a plume of smoke in the shape of the Lord Mayor's coach. 'Allow me to explain,' he said and then went on to do so. 'I must confess some puzzlement, young Rizla, regarding you doubting the existence of God, as to my personal knowledge you watched the crucifixion of Christ on the screen of the Chronovision and met his many-times great-grandson, Lord Tobes.'

'I am a teenager,' I explained to the guru's guru. 'I am inconsistent and contradictory as the mood takes me.'

'Quite so,' said Mr Rune. 'But to me the existence of God is, as our American cousins might put it, "a given". Without the existence of God and the orders of beings He created, angelic and otherwise, magic, the High Magick, could not function. Professor Campbell sought to discover the God Particle because it is this particle that constitutes the ether, the very medium along which magic is transmitted, as it were.'

'And you are saying that he found it and in doing so put himself into the unfortunate situation that he is now in?'

Hugo Rune flicked ash from his cigar with his little pinkie finger and shook his large head sagely. 'No,' said he, 'I am not. Professor Campbell did *not* discover the God Particle. Because the God Particle *cannot* be discovered. The evidence of God's existence is essentially esoteric and exclusively within the realm of belief. There can never be solid evidence that you can hold in your hand. God is God, Rizla, He knows everything and He is everywhere. Everything is composed of God Particles, everything.'

'I am as confused as ever I was,' I said.

'Now that *does* surprise me. For I have only devoted several lifetimes to this study and still confess to knowing but little. I naturally would have thought that a present-day teenager could pick up such matters within half an hour.'

'You are being sarcastic,' I observed. 'So fair enough. But what *did* happen to the professor? And can he be restored to health and normality?'

'Professor Campbell is dead,' said Hugo Rune. 'His mortal form dissolved into the ether. No magic that I or any other Magus living possesses can restore him to life. Presently the psychic echo of him that I outlined through the employment of this sanctified cigar will vanish for ever. Clearly he worked out the formula, the equation necessary to prove the existence of the God Particle. Such a formula or equation would constitute the strongest spell in the universe. The war would certainly be won in an instant by the country that possessed such a spell and knew how to use it correctly. And he read it aloud. I suspect that his calculations were only ninety-nine-point-nine per cent correct. And so he became subject to the scourge of all clumsy magicians, the *three-fold law of return*, whereby an incorrect calling is reflected back upon the caller with triple force. Most unfortunate for the professor, but fortunate for the Allies.'

'How so fortunate?' I asked. 'The spell does not work. Quite to the contrary in fact.'

'Precisely,' said Hugo Rune. 'But the Nazis aren't to know that, are they? And so when one of the high muckamuck magicians recites it, he too will go the way of Professor Campbell. Hopefully taking a few of his close-by companions-in-infamy with him.'

'But the Nazis do not have the professor's spell, do they?' I said.

'Oh yes they do,' said Hugo Rune, 'or at least they soon will.'

'How so?' I asked again, and I really sighed as I asked it.

'Because the Nazi spy working in the professor's house will be transporting it to them even now.'

'Will they?' I said. And now I was really confused. 'And how could you possibly know *that*?'

'Because you and I met her only a short while ago. She opened the front door and directed us to the cellar laboratory. Did you not notice that she was in a great hurry to get us down there? It was so that she could flee before her identity was discovered. She had found what she was looking for and was making good her escape with it.'

'But how did you know that she is a spy?' I asked.

'Because I recognised her, Rizla. She is Countess Lucretia. The wife of my arch-enemy Count Otto Black. You will recall that I put paid to the evil count in the nineteen sixties. But these are the nineteen forties and he is alive and well and in the employ of the Nazis.'

'Oh,' I said. Which was all I had. But then I said, 'But surely she recognised *you*.'

'Of course she did, Rizla. I did introduce myself to her. And I'm sure that it amuses her greatly to think that she has pulled one over on me. I certainly hope that it does, anyway.'

'And so the case is over,' I said. 'And I suppose it is a satisfactory conclusion. Although not for poor Professor Campbell.'

'Caught in the cosmic crossfire, as it were. Regrettable, but these are troubled times. Ah, Rizla, I see a bus coming, let us return to town and take tea.'

But I shouted, 'No!' And then I shouted, 'Run, Mr Rune. Back into the house, run.'

And Mr Rune, seeing that I meant what I said and clearly sensing that something was deeply amiss did that very thing.

We dived through the open doorway, slammed the door behind us, rushed down the hall and into the kitchen. And not before time did we do this, because so great was the explosion that followed that it brought down the front of the house, lifted the roof and chimney pots and cast them far beyond the back garden.

Coughing and gagging somewhat, we raised our ducked heads and Mr Rune took to dusting down his tweeds, before patting me on the shoulder.

'Stirling work,' he said to me. 'You saved our lives, Rizla. But how you knew what was coming, I confess that I do not know.'

'It was a bus,' I said.

'Yes, Rizla, I am well aware that it was a bus.'

'It was a Number Twenty-Seven bus,' I said.

And then there was a moment's pause.

And then Mr Rune said, 'And that is supposed to be significant, is it?'

'Well, I did not know it was going to blow up,' I said. 'I thought it was going to run us over.'

'I am still in the dark, I regret. And such a lack of illumination suits me not at all.'

'I had a vision,' I explained, 'on the top deck of the tram. An old ragged man warned me to run when I saw the number twenty-seven. I thought it might be a door number, or something. I was not expecting a bus. And certainly not an exploding bus.'

'Packed with dynamite, I suspect, and certainly intended to destroy us. So, it was a vision that warned you.' And Hugo Rune nodded thoughtfully. 'And did this vision have a name?'

'He did,' I said. 'He said that his name was Diogenes.'

'Excellent, splendid, A-one and dinky-do. It would appear that you have a guardian angel watching over you. How appropriate considering the nature of our first case.' And Hugo Rune flung an imaginary hat into the air. 'Then this first case is now most successfully concluded. Diogenes of Sinope, my dear Rizla, was a Greek philosopher. He eschewed all domestic comforts for a life of austere asceticism. He lived in squalor and preached on self-sufficiency. A tarot card is based upon him. And the name of that tarot card is—'

'THE HERMIT?' I said.

And Hugo Rune nodded.

'It's time for tea,' he said.

JUSTICE

14

JUSTICE

I did not immediately take to Lord Jason Lark-Rising.

He appeared upon Mr Rune's doorstop on a Monday morning in early March, while Mr Rune and I were recovering from the after-effects of a particularly heroic five-course breakfast. Waistcoat buttons had been undone, and bellies gently massaged.

'Get the front door, Rizla,' cried Hugo Rune, 'before that young jackanapes has the knocker off it.'

As Lord Jason had yet to reach out for the knocker, I hastened, though sluggishly and unenthusiastically, to oblige the great man. Loud knockings would not suit either of us at that particular time.

Time, always time, and upon this occasion my timing was poor. I swung open the door as Lord Jason groped towards our knocker. The young aristocrat was clearly distracted, for he took hold of my nose and attempted to knock with it.

Which greatly amused a lady in a straw hat who was passing by at the time, but failed to bring joy unto me.

'Dashed sorry, old bogie,' said his Lordship, releasing his grip and examining his fingers with distaste. 'Wish to see Rune, go fish him out for me, do.'

I eyed up this fellow and I did this with similar distaste. I had seen him around and about in the borough, whilst I was strolling in the company of Mr Rune, who still would not let me go out on my own. And the Perfect Master had pointed him out and told me all about him.

He was born to heroic stock; the bloodline of the Lark-Risings could be traced back to the time of Richard the Lionheart, when one of Lord Jason's ancestors had saved that monarch's life by decapitating a Mussulman who was taking a swing at him with a great big pointy sword. And so it had gone on since then, with the Lark-Risings performing noble deeds for King and country down through the ages and right up to the present day.

And in this present day that I now inhabited, there were still many members of the aristocracy to be found living upon Brentford's historic Butts Estate. It was later, during the October mini-uprising of nineteen fifty-one that those who did not flee found themselves up against the wall. Brentford's brief revolution and instigation as an independent communist republic had not proved popular with the locals, who soon ousted the ruling junta.

These in turn fled, including, my Aunt Edna told me, a certain local baker who had risen to prominence in the mini-revolution and who had it away upon his heels to Cuba. I think my Aunt Edna had quite a 'thing' for that baker Mr Castro.

But that was for the future and this was for the now. Before me, on Mr Rune's doorstep, stood this young aristocrat. Surely hardly older than myself, but with that confident bearing and authoritative manner that marked him out from a common-as-mucker such as myself. Naturally I was jealous – well, of course I was. He was very good-looking and very well dressed and he came from a very good family.

'Mr Rune is away on important business,' I said, closing the door upon Lord Jason Lark-Rising.

'Oh no I'm not, young Rizla,' boomed a voice from within. 'Allow His Lordship entry at the hurry-up.'

'Apparently he just returned,' I said and allowed his Lordship entry.

There was something very vibrant about this young man. He veritably bounced past me into the hall and pranced into Mr Rune's study.

I followed him in and a certain joy was brought to me as I noticed the immediate change in his demeanour when he found himself in the presence of Hugo Rune.

A certain humility manifested itself.

'Good day, sir,' said Lord Jason. *Sir!* I liked that. 'So sorry to trouble you, but something has come to my notice that I felt I must bring to yours. So to speak, suchlike and so on.'

'Please seat yourself,' said Hugo Rune. And directed Lord Jason to *my* chair. 'Rizla, fetch coffee, if you will.'

'And if I will *not*?' I asked, huffily.

'You will, Rizla, you will.'

And so I did. And I returned with it, in the bestest pot, with the bestest cups and saucers on the very bestest tray. And I did so in time to hear Mr Rune cry, 'Now here's a thing and no mistake. The sheer unbridled gall.'

So I set down the coffee tray upon an occasional table which no doubt had been yearning for an occasion such as this to arrive and I asked Mr Rune what the trouble might be.

'This letter,' said Himself. 'Delivered anonymously to the house of Lord Jason. Here, read it aloud, if you will.'

'Oh I say,' His Lordship protested. 'It's not for common folk like him.'

But Hugo Rune stilled this protest with a gesture. 'My amanuensis Rizla can be trusted,' he said. 'He is my valued companion. Now, Rizla, please read it aloud. And also let us have your observations.' And he handed an envelope to me and I took this, examined it and said the following things.

'A cheap envelope,' I said, 'which could have been purchased anywhere; no stamp, so as you say, hand-delivered. Opened with a paperknife.'

And Hugo Rune said, 'Bravo.'

I drew the letter from the envelope and opened it up with care. 'Folded seven times,' I said. 'Rather unusual and unnecessary. But typed—' and I examined the typing carefully '—upon a somewhat superannuated typewriter, which has given several distinctive features to the print. And now the contents I shall read aloud.'

And so I did.

Dear Scum

I read. And, 'Ahem,' went I.

Dear Scum,
Know that the war is lost for you and your kind, you who
have squeezed this country until the very pips bled. A Dawn
of Gold shines from out of the darkness. Your end is nigh
and know this too. We will take back what is ours, starting
with your National Treasure. Before the Dawn comes. This
shall be the first sign of our power.

'It is not signed,' I said. And I turned the letter over. 'That is all it says.'

'And what do you make of it, Rizla?'

'Poison pen letter,' I said. 'From some local nutter who has it in for the swells.'

'There is a great deal more to it than that, methinks. Pour coffee, if you will.'

I returned the letter and envelope to Mr Rune and poured coffee. Lord Jason helped himself to three spoonfuls of ersatz sugar and a Bourbon biscuit that I had set aside for myself. I sat down at the now-occasioned table and awaited further developments. These were not too long in coming.

'National Treasure,' said Hugo Rune. 'Now what would you take that to be, Rizla?'

'A plot to kidnap George Formby?' I suggested.

'Try once more.'

'Not Vera Lynn?' And here I shrugged. 'I have never liked her much anyway.'

'No, Rizla,' said Himself. 'It is referring to *the* National Treasure. It is referring to the Crown jewels.'

'Oooh,' I went and I whistled as I went. 'A plot to steal the Crown jewels, how exciting.' But there *was* a certain tone to my voice. One that more than merely hinted that I was not convinced.

'Are you suggesting that I am wrong?'

'Why, perish the thought,' said I. 'But come on now, Mr Rune, that is a letter from a loony.'

'Would you care to wager on this matter?'

'Well . . .' But I knew far better than to bet against Hugo Rune. 'I will keep my money,' I said. 'Or would if I had any. Do you not think it is time that you started paying me some wages?'

But Hugo Rune was having none of *that*. ' "Before the Dawn comes," ' he quoted. 'Which I must take to mean that the Crown jewels are to be stolen tonight.'

But I shook my head at this. 'Oh, please,' I said. 'The Crown jewels? This will be only our second case, if it proves to be a case at all. The theft of the Crown jewels is a Crime-of-the-Century sort of occurrence. Surely that would merit it being at least our eighth or ninth case?'

And, pleased with the persuasiveness of this argument, I took to supping my coffee.

'I shall take the case,' said Hugo Rune to Lord Jason. 'Is your Uncle Rottweiler still an equerry at Kensington Palace?'

Lord Jason nodded.

'I already have an OBE and a Victoria Cross,' said Hugo Rune. 'When I save the National Treasure, I think perhaps a very special one-off knighthood would be in order, in honour of that particular day. What say you?'

And Lord Jason nodded once more.

'Ludicrous,' I said. And I threw up my hands, nearly taking my left eye out with my coffee spoon.

'Well, ludicrous or not, it takes my fancy. Pluck a card from the deck and we'll be on our way.'

'But my breakfast has not gone down yet,' I complained.

'A card from the deck, young Rizla.'

And I plucked a card from the deck.

15

The card I plucked was JUSTICE. But I confess that I did not simply pluck it at random. I plucked it out of sheer wilfulness, as I could see absolutely no connection whatsoever between JUSTICE and the Crown jewels. So, in my own small way, I was simply trying to be unhelpful.

'Can I come along with you?' asked Lord Jason Lark-Rising, the bounce once more returning to him. 'I have all manner of skills that you might wish to put to good use.'

'I think not,' said Hugo Rune. 'Rizla and I work as a team. Although I appreciate your offer, I must decline it.'

And *I* appreciated *that*. Yes, we were indeed a team and it was a real joy to hear Mr Rune confirming this.

'I could drive you in the Rolls,' said the young aristo.

And so we two became three and I got a right old sulk on.

'Perk up, Rizla,' said Hugo Rune as he lolled in the back seat, window half-down, languidly waving to folk we passed by.

'I *am* perked up,' I said, but I was not.

Lord Jason lolled beside Hugo Rune.

I was doing the driving.

All right, I *was* driving a Rolls-Royce 1938 Phantom Fandango XR6, which is not something that you do every day and is really rather quite special. But it should not have been *me* doing the driving. I should have been sharing in the back-seat lolls. *And* Mr Rune made me wear a chauffeur's cap!

'I would have been quite happy to drive,' I heard Lord Jason say to Hugo Rune. 'I'm really becoming quite good at it. I hardly run over anyone much any more. Anyone important anyway.'

'Rizla needs the practice,' Mr Rune replied. 'One day soon he might be driving a tank, so he needs to get his bearings.'

Driving a tank? I shook my head. But later I did *not* drive a tank!

'I see you have a cocktail cabinet,' Hugo Rune observed. 'What say you knock us up a couple of Dive Bombers?'*

'Pip pip,' went His Lordship. And I drove on in silence.

We certainly got some looks from the London populace. But not many of these encompassed admiration or respect. These wartime years saw the class system starting to erode. Those who had once bowed their heads and tugged at their forelocks were straightening up. Change as well as smoke was in the air.

I called back over my shoulder to my passengers, who now were growing somewhat rowdy in the back. 'Will you please stop that raucous singing?' I called. 'And tell me, Mr Rune – should I be driving to the Tower of London, or are the Crown jewels kept somewhere safer from the bombs? The vaults of the Bank of England, or suchlike?'

'They are still in the Tower,' came the somewhat drunken reply. 'As the Royal Family remain at Buck House, so the Crown jewels remain at the Tower. It's a PR exercise really, something to lift the spirits of the masses. "We're all in this together" and all that kind of guff.'

'Oh dear, oh dear,' I was heard to say. But no one heard it but me.

It is a fair old journey from Brentford to the Tower of London and by the time I had reached my destination my passengers were in a state of advanced inebriation, giggling like girlies and falling about in laughter at the slightest no-good-reason-whatsoever. It was quite disgraceful behaviour and I was rightly appalled.

'We are here,' I said, as I drew the Roller to a very sudden halt outside the Tower, which dispatched Hugo Rune and Lord Jason into a giggling heap on the floor. 'We have arrived.' No yellow lines in the nineteen forties. You could park where you wished. 'What exactly are we going to do now?' I asked. 'Neither of you is in any fit state to conduct any kind of investigation.'

'You go by yourself, Rizla,' called Hugo Rune, attempting without success to light a cigar whilst still on the floor and setting fire to Lord

---

* Hugo Rune's favourite cocktail, comprising: 1 part absinthe, 1 part liquid ether, 2 parts laudanum and a glacé cherry. Neither shaken nor stirred, but drunk with extreme caution.

Jason instead. 'Investigate away and return later to report your findings.'

'While you get your head down for a little nap, I suppose.'

'What a fine idea. Go on, now.'

And so I left the Rolls-Royce and its drunken cargo and traipsed over the drawbridge and into the Tower's environs. I had never been to the Tower of London before and I *was* quite impressed by it. Impressed but *not* well favoured. As I had not taken to Lord Jason, I did not take to the Tower of London. It was leaden. Heavy. Grim. Foreboding. Its atmosphere weighed upon me. Many evil deeds had been committed there and you could almost feel them.

I did a little shiver and plodded into the central courtyard. To find my passage blocked by a beefeater.

And a great big beefeater too, he was. And one with a certain attitude.

He wore the traditional duds of the beefeater. Those of a meaty persuasion. The mutton-chop sideburns, the leg-of-lamb shoulder epaulettes, the ham-hock trouserettes, with their distinctive T-bone stripes. The porterhouse shoes and pig-knuckle anklets. Jugged-hare shirt and club-sandwich tie.

And not everyone can pull off a look like that. He regarded me as if I were a stain on his pork-sword cravat and asked just what I wanted.

'I have come to see the Crown jewels,' I replied, bringing my smile into play.

'Well, you can't,' said he. Ignoring my smile and offering me a glare.

'But surely the treasure house is open to the public.'

'Not today it's not.'

And I asked why this was.

And received in reply words to the effect that I should take myself away to a place far distant and engage in sexual intercourse.

'I do not think you quite understand,' I said. And I stood my ground. 'I have reason to believe that an attempt will be made today to steal the Crown jewels. I have been sent to reconnoitre and report back to my superior.'

And would not you know it, or would not you not, the beefeater then told me that I was not a male person, as I had been given to believe throughout my life, but rather, indeed, the personification of female genitalia.

And this I found offensive.

'Your social skills are somewhat lacking, my fine fellow,' I said to him. 'I demand to speak at once to your supervisor.'

Now this demand I knew usually puts the fear of God into any truculent minion of the service industry. And I folded my arms to show that I meant business. And would not be budged until I had found satisfaction.

And would not you know it, or would not you not, he now bawled that I was to 'get out and ******* well stay out', and he dragged me from the courtyard and he flung me out on my ear. And I bounced across the drawbridge and came to rest in a kind of twisted mess upon hard gravel, which really brought on a serious sulk.

I lurched to my feet and dusted down my tweeds. And pondered over just what I should do next. Return to the Rolls and bewail my lot to the probably-now-snoozing Hugo Rune? No, I would have none of that. I was not going to stand for being treated so shabbily. I *would* speak to that fellow's supervisor. And I would—

And then I was all but run over by a horse-drawn brewer's dray. 'Out of the way!' cried its driver, as big-hooved horses marched by.

They were magnificent beasts and exuded the smell of 'horse' to a degree that reached beyond 'pungent' into nasal realms that were best left unexplored.

I jumped back and covered my nose as the brewer's dray rattled by.

They clearly drank a lot of beer at the Tower of London. One of those traditions or old charters or somethings that you read about, I supposed. Like boiling sparrows as a palliative against bicycle saddle sores only when the moon is in its final quarter and there are more blue tulips in the park than you can reasonably shake a stick at. Or was I thinking of something else entirely? Or had I perhaps suffered concussion and was not thinking clearly at all?

The dray rolled into the Tower of London.

And I, having surreptitiously shinnied on the back, rolled with it.

I covered myself up with horses' nosebags and maintained the now legendary low profile. If I could sneak down from the dray and sneak past the foul-mouthed eater of beef then I might be able to sneak into the treasure house and see whether the Crown jewels were still secure or whether someone had sneaked them away.

And then something happened that was so utterly wonderful that I could scarce believe it to be true. It was something that schoolboys of my generation, when I *was* a schoolboy and it *was* my generation, dreamed above all other things would happen to them. It was a Boy's Own Adventure thing. An Enid Blyton moment.

The driver brought the dray to a halt in the courtyard. He climbed down from his high seat and spoke in whispered words to the surly beefeater. And he spoke in the fashion that made my dreams come true.

As I heard: 'Mumble mumble mumble *secret plan*. Mumble mumble *steal the Crown jewels*. Mumble *international conspiracy*. Mumble mumble mumble mumble mumble *A Dawn of Gold shines from the darkness*. Mumble mumble mumble.'

'Well, that explains everything,' I said to myself, but quietly. 'I will follow these villains and see what is indeed what.' And I peeped out from my hideaway beneath the nosebags and watched as the drayman and the beefeater sidled off across the courtyard and entered a great stone tower.

I then climbed from my hideaway and did *certain things*, which seemed appropriate to do. And then I followed the two would-be stealers of the nation's treasure, in that ducking, diving, skulking, creeping-along fashion that is greatly favoured by the ninja.

And I did it with considerable style.

I crept into the mighty castle keep kind of jobbie and along stone corridors, my heart pounding fiercely and my head all swimming with fear. I did not know quite what would happen if I found myself in confrontation with these criminal types. But I supposed that it would be nothing nice for me.

And then I heard them once again.

'Mumble mumble mumble,' they went. '*Drugged all the real beefeaters* mumble mumble. *And told the public to* **** *** mumble mumble mumble. *So let's get this done and hump the jewels into the fake beer barrels on the dray*. Mumble mumble mumble.'

'They might think that they have all the loose ends tied up,' I whispered to myself, 'but they have not reckoned with Rizla.'

And then I felt something cold at the nape of my neck. And then I heard those words that I had no wish to hear.

And that something cold was the mouth of a pistol.

And those words were, 'Put up your hands.'

16

At a gun-muzzle's end I was urged along stone lanes.

The treasure house itself proved to be smaller than I had imagined. A simple circular room with an armoured showcase at its centre. Within this showcase treasure twinkled. And without, the bogus beef-eater and the duplicitous drayman worried at the glasswork with big sledgehammers.

'Comrades,' called the scoundrel who muzzled me forwards. 'See what I 'ave 'ere. A young toff who's wandered far from 'is 'ampshire 'ome.'

The bogus eater of beef did growlings.

As did the dodgy driver of the dray.

'I sent that young ***** packing!' growled the beef-eating one. 'But now as he's back and smelling strongly of horses, we'd best slit his throat.'

'No, hold on, hold on there,' I said, raising my hands even higher than they were already. 'There is no need for any throat-slitting. No need at all.'

'And I'll agree to that,' said he that drove the dray.

'Thank you,' I said. 'I appreciate you doing so.'

'And we'll appreciate *you*. It's a long haul to our destination by steamer. You'll provide us with entertainment.' And he winked most lewdly and licked at his lips. 'And then you'll be meat for our bellies.'

'What?' went I, in an outraged manner, and one not lacking for terror. 'This is not the way things are done in Boy's Own Adventure books. I recall no mentions of homosexual gang-rape and cannibalism.'

'Don't you know there's a war on?' said the villain with the gun at my neck. 'It's all bestiality and phlebotomy nowadays.'

'And chezolagnia,' said the drayman. 'Not to mention emetophilia and coprolagnia.'

'And hierophilia and mammagymnophilia,' said the bad beefeater in a tone that suggested he actually knew what those words meant.

'Hm,' I went. And I took another tack. '*I* would not want to be remembered like that,' I said. 'Not if *I* were making history.'

The drayman gave me a bit of a stare. The beefeater just went, 'Eh?'

'You are revolutionaries, are you not?' I said. 'Your names will go down in history as the brave comrades who liberated the symbols of the monarcho–capitalist tyranny. I would not want my grandchildren to read that I had performed such noble deeds for the people, then rounded them off with a session of bum-banditry followed by a nosh-up of human hamburger.'

There was a pause, then a pause for thought. With each man alone with his own, as it were.

'There's truth in what 'e says,' said the holder of the gun. And his comrades nodded their heads.

'So we'd best not mention it when we get interviewed by the 'acks from the local newspaper.'

'What?' went I. And, 'But,' as well. But all to no avail.

'Pick up an 'ammer,' said the gun-toting anthrophagus pervert, 'and get stuck in to the treasure case.'

And so, downcast and shoulders slumped, I slouched over to the treasure case, hauled up a spare sledgehammer and took to the swinging of it.

Which, as it happened, I rather enjoyed. But then, after all, who would not have? For it was also a childhood dream of boys of my generation to be involved in a really big crime. A Great Train Robbery. The snatching of gold from the Bank of England. The Kidnapping of Diana Dors. I was playing a part in the making of history here. If these monsters actually escaped with their booty and I did not wind up feeding their fetishistic fancies or their grumbling guts, then I would go down in the history books as one of the super-criminals.

But then another thought struck me and did so with some force. I had lived up until a month ago in the nineteen sixties. And although I had never been a particular fan of history, I had read about the Crown jewels. And I had not read that they had ever got stolen during the war, especially not by *me* as one of the robbers. They had not.

But then another thought struck me, which rubbished the former.

The history that *I* had been taught did not record that America had been reduced to a nuclear desert and that Germany had won the war.

But—

And then I received a clip around the ear.

'Stop standing there staring into space with your mouth open, you *** ****** *,' shouted the beastly beefeater, 'and get stuck into that showcase!'

And so I did and they did too and soon the glass was flying. And no alarms went off, for these were the days before pressure-sensitive pads and laser trips and all that kind of hi-tech security caper.

Soon we were all dipping in through the holes we had smashed and pulling out crowns and sceptres and orbs and things of a right royal nature. And the drayman placed Queen Victoria's diamond crown upon his head and his comrades guffawed, and I found myself holding King Charles the Second's Sceptre with the dove, which was originally made for his coronation in sixteen sixty-one. Which was rather special and I knew in my heart that this was all very wrong. Whatever one felt about the monarchy, stealing the Crown jewels *was* wrong. And surely it was heresy or treason, or something, and did they not hang you for that?

'Give me George the Fourth's State Diadem, once worn by Princess Alexandria,' said the drayman to me. 'And empty your pockets too. I saw you slip the One Ring of Power™, otherwise known as Isildur's Bane™, into your trousers.'

'I never did,' I said. But I had.

They crammed the golden regalia into sacks. The drayman fetched a wheelbarrow from his dray and they had *me* load it up. 'Now push it to the dray,' he said and I did not have any choice.

The sun was already going down, which came as some surprise. I did not know that we had been in the treasure house for such a length of time. But darkness *was* falling and searchlights were windscreen-wiping the sky. I gazed up at the barrage balloons that hung above the Tower. What exactly *was* the purpose of those?

And I sniffed at the air of wartime London and that air smelled grim.

'You will not get away with this,' I told my captors. 'You should just make good your escape and have done with it. I will put back the jewels and we can just pretend that none of this ever happened.'

And the wielder of the gun clipped me hard on the head with it and counselled speediness of action in favour of unrequested jaw-motion. 'Move it and shut it,' he told me.

'But—' But I was wasting my time.

But then I heard the air-raid sirens sound.

'Aha!' I went in an I-told-you-so fashion. 'Now you will have to stay put. You cannot drive this dray through the streets during an air raid.'

And then the blighters laughed at me. And the drayman, who seemed now to be doing most of the talking, told me that brewers' drays always had free passage during these otherwise publicly restricted periods.

'I am appalled,' I said and I truly was. But they hastened me onto the dray and the drayman whipped at his horses.

And then those *certain things* that I had done before I followed the drayman and beefeater became manifest. And the drayman suddenly flew from the dray and was dragged at the ends of his reins across the courtyard by his horses.

For I had disconnected them from the dray. Which I, at the time, had thought rather clever. Although not quite so much at this particular moment, because at this particular moment both the beefeater and the gun-wielder set about me something wicked. Reasoning, quite rightly, that I was to blame for the painful fate of their comrade.

And when, at length, they were done with venting their collective spleen upon my person, they left the dray, gathered up their fallen partner in crime, led back the horses and reconnected them to the dray.

Which left me thinking that amongst the *certain things* that I had done, telephoning for the police should have been included.

'What else?' demanded the scuffed-up drayman now looming over me. 'What else did you do?'

'I loosened all the barrels so they would fall off when you went over a bump,' I managed to say, though it pained me in many ways to do so.

I received a bit more kicking while the drayman retightened the stays that held the barrels in place. And then we set off.

Which would have been nice, I suppose, a jaunt on a horse-drawn brewer's dray. Had my own circumstances not been quite so dire at that particular moment. And had not this dray been conveying the stolen Crown jewels away through the streets of London.

The drayman and the gunman sat up front.

The bogus beefeater sat upon my head at the back.

And the horses all went *clip-clop-clip*.

And searchlights beamed in the sky.

Presently we reached the East India Dock Road. Which led to the East India Docks. And unmolested we travelled with naught to be seen of folk on the streets but for the occasional group of firefighters loading crates of beer onto their tenders, or members of the Home Guard stripping lead from the roof of St Stigmatophilia's Church.

And I sighed beneath the big bum bearing down upon my head and I felt quite disillusioned about the Blitz Spirit and hands holding hands and a nation united in a time of crisis.

'This is a rotten world and a rotten age,' I mumbled, 'filled with rotten people doing rotten things and I hate it.'

'Shut up,' said the sitter and he farted on my head.

London's docks had taken a brutal pounding from the Luftwaffe bombs. How anything could function now was well beyond me, but somehow it did, and a small tramp steamer lay at anchor somewhat out from the shoreline.

The villains, myself and the stolen booty were soon in a rowing boat and this was soon out into the river and alongside the steamer. Then we were shortly up and aboard and off down the night-shrouded river. They tossed me through a hatchway into a stinking hold and locked that hatchway upon me.

Which left me alone, to muse upon matters generally and draw my own conclusions as to how I felt about them. Specifically.

But I did not have too long to dwell upon man's inhumanity to man and the unfairness of it all, because the hatchway suddenly opened and I found myself being hauled forth onto the darkened deck. I was most saddened by this hauling forth, as I feared that the fate awaiting me was that fate which had befallen many a cabin boy aboard a pirate brig.

But not as yet, or so it seemed, because I then found myself in the company of a rather pretty lady, who held up a ship's lantern before me and asked me politely whether I would care to join her in her stateroom.

Which I did.

It was a rather well-appointed stateroom as it happened, done up in a somewhat antique style that put me in mind of illustrations I had seen of Captain Nemo's sitting room in the *Nautilus*.

The rather pretty lady sat me down in a leather-bound captain's chair and poured me a glass of red wine from a ship's decanter. I viewed her as she did this and I have to say that there was something not altogether right about this beautiful creature. Which is not to say that there was something *wrong*, just something *different*. She had an ethereal quality about her. An other-worldly quality. And had I believed in such things, which as a rationalist I naturally did not, I might well have supposed that she was one of the fairy folk.

'I really must apologise for the behaviour of the beastly men who captured you,' she said. 'I had not given them my permission to do so. They were simply to retrieve what is ours and return it to me. They will be punished for their transgressions.'

'Right,' I said and I nodded my head. 'I have no idea at all what you are talking about,' I continued.

'You held the ring in your own hand,' she said to me. 'You know exactly what I am talking about.'

'The Ring of Power™?' I asked. 'Also known as Isildur's Bane™?'

'The very same. A great sorrow exists in the land from which I come. A sorrow that can only be lifted when that which was stolen from us is returned. The Ring of Power ™.'

And I nodded once more, most thoughtfully. 'I did think it was a little out of place amongst all the other jewels,' I said, *'them* being real and *it* being the fictional creation of J. R. R. Tolkien™. But then what do I know? Because after all, there is a war on.'

'I am Princess Roellen of Purple Fane,' said this lady to me. 'My realm extends from the Mountains of Ffafiod to the Sea of Garmillion, encompassing the forests of Caecomphap and Pemanythnod.'

'Ah,' I said, 'and pardon me for mentioning it, but none of these names, including your own, would appear to be *trademarked*.'

'The meaning of your words is lost to me,' said Princess Roellen, without the *trademark*.

'*The Lord of the Rings™*,' I said. 'Although, now that I come to think of it, I do not believe it was published until the nineteen fifties. But if push comes to shove, I can always blame it on the Chevalier Effect. Could I have some more wine, please?'

And the princess poured me more wine.

'You understand,' said she, 'that now I have told you of these matters, I cannot allow you to return to London.'

'Oh dear oh dear,' I said. 'And just when I thought that things were looking up. So the future that awaits me is that of the sex toy and the sandwich?'

And at this the princess grinned somewhat coyly. 'We have only just been introduced,' she said. 'Such forwardness is not our natural way in Purple Fane. Although I am never averse to a bit of hobbit-ophilia.'

'I am now truly confused,' I said. 'Am I to be rogered and eaten by the jewel robbers, or not?'

'Absolutely *not*,' said the princess. 'Unless that is what "tugs your elfin bell", as it were.'

'It is not,' I said. 'So what *are* you talking about?'

'If you wish,' said the princess, 'you may return with me to Purple Fane, a land of great beauty untouched by war. Where our people exalt in their liberty. Where justice is the foundation upon which our society rests. And where women outnumber men by twenty to one. What say you to this prospect?'

'Well,' I said, 'I will have to give the matter some thought.'

17

Have to give the matter some thought?

I perhaps lied about this.

'You are asking,' I said, 'whether I would care to leave war-torn London and come with you to what can surely be described as nothing less than an Earthly paradise?'

'I think you will find it to your liking,' said the princess. 'Would you care for more wine? And have some sweeties too. You will be a hero in our land, for returning that which was stolen from us.'

'A hero,' I said and I sipped at my wine and accepted a sweetie too. The prospect of returning with this beautiful creature to Narnia™, or wherever it was that she had come from, leaving the horror of London behind was certainly tempting.

To put it mildly.

And of course—

But then there was a terrible
WHOOMPH!
And things went black for me.

18

And I awoke to find myself aching in places that I never even knew that I had, in the sitting room of Mr Hugo Rune.

'Oh no!' I went and tears leaped to my eyes. 'I dreamed it, I know I did. None of it was real.'

And Mr Rune did pattings at my shoulder and offered me whisky to drink. And although I have never been particularly good with whisky, as it tends to catch on the back of my throat and I find myself spitting it all down my front, on this occasion I took it gratefully and poured it into my mouth.

'She was so beautiful,' I said. 'I should have known it was too good to be true.'

And Mr Rune now took my glass and filled it up once more. 'The tramp steamer was torpedoed,' he said. 'You have Lord Jason here to thank for saving your life.'

'Hi de ho,' went Lord Jason, grinning over Mr Rune's shoulder and waggling fingers at me. 'We asked the Royal Navy to hold fire until I'd rescued you, but they got a tad trigger-happy.'

'But how did you—' And I looked from the one to the other of them and asked just what had happened.

'To be frank with you, Rizla,' said Hugo Rune, 'I was not entirely frank with you.'

'Now this *does* surprise me,' I said, as it did not surprise me at all.

'Firstly, Lord Jason and I did not really get tiddly in the rear of the Roller. We only acted that way—'

'So you could be a hero,' Lord Jason put in.

'Quite so,' said Hugo Rune. 'We were looking out for you, of course, so that no harm came to you.'

'But they beat me up,' I protested, 'on the brewer's dray. And a bogus beefeater sat on my head. And farted too, as it happens.'

'No *lasting* harm,' said Hugo Rune. 'I would have stepped in if they'd actually decided to kill you.'

I did *not* say, 'Well, that is a relief,' because frankly it was not.

'We wanted the whole gang, you see,' Mr Rune continued. 'We wanted to know where they went and how they meant to escape.'

'We followed in a submarine,' said Lord Jason. 'Mr Rune is a friend of the captain and he let me steer some of the way.'

'They will no doubt be able to rebuild that bridge,' said Hugo Rune. 'But to continue: once out at sea the naval chappies decided that the best thing was simply to torpedo the tramp steamer and send all the villains to the bottom of the sea.'

'And me with them,' I said.

'Hence Lord Jason's bravery. He swam over, fought off villains and rescued you.'

'Well, thanks very much indeed,' I said to Lord Jason. 'And what about the Crown jewels? Did you rescue them too?'

'Ah,' said Hugo Rune. 'Ah.'

' "Ah"?' I said. 'Does that mean "no"?'

'It does mean no,' said the Perfect Master. 'The Crown jewels have gone to Davy Jones. But let us not worry for that, they'll be back on display tomorrow.'

'Davy Jones is going to return them, then, is he?' I asked. As I tipped more whisky into my mouth.

'Not as such, Rizla. Which is where the matter of me being frank with you must be brought into play. You see, the Crown jewels are not really the Crown jewels, which is to say that they are only reproductions of the real Crown jewels.'

'Oh,' I said. 'I see. The real Crown jewels are in a safe place.'

'No, my dear Rizla, they're not. The real Crown jewels were broken up and sold at the beginning of the war to raise money for tanks. But this is top secret, so you can't breathe a word of it.'

'So it was all a waste of time,' I said. 'The robbers stealing fake Crown jewels and me getting the hiding of my life for no good reason at all. There really is no justice in this world and I have really had quite enough.' And I finished my drink. And I put down my glass. And I folded my arms and I sulked.

'Well, I must be toddling along now,' said Lord Jason. 'Have a dinner date at my club. The Diogenes. Pop in some time if you're passing, toodle-oo.'

And with that he left. Though I thanked him once more as he did so.

'Another small helping of whisky,' asked Hugo Rune, 'to warm up those cockles of yours?'

'I am disgusted,' I said, 'by the whole thing. There is no justice in this world and everything is evil.'

'There is *some* justice,' said Hugo Rune. 'And although unwittingly, you played your part in bringing it to be.'

'How so?' I asked, for I was baffled by this.

'A small, or rather not so small, matter of a certain ring.'

'A certain ring?' I said in surprise. 'And what certain ring would this be?'

'The Ring of Power™, perhaps,' said Hugo Rune, 'which now is once more in Purple Fane in the hands of a certain princess.'

'You are telling me that she was real?' I said. 'That I did not dream her? That she really exists?'

'Of course,' said Hugo Rune. 'But I did not wish to discuss the matter in front of Lord Jason. He is a member of the aristocracy, after all. In fact it was one of his ancestors who stole the ring and presented it as a gift to a medieval King of England.'

'Would you mind just explaining a little bit more,' I said. 'I really am completely baffled now.'

'The princess came to London to recover the ring, but having visited the treasure house at the Tower, she knew that she could not recover it alone. And so she hired certain East End revolutionaries to make a political statement and send a letter to Lord Jason's family. I rather suspect that the princess put that idea into their heads − it was a good diversion, as then no one would ever suspect the real reason for the theft.'

'And you reasoned all this out for yourself?' I said.

'Well, not entirely − the princess did tell me some of it, when I pulled her from the sinking tramp steamer.'

'But you said that she was probably back in her magical kingdom by now.'

'I arranged transportation myself,' said Hugo Rune. 'It seemed the just thing to do.'

'The *just* thing to do?' And I shrugged as I said it. 'As in the card I picked, JUSTICE.'

Hugo Rune nodded. 'And even though my knighthood must wait

until another day, it would seem that all's well that ends well. Although one thing still remains to be done.'

'And what is that?' I asked.

'You really need to take a bath, young Rizla. You smell most odiously of horse.'

THE HANGÈD MAN

19

THE HANGÈD MAN

'What know you of Bletchley Park?' asked Hugo Rune one day.

The day was a Sunday early in April and we were out a-strolling.

'Actually, I know quite a lot,' I said, in ready reply. But speaking then in muted tones, for walls had ears and we *were* digging for victory. 'It was known as Station X and it was there, under the leadership of the now legendary Alan Turing, that a hand-picked team of polyglots were gathered together to crack German codes. Using Enigma machines and an early computer called Colossus, which was designed and built by the gloriously named Tommy Flowers at the Post Office Research Station in Dollis Hill.' And I did blowings onto my fingernails and mock buffings of these onto my tweedy lapels.

'I assume these blowings and buffings are to signify your smugness at knowing so much,' observed the all-knowing one.

'I would hesitate to use such an emotive word as "smugness",' I declared. 'But you must be impressed by the extent of my knowledge on this subject.'

'Must I?' asked Mr Rune. Affecting an attitude of yawning distraction.

'So, are we going there? Is there a case? And will I get to meet the now legendary Mr Turing?'

'Something of a hero to you, is he?' Mr Rune ceased his strolling and gave me a beaming smile.

'Him and Barnes Wallis,' I said, 'the man who invented the bouncing bomb. I would really love to meet him.'

'And so I suspect you shall. But I see that our strollings have brought us into the close proximity of The Purple Princess, so why should we not take ourselves inside for luncheon and libations?'

This I felt to be a rhetorical question and so I followed Hugo Rune inside.

I greatly enjoyed our visits to The Purple Princess. It was, after all, and I feel that no harm can now come from me revealing this fact, the very pub where in nineteen sixty-seven I had engaged in my underage drinking. In the pleasant company of my good friends John Omally and Norman Hartnel.

The Purple Princess stood four-square on the corner of Ealing Road and Brook Road. And as any sporting gentleman will tell you, Brook Road is *the* road in Brentford. For it is *the road* where stands Brentford Football Ground.

The interior of The Purple Princess, then, as now, was, and is, one to inspire confidence in what lies beneath its pump handles: beer of an excellent nature. It plays host to a fine collection of Victorian fixtures and fittings and assembled bar paraphernalia. And has six hand-drawn ales on draft, a selection only bested by The Flying Swan, an establishment noted for its eight fine ales. And which, under the management of Neville the part-time barman, boasted a policy of absolutely *no underage drinking*.

And thus and so we took our ale at The Purple Princess.

The barlord of this drinking man's Valhalla was a gentleman by the name of Paul, who went, for reasons known only to himself, by the name of Fangio. Fangio combined bar management and black marketeering into a pleasing composition and he, like his bar, stood four-square, prepared to take on all comers.

On this particular Sunday in April he was placed behind his bar counter, his ample frame housed within a siren suit, his brain-filled bonce shaded beneath the brim of a bowler hat and him holding forth upon the quality of mercy, which in his opinion had to be strained more than once in a while.

He greeted us with a cheery, 'Good day there, Mr Rune, Rizla,' enquired as to our drinking tastes, tugged upon the appropriate beer-pull and then asked Mr Rune whether he might ask him a question.

Mr Rune tasted beer, found it pleasing and nodded his head in the affirmative.

'It is this way, Mr Rune,' said Fangio. 'Myself and my colleagues here,' and he indicated himself, and his colleagues, these being a certain Old Pete and a certain Squadron Leader Lancaster, who had happened by on the off chance of an off chance, or some other reason beyond my understanding but which probably involved buying nylons for ladies, 'have been discussing whether the dog is really Man's best friend. Old Pete here says yes that it is. But the squadron leader says no that it isn't and that a good woman can be a man's best friend and a better thing to cuddle up to on a dark and stormy night. And he has a wife *and* a dog. And so we would be grateful if you would offer a casting vote. You being all so all-knowing and suchlike.'

And Hugo Rune nodded once more. And then spoke words of wisdom. 'It is the way with me,' he said, 'never to take any given proposition at face value. One must test a proposition in order to see whether it is to be found wanting. Do you agree?'

And Fangio's head bobbed up and down, taking its bowler hat with it. And Old Pete nodded his snowy scalp and the squadron leader said, 'Tally-ho.' And twiddled his ample moustaches.

'This said,' continued Mr Rune, 'my suggestion would be that the squadron leader should test out the proposition himself.'

'How so?' asked the squadron leader, now twiddling his chin.

'Lock both your wife and your dog in the boot of your car for an hour. Then open up the boot and see which one is the most pleased to see you.'

It was at moments like this that I understood just how Hugo Rune's clear and uncluttered reasoning raised him that extra head and shoulders above the common man.

We left the gentlemen at the bar counter to nod their heads and comment upon Mr Rune's genius and took ourselves off to the corner booth that was permanently reserved for the Magus, lowered our bottoms onto comfy chairs and took to tasting ale.

'That was very impressive,' I said to Hugo Rune.

'A simple enough test, I would have thought,' Himself replied.

'No, not the boot-business,' I said. 'That was an appalling idea. I am talking of course about the way that by saying what you did in the way that you did, you somehow managed once again to avail us of two beers without paying for them.'

'Sssh!' went Mr Rune, pressing a finger to his lips. 'Let us not forget the matter of the walls having ears.'

'It is never far from my thoughts,' I assured him. 'But speak to me now of Bletchley Park. Are we going there?'

'We are indeed,' said Hugo Rune. 'This telegram arrived this very morning. Kindly give it your perusal, then feel free to flesh out a sentence or two with some ill-conceived theorising.'

'Hm,' went I and I accepted the telegram.

It read:

MURDER AT STATION X STOP
FEAR AREA COMPROMISED STOP
REQUEST YOUR IMMEDIATE ATTENTION STOP
M STOP

I handed back the telegram and took to twiddling *my* chin. And further tasting of my ale. And twiddling my chin once more.

'It would appear,' said I, 'that there has been a murder at Station X and Mr McMurdo fears that the area has been compromised and is requesting your immediate attention. So, in my opinion, I—'

'And have to stop you *there*,' said Hugo Rune. 'But it would appear that this is to be our next case. Do you have the remaining tarot cards upon your person?'

'I always carry them with me,' I said.

'Then whip them out and pluck one from the deck.'

I dug into my inside jacket pocket, where I kept the cards, which were already growing somewhat dog-eared at the edges. 'I really do not see the purpose in me doing this,' I complained. 'If you have the case, why *do* you need me to pick a card?'

'Because it is how business is done, Rizla. Have I taught you nothing? Pick a card and no more of your stuff and nonsense.'

And so I picked a card at random and the card I picked was THE HANGÈD MAN.

'That's a particularly gloomy-looking card,' I observed. 'I do hope that it will not mean either you or I having an early-morning appointment with Mr Pierrepoint.'

'You know the hangman's name?' said Mr Rune.

'Another of my heroes, I'm afraid.'

'But not one I hope you'll be meeting. But it is an intriguing card and one that will no doubt have a certain resonance. We will need transportation to Bletchley Park. I have retained the keys to Lord Jason's Rolls-Royce, but I don't think you'll be up to driving.'

'I have only had one beer,' I protested. 'I will be fine.'

'We have lunch to take,' said Hugo Rune. 'And I observed two guest ales on the hand pumps.'

'Hm,' went I, once more. 'It is always a shame to pass up a guest ale.'

'My opinion entirely. I think we should presume upon the squadron leader to provide us with transportation.'

And so we did.

We took a suitably heroic luncheon, which included a haunch of venison, which had apparently 'fallen off the back of a Harrods van'. A selection of vegetables which had, we were given to understand, 'fallen off the back of an ENSA catering truck'. And a bottle of Château Lafitte, which had taken a similar tumble from the rear of yet another carelessly secured vehicle, but had landed safely and softly in the hands of Fangio.

Waistcoat buttons were once more undone. Cigars (we did not ask) we secured from Fangio. These cigars were then smoked, in the company of brandy. And, after a little snooze, Hugo Rune announced that it was time to go and that I should cease my slacking, as work of National Importance awaited us.

He then awakened the squadron leader, who was taking a similar snooze. Although his was punctuated by various mutterings and mumblings, of the, 'Good Lord, woman, it's the size that matters,' and, 'Take tea with the parson? Not with my back,' persuasion. And told him that we must requisition the squadron leader's mode of transport as the fate of the nation depended upon it.

'Need to get back to Ruislip by sparrow-fart though,' said the squadron leader. 'Think you can do that? Can I come along for the ride?'

Hugo Rune nodded that this was acceptable. Told me to expect a long, but exciting, night and told me also, as I kept asking more than just once—

That *yes* I *would* be meeting Alan Turing.

20

We travelled in an Armstrong Hepworth-Stapleford RAF staff car. And it was *not* the most enjoyable ride of my life. It is a long haul from Brentford to Bletchley Park and more than once the air-raid sirens screamed.

And we moved on as the bombs rained down and the sounds and the sights were terrible. The mindless destruction sickened me and made me fierce and angry. The Allies *would* win this war, right would prevail against wrong and *I* would do all that I could to aid Hugo Rune in whatever it took to achieve this end.

It was late in the evening when we finally arrived and what with the blackout and everything, I would not have been able to discern much of the mansion itself had it not been for the fine full moon that swam in the cloudless heavens.

This was a wonderful Victorian pile and as a great fan of Victorian architecture, I was thrilled at the prospect of going inside. But even more thrilled at the prospect of meeting Mr Turing.

I have always had this thing about back-room boffins. Other boys at my junior school chose more obvious heroes to emulate and praise. Douglas Bader with his tin legs. And curiously now as I now remember it, Lord Jason Lark-Rising, who performed great feats of valour. But as I never saw myself as ever likely to be any kind of a hero, in the sense that, in all truth, I would probably never actually have the guts to do anything *really* brave, I liked to read of those other heroes who worked quietly away cracking codes, inventing marvellous weapons and 'being-the-brains-behind'.

I always fancied 'being-the-brains-behind'.

'Pacy-pacy, Rizla,' called Hugo Rune to me as he stepped from the staff car and onto the gravel drive. 'When attacked by a grand piano, you had better not play for time.'

And I marvelled at the brains behind *that*.

Squadron Leader Lancaster bumbled along in the wake of Hugo Rune. And I wondered whether indeed *he* was a hero. Had he shot down Heinkels and Messerschmitts? Did he have any artificial body parts?

Would they make a film about him after the war, with Kenneth More or David Niven in the starring role?

Hugo Rune rapped upon the big front door with the pommel of his stout stick. Then called, 'Open up there,' through the letterbox. But nothing stirred. All was silent. Silent, that is, but for the muffled sounds of distant bombing. And the call of a nearby owl.

'Most curious,' said Hugo Rune. 'And most alarming also.'

'Perhaps they are having an early night,' I suggested. 'After all, they did work very hard. Well, *do* work very hard. Or perhaps they've taken to the shelters and not heard the all clear?'

Hugo Rune did shakings of the head. 'They work around the clock,' he said. 'And do you see that window up there?'

'Top floor, beneath the copper dome?' I asked.

'That very one. That is Winston Churchill's room. He spends a great deal of time here. And he should be here tonight.'

'Winston Churchill,' I said. And I whistled as one would. I mean, *Winston Churchill.* 'Will I get to meet *him*?' I asked. As Hugo Rune struck the door once more.

'Hopefully not,' replied the Magus. 'I don't think you'd take to him at all. And he certainly would *not* take to you.'

I opened my mouth to protest at this, but instead said, 'There is an open window.'

And Hugo Rune asked where and I told him.

'Up there, on the first floor. I could perhaps—'

'You could indeed.' And with a single, and might I say *violent*, motion, Hugo Rune hoiked me from my feet and propelled me skywards. And I made the wailing, as of a lost soul, and floundered about with my hands in the hope of gaining some purchase.

Which I did amidst the climbing ivy. And puffing and blowing in, I admit, a most *un*heroic fashion, I shinnied to the windowsill, then wriggled in through the open window.

I slid untidily to a carpeted floor, struggled to my feet and gently parted the blackout curtains. Soft candlelight welled within this room, which appeared to be some kind of office. There were many papers all littered about and I noticed that drawers had been pulled from a pine desk and emptied onto the floor. This did not look *good*.

I returned to the window and stuck my head out of it. 'There is an office up here,' I called down, 'and it looks all ransacked. I will come down and let you both in.'

I left the ransacked office and found myself upon a wide landing. I thought about calling, 'Hello, is there anyone there?' but I chose not to. There was something altogether uncomfortable about the silence in this great house. Something oppressive. Something somehow alien.

I made off down the stairs at the hurry-up, crossed a marble floor and opened up the big front door.

'Things are not right at all,' I whispered as Hugo Rune entered the house. 'There is a terrible atmosphere here – can you feel it?'

'I feel it and more,' said Himself. 'There is evil afoot in this place.'

'Perhaps I should just wait in the staff car,' said Squadron Leader Lancaster, giving up all hopes of ever being played by David Niven.

'No, come along, do.' And Hugo Rune chivvied him in. He then closed the door and requested that I turn on the lights. I clicked at the switches.

'The lights do not work,' I said. 'The office upstairs is candle-lit. Perhaps there has been a power cut, so they have all gone down to the pub.'

'Perhaps we should go there and check,' said the squadron leader. Whose film part, if any, now seemed likely to be filled by Charlie Drake, or Kenneth Williams at best.

'No electrics and no signs of life,' said Hugo Rune, raising his stout stick in the fashion of Moses calling upon the waters of the Red Sea to part. 'We must step carefully, Rizla. But boldly too, I think.'

He then clocked the squadron leader on the head.

I opened my mouth to ask why as I watched that fellow sink to the floor.

Hugo Rune replied that it was all for the best and that I should follow him.

After which he did that thing with his stout stick again – the bringing-light thing that he had done in the tunnel of the London Underground. And the stout stick's pommel cast a beam of light before us and I followed Mr Rune.

'What do you think has happened here?' I whispered. 'You always have a theory. Or an answer before a question has even been asked. So what do you think about this?'

'If you are asking what I suspect, Rizla, then I must say *the worst*. But in order to learn what has specifically occurred, we must find a survivor.'

And I did not like the sound of that word at all. 'Do you think then that there has been some kind of massacre here? This establishment is top secret, surely.'

'This way, Rizla, come.'

We passed under a Gothic arch, all decoratively diddled in the Arts and Crafts style, and entered what was surely the operations room.

There was a great world map on the far wall, acupunctured all over by myriad coloured flag-pins.

There were rows of desks and upon these desks were the amazing Enigma machines. I had never before seen one up close and the temptation was great to have a little tinker.

'Tinker ye not,' said Hugo Rune. Which made me think that indeed the part of Squadron Leader Lancaster should be played by Frankie Howerd.

'And oh dear me.' And Hugo Rune held high his stick and gestured with his free hand towards the floor.

I peeped past his elbow and gave out with a low, slow whistle, and then I said, 'Oh my goodness, what is *that*?'

Before us, and twinkling slightly in the magical light, was a blackened shape. As it were a shadow or silhouette cast upon the carpeted floor. And the more I looked upon it, the more I became aware of just what it was and just how nasty also.

'It is the shape of a man,' I whispered. 'The shape of a man who has been flung to the floor. But the shape is formed from ashes.'

'That's just what it is, young Rizla. And I have seen such a phenomenon before. A case of Spontaneous Human Combustion.'

'Golly gosh and things of that nature generally,' I said. 'I am now once again most confused. You think that we have stumbled upon that rarest of all rare Fortean phenomena – a case of *Mass* Spontaneous Human Combustion?'

And Hugo Rune clocked me with his stick.

Although not sufficiently hard as to induce unconsciousness.

'Ouch,' I said, as to do so was appropriate at this time.

'Buffoon,' said Hugo Rune. 'This is not the work of God.'

'*The work of God?*' I said. In considerable surprise. 'Are you telling me that Spontaneous Human Combustion is really caused by God smiting people down with a thunderbolt, or something?'

'You have, perchance, a better explanation?'

'Well,' I said, 'I read this article about an experiment that these scientists did with a piggy's leg and a gentleman's pyjama bottom. There is this effect called the slow-burning candle—'

But Hugo Rune raised his stick once more.

'But if you say God, then God it must be,' I said.

'But this is *not* the work of God.' And Hugo Rune stepped over the blackened shape and approached the big wall map of the world.

And this he examined at considerable length.

I stood and shuffled my feet. There were the ashes of a dead person right there on the carpet before me and I did not like that very much. I quite fancied being off on my way. Perhaps I would get to meet Mr Turing another day. But for now all I wanted was to be out of this house of oppressive gloom and body ashes and away to my cosy bed.

'This is all most interesting,' said Hugo Rune suddenly.

So suddenly in fact that I all but dampened my trousers.

'It would appear that the progress of the war that is displayed upon this map scarcely mirrors that which is displayed daily before us in the news-sheets.'

'And *that* surprises *you?*' I said.

'I know that propaganda naturally plays its part in the War Effort,' said the Perfect Master, 'but this is something more. This map shows military ground offensives that are either presently underway, or are planned soon to be so. But these are the most extraordinary strategies. These put me in mind of a game of chess. And I do like a game of chess.'

And indeed Mr Rune *did* like a game of chess. He had taught me how to play, but *not*, so it seemed, how to *win*. And Mr Rune did not play chess upon the standard sixty-four-square board. He had created a somewhat larger board with two extra rows of squares. To accommodate the extra chess piece he had invented. This piece stood to either side of the castle on the new squares of the board. This piece was introduced to me as *The Gentleman*. And as I examined one of these extraordinary pieces, I discerned it to be a small and beautifully carved facsimile of Hugo Rune himself, shaven head and stout stick and everything.

The Gentleman, I was informed, was a rather special chess piece. He could duplicate any movement made by any other piece, including the horsey. And could not be taken, no matter the circumstances. I only played chess with Mr Rune twice. The first time he huffed one of my bishops and the second, one of his *Gentlemen* took all of my pieces, including both of *my Gentlemen* and my King. Mr Rune then poked one of his *Gentlemen* up my left nostril and made me pay a forfeit.

I decided at this point that chess was *not* the game for me.

'It's a work of genius,' said Hugo Rune, gazing at the big wall map of the world. 'But of unworldly genius. With these strategies the Allies will surely trounce the Germans. Although at great human cost. Indeed—' And he stepped back from the map and gestured with his effulgent stick. 'Do you see it, Rizla, do you see it?'

And I gazed too at that map and I saw it.

The flag-pins that represented Allied troops, regiments and units and squadrons too of planes, were tipped with black, the Nazis' tipped with red.

And these black flags' pin-tips formed, it seemed, a great pictorial representation upon that map of the world. And if one stepped back, as I did, and took to slight squintings of the eyes, it was quite clear that they formed a recognisable shape.

And this shape, it seemed, was that of a hangèd man.

21

'What does it mean?' I asked of Hugo Rune. 'What does it mean and what is going on in this place?'

And I think he might have told me, because he probably knew, but he did not get the chance to speak, which was in itself most odd for Hugo Rune.

Because a door, which was clearly camouflaged because neither Mr Rune nor I had noticed its presence, suddenly flew open to the right of the great map and a fellow staggered through the opening and dropped to the floor in a crumpled tweedy heap.

Hugo Rune gazed down upon this tweedy heap and said, 'Step lively Rizla and meet Mr Alan Turing.'

22

We revived, as best we could, the back-room boffin of a hero with the contents of Hugo Rune's hip flask.

The back-room boffin came to and coughed somewhat and spluttered.

'Alan,' said Hugo Rune. 'Are you feeling yourself now?'

'I was searching in my pocket for my keys,' said the other. 'I'll thank you to keep a civil tongue.'

And sadly I shook my head and hoped against hope that I was not about to find myself on the receiving end of a load of ghastly double entendres and cheap knob gags. This, I knew, was *not* what Alan Turing was all about. Although it would be right up Frankie Howerd's back alley. So to speak. I helped the hero into a chair and dusted down his tweeds. He certainly had a noble look to him. A noble look and a famous one too. He had one of those big square heads that film stars and politicians seem always to have. They look so big and square when you actually see them in the flesh that it is as if you are seeing one of Gerry Anderson's puppets brought to life. And it was indeed the case here that Alan Turing bore an uncanny resemblance to Brains out of *Thunderbirds*. I was very taken with his suit, though. Boleskine tweed, like my own, but in the blue. The man had class.

He had extremely twinkly brown eyes and these now stared at Hugo Rune.

'Hugo,' said Alan Turing. 'What are *you* doing here?'

'The matter of the murder,' the mage replied. 'McMurdo from the Ministry called me in, as it were.'

'You should go,' cried Alan Turing. 'Go at once!' And he stared now at me. 'And take your catamite with you.'

'Now steady on,' I said. 'I am an acolyte, me.'

'It's out of control,' Alan now cried. 'I fear it will kill us all. In fact I am certain that it will. Go now. Run while you still can.'

'Where is the rest of your team?' asked Mr Rune, downing the last of his hip flask's contents. 'Not all dead, as that fellow there?' And he gestured to the ashes on the floor.

'Outside, in the Anderson shelter.'

I wondered whether Gerry Anderson had invented *this*.

'They are all safe,' Alan continued, 'as long as they do not come back in here.'

'So why are you here, my friend?' Mr Rune asked.

'I must pull the plug. It is my folly that has brought this upon us. I must, if needs be, pay the price.'

'I think,' said Hugo Rune, 'indeed I *know*, that you must now tell me all that *you know* regarding this matter.'

'I must destroy it. You must leave.' Alan Turing fluttered his hands about in a futile fashion, imploring that Hugo Rune and I depart.

'I must know all that *you* know,' said Hugo Rune. And with that said, he now hoiked Alan Turing to his feet and dragged him from the room and from the hall and from the building.

And then sat him down upon the gravel drive.

'Tell me all,' said Hugo Rune. 'Tell me all, and now.'

Alan Turing huffed and puffed, but then he told it all.

'It is this way,' he said, his big face lit by the moonlight. 'As you must know, this unit has been assembled to crack German codes. Each member of the team is a genius in their own field. Each was required to pass a test, solve the *Daily Telegraph* crossword in less than twelve minutes—'

'I can do that in eight,' said Hugo Rune. 'Whilst holding my breath.'

'I have not the slightest doubt that you can,' said Alan. 'But we are not as you. But we are gathered here to beat the Germans in our way. And I did what I did in good faith and through the honest wish to aid my country. You must understand that.'

'I will understand it better when you explain it to me,' said Hugo Rune. 'Although a light is slowly beginning to appear at the end of a long, dark tunnel. Would I be right in believing that you are referring to Colossus?'

'The computer built by Tommy Flowers,' I said, 'at the Post Office Research Station at Dollis Hill.'

'The same,' said Alan Turing. 'Are you with MI6?'

I shook my head. And shrugged my shoulders. And then I scratched at my nose and twiddled my chin.

'I see,' said Alan Turing. 'A Freemason, I understand.'

I looked at Hugo Rune. Who rolled his eyes.

'Colossus,' said Alan Turing. 'A work of genius if ever there was one. You see, Hugo, there are certain things that cannot be improved upon. Certain mathematical theorems. Certain works of engineering. The Merlin engine for the Spitfire. The Tesla coil. These things have been designed and built to the best standard humanly possible and they simply cannot be improved upon. Such was Colossus. But *I* improved upon it. I added extra components. I upgraded its memory banks. I improved upon perfection. And that a man must never do.'

'That, by definition, a man *can never* do,' said Hugo Rune. '*So* what *did* you do, Alan?'

Alan Turing gave a great sigh. 'I gave it life,' he said.

And I gave a gasp as big as his sigh. 'You gave it *what*?' said I.

'Life,' said Alan Turing. 'Colossus lives. It is a thinking machine. It now thinks independently of those who programme it. It has its own—'

'Artificial Intelligence,' I said.

'Yes,' said Alan Turing. 'I couldn't have put it better myself. That is what it has. Artificial Intelligence. It learns, it thinks. It makes its own decisions.'

'The flags on the great wall map?' said Hugo Rune. 'The strategies, as in a great game of chess?'

'The work of Colossus.'

'A work of unworldly genius,' said the Magus.

'Indeed, indeed.' And Alan Turing nodded his big square head. 'It thinks for itself and it is now in command of the Allied offensive against Germany. It is, in effect, running the war from this side of the English Channel.'

'And Churchill?' asked Hugo Rune.

'He loves every minute of it. Because when we win the war he will take all the credit. No one is ever going to believe that a machine constructed from wires and valves did all the thinking and planned all the military campaigns, are they?'

'It is not in any history book I have ever read,' I said.

'What?' asked Mr Turing.

'And how long has this been going on for?' asked Hugo Rune.

'About six months.'

'And would you say that we are winning the war?'

'Undoubtedly so.'

'And so where, exactly, is the problem?'

'The problem,' cried Alan Turing, his voice rising to an alarming pitch, 'is that it has started killing my staff. It is eliminating those it considers to be slackers, or not contributing sufficient new ideas regarding the winning of the war. It thrives upon ideas. Ideas are its brain food, as it were.'

'How many dead?' asked Hugo Rune.

'Four,' said Alan Turing. 'Mavis the tea lady. She was the first to go. Colossus said that she made the tea too weak. That the operatives needed the *noblesse* of strong tea—'

'Have to stop you *there*,' said Hugo Rune. 'Colossus *said* this? Colossus *speaks*? And *noblesse*?'

'I installed a frequency modulator linked to a vibrating diaphragm. The resultant oscillations mimic speech of a rudimentary nature. It uses words such as *noblesse* and *chivalry*. It thinks it is King Arthur.'

I said, '*What?*'

Mr Rune said, '*What?*'

And again we said, '*What?*' together.

23

'You must surely know the legend,' said Alan Turing, 'that in England's darkest hour, when all seems lost and the realm is threatened with overthrow, King Arthur and his knights will stir from their slumberings beneath Avalon and save us from the oppressor.'

'I consider this to be more than mere legend,' replied the Magus. 'But as to whether this machine of yours is possessed by the spirit of Albion's greatest warrior King, such a proposition I would need to test.'

'It cannot be Arthur.' Alan Turing wrung his hands in wretchedness. 'And it is I who must deal with this matter. I pulled the fuses from the mansion's fuse box, but still Colossus functions. I know not from where it draws its power. But from wherever that is, it must be cut off.'

'There can be at times a very fine line between magic and technology,' said Hugo Rune, 'and sometimes there will be no line at all. I shall deal with this, Alan; you must stay here.'

Alan Turing rose to take issue with Mr Rune's words. But Mr Rune's stout stick came down firmly on his head.

'Your smiter is working overtime tonight,' I observed as I caught the floundering back-room boffin and lowered him gently to the ground.

'I have never matched wits with such an adversary before,' said Hugo Rune, polishing the pommel of his big stout stick. 'It will certainly be a challenge. Do you dare to accompany me, young Rizla?'

'Well,' I said, and I thought about this. I do consider myself to be a brave boy. But, as I have said, there are degrees of bravery. And as to whether I possessed bravery to the standard required to qualify for heroic status, that was open to question.

'Your timidity is understandable,' said the Perfect Master.

'I am *not* timid,' I said. 'I am . . . well . . . yes, I *will* join you, Mr Rune. I will. Yes. I will.'

'Good lad.' And the great man patted my shoulder. 'Let us get this done before the rising of the sun, so we can have the squadron leader back to his squadron in time for his breakfast.'

I went, 'Hm,' and followed Mr Rune.

I knew from what I had read of Bletchley Park that Colossus occupied what had once been the ballroom of the mansion and I had a pretty good idea of what it looked like, and so, with an inevitability that was little less than inevitable, it came as no surprise to me whatsoever to discover that the huge computer was located some-where altogether different and looked absolutely nothing like any photograph I had ever seen of it.

'Down to the cellar,' cried Hugo Rune.

And down to the cellar went we.

The first thing that I became aware of was a humming vibration. It fair put my teeth upon edge. And there was that bumper-car electric sparks smell, mingled with something all-consumingly cheesy that I did not recognise.

'The scent of amaranth,' said Hugo Rune, testing the air with a sensitive nostril. 'A fragrance brought back from Jerusalem during the Crusades. King Arthur's favourite, I do believe.'

'The Crusades?' I whispered. 'Since when was King Arthur around at the time of the Crusades?'

'A rather poorly constructed question,' said Hugo Rune. 'So please hush now and do not speak unless I request you so to do.'

'All right.'

'Did I request that?'

'No.'

'Shut up!'

And we continued in silence.

The hum grew louder, the smells grew smellier and then suddenly—

'Halt!' The voice came as if down a crackling telephone line, or from some even more crackling ancient 78 rpm record. 'Halt and bend the knee.'

Hugo Rune knelt and I did likewise. Hurriedly.

'Who dares to trouble the Monarch unannounced?' asked the voice.

'A loyal knight, my liege, with his squire,' replied Hugo Rune.

'Advance then and be recognised.'

And Mr Rune rose and I rose also. And we two approached Colossus.

And I have to say that I was mightily impressed by what I saw and mightily afeared by it also.

Colossus sat upon a kind of makeshift throne, constructed apparently from the detritus of the cellar. Discarded packing cases, old steamer trunks, several pairs of stag antlers cunningly laced together. And Colossus resembled a man. He was a good and proper nineteen-forties science-fiction-movie-style robot. Most of his parts were cylindrical, the head, body, arms and legs. And all the parts were heavily riveted and all of a metal buffed and polished. He had oblong, letterbox-shaped slits for eyes and mouth and within these slits there was the suggestion of movement. Of cogs slowly grinding together. Of little wheels turning. Of glowing valves and twinkling lights. The robot's hands were jointed and dexterous; its feet had pointy toes.

And upon its head sat a paper crown, of the Christmas cracker persuasion.

I viewed this mechanical apparition with considerable misgivings. I could not see any external wiring. No power leads or plugs that might be wrenched suddenly from sockets. This creation exuded an aura of power and confidence. It had the look of something that would not be easily dealt with.

'I am Arthur, King of all the Britons,' it said. 'And who are you to trouble my cogitations?'

'I am Rune,' said Hugo Rune. 'Though you, sire, will recall me as Merlin.'

My mouth grew wide and ached to utter words. But I shut it up and kept silent.

'Merlin?' The robot leaned itself forwards, metal creaked on metal, cogwheels whirred and whizzed. 'Merlin?' it said once more. 'So long ago. So much time has passed.'

'I am here, sire,' said Hugo Rune, 'as ever loyal and ready to serve you.'

'Merlin, Merlin.' The robot nodded its head. 'We can use your magic here in this benighted time.'

I looked up at Hugo Rune; his face wore an unreadable expression.

'Where are my knights?' asked the robot. 'My knights of the rounded table? What of Lancelot and Galahad and Berty?'

'They race upon their mighty steeds to join you, sire.'

'That is good. That is good. There is so much to be done. So many battles to be waged. No war such as this have ever I seen. Such evil. Such weapons. How has this come to pass?'

'With the passage of time, sire. Much time has passed. Much progress has been made.'

'Progress?' The robot laughed. Its laugh, though, was hollow and somewhat resembled small stones being shaken about inside a tin can. 'You mock me with your words, Merlin. Progress? Look at your King. I am locked within this suit of armour, unable to free myself. Such weirdery as this there never was. And you would call this progress?'

'Much progress has been made, but little of value has been learned,' said Hugo Rune. Which I considered somewhat profound.

As so, it appeared, did the robot.

'But you have not changed, Merlin,' it said. 'Still as bald and well knit. Forever in love with your trenchering.'

I did flinch somewhat at this, as I knew that Mr Rune never took kindly to remarks regarding his portliness.

'I'll dine with a less heavy heart once our enemy is defeated,' he said to the robot. 'I observed your battle plans upon the map upstairs. Such a campaign, although costly, must surely find success.'

'So it is to be hoped.'

As I listened to the crackling telephone voice of the robot, I thought to discern emotion in its words. A certain sadness, a wistfulness, a loneliness also. And as it spoke, I sensed an overwhelming exhaustion.

'Why sit you here, my Lord,' asked Hugo Rune, 'in this dark and dampness? There are fine rooms above that would surely serve you better.'

'No,' said the robot. 'Here I must stay, until all I am called to do is done.'

'Would you not see the light of day once more? Touch mighty oaks that were not yet acorns in our days?'

'No!' And the robot shook its head most fiercely. 'Here must I stay until all is done. I will burn those who fail me with this.' And electrical sparks grew brightly at its fingertips and arced up into the floorboards forming the ceiling above. 'Those who will not obey will be subdued or destroyed. Already have I slain several who I discerned to be spies.

But it is here I must remain, beneath the earth, until I have triumphed. And then I shall rise again and take my rightful place upon the throne of England.'

'Then here I stay also,' declared Hugo Rune, placing his hand on his heart. 'Together we will sing the songs of old and recount the valorous tales. Squire, bring ale for the King and I.'

And I almost said, 'The King and I?' But I thought better of it.

'Ale,' I said. And I bowed my head and backed from the sinister cellar.

It took me a considerable time to find any ale. But at last I managed to locate two bottles of Fuller's ESB. And these in the jacket pockets of the still-unconscious Squadron Leader Lancaster.

I returned to the cellar with much trepidation.

And two bottles of beer.

But I had only reached the foot of the stairs when it hit me that something had changed. Something was altogether different. The humming sound had ceased to be, as too had the curious smells.

Hugo Rune sat at the foot of the throne. His head was in his hands.

The robot sat on the throne itself. But its head lolled to one side. In the manner of a man who had been hangèd.

'What has happened?' I asked Mr Rune. 'Did you kill it? Are you all right?'

The Magus turned his face up to me and I saw tears in his eyes.

'He is gone now,' whispered Hugo Rune. 'I have sent him on his way.'

I looked towards the robot and noticed a dent of considerable size on the crown of its head. And I looked down towards the floor, where lay Mr Rune's stout stick.

And Mr Rune's stout stick was broken, all but snapped in half.

'You did kill it,' I said to Mr Rune. 'And you sent me away so that I would not see you do it.'

'Now is not his time,' said the Magus. 'I have returned him to his slumbers.'

I shook my head. And I said, 'No, you are not telling me—'

'That it *was* the spirit of King Arthur, lodged within the framework of a machine?' Hugo Rune did wipings of a tear. 'That is what I *am* telling you, Rizla. Because that is what it was. What *he* was.'

'No,' I said. 'But then, if it *was* King Arthur, why did you strike him with your stick? Surely, as you said, his battle plans will win the war. Surely that is what we want.'

'The plans will remain in place,' said Hugo Rune, hauling himself to his feet. 'And Mr Turing will restore this machine and this machine will help us to win the war.'

'Oh, hold on,' I said. 'I see this. The robot was not really possessed by the spirit of King Arthur at all. That was some kind of glitch. You have disabled the robot so that Mr Turing can sort out the glitch and use the machine to help win the war.'

And I once more did those buffings of my fingernails upon my tweedy lapels.

But Hugo Rune had no comment to make and we left the cellar in silence.

THE CHARIOT

24

THE CHARIOT

What happened at Bletchley Park deeply affected Hugo Rune. He was silent for days and when finally he spoke again his words were gruff and unfriendly.

I really did not know what to say, but I felt that the Bletchley Park case had not really been brought to anything even vaguely resembling a satisfactory conclusion. I had never got to chat with Alan Turing and the entire case seemed to simply terminate in nothing more than a cop-out ending. And so, when a week had passed, and a most uncomfortable week at that, I felt up to tackling Mr Rune on the subject.

'I really must know,' I told him over breakfast. Mine was a big one and his merely toast. 'I really must know what all that business was about back there at Station X. Was it really the spirit of King Arthur? And were you really Merlin?'

Hugo Rune looked up from his toast, a faraway look in his eye. 'I might tell you much, young Rizla,' he said, 'but whether you would believe any of it, that is quite another matter entirely.'

'I have learned that although it can be uncomfortable, it is always better to believe you rather than to doubt your words,' I said, 'so please tell me what it was that affected you so deeply.'

'The re-meeting of an old friend under quite the wrong circumstances.' Hugo Rune munched toast, but with little joy or gusto.

'Then it *was* King Arthur, and *you*—'

'Let me tell you a story,' said Hugo Rune. 'You can believe it, or believe it not, the choice is entirely yours.'

I nodded with the head of me and tucked into my breakfast.

'There is an Eastern Esoteric tradition,' said Hugo Rune, 'that at the beginning of time, the angels of God penned the pages of a great book. Within this book were listed the names of every person who would ever be born, live and die upon the Earth.

'As each person dies, his or her name is crossed out in the great book. When every name is finally crossed out and there are no more men upon the Earth, so then will this great book be closed for the last time and placed in a great bookcase, beside many other such books that listed the names of many others of many another world.'

I raise my eyebrows to this, but kept on eating my breakfast.

'Now,' said Hugo Rune, 'knowledge of the existence of this great book, and knowledge of its whereabouts, reached the ears of a certain evil man. Exactly how this evil man bribed the angels that guard the great book I do not know, but bribe them he did, to this end: that his name be cut from the book. And once cut from the book his name could never be crossed out. And so he would live for ever.'

'That is very ingenious,' I said. 'If somewhat far-fetched.'

'Do you wish me to continue or not?'

'I do,' I said. And I did.

'This evil man is Count Otto Black,' said Hugo Rune. 'I have killed him at least three times by my reckoning, but back he comes, as chipper as ever.'

'So what is this?' I asked. 'Some personal quest of yours, to track down this particular man and seek to destroy him?'

'It is for me to deal with Black because I am forever linked to him. Allow me to explain, Rizla. A page of a book has two sides and when a name on a page was cut from that great book it had another name upon its other side. When Count Otto Black had his name cut from the great book, *my* name was on the other side of this cutting.'

And I then choked on my breakfast.

And Mr Rune had to pat me on the back and fetch me a glass of water.

'Are you telling me that you are some kind of immortal?' I asked Hugo Rune.

The Magus nodded his head. 'My name was Merlin. Count Otto's name was Mordred, an evil knight at the Court of King Arthur.'

I did whistlings and shakings of the head. 'That is pretty far out,' I said. 'To use the patois of the sixties, that really freaks me and I cannot get my head around it.'

'Perhaps it would be better not to believe it – after all, I might just be winding you up.' And Hugo Rune winked and I saw his face lighten.

And then he stole my sausage.

We had come to the month of May and I was not altogether sure that we were furthering the War Effort and helping to free Europe from the impress of the Nazi jackboot. There was an unremitting sameness about the days. The wail of the sirens, the horror of the bombings. Although, to my wonder, I almost seemed to be growing used to the bombings. Was I developing the Blitz Spirit? Surely not. I was perhaps merely growing numb.

But that ever-present possibility of death certainly seemed to make life brighter. Jokes seemed funnier, food tasted better, drunkenness was somehow more drunken. I had not cared much for our silent week, but if now Mr Rune's spirits were rising once again then it seemed appropriate that we should celebrate this with a drink.

'The Purple Princess will be open,' I said, consulting my wristlet watch. 'We did take a rather late breakfast and it is nearing twelve of the midday clock.'

'You are suggesting luncheon and libations?'

'Well, libations at least, and you will have to pay as I am wageless, as ever.'

'We'll take a drink,' said Hugo Rune, rising and stretching and smiling as he did so. 'But as to actually paying, that would be a matter for discussion.'

There were many cardboard boxes upon Fangio's bar counter. These were stamped with numbers and symbols suggestive of a military origin.

'Fell off the back of a tank?' I enquired when Mr Rune and I had reached the counter.

'Gremlins,' said Fangio, bobbing up and down behind the boxes.

'Two pints of that guest ale, Sans Serif,' said Hugo Rune. 'And then you might explain about the gremlins.'

Fangio pulled pints, cleared boxes to the right and left of him, then pushed these pints across his counter towards our hands.

'Gremlins,' he said once more. 'You must surely have heard the term used. It's a military term – when the mechanical gubbins of something go all to pot, the military folk say "it's got gremlins".'

'That is just a term, Fange,' I said, 'like saying "there is a spanner in the works".'

'And I've got those spanners too,' said Fangio. And he hoisted one up from behind the bar and banged it down on the counter.

'That is a big one,' I said to Fange.

'It's size that matters,' said the barlord. 'Or at least that's what Squadron Leader Lancaster is always saying in his sleep. Did you hear that he got a knighthood? Solved some murder at somewhere called Station X, apparently.'

I looked at Hugo Rune.

He looked at me.

And our looks were far from pleasing.

'So,' said the Magus, tasting ale, 'regarding these gremlins. What do they look like and what do they do and how much are they by the gross?'

'I cannot answer those questions with any degree of precision as of yet,' said Fangio, his face like a cloudy autumn sky. 'I can't seem to get the tops off the boxes.'

Oh how we laughed.

'Til we stopped.

'But I will,' said the publican. 'And when I do, you will be the first to have first dibs, as I live and breathe.'

We took ourselves away from the counter to Mr Rune's private corner.

'Gremlins indeed,' said I.

'Are you expressing some doubts regarding our black-marketeering barlord's latest acquisitions, young Rizla?'

I shrugged and said, 'I suppose not.'

'You should know now never to favour the natural over the supernatural. An illogical explanation will forever trounce its logical counterpart.'

'I am not altogether sure about that.'

'Then what about this?' And Hugo Rune fished the morning's paper from his pocket and tossed it onto the table before me.

'More toot and propaganda?' I queried.

'That and more. You will notice that certain military campaigns have proved most successful. Campaigns that you saw represented by flag-pins on a wall map at Bletchley Park.'

I perused the front page of the paper and mouthed the word *impressive*. 'So Colossus is back on line and all is hopefully well,' I said.

Himself nodded, then prodded at the paper. 'It is this article that interests me,' he said. 'Read it and tell me what you think.'

The article was ringed in pencil.

I read it aloud.

SIGNS AND PORTENTS IN THE HEAVENS

A BRENTFORD shopkeeper, Mr Norman Hartnel, telephoned our offices to report an extraordinary phenomenon in the sky above the borough last night. Mr Hartnel (27) said that he had witnessed a huge wheeled craft apparently pulled by flying horses. Mr Hartnel is teetotal. Did other readers witness this?

'Norman Hartnel,' I said. 'The father of one of my bestest friends. But wheeled craft, pulled by flying horses, what of this?'

'What of this indeed, young Rizla. Have you the tarot cards about you?'

'Yes, as ever,' I said. And I patted my pocket.

'Then dip your hand in and pull out a single one.'

I dipped my hand in and did as I was bid.

Examined the card and said, 'It is called THE CHARIOT.'

'With winged horses and all?' asked the Magus.

'With winged horses and all,' I said. But there were no winged horses.

'Then that would seem about right. Drink up, Rizla, and then we'll take luncheon and then we'll see what we'll see.'

25

I was really rather looking forward to meeting up again with Old Mr Hartnel. Or *Young* Mr Hartnel, as he was now.

Mr Rune still maintained his vigilance when it came to me wandering alone upon the streets of Brentford. He hinted that dire consequences could result. And these hints included the hint that I might somehow create a quantum paradox which would bring about the destruction of the universe by triggering a transperambulation of pseudo-cosmic anti-matter. Although personally I felt that he was over-buttering the curate's egg.

But wander I did *not*. And my only strollings through Brentford were done in the company of Hugo Artemis Solon Saturnicus Reginald Arthur Rune.

And, after considerable lunchings and liberal quaffings of guest ales with names such as Caslon Old Face and Baskerville Bold, we said our farewells to those at The Purple Princess and took ourselves down the road a piece to Norman Hartnel's corner shop.

Oh yes indeed, and I gazed in through the windows, which then were most clean and most polished. Oh yes, there the Wild Woodbine flowered upon colourful show cards and stand-up displays. And there too were many other products of the tobacconist's and confectioner's persuasion. Products that I had no knowledge of. Which had clearly never made it through to the nineteen fifties and sixties.

I spied Atomic Tipped, 'a brand-new concept in smoking pleasure, containing 15% strontium 90'. Also lead-flavoured crisps. Tiger-eye toffees (containing real toffee). And X-Ray Gums, each gum 'bathed in the health-giving rays of the X'.

And I felt somewhat cheated. We never got to taste such goodies in the austere fifties. These people of the nineteen forties never knew quite how lucky they were.

A doodlebug whistled overhead.

And I choked on my thoughts.

'Right, now,' said Hugo Rune, bringing my progress towards the shop door of Mr Hartnel to a halt with his brand-new smart stout stick. 'Just a minor matter or two before we proceed. You have previously entered this establishment, have you not?'

I nodded that I had. Previously, in the future.

'And so you have met Mr Hartnel?'

I nodded that this was the case.

'Then I want none of it,' Hugo Rune said.

'None of *what*?' I asked, most baffled.

'None of your jiggery-pokery, my fine fellow. It might just cross your mind, in the spirit of mischievousness, to impart something to Mr Hartnel in the hope that he might act upon it. So that, when we return to the future, you can check whether he did and if he has, then do some more of that foolish nail-buffing buffoonery that you have become so fond of.'

'Such a thing has never crossed my mind,' I said, although I suppose my thoughts had indeed been moving in this, or a somewhat similar, direction. I had been thinking that I could perhaps make some prediction that Mr Hartnel would pass on to his son. One that I could then take the credit for. Because, and I *did* know this well enough, no one was ever going to believe that I had travelled into the past with Hugo Rune. So – perhaps—

'No!' said Hugo Rune. 'It is one of the reasons that I keep you from wandering the streets alone. It can do great harm. Swear to me that you will do no such thing, nor any other such thing. Now swear.'

And I spat onto my finger and said, 'See this wet, see this dry, cut my throat if I tell a lie.' Though frankly it pained me to do it.

'Good enough,' said Hugo Rune and led the way inside.

And it smelled the same! It actually did. Although the last time I had smelled it, it bore the taint of the Bottomless Pit that Norman junior had uncovered in the kitchenette. But now the shop smelled as it should and looked as it should. And it looked and it smelled wonderfully.

Newer, but basically the same.

But for the boxes, of course. And there were many of these, stacked upon floor and countertop. Cardboard boxes they were, bearing numbers and symbols suggestive of a military origin.

I looked at Mr Rune.

He looked at me.

And both of us spoke the name, 'Fangio.'

And up from behind the counter bobbed the head of Mr Hartnel. And that head gave me something of a start, so closely did it resemble the looks of *my* Norman.

Like father like son indeed. But somewhat spooky when seen in this order.

'How might I help you, gentlemen?' And Mr Hartnel took from the top pocket of his brown shopkeeper's coat a pair of pince-nez and slotted them onto his nose. 'Ah,' he said. 'Mr Rune. And who is this young schoolboy with you? A regular scallywag, he appears to be. Would you care for a toffee, young fellow?' And he dug into an open toffee jar upon the counter and proffered a toffee to me.

'No thank you,' I said, taking half a step back. 'And I will have you know that I am not a schoolboy. And also that offering sweeties to children is not considered politically correct.'

And Hugo Rune smote me with his stick.

And, 'Ouch!' I cried, with very good reason.

'Not off to a good start,' the Magus whispered gruffly into my ear. 'Keep silent and keep your wits about you.'

And I rubbed my ear, where the smiting had smitten, and nodded my head that I would.

'He can be a naughty boy,' said Hugo Rune to Mr Hartnel, 'but he generally responds to a good smacking.'

'Would you care for me to lay into him?' Mr Hartnel asked. 'I've been practising my smacking lately and also my jumping-out. Please observe.' And he ducked down beneath the counter level then suddenly jumped out further along, to most alarming effect.

I fell further back in shock.

And Mr Rune said it was 'nice jumping-out'.

'Thank you,' said Mr Hartnel. 'So would you care for me to take a swing or two at him for good measure?'

'I'll bear it in mind, should the need arise,' said Himself. 'But for now I am here upon more pressing business.'

'The cigars that you ordered, of course. Although, and it pains me greatly to mention this matter. A matter regarding your account. It was agreed that it would be paid six-monthly. And now six years have passed.'

'Good God, man!' cried Hugo Rune, throwing up his stick-bearing hand. 'Don't you know there's a war on?'

'Well, of course, yes. I'm so sorry to bring the matter up.'

'Then just don't do it again. I am here upon far weightier affairs than a few pounds' worth of cigars!'

'A few *hundred* pounds' worth,' said Mr Hartnel, in the tone that is known as 'hopeless' and the manner known as 'doomed'.

'Details, details. I am here at the behest of the Ministry of Serendipity.' And I raised my eyebrows to this. For I knew we were *not*. 'Are you aware of this august body?'

'Absolutely,' said Mr Hartnel. 'They are a secret organisation that represents the real power behind throne and Government.'

I raised my eyebrows also to this. The Ministry of Serendipity was both of these things. But it was also *Top Secret*.

Mr Rune and Mr Hartnel joined hands in a certain fashion. And I noticed for the first time that Mr Hartnel wore a Masonic ring upon his left-hand pinkie finger.

'Quite so,' said Hugo Rune. 'And I am here regarding your vision.'

'The chariot drawn by the winged horses, as the local rag reported it? How might this be of interest to the Ministry?'

'The Ministry takes an interest in *all things*.' Hugo Rune put great emphasis on the final two words of this statement. 'These boxes here, for instance.'

'Ah,' said Mr Hartnel, his face taking on a haunted expression. 'I'm disposing of them. They're gremlins. The very scourge of the War Effort. As a member of the Home Guard I have taken on the responsibility for disposing of them. They're not too easy to get rid of, you see, but I'm doing my best. Fangio at The Purple Princess kindly took a load off my hands.'

I looked up at Hugo Rune.

And he looked down at me.

'You are *disposing* of them?' said the mage.

'Oh yes, they're terribly dangerous. They can break anything. Between you and me, and I say this to you as you are of the Brotherhood and my walls have no ears at all. These gremlins were developed by the Ministry of Serendipity. They were to be dropped by parachute onto German armament factories to disrupt production. The Nazi War Machine is gremlin-free, you see. But the gremlins multiplied and now they must be disposed of.'

'Then why not simply drop them on Germany?' I asked.

'He's speaking out of turn again,' said Mr Hartnel. 'Should I take off my shoe and belabour him with it?'

'It's tempting,' said Hugo Rune. 'But no. However, his point is well made. Why did the RAF not drop the gremlins on Germany?'

'They tried, but the gremlins got free in the aircraft, ruined the control systems, brought down an entire squadron. That newly knighted Squadron Leader Lancaster parachuted into the English Channel. It was three days before he was washed up at Dover and then he got arrested and interrogated – they thought he was a German spy.'

Both Hugo Rune and I grinned somewhat at this, which perhaps was not altogether nice of us.

'Anyway,' said Mr Hartnel, 'I am now in charge of the disposal of these gremlins, before they can do any more damage.'

Hugo Rune nodded thoughtfully. 'And how do you propose to do that?'

'Well,' said Mr Hartnel, 'between you and me, I thought I'd just dig a hole under the kitchenette and bung them all into it.'

'*No!*' I screamed. 'You must not do *that!*'

And Mr Hartnel hit me with his shoe.

26

The shoe-hitting scarcely quietened me down and I made loud my protestations that Mr Hartnel should not engage in any excavation work within his kitchenette.

Hugo Rune hauled me from the premises and demanded an explanation. And when I gave it to him, he stroked at his chin and nodded his head and said the words, 'Well done, Rizla.'

'I did the right thing by speaking out?' I asked.

'You did. Now say no more and leave all further speaking to me.'

And we returned inside.

Mr Hartnel was nowhere to be seen. But I suspected that I knew what was coming and so did not fall back in alarm a second time when he jumped out on us.

'Bravo,' said Hugo Rune, miming the clapping of hands. 'Now, as time and the tide wait not even for Norman, I suggest that we get down to business. Tell me everything you can remember about this vision of yours and in return I will take personal responsibility for the disposal of the gremlins, to save you soiling your sensitive hands with the digging.'

'Sensitive hands?' said Norman Hartnel. 'Well, my mother did say that with hands like mine I should be a pianist. But then she came to a sad end when she was attacked by a piano.'

I mouthed, '*What?*' but did not say it aloud.

'The vision,' said Hugo Rune.

And Mr Hartnel told us what he knew.

'It came about this way,' he told us. 'I am a member of the Church of Banjoleleology. I know the local paper has damned it as an End Times Cult and scorns and condemns our credos, but we are good people, Mr Rune, who mean no harm to others. All we ask for is the freedom to worship in the church of our choice. And the council agreed that as long as we eschew the practices of human sacrifice and drinking the blood of children, then we should be left to our own devices and desires.'

'Quite so,' said Hugo Rune. 'Do you dance around in your bare scuddies at all?'

'Most of the time,' said Mr Hartnel. 'Particularly on Thursday nights at nine at the Good Shepherd Hall in South Ealing Road.'

'Many lady members?' Hugo Rune enquired.

'They outnumber gentlemen two to one.'

'I might swing by next Thursday,' said the Perfect Master. 'Now pray continue with your most interesting narrative.'

And Mr Hartnel continued.

'The Church of Banjoleleology holds to the belief,' he continued, 'that George Formby is an Ascended Master and that the lyrics and chord-sequences of his songs contain occult wisdom that might be garnered through the practice of strict ritual—'

Hugo Rune nodded.

'And the imbibing of strong hallucinogenics.'

'I'll tag Thursday night in my diary, then.'

And Mr Hartnel continued.

'To be entirely honest with you, as you are a Brother Under the Arch, we have not as yet garnered any specific knowledge. But we work hard at it, with the drugs and the frenzied dancing to his records.'

'Most worthy,' said Hugo Rune. 'But am I to understand that the vision of the flying chariot occurred when you were under the influence of strange drugs?'

'Oh no, certainly not. I was on my way to the service when I was granted the vision. I told the congregation and all agreed that I had been greatly blessed. There was much bare-scuddy dancing right up close that night, I can tell you.'

'A flying chariot?' said Hugo Rune.

'It was nothing of the sort,' said Mr Hartnel. 'That is the way the local rag reported it, but that is not the way it was. I did *not* see a flying chariot. What I saw was George, astride a motorcycle combination, and he was riding in the TT Races.'

Mr Rune looked momentarily baffled.

Happily the moment soon passed and he was once more himself.

'A motorcycle combination?' he said. 'With George at the throttle, as it were?'

Mr Hartnel made a 'so-so' face. 'I admit that I told the congregation that it *looked* like George. But to be totally honest, it did not look *too much* like George. The fellow who drove the motorbike was long and gaunt and heavily bearded and he wore a long black leather coat, the tails of which trailed out behind him as he flew along.'

Hugo Rune nodded. Thoughtfully.

'And one more thing,' said Mr Hartnel. 'It wasn't a vision. It was the real thing. I heard the stuttering of the engine and what I saw was solid as solid could be. It flew over Brentford and vanished into the clouds in the direction of Isleworth.'

'Thank you very much,' said Hugo Rune. 'My colleague here will return later in the day to collect the boxed gremlins. The information you have supplied will be of considerable interest to the Ministry. Farewell, Brother.'

And Hugo Rune gave a curious salute and he and I departed.

'And what do you make of all *that*?' I asked when we were once more a-strolling.

'Much,' said the Magus. 'Much indeed. And all of it alarming.'

'It seems the day to be alarmed,' I said. 'That Mr Hartnel had me greatly so with his jumping-out. What do you make of it all? Is he simply a stone-bonker?'

'A stone-bonker, Rizla? Certainly not. Think about what he said. The motorcyclist in the sky. Long and gaunt and heavily bearded, wearing a flowing leather coat. Ring any funeral bells, young Rizla?'

'Count Otto Black,' I said.

'The count if ever it was him. Have you come to any conclusions yourself, regarding this?'

'Only that it is best not to draw any conclusions until you are in command of *all* the information.' And I came *so near* to doing that annoying nail-buffing thing once more. But happily resisted the temptation.

'How about hazarding a guess, then?'

'Ah, well,' I said. 'If it is a guess you are wanting, then how about this one? Count Otto Black has made contact with space aliens and they have furnished him with advanced technology. He was testing out some kind of new-fangled flying craft, possibly powered by the ever-popular, yet enigmatic, transperambulation of pseudo-cosmic anti-matter, when Mr Hartnel saw him.'

And I ducked the coming blow.

But the coming blow never came.

'You might well have something there,' said Himself. 'We will play this one close to our chests.'

'How so?' I so enquired. 'The count has flown away. This happened the night before last – he will be long gone by now.'

'I think not,' said Hugo Rune. 'As I told you, our names are forever linked. And even though he is evil and in the pay of the Führer, he is never far away from me.'

I nodded my head at this intelligence. 'I suppose the Nazi fashions would suit him,' I said. 'All that SS-black-and-leather look. Right up his street, really.'

Hugo Rune did chucklings. And I was glad for them.

'One thing that always puzzled me about the SS,' I said, 'was that they had skulls on their caps. Did they never look in the mirror and say, "Hang about, we have the skulls on our caps. Surely that makes us the baddies?"'

And Hugo Rune did further chucklings.

Causing more gladness from me.

'So what are your plans?' I asked, when we had strolled some more. And *not* in the direction of The Purple Princess, which would have been my first port of call.

'We are going to my workshop,' said the Magus. 'Well prepared is best prepared and things of that nature generally.'

Now this was the first I had heard of Mr Rune possessing a workshop. The concept of such a thing seemed to me absurd. The term 'Hugo Rune's workshop', an oxymoron. Here was a man who ordered the best and expected to have the best delivered to his door. And would possibly one day pay for this best, but probably not in this lifetime. But *own a workshop*? People did *work* in a *workshop*! Hugo Rune?

'Stop it, Rizla!' cried Hugo Rune, raising a fist to his temple. 'I can tell what you are thinking. I said that I *owned* a workshop. I did not say that I ever *did work* in my workshop.'

I breathed a sigh of relief. 'It would certainly have played havoc with your image, as far as I am concerned,' I said.

'Just follow me,' said Hugo Rune.

And follow him I did.

He led me to the St Mary's allotments, where Brentford's horticultur-alists worked their special magic. It was not somewhere that I regularly visited, although as a child I had caused my fair share of havoc amongst beanpoles and water butts. And yes, it looked just the same.

With just one notable difference.

There was a great big hut in the centre of the allotments, a very well-constructed, indeed formidable-looking hut. All corrugated iron and steely rivets.

Hugo Rune was once more at his watch chain, where he selected yet another key and unlocked a mighty padlock. And then he turned to me and said—

'Rizla, I know that I can trust you and so I do not need to impress upon you that you must never speak of what you are about to see. It is my secret. And it will be your secret also. Do you understand this?'

'I do,' I said and I nodded my head.

'And do you swear never to divulge what you see?'

'Not even in the pages of a book that I might pen sometime in the far future?' I asked.

'Other than for those.'

'I swear,' I said. And I saw it wet and I saw it dry once more.

'Then follow me once more.'

Hugo Rune swung open the door and led me into darkness. He shut and bolted this door behind us, bringing on greater black. Then I heard the clicking of a switch, light welled and I became aware that we were travelling downwards. As in a lift descending into the very bowels of the Earth. And I do not make this statement lightly, because we were travelling down and down and down.

My ears began to pop and Hugo Rune offered me a boiled sweet to suck, which certainly took the edge off.

And down and down we went and down and down some more.

'It is very very deep down, your workshop,' I said.

But Hugo Rune said nothing.

Presently the lift halted and we had reached our destination. There was a door before us and the Magus slid this open.

I stared into what lay beyond.

And then I all but fainted.

27

I stood as if within a vast cathedral. A climbing triumph of High Gothic. The columns contained cloisonné coffering in the champlevé style. Sheltered cameo-crusted capitals supported a calotte which rivalled that of the basilica of João de Castilho. But for the subtle differences of the Diocletian diaper work. And the bas-reliefs of booger men and banjos.

'What is this place?' I managed, in a strangled kind of voice.

'Come, Rizla,' Mr Rune said, kindly. 'Surely you recall this style of architecture. We are in one of the Forbidden Zones*, those hidden areas that are not to be found upon any map, where all that is "lost" or "missing" is ultimately to be found. You see, it all began when—'

'Yes,' I said and I nodded as I said it. 'I *do* remember. We discovered the Chronovision within such a cavern as this, beneath the streets of Brighton.'

'And I have appropriated this one for myself,' said Hugo Rune. 'Requisitioned it, as it were, for our old friend the War Effort.'

I gazed all around and about, my jaw hanging slack in awe. There were many tables, or workbenches, dwindling into the distance, and upon these rested many outré items.

Complicated contrivances, wrought from burnished brass, heavy on the cogwheels and ball-governors. Constructions resembling the interiors of mighty clocks, clicking and clacking as wheels slowly turned and curious business was done.

'What are all these mind-boggling things?' I asked of Hugo Rune.

The Magus, stepping to a bench, toyed with an intricate engine. 'Many are inexplicable conundra,' he said, 'built from plans discovered in the lost notebooks of Leonardo da Vinci. Others once belonged to Cagliostro and the Count of St Germain, who designed

---

* For a full explanation see *The Brightonomicon*. But a brief explanation follows here.

them for the improvement of diamonds. Over there, the wheel of Orffyeus, a perpetual motion device that has been turning at precisely twenty-three revolutions per minute for more than three hundred years.'

I shook my head at the wonder of it all. 'And all these marvels belong to you?' I said.

And Hugo Rune did noddings of the head.

'Then why not give them to the world? Or *sell* them, if you prefer. An ever-spinning wheel could replace the internal-combustion engine. Such miracles as these could change the world.'

But now the sage did shakings of the head. And sad they were, the shakings that he did.

'Alas no,' said he. 'Such wonders as these must never find their way to the world above. As with the Chronovision, only evil would come of it.'

'That cannot be true,' I said. 'You are just being selfish.' And even as I spoke those words, I wished I had not done so.

'No, Rizla, no,' cried Hugo Rune. 'You fail to understand. These machines confound all scientific principles. Here, see this, for this is what we've come for.' And he drew my attention to a disc of dull metal about the size of a manhole cover that lay on a nearby table and upon which there rested several house bricks.

'A pile of bricks, on a metal disc,' I remarked. 'Perhaps one of the less-impressive items to be found in this hall of dreams.'

'You think so?' And Hugo Rune flung aside bricks and hoiked up the disc of dull metal.

It was a half-decent hoik and what followed it had my heart rate increasing and my throat turning dry.

He literally balanced that disc of dull metal upon a single finger and then released it into the air.

But it did not fall; it yet remained there, all still and a-hover, defying the law of gravity.

'Wow,' I said, when I could say it. 'What in the Underworld is *that*?'

'That is Gravitite, young Rizla, created by a certain Professor Kaleton. It does not wholly defy the law of gravity. It is actually falling, but only by an inch or two a year.'

'Now *that* would certainly help the War Effort,' I said. 'And do not go telling me at all that it would not.'

'Absolutely not,' said Hugo Rune. 'In fact, it will be helping the War Effort this very night. *It* with the help of *you.*'

And there was something in the way that he said that which I found unappealing, and when he explained to me exactly what he expected me to do, I—

'No!' I said. 'I could never to *that.*'

'But with training, young Rizla, right here, under my supervision, there is no telling what you might be capable of.'

'But I might die.'

'This is a possibility. But if I were a betting man I would say that it was a long shot. At most you might expect some injuries and a degree of hospitalisation.'

'Then *no* once more,' I said. 'I will not do it.'

'Why not give it a little go now? You never know, you might like it.'

I shook my head. And then I ceased with this shaking. Because, after all, what was being offered to me was every schoolboy's dream. Well, every schoolboy's dream after the one about being able to turn invisible at will and sneak into ladies' bedrooms.

This dream was the other dream. The one about being able to fly.

'You are saying to me,' I said to Hugo Rune, 'that the disc of dull metal floating there can support my weight and that on it I would be able to fly through the sky?'

'You read comic books, do you not, Rizla? You have surely read tales of the Silver Surfer™.'

'The Silver Surfer™,' I said, and I did that whistling thing that I did in moments such as these.

'You would surf through the clouds, Rizla. Imagine that.'

And I *could* imagine *that.* Because I *had* certainly dreamed about *that.*

'How do you work it?' I enquired, in a sheepish fashion.

'It is simplicity itself,' the Magus explained. 'Here, let me demonstrate.' And he shinnied up onto the table and climbed aboard the disc. And it simply hovered there, bearing his weight and defying more laws of gravity and suchlike than I dared think about.

'Angle it up at the front and it will rise, down and it will lower, same to swing right or left, a little pressure here, a little pressure there. Lean forwards to make it move forwards, back to make it move back.'

And then he took it up for a spin. Up into the very cathedral-like dome of this subterranean phantasmagoria. And there he performed loop-the-loops and victory rolls and emergency stops and roller-coaster mimickings.

And to say that I was impressed would be—

'Let me have a go!' I shouted. 'Let me have a go!'

And yes, all right, there were moments when I surely might have died. And I came near to many a tumble and many a horrid crash. But during the next couple of hours I steered that magical disc through the air of that underground fastness. And really became most adept.

Hugo Rune made free with mighty clappings and seemed to be in the very best of spirits. 'Bravo, Rizla,' he called to me. Again and again and again.

I do have to say that it took considerable persistence on his part to lure me down to the flagstones. I think I must have become convinced that the sky was really my natural habitat. I was enjoying myself *so much*.

'So now what say you?' asked Hugo Rune. 'Do you think you are up to the challenge?'

'I certainly am,' I said. And I am sorry, but I did that nail-buffing thing.

'Then we must make our plans. I want no harm to come to you and there are certainly dangers ahead. I will explain all and you will listen. What say you to this?'

Well, I did not really say anything much.

I just nodded my head.

28

It was somewhat later that we fell into dispute.

I never argued with Hugo Rune, because on those rare occasions when the mighty force of his intellect did not flatten all opposition, the similarly mighty force of this stout stick would find itself brought into play.

But I really *did* think that I had a point this time and I *was* prepared to argue about it.

'I do not care what you say,' I said. 'I think I *should* have one and that is all there is to it.'

'And I think that you shouldn't!' roared Himself, and his deep voice boomed all around and about the high-domed roof.

'Oh, come on,' I said. 'It is only fair. If I am going to behave like a superhero then I should be dressed like a superhero.'

'You should be incognito. Unrecognisable. In high camouflage.'

'Yes,' I said. 'But that is the point. Most superheroes wear their costumes as a disguise, so that the rest of the world does not know who they are. I could wear these for a start.' And I took up a pair of goggles.

'No, don't look through those,' cried Mr Rune.

But I had and I went, 'Wow!'

Followed by, 'X-Ray Specs!' and, 'I can see right through your clothes!'

And then, 'Oh my goodness me,' and I removed the X-Ray Specs and returned them to Mr Rune.

But I still thought that I should have a superhero costume and so finally we reached a sort of a compromise.

I was given another pair of goggles, a bright red fez, a polished breastplate from one of the many suits of armour that stood all around and about and a Sam Browne belt with several pouches attached to it, which I felt had a certain caped-crusader quality.

'And I need a cloak,' I said.

'I am beginning to think that Mr Hartnel's methods of child training hold to a certain merit,' said the guru's guru. But he took himself off to a distant cupboard, returning soon with a fine long black velvet cloak. And with that he also gave me a certain something that he assured me in whispered words would be essential to the success of my mission.

I togged up in all and said, 'What do you think of me?'

And Hugo Rune stifled jocularity. 'To paraphrase someone or other,' he said, 'if you scare the enemy as much as you scare me, then we'll all be home in time for *Jackanory*.'

The lift went up and we went with it. Me in my superhero outfit, seated on the floating disc of metal. Mr Rune tapping his stout stick on the floor and checking his pocket watch.

'Oh no,' I said. 'I do not have a name. I cannot be a superhero if I do not have a name.'

'How about Puppy Boy?' asked Hugo Rune.

'Certainly *not*!' I said.

'Badly Dressed Boy? The Flying ★★★★Wit? The Masked Buffoon? The—'

'Stop it,' I said. 'Do not be so unkind. You are the all-knowing one. You should know a good name to call me.'

There was a moment of silence then. Followed by Hugo Rune saying, 'Well, Rizla, the wingéd chariot concept, being put about by the reporter of the local rag, was clearly designed to inspire. So why not something appropriately inspirational? I hereby name you Captain England.'

'There *is* Captain America,' I said.

'All too generalised,' said Hugo Rune. 'Let's call you Captain Brentford.'

'There is *still* Captain America,' I said.

'Then let us outrank him. How about Wing Commander Brentford?'

'That does not sound much like a superhero.'

'Oh dear,' said Hugo Rune. 'We seem to have reached ground level. You'll just have to be known as the Superhero Who Dare Not Speak His Name.'

'Captain Brentford it is, then,' I said. And I saluted.

'Captain Brentford it is, then. Good boy, Rizla.'

It was now the evening and all around was dark. Very dark, as everywhere was blackout. The moon was scarcely a crescent, but the stars were shining down. I shivered and I raised my tweedy collar.

'I think perhaps now,' I said, 'would be the time for you to outline your plan. I know it involves me flying up into the sky and engaging Count Otto Black in some kind of aerial combat, but so far I find myself short of a battle plan. This is not going to be a kamikaze mission, is it?'

'I have assured you otherwise.'

'You did hint at hospitalisation.'

'Oh come come, Rizla.' And Hugo Rune plucked a cigar from his case and inserted it into his mouth. 'Don't go getting all timid again. You have the certain something that I gave to you earlier?'

There had been a degree of secrecy regarding this certain something. A certain furtiveness had been involved in Mr Rune passing it to me and whispering into my ear.

'I have it,' I said. 'Under my cloak.'

'Then do with it as you should, when the moment presents itself.'

'Well,' I said, 'that is all well and good, but I do not see how—'

But Mr Rune did *sssh*ings with his finger pressed to his lips and then this finger pointed to the sky. And I screwed up my eyes and did some peerings and also screwed my ears up and heard some sounds.

Sounds were these as of an aged motorbike. The coughing and spluttering of a four-stroke engine. And these sounds came not from a nearby road. These sounds issued from above.

'It *is* him,' I whispered. 'He has returned.'

'Prepare yourself, then, Captain Brentford.'

The stuttering, coughing motorbike sounds drew nearer and nearer and then we espied in the heavens a single headlight cleaving the darkness before it. And less than one hundred feet above we could make out the shape of a long gaunt figure astride an ancient motorbike, which was attached to a similarly antiquated sidecar. And even though this figure was shrouded in darkness, there was absolutely no doubt in either Hugo Rune's mind or my own that this was none other than the arch-enemy of my noble friend.

The evil Count Otto, it was he.

Hugo Rune lit his cigar and drew upon it deeply.

And then a voice called down from on high that fair put the wind up me.

'Rune,' called this unholy voice, for such a voice it was. 'Rune, you plump scoundrel. Surely that is yourself I see there, lurking. Sucking on some cheap cigar that you conned from the local wide boy.'

Hugo Rune did wavings unto me and I understood the meanings of these wavings and converted these meanings into motions.

'Black,' called back the Magus. 'What is that dilapidated contraption that you perch upon? You look like an organ-grinder's monkey.'

'State of the present art, my fat friend. And it has a trick or two up its technological sleeve. Here, have a taste of *this*.'

And Count Otto Black delved into his sidecar and then many small queer things rained down.

And great were the explosions all around and about the allotment. Old Pete's shed took fire and many a sprout bed went to wrack and ruin. The laughter of Count Otto Black poured forth from up above. And I feared greatly for Himself.

'You'll have to do better than that, you pungent turd,' called the voice of Hugo Rune. From somewhere now in hiding, but large and loud as life.

'Just a tiny taste of what is to come, you porkie pie. The Reich's terror weapon programme expands daily. Great are the advances made. Soon the whole world will cower before the power of the Führer.'

'What is it with madmen and facial hair?' called Hugo Rune in return. 'That Nazi oaf with his bog-brush moustache and you with your verminous facial furnishings. Should I introduce you both to my barber? A wash and brush-up would certainly do the pair of you no harm.'

And down poured further ordnance and damned were many crops.

And Count Otto Black made free with that manic laughing that is always so popular with the supervillain.

And it crossed my mind that in order to beat a *super*villain, the most suitable person to employ for the job would be a *super*hero. And so, as the count now delved into his sidecar once more and sought to drag out a particularly large killer-bomb-type arrangement, I did a kind of 'ahem' which focused his attention.

'What?' went he, Count Otto Black. 'What do we have here?'

And I hovered there above him. There in the pale moonlight.

'I am Captain Brentford,' I called out. 'And you are dead, mother-f★★★er.' Which was not perhaps the most appropriate thing to call out, given the period and suchlike, but I was a bit overexcited and it just popped out, so to speak.

'Captain *what*?' And Count Otto laughed once morè. He laughed once more, then he stopped.

'So how exactly are you hanging up there?' he asked. And he raised himself from the seat of his hovering motorcycle and tried to reach up to my feet.

I angled up the Gravitite disc and swung away out of reach.

'A rather natty device,' said the count, 'and one, I think, that would certainly further the ends of the Fatherland. What say I offer you one million pounds in exchange for your metallic ride?'

'A million pounds?' I said. And certain thoughts ran through my head.

'A million pounds. Here, I have a pouch of diamonds in my pocket, kept for such an occasion.'

'A million pounds?' I said again. And I gazed down at the gaunt figure below me, astride the hovering motorcycle combination. His pinched features were lit by the fires beneath, blazing upon the St Mary's allotments. Above, the moon and stars; below, this man. This *evil* man.

'A million pounds,' he said once more. 'Down just a bit and it's yours.'

And I leaned forwards and dropped down a tad, oh so near to those long, thin fingers.

'Here,' cried Count Otto Black. 'See the diamonds. They are for you.' And he dug into his jacket and then he pulled out—

A gun.

And I cried, 'No, this is for *you*.' And I flung down a certain something.

Mr Rune confessed to me later that he genuinely feared for my life at that moment. He confessed that he had never tested a piece of Gravitite to see whether it could withstand an onslaught of bullets.

Happily the piece I rode upon could and the bullets fired by the count ricocheted down and bounced about his motorbike causing certain damage.

But the cry of horror that rose from his thin-lipped mouth, hidden somewhere beneath the great black beard, came not because of ricocheting bullets. It came because of the fact that the motorcycle engine, the inexplicable antigravitational engine, suddenly coughed rather loudly, then faltered, then died, which caused his mount to plummet.

There were clickings and whooshings and fallings and down went Count Otto Black. His descent arched over the allotments, and over the football ground and over The Purple Princess. And when he finally met terra firma, it was in the Thames.

We took an evening drink in Fangio's bar.

'And what in the name of all that slips out of a rear entrance when officials' backs are turned are you supposed to be?' he asked me, as Mr Rune and I approached the counter.

'I am Captain Brentford,' I said. 'Oh damn, there goes my secret identity.'

'Two pints of Helvetica Narrow please,' said Hugo Rune. 'And double whisky chasers – Captain Brentford here just struck a mighty blow for freedom.'

'Did too,' I said. 'Shot down that mother★★—'

'Rizla!' said Hugo Rune.

'Oh, it's Rizla, is it?' said Fangio. 'I didn't recognise you. I thought you were a superhero. And we don't get many of those in this bar. There's only Rat Boy over there in the corner, gnawing cheese, and Bad Advice Man, who personally advised me to avail myself of a load of boxes of gremlins from Norman at the corner shop. One of which I did notice you slipping into your coat earlier in the day, Mr Rune. And you're quite welcome to it too, I might say.'

And I looked at Hugo Rune.

He looked at me.

And Hugo Rune said, 'This very gremlin was indeed that "certain something" that you, Captain Brentford, emptied from its box onto the flying motorcycle's engine, and it had the desired effect – do you not agree?'

'Oh, I do,' I agreed. 'It certainly put paid to his flying chariot.'

'Hey, hold on now for a minute,' said Fangio. 'How come that manhole-cover affair that you've brought in with you is hovering right there in the air?'

'It isn't,' said Hugo Rune. 'It is an optical illusion. Now two more beers and chasers please, and two packets of those new potato-flavoured crisps. The ones with added Kryptonite.'

THE HIGH PRIESTESS

29

THE HIGH PRIESTESS

'But is he dead?' I asked of Hugo Rune.

'Of course he isn't,' Hugo Rune replied. 'He noodled about on that sky-bike of his merely to taunt me. And flaunt the superior technology of his fascist cronies. But you put a spanner in his works.'

'Yes,' I agreed. 'And I have been thinking about that. I reckon Captain Brentford should take to the skies on a regular basis. Knock those German Blitz-planes for six. Save the day generally and indeed things of that nature. What do you think?'

'I think that you have been drinking,' said the Perfect Master. 'I know that I have and I am beginning to feel the benefit.'

For indeed we had been drinking at The Purple Princess. It was another Sunday afternoon and this one in June, as it happened, and we were celebrating something or other, which, in the midst of all the celebrating, had somehow, now, been forgotten.

'So what do you think?' I said to Mr Rune. 'Should Captain Brentford take to the skies once more?'

'Not at present, Rizla. I think our next case will be strictly ground-level.'

'Oh,' went I. 'We have a new case, do we? This is new, as it were.'

'I am weighing up the pros and cons,' said Mr Rune, 'in order to see whether I can fit it in.'

And I made laughter at this. 'We have not done anything for the last three weeks,' I said, laughing still as I said it.

'*You* have done nothing,' quoth the mage, 'but Rune's mind never sleeps. I cogitate, Rizla. I tread the interdimensional landscapes of the id.'

'And you dine,' I added. 'And smoke cigars and drink the finest wines. Not bad during a period of national austerity and rationing.'

'You wish me to starve like an anchorite?'

'Certainly not,' I said. 'I love the dining out. But tell me about this possible case that you are weighing up the pros and cons of.'

'Do you recall our first case? Regarding the tragic demise of Professor Campbell?'

'I doubt I will ever forget it,' I said. 'I had nightmares for weeks.'

'Well, I have received yet another telegram from the egregious Mr McMurdo at the Ministry of Serendipity. More problems with their boffins, it appears.' And Mr Rune tugged a crumpled telegram from his waistcoat pocket and flung it in my direction.

I lowered my pint of Times Roman and took up the telegram from where it had fallen into the leavings of my bread and butter pudding. I viewed this missive and read from it aloud.

EMERGENCY STOP COME TO MINISTRY AT ONCE STOP
PROJECT BBT IN DANGER STOP NEED YOUR HELP NOW STOP

'Golly and gosh,' I said to Mr Rune. 'This does sound a bit urgent. Did this arrive today?' And I examined the crumpled paper.

'Last week, actually.' The Magus yawned. 'But it's all such a fag. Project BBT is always in danger. And always on the verge of a breakthrough. But never actually makes a breakthrough. I tire of it, truly, Rizla, I do.'

'Might I ask what Project BBT is?' I enquired.

'You might,' Himself replied.

'And would there be any likelihood of you telling me, do you think?'

Hugo Rune made louder yawns. 'Get the drinks in, then, and I will,' he said.

'I have no money,' I replied. 'You never pay me any money at all.'

'I said get the drinks in, Rizla. I do not recall telling you to pay for them.'

'Quite so,' I said and I toddled off to the bar.

Fangio was holding forth to all and sundry upon the subject of dogs.

'Dogs *again*, is it?' I enquired as I ordered two more pints of Times. 'I recall that chat about Man's best friend.'

Fangio laughed and handed me the Sunday paper.

SQUADRON LEADER JAILED IN
WIFE-IN-BOOT SCANDAL

'Oh, jolly good,' I said. 'That will amuse Mr Rune. So what is it about dogs today then, Fange?'

'It's not dogs in general,' said the barlord, 'but rather one in particular. Did you ever hear the story of the Devil Dog of Mons?'

'No I did not,' I said, 'but I certainly like the sound of it.' And I sipped at my newly drawn ale, ignoring Mr Rune's frantic beckonings to bring his over.

'Go on then, Fange,' I said. 'I have a moment or two spare before I have to swing off on a new case.'

'Right then,' said the barlord. 'It is this way. During the First World War, the Allied soldiers inhabiting their trenches at Mons swore that they saw at night the shape of a huge hound that roamed no-man's-land feasting upon the corpses of the newly slain.'

'How absolutely horrid,' I said. 'Tell me more.'

'Well then,' Fangio continued, 'many folk didn't believe this tale. They said it was hysteria or shell shock or suchlike. But after the war, a hospital nearby on the German side of the enemy lines was liberated and it turned out that an evil doctor called Baron von Bacon had been performing terrible experiments there. With dogs and men.'

'Go on,' I said. And I turned my back on the flapping Mr Rune.

'It seems,' said Fangio, 'that Baron von Bacon had taken the brain from a dying German soldier and transplanted it into a German wolfhound. And that was the creature that roamed no-man's-land.'

'And did they ever find this monstrous hound?' I asked.

'Never,' said Fangio. 'Nor indeed any trace of Baron von Bacon. Well, not perhaps until now.'

'Oooooh!' I said and I made a scaredy face.

'It's no laughing matter,' said Fangio. 'Recall that enemy bombing of the St Mary's allotments a few weeks back?'

I did indeed, but I had not divulged the extent of my knowledge to Fangio.

'Well, something odd got uncovered on Old Pete's plot. Thrown up by the explosions. A big coffin-type box it was. But by the time Old Pete got to it, it had been busted open. Inside the coffin-type box he found lots of screwed-up German newspapers that dated back to the end of the First World War. At that time the allotments were briefly used as a prisoner-of-war-camp. All kinds of odd stuff was said to have been moved in and out of those allotments around then. Old Pete talks about antique brass machinery and stuff that had found its way back to England after being "liberated" by the Allies. It went onto the allotments, but no one ever saw it leave. Anyway, this German newspaper seemed to have been used to pack two things, because although the things were gone, their shapes were left behind.'

'And let me guess,' I said. 'The shapes were of a man and a gigantic dog.'

'You have it in one,' said Fangio the landlord. 'Or two, if your counting is precise.'

'And does Old Pete still have this coffin-type box?'

'Chopped it up for firewood, I believe.'

'And so no actual proof exists at all?'

'Not of the coffin-type box, no.'

'Nor that it contained Baron von Bacon and his Hellish Man-Hound.'

'But for these,' said Fangio, and he handed me—

'Dog tags,' I said. And I read the name on them. 'Baron von Bacon,' I said. And I was truly impressed. 'Are you selling *these*?' I asked the barlord.

'If the price is right,' he said.

I shook my head and returned with my pints to Hugo Rune.

'Jaw jaw jaw,' said the guru's guru, 'and my ale growing warm whilst you do so.'

'But you will notice that I did not actually pay for the beers,' I said, placing same on the table.

'Buff your fingernails upon your lapel and feel the weight of my stout stick,' said Hugo Rune, tasting and approving of the ale.

'Fangio just told me a really creepy story,' I said.

'Baron von Bacon's Hell Hound, I suppose.'

'It might be running loose on the allotments – what do you think?'

'I would not totally pooh-pooh the idea. I recall that back in the nineteen twenties I visited a freak show at Blackpool Tower Circus. And there I viewed a most extraordinary exhibit. I remain uncertain even to this day as to whether it was simply a poor imbecile that was being displayed, or, as the showman claimed, the Man with the Brain of a Dog.'

154

'It was a two-way transplant?' I managed to say. 'Now that is *really* horrid.'

Hugo Rune just shrugged and said, 'So, would you care to hear something about our potential case now? Or would you prefer me to spin you a few more horror stories? I can far outrank anything Fangio might have in his repertoire.'

'Of that I have no doubt,' I said. 'So please tell me of Project BBT.'

Hugo Rune sipped from his glass then told *his* tale to me.

'BBT, young Rizla, stands for "Big Band Theory". A little touch of humour there from the Ministry, I believe. It is all to do with sound and the influence of sound. A top-secret scientific team is working upon musical weaponry. Music, Rizla. Music that when played will influence the hearer to take certain actions.'

'Such as *dance*?' I suggested. 'I think that is called Dance Music. It works, that one, I can vouch for it.'

'Not *dance*, Rizla. Go into trance. Become susceptible to instructions, to orders. Music that, when you listen to it, puts you into a receptive frame of mind. Imagine it, Rizla – you fly over the enemy lines in a helicopter with the music playing from loudspeakers, the enemy soldiers become entranced, then you order them to surrender and they do. War over, no more shots fired.'

'Excellent stuff,' I said. 'Just what the War Effort needs. So how is it coming along? Have they got it perfected yet?'

Hugo Rune did raisings of the eyebrows. 'What do you think?' he asked.

'I think perhaps *not*,' I said. 'Which is why you said that they are always on the verge of a breakthrough, but they never actually *have* a breakthrough.'

Hugo Rune nodded, slowly. 'But they do play *a lot* of music,' he said. 'And really really *bad* music, Rizla. The Big Band that they have, that plays the music they write for it, well, Rizla, frankly, they're *rubbish!*'

'Perhaps the theory might be put into practice if they got a better band,' I suggested.

'Brilliant deduction, Rizla. I have been suggesting that for the last four years. I suggested Lew Stone and his Orchestra, with Nat Gonella on vocals.'

'And they did not listen?'

Hugo Rune shook his head. 'And now some kind of disaster has struck them, probably of their own silly making, and I am expected to drop everything, rush along and sort it out.'

'Or perhaps lay aside your pint pot and gently *stroll* along after a hearty lunch,' I said.

And Hugo Rune sighed most deeply.

'Come on then, Rizla,' he said as he sighed. 'Let us away to the Ministry.'

30

Mr McMurdo did *not* seem happy to see Mr Rune. But I was rather heartened to see that Mr McMurdo appeared to be his normal size once more.

Hugo Rune smiled upon Mr McMurdo and said, 'Jolly spiffing to see you returned to your old self again, M. Those magic coffee beans I sent you got the job jobbed then, it would appear.'

'It would appear so, would it?' And Mr McMurdo turned sideways and would not you know it, or would not you not, he all but entirely vanished. Because although he looked normal and man-sized from straight on, turned sideways he was no thicker than a piece of paper.

'Ah,' said Hugo Rune. 'You'd better not go out then on a windy day.'

'Windy day? I'll . . . I'll . . . I'll . . .' And Mr McMurdo flapped his papery arms.

'But look on the bright side,' said Hugo Rune. 'If you ever forget your house key, you can simply slip yourself under the front door.'

And Mr McMurdo let out a terrible howl.

'But enough of such larks,' said Hugo Rune. 'I am confident that I will be able to sort you out eventually. Let us speak of more important matters. Those pertaining to Project BBT, for instance. Tell me, exactly what is the problem this time?'

'The problem, Rune, is that half of the team are now dead. No one knows how they died. Post-mortem examinations suggest the possibility of a viral infection.'

'Germ warfare?' I said.

'I'm talking to the organ grinder,' said Mr McMurdo, 'not the—'

But he did not finish that bitter sentence. Because Hugo Rune suddenly sneezed. And the force of his sneeze propelled the wafer-thin Ministry man away to the room's far corner, where he fluttered to rest beside a brass coffee table that was shaped like the *Sloop John B.*

'Bless you,' I said.

And Hugo Rune grinned.

And Mr McMurdo went spare.

'Don't get yourself all in a *flap*,' said Hugo Rune, hastening in a most leisurely fashion to help up the flimsy fallen fellow. 'But do answer my acolyte's most pertinent question. *Do* you suspect germ warfare?'

'We cannot tell. Hey, put me down.' For Hugo Rune was now rolling up Mr McMurdo.

'Oh do pardon me,' said Himself. 'I was going to pack you away for safety inside a cardboard tube. Would you prefer me to place you back upon your chair?'

The exasperated sounds that issued from the lips of Mr McMurdo suggested that indeed this would be his place of preference. And also that he dearly wished to wreak a terrible revenge upon his tormentor.

Hugo Rune placed him upon his chair and then took himself over to the drinks cabinet. 'What *did* the post-mortems reveal?' he enquired as he poured out a G & T.

Mr McMurdo fought to control his emotions. 'Scrambled,' he finally managed to say. 'Their internal organs had turned to mush. The introduction of some flesh-eating virus into the music labs seems probable.'

Hugo Rune did noddings of the head. 'Did you have the laboratories fumigated?' he asked.

'Extensively and three times over. And all the bodies cremated. No virus could live through that, believe you me on this.'

'Oh, I do,' said Hugo Rune. 'I only regret that now we will not be able to find a sample of the virus and test it to ascertain a possible source.'

'Hardly necessary,' spat Mr McMurdo. 'Berlin would be the obvious source, I would have thought.'

'Would you now, would you?' And Hugo Rune sipped at his drink. I made the kind of face that implied that I would not have minded a drink myself. But Hugo Rune clearly had weightier things on his mind and ignored me.

'Are the technicians and musicians back at work?' he asked.

'They are,' said Mr McMurdo.

'Then I will hasten there,' said Hugo Rune. 'Call a cab for myself and my companion, Mr McMurdo, if you will.'

Mr McMurdo glared at Mr Rune.

And Mr Rune was forced to make the call.

'What a two-dimensional fellow, that Mr McMurdo.' Mr Rune chuckled as he and I hurried across war-torn London in the back of a high-topped London cab. Driven by a high-topped cockney cabbie.

'You ride him a little too hard,' I said. 'He could make life very difficult for you, I am thinking.'

'Not until he is restored to full dull normality, *I'm* thinking.'

'And *I* am thinking that such a restoration will not be occurring in the foreseeable future.'

'If at all,' said Hugo Rune, taking out a fine cigar and slotting it into his mouth.

'I will just bet that you have not paid Mr Hartnel for that,' I said.

'I'll just bet you're right,' said Hugo Rune. 'And I'll tell you what, Rizla, if you help solve this case, I will give you one of these cigars as a reward.'

'How very generous,' I said.

'So, pick a card, why don't you?'

And I dug into my pocket and brought out the tarot cards.

'Look at the state of them,' said Hugo Rune. 'What a mess you've made.'

'Shall I pick one at random, or shall I choose one?' I asked.

'I think upon this occasion that you should choose one – go on.'

So I fanned out the cards and examined them and then I said, 'This one, I think.'

'Are you sure?'

'I am certain.' And I held up THE HIGH PRIESTESS.

'I was rather hoping that this particular card would not be chosen until a much later case,' said Hugo Rune. 'It is a very powerful card. Let us pray that we are up to the challenge.'

'I do not believe you have ever explained to me the full significance of these cards,' I said to Mr Rune.

'Have I not, Rizla? Then I really should do that, shouldn't I?'

'Yes,' I said. 'And—'

''Ere you go, guv'nor,' called the cockney cabbie. 'We're 'ere.'

I took myself a little ways up the road to avoid watching Hugo Rune deal with the matter of the fare. In no time at all, it seemed, he joined me, polishing the pommel of his stout stick on his leg and whistling the Lew Stone classic 'East of the Sun (and West of the Moon)'.

We were now in a crowded area of London that was new to me. Somewhere in the West End, Soho-ish, but not quite. In a street called—

'Tin Pan Alley,' I read aloud. 'There never was really a street called Tin Pan Alley.'

'Of course there never was, Rizla, that would be absurd.'

'Then how?' I asked.

'It's an *alley* called Tin Pan Alley, *not* a *street*.'

'It is all so simple when it is explained. Would you care to lead the way?'

'Do you think you would be able to find the secret establishment yourself, if I chose not to?'

'Not really,' I said and I shook my head to signal I would not.

'Then follow me.' And striking passers-by to the right and left of him, Hugo Rune forged his way into the crowd and I followed on close behind.

'This would be the place,' cried he, stopping suddenly and causing me to collide with his back and bottom parts.

I looked up at the shopfront now before me. 'It is a tobacconist's,' I said. 'And I see they have Wild Woodbine in stock.'

'The door next to the shop entrance,' said the Magus. 'See the brass plates here?'

I saw the brass plates there and read from them aloud.

' "Naughty Boys Get Bottom Marks, Third Floor",' I read from one. ' "The Sorority Stable of Pony Girls, Second Floor",' I read from another. ' "Hilda Baker's Love Dungeon, Basement Floor",' I read from a third.

'You're not *really* reading from the brass plates, are you?' asked Hugo Rune.

'No,' I said. 'I am reading from these postcards that are stuck all over the wall above them. 'What is "goldfish nipple training", do you think?'

'Not something to engage in lightly, without the aid of spats. Or perhaps that should be sprats. But read from this brass plate now, or feel the weight of my stick.'

' "Roberta Newman's Academy of Music",' I read. 'Could we not visit the pony girls first?'

Hugo Rune shook his head and sighed. Then pressed a brass bell push.

Roberta Newman was not your average music teacher. She had a certain burliness. A certain broadness across the shoulders. A certain stubbliness about the chin. She wore a heavily corseted Edwardian-style black and lacy evening gown and much in the way of jet jewellery, and favoured wellington boots and long rubber gauntlets.

And I felt sure she was wearing a wig.

And owned to an Adam's apple.

And when she spoke she did it gruffly, and with a German accent.

I was about to whisper to Hugo Rune that I had solved the case immediately. And that this was a German spy who had done away with the real Roberta Newman and dressed himself up in her clothes. But Mr Rune and the bogus music teacher were now having a bit of a hug and saying how good it was to meet once more and how the other did not look a day older and had the years not been kind.

'But it is a bloke,' I began. But I did not get to the 'a bloke' bit because Mr Rune put his hand over my mouth and told me to be polite.

'Roberta and I have known each other for many years,' he said. 'She once actually came close to beating me in a game of chess.'

'And I would have too,' said Roberta, 'if you hadn't poked one of your *Gentlemen* up my nose and "accidentally" kicked the board over.'

'Hm,' I said. 'Well, hello, Miss Newman, or is it *Mrs* Newman?'

'It's *Miss*, dear,' said Roberta. 'And you'd be the latest Rizla, I suppose. Hugo goes through them like pocket hankies at a Vera Lynn concert.'

'What?' I said.

'She jests,' said Hugo Rune.

'I don't,' mouthed Roberta, shaking her head. 'But welcome to my Academy.'

And I looked all around and about at the Academy. It appeared to be a single room, small and dingy, lit by a tiny window and heavily cluttered with instruments and instrument cases and piles and piles of sheet music.

'This is *it*?' I enquired.

'Faith, no.' And Roberta Newman put a big hand to her chest and gave a little giggle of a laugh. 'Follow me.'

And she opened up a cello case that stood against a wall. And climbed into it. And then Hugo Rune climbed into it also, beckoning with his vanishing hand for me to follow.

And though it seemed impossible that three people could actually fit into a cello case, or even two or one, I followed on.

And I was grateful that I did.

For what I saw next was amazing.

31

'By Crom!' said I, which made for a change, but quite expressed my surprise. 'Are we in one of the Forbidden Zones, or is this Narnia™?'

I had emerged from the other side of the cello case into a weird world of whiteness. Mr Rune stood adjusting his tweeds while Miss Newman tinkered with her jet.

'You're in between,' explained Himself. 'This place is neither one thing nor the other, neither in one place nor elsewhere. It is a singularity. And as far as is known, the only one of its kind in the London area.'

'How big is it, then?' I asked, because even though all I could see was whiteness, which might have been white-painted walls, I had no way of knowing whether indeed these were walls and if they were, then just how close they were.

It was an odd place to be sure and I took not to it.

'I feel all uncomfortable,' I said to Hugo Rune. 'I do not think that people are supposed to be in a place such as this is. Or is *not*, as the case might be.'

'Or might *not* be,' said the guru's guru. 'But let us face it, Rizla. It is only the man who knows where he is who knows where he should be.'

'We work here because of its perfect acoustic,' said Miss Newman. 'Shout as loudly as you can. Go on – see what happens.'

I did shruggings of the shoulders and then I shouted. Not perhaps quite as loudly as I *could* have shouted. But loudly enough, I felt.

But to my great surprise, my shouts sounded no louder than my previous spoken words. And, having made further attempts at creating a racket with louder and louder shoutings, I was forced to give up as each showed no increase in volume.

'That is very odd,' I said.

'Pardon?' said Mr Rune.

'I said, no, well, never mind. So how does it do that? Or *not* do that, if that is the case?'

'Nobody knows,' said Miss Newman. 'Come with me now and I'll show you the labs and where the evil was done.'

She led us through whiteness and further whitenesses, passing fellows in coats of white who carried white clipboards and pens, to a room with definite walls but no windows. Here, on a number of stands, hung what looked to be some cut-off oil drum end sections. These were all burnished steel and the tops had indentations neatly pressed into them.

'Behold the future of music,' said Miss Newman, proudly.

'Steel pans,' I said. 'Like Trinidadians play in the Notting Hill Carnival. I learned to play the tenor pan at school – would you like to hear "Yellow Bird"?'

Mr Rune now glared me daggers.

'Oh,' I said and fell silent. 'Sorry.'

'Steel pans?' said Miss Newman. 'Trinidadians?' said Miss Newman. 'Notting Hill Carnival?' said Miss Newman also.

'He daydreams, poor half-witted boy,' said Hugo Rune. 'The strangest things come out of his mouth. I feel it best to ignore them.'

'Quite,' said Miss Newman. 'Well, although these instruments *are* made of *steel* and could be described as pans, we call them the Mark Seven fully chromatic/acoustic metallic idiophones.'

'But of course,' I said, 'that makes it all so straightforward. Then tell me, were these instruments invented right here?'

'Right here and by myself. They are, as you see, constructed from the end sections of oil drums, with an approximately eight-inch skirt. This department runs on a shoestring. In order to create new instruments we have to improvise. We reinvented the ocarina here. Hugo has our prototype and we'd really like it back.'

'Soon, soon.' And Hugo Rune did wavings-away with his hand. 'But for now speak to us of the Mark Seven. How is it an improvement on the Mark Six, for instance?'

'The Mark Seven doesn't give you spots,' said Miss Newman.

Which brought confusion unto me.

'Allow me to explain,' said Miss Newman. 'As Hugo has probably told you, we here in the music labs are seeking to create instruments that can bring about emotional and psychological change in the persons who hear them played. We have so far created a penny whistle that puts you off cornflakes, a pair of maracas that bring on an irresistible urge to run for a tram and an entirely new form of harmonica that only works when you suck it.'

I looked at Hugo Rune.

Hugo Rune, at me.

'Right,' I said. 'Well, this is a very interesting line of research. What exactly does the Mark Seven steel pan do?'

'It makes you want to dance,' said Miss Newman.

And I recalled the conversation I had had earlier with Hugo Rune at The Purple Princess.

'And Big Band Theory leads me to believe that the greater the number of Mark Sevens assembled in a single place and played together, the greater would be the number of people within their range of sound who would feel the urge to dance,' continued Miss Newman.

'I am beginning to understand,' I whispered to Hugo Rune, 'why you were not particularly keen to come here.'

'It is rude to whisper,' said Miss Newman. 'And due to the acoustical anomaly of this singularity, I heard every word of your whisperings.'

'Sorry,' I told her. Not so loud, but clear.

'Would you care for me to demonstrate the Mark Seven?' Roberta Newman asked of Hugo Rune. 'I am experimenting with forms of calypso. I think that I am definitely on to something.'

'My dancing days are sadly at an end,' said the Magus. 'Though once I tripped the light fantastic with debutante divas, I am now reduced to a soft-shoe-shuffle at the butcher's bacon counter.'

'You jest, of course,' said Miss Newman, making a winsome expression that put my teeth upon edge.

'I certainly do,' said Hugo Rune. 'I could out-hoof Fred Astaire, any month with an R in its name. But we must get down to business. How many died here and where did they die?'

Miss Newman walked us around and about and pointed to here and to there.

'And here,' she said. 'And there,' and she pointed. 'Four of my top technicians. I've been sent no replacements, you know. If I lose many more, this entire research facility will have to be closed down. And right when we are on the very verge of a breakthrough.'

Hugo Rune and I once more exchanged glances.

Although no words were exchanged.

'Would you mind, dear lady,' enquired Hugo Rune, 'if my assistant and I had a little poke around by ourselves? I am sure you have much to do. Especially now, with the shortage of staff.'

'You have no idea.' And fluttering her eyelashes and diddling her jet, the burly woman left us to get on.

'That *is* a bloke,' I said to Hugo Rune. 'And do not go telling me that it is not.'

'Of course it's a bloke, Rizla. But we must be polite and pretend not to notice. These are not the swinging sixties. I have known "Roberta" for many years. He risks a prison sentence for dressing as he does.'

'Looking like that *should* be a criminal offence,' I said. 'And *I come* from the swinging sixties.'

'Shame on you, Rizla. But pay attention now, we have a case to solve and I feel that if we are not quick about it, others will come to grief.'

'You have a theory?' I asked. 'Then please share it with me, for I am totally in the dark.'

'So, no prize cigar coming your way, then?'

'I remain quietly confident,' I said. In a manner that implied that I did, no matter how unlikely it might appear.

'Let us search for clues,' said Himself, and search for clues we did.

There was something about the all-over whiteness of this singular singularity that fair put my teeth on edge. I had felt uncomfortable when I entered and the discomfort seemed, if anything, to be on the increase. The air here had an almost liquid quality to it and things did not diminish in size the further you were away from them.

'I hate it here,' I told Hugo Rune. 'And for that matter, much as I enjoy your company, I hate this war and really wish that I was back in my right time and all of this was over.'

'And the war won by the Allies?'

'Quite so.'

'And all nice and normal again?'

'That is right.'

'And your Aunt Edna sending you off to find a respectable job-for-life?'

'Let us search for clues,' I said. 'I bet I find one before you do.'

But I lost *that* bet.

'See here,' said Hugo Rune, some moments later and poking around in what might have been a corner of the room we occupied, but might equally not have been. 'Tell me what you think of this, young Rizla.'

I ambled over through the whiteness and knelt down beside Himself. 'You see that, Rizla?' he said to me. 'Grey smears upon the whiteness below – now what do you make of those?'

'Aha,' I said and I straightened up and did some feeling around. 'I believe that to be the scuff-mark of a door that rubs upon the floor and . . . yes.' Something clicked and a bit of a door swung open.

'Very good, Rizla, you have earned yourself a cigar band.'

I peered in through the open doorway. 'Ah no,' I said. 'It is nothing special, just a big cupboard with lots of musical instruments in it.' And I went inside and did some poking about.

'What is *that*?' I asked Hugo Rune.

'A crumhorn,' he replied.

'And *that*?'

'A *viola d'amore*.'

'And what about *that*?'

'That, as you know, is a ukulele, Rizla. And *that* is enough of *that*.'

'I have noticed the severe lack of running gags in our present adventures,' I told the Magus. 'What is *that*, by the way?'

'That is a girdle, Rizla. A form of ladies' foundation garment. And a size eight. One for a little lady, methinks.'

I rummaged about amongst instrument cases. 'There is a pair of ladies' shoes here,' I said. 'In this ukulele case.' And I flung the ukulele case aside. 'Small size too and a flowery frock and a lady's straw hat also.'

'Any gentlemen's clothing to be found?'

I rummaged some more and some more and then said that there was not.

Hugo Rune took the foundation garment and gave it a bit of a sniff.

'I think you will probably find *that* is a criminal offence,' I told him. 'Especially if you steal them from washing lines.'

'Buffoon, Rizla. But these are our clues and the case is all but solved.'

'Right,' I said and I made a certain face.

'Think, Rizla, think,' said Hugo Rune. 'You can reason it out.'

And I thought.

'Are you *really* telling me,' I said at length, 'that these clothes are *really* the clue that will lead us to solving the case?'

Hugo Rune nodded his head and told me he did.

'Then I should be able to reason it out.'

And perhaps I might have done so there and then. Had there not been a sudden interruption. A fellow in a white coat, with a clipboard in his hand, came busting into the instrument storeroom and fell down at the feet of Hugo Rune.

'Bless you, my son,' went Himself. Bringing his blessing finger into play.

'I've not come for a blessing.' The fellow in the white coat struggled up. 'I tripped on a ukulele case that some fool must have carelessly flung aside. There has been another murder, Mr Rune!'

32

We followed the white-coated fellow, who led us at length to the corpse. A number of similarly white-coated fellows stood about their fallen companion, clipboards under their arms and a-wringing of their hands.

Miss Newman was kneeling down by the body with big tears in her eyes.

Hugo Rune cleared a path for us with his stout stick and cried out the words, 'Don't touch anything!'

'I loosened his collar,' blubbered Miss Newman. 'I thought he was having an epileptic fit or something.'

'If this is the virus at work,' I whispered to Hugo Rune, 'we could all now be in a lot of trouble.'

'We all heard *that*,' cried a fellow in a white coat. 'And that seems good cause for panic.'

And panic they began to do and run they were about to.

'No!' shouted Hugo Rune. And even the weird acoustics were unable to muffle his shout. 'You will *not* panic. You will return quietly to your work. This is *not* the work of a virus. You are all intelligent men – has it escaped you that a deadly virus is not selective in whom it kills? If this, as the other deaths, was caused by some deadly virus, you would all have been struck down by it by now.'

A fellow in a white coat spoke up at this. 'If it was a slow reactor,' he said, 'say, passing on the viral chain through an elliptical navigation of the—' But his words were brought short by the stout stick of Mr Hugo Rune.

'Return to your work,' the guru's guru said. 'I will take charge here.'

Grumbling and mumbling, the men returned to their work.

'Escort Roberta back to her office, Rizla,' said Hugo Rune to me. 'Sit her down, fetch her a nice hot-water bottle, splash a bit of lavender water on her wrists and, if needs be, employ the bottle.'

'I can manage by myself,' said Miss Roberta Newman. And with that said, she upped and tottered away.

'Quickly, Rizla,' said Hugo Rune. 'Off with his coat and pants.'

'Certainly *not*!' I said, appalled. 'I do not know what you think you are up to, but I will not get involved.'

'We are checking for needle marks to see whether this man has been injected with poison.'

'Oh, I see.' And I helped Hugo Rune take down the dead man's trousers. Though I certainly did not enjoy the experience.

'He is wearing special garters to keep up his socks,' I said. 'And what is *this* – a gentleman's girdle, is it?'

'Think about yourself, Rizla,' said Hugo Rune. 'We wouldn't want people to get the idea that you harbour a morbid interest in corpses' undergarments.'

'No we *would not*!' I agreed. 'But I do not see any needle marks.'

'Then we must turn him over.'

'Must we?'

'Yes.'

So we did turn him over and we did peep into intimate places, but we found no needle marks. But to my horror I now noticed that the corpse was beginning to leak blood. From every available orifice.

'That is me done,' I told Hugo Rune. 'I will find something to cover him up with. That is most disgusting.'

Thus saying, I departed at the hurry-up and went in search of a temporary shroud. And I wondered, *Should I phone for an ambulance also?*

I ambled down this corridor and that, if corridors they actually were, and managed to get myself a bit lost. Eventually I happened back at somewhere that I recognised, but this was not a laundry room, but rather the room that housed the Mark Sevens.

I smiled upon those Mark Sevens. So, steel pans were invented right here, in London, were they? By a female impersonator working for the Ministry of Serendipity?

Aha, I thought to myself. *That might explain why history does not record this fact, but prefers the tale that they were created in Trinidad from oil drums left by the American Air Force.*

'It is all so simple once it is explained,' I said to myself. And then I thought to myself, *I would not mind having a little go on those steel pans. Not that I could ever actually say to anyone that I had. But just to satisfy myself that I had played upon the prototypes before they came into the public domain.*

I glanced all around and about me. But there was no one to be seen. So I sidled over to those pans, picked up the pair of sticks that rested upon one of them and examined the playing surface.

'A somewhat curious configuration,' I said. 'That is neither your Invaders, nor your fourths and fifths.' For I knew a little about steel pans and how their notes were laid out. It is all to do with making use of the concordant and sympathetic harmonies and upper partials.

These things matter.

I had a little tap at the nearest indentations, thereby eliciting a most horrible deadpan note. 'Oh dear,' I said. 'This pan has been really badly tuned. Hugo Rune was certainly right about what goes on here.' And then I tapped upon another, bringing forth a dire twang that set my teeth to rattling. 'It is complete rubbish,' I said. 'You could never get any kind of decent tune out of this. No tune whatsoever, I suspect.' And I thrashed randomly about, creating a hideous cacophony, which although not loud, due to the outré acoustics, was certainly horrible in every single sense there was of the word.

And then I went down in an untidy heap. Knocked from my feet by a blow. And then further blows rained down upon me and I shouted (in a futile fashion) for them to stop. 'Get off me,' were the words I used. 'Why are you hitting me?' were others. 'Help!' was a single one also.

'What did you think you were doing? Who gave *you* permission to play the Mark Sevens? You beastly boy, you need some discipline.'

Which caused me to become aware that it was Miss Newman who was slapping me all about. Which somehow made it even more wrong. And certainly much more undignified.

'Unhand me, you weirdo.' And I struggled up, prepared to defend myself. 'I will clunk you on the button if I have to.' And I raised up both of my fists.

'Oh bless me, I am so sorry.' And the she-male started to dust me down, but I did backings away.

'I really am so sorry,' she continued. 'But you must understand. They are experimental instruments. Precisely tuned.'

'They are *terribly* tuned,' I said to Miss Newman. 'Give me a ball-pane hammer and half an hour and I will knock a half-decent set of scales into them.'

'No!' And Miss Newman threw her hands up. 'Horrid mental boy. Why does dear Hugo employ such awful boys? When you come to a sticky end like the others, it will serve you right.'

'I am sorry I touched the pans,' I said. 'I came looking for something to cover up the body. I am sorry that I have upset you so much.'

'All right then. No harm done, I suppose. I shall lead you to the laundry cupboard – follow me, if you will.'

I was led to the laundry cupboard and then to the corpse and this I covered up.

'I think you should both leave now,' said Miss Newman. 'Your bad boy servant here has behaved most naughtily, Hugo, I'd like you to take him home.'

'I only had a little tap on the Mark Sevens,' I told the Magus, 'and they are completely out of tune. The notes they raise when you strike them are horribly discordant. They literally make you feel sick.'

'Take him home, *please*,' said Miss Newman.

'I think I now have all the evidence I need,' said Hugo Rune.

'And so you will depart?' asked Miss Newman.

'Not perhaps quite yet. So you couldn't get a tune out of the Mark Sevens, Rizla?'

'He was doing it all wrong, please take him home.'

'I have some knowledge of music and harmonics,' said Hugo Rune. 'I'm sure I could tease a jig or two from these errant instruments.'

'You do not have sufficient security clearance,' Miss Newman wailed. 'Please leave me alone with my grief. The dead man was a close friend of mine – have some respect for him, if not for me.'

'Let us return to the pan yard, as it were,' said the Magus, 'and see what we shall see.'

'Oh no you don't.' And with a suddenness that certainly surprised me, even if it failed to raise even a hint of surprise from Mr Hugo Rune, Miss Newman tugged a Luger pistol from somewhere and pointed it at us.

Well, mostly at Hugo Rune, as it happened.

'He is the murderer!' I cried, pointing at Miss Newman. 'I suspected it from the moment I saw this person. I certainly should be given that cigar.'

172

'Perhaps you'll be able to smoke it through the hole in your chest,' said Miss Newman, the Luger now swinging towards me. 'But I am intrigued, Mr Hugo Rune – how did you know it was me?'

'I did not,' said Hugo Rune. 'Not until Rizla mentioned the cacophony of the steel pans. And your anxiety that no one should touch them but yourself.'

'All right, I am lost again,' I said. 'What have the steel pans got to do with the murders? And is this or is this not Miss Roberta Newman?'

'Will you tell him, or should I?' asked Hugo Rune.

'Tell him in Hell,' said Miss Newman. Who then did squeezings on the trigger.

'You must always be careful to release the safety catch,' said Hugo Rune. And Roberta Newman glanced down at the gun and Himself struck out with his stick.

The baddie went down in a flutter of lace and a pitter-patter of jet.

'Let us open her up,' said Hugo Rune, 'and see what we have inside.'

And with that he put his boot to the fallen figure and flipped it over onto its front.

'Unlace the corset, Rizla.'

'No, I am not too keen,' I said. 'And now not altogether sure what is going on. Would you please mind explaining it to me?'

'I will as you unlace.'

And so I unlaced and Hugo Rune spoke, and this is what he said. 'The operatives who died,' said Hugo Rune, 'did not die from some flesh-eating virus, although the effects were very similar. Their internal organs were turned to pulp. And how was this evil done?' I shook my head to show that I did not know and Hugo Rune continued. 'Infrasound,' he said. 'They were killed by the Mark Seven pans being played in a certain rhythm, creating a deadly frequency of sound in a standing wave capable of literally scrambling the organs of anyone positioned on the audience side of the pan. The idea being to bring this project to its knees and have it cancelled altogether.'

'And why am I unlacing this corset?' I asked.

'Why, to see just who we have inside.'

'*What?*' I said. And I really meant that *what*.

'It is my old friend Roberta Newman,' said Hugo Rune. 'Well, *outwardly* at least. And the Miss Roberta I knew would never become a traitor. But, oh, what have we here?'

And I gazed down at the spine of the fallen person. Now exposed to us as I had undone the corset.

'Do not tell me that is what I think it is,' I said.

'If you think it is a zip-fastener,' said Hugo Rune, 'then that is what it is. But if you would rather I didn't tell you, then I will not.'

'I do not want to unzip it,' I said, and I stood. 'There is bound to be something absolutely horrid in there. A demon monster, or something, perhaps.'

'Or a slender girl,' said Hugo Rune. 'One whose clothes you discovered in the instrument storeroom.' And he now stooped and unzipped the zipper, though I turned my face away.

But when I looked back there were two bodies lying on the white floor. A rather deflated-looking one which had so recently been that of Roberta Newman. And beside that, one of a small and beautiful, yet bloody, young woman, who even now Hugo Rune was helping to her feet.

'Rizla, allow me to introduce you to Count Otto's daughter, Citrus,' said the Magus. 'It is quite the family business with the count, is it not? Recall that I sniffed the foundation garment in the storeroom? I detected a certain Germanic perfume – Edelweiss for Fräulines, a favourite of the Black family women.'

'But how was *she* inside *that*?' I asked. Gaping down at the corpse and all but throwing up.

'The work of the sinister Baron von Bacon, creator of the Hellish Man-Hound of Mons. Recently resurrected from his self-imposed human hibernation beneath Old Pete's allotment patch. He must have hollowed out Roberta Newman, allowing Citrus to take up residence inside and work the outer remains of the body like a puppet. Clearly a portion of Roberta's brain was retained, which would account for the intact memories of myself and the continued running of this establishment. Ingenious, if somewhat gruesome, wouldn't you agree?'

'I really do think that I am now going to be sick,' I said.

And, regrettably, I was.

And not just the once, as it happened.

Because later, whilst celebrating our success at having solved the case, and drinking many celebratory pints of the latest guest ale,

Human Serif, Hugo Rune actually gave me one of his cigars, saying that I had earned it.

And I tried hard to smoke that very cigar.

A cigar that, as was the way with Hugo Rune, had been previously soaked in rum.

It turned out to be a horrible cigar.

And I, once more, was sick.

THE SUN

33

THE SUN

It was a Tuesday early in July when the arrival of a parcel caused great excitement in our household.

Hugo Rune examined this parcel and gave it a little shake. 'This fellow has travelled far,' he said. 'From Switzerland, by the postmark, and through several diplomatic bags.'

'An early Christmas present?' I suggested. 'It does look somewhat bashed about. I hope whatever lurks within is not broken.'

'I'm sure I would have packed it properly,' said Mr Hugo Rune.

'Sure *you* would have packed it? I do not understand.'

'Examine the handwriting of the name and address,' said Hugo Rune and handed me the parcel.

I examined this writing with care and then said, 'It is *your* hand-writing!'

'Exactly, Rizla. Packed up and posted to me by my other self. The one who resides naturally in this time period. And resides presently in Switzerland.'

'Wow,' I said. 'That is deep. You have sent yourself a present. That seems rather generous of you.'

'No present, this. I must study the contents of this parcel in private.'

And with that Hugo Rune left the room and took to his bed for two days.

I was rather bored without him and I did wonder whether I might just take the opportunity to slip out and have that wander around the borough that I had been promising myself. But I *had* sworn upon an actual stack of Bibles that I would not.

And so I did not.

I perused the daily papers and it did amuse me slightly, although perhaps it should not have, to read a tiny piece on an inside page entitled

PRIESTESS FLIES FROM HER FLOCK

Lady Citrus Black, convicted spy and murderess, and leader of an End Times Cult formed from her fellow inmates at HMP Holloway, escaped last night in a daring fashion that has left prison authorities baffled. She apparently picked the lock on her cell door and stole up to the cell-block roof. And after that was never seen again.

'I rather suspect that her father popped by on his motorcycle combination to pick her up,' I said to myself. And it did make me smile just a bit, because although I *had* picked the tarot card depicting THE HIGH PRIESTESS, it was only *now* with the reading of this newspaper piece that it had even the vaguest connection to our previous case.

Another thing that had occurred regarding that last case, which made me smile a little too, was the matter of the Mark Seven gut-mashing sonic terror-weapons, otherwise known as steel pans. I had asked Mr Rune what was going to happen to the Mark Sevens. Surely, I said, they represented that great breakthrough which the BBT Team had been hoping for and could be used in the winning of the war. Which would at least have paid some kind of posthumous tribute to poor Miss Roberta Newman.

But to my surprise and disappointment, Hugo Rune had said, no, they would not be used. And had gone on to explain that they represented another of those mysterious anomalies that were not supposed to exist in this time period. And that if they *were* utilised, even in the cause of good, there could be dire future consequences.

'And so what will become of them?' I had asked.

'They'll be disposed of,' Hugo Rune replied.

And they were. In a way. They were flown off in a transport plane to be dumped into the sea. But word reached me, through Lord Jason Lark-Rising, now a dashing Spitfire ace, that the plane had run off course and crashed into shallow water just off the coast of Port-of-Spain, Trinidad.

And that before authorities had been able to secure the area, locals had thoroughly looted the plane.

Which, I suppose, sort of put history straight.

But I *was* having my doubts as to where, if anywhere, things were leading. We had solved five cases so far, which meant that the next would be our sixth and we would be halfway through our mission. But as to what we were actually doing to stop the Germans developing the atomic bomb, destroying America and winning the war, I was not quite sure at all.

On the third day Hugo Rune rose again. He appeared at the breakfasting table, the opened parcel in his arms, deposited it into my lap and availed himself of my breakfast.

'I want you to read all the way through this, Rizla,' he told me. 'Take notes if you wish, but make yourself thoroughly conversant with the contents. I feel that this is the catalyst I have been awaiting.'

'I will just finish my breakfast,' I said, reaching out.

But he waved me away and that was that for my breakfast.

I took the parcel into Mr Rune's study, sat down in the fireside chair that had been designated as mine, tipped out the contents and gave them a thorough perusal.

A biffed-about box file with the words

PROJECT RAINBOW
ABOVE TOP SECRET

---

printed on it reached my gaze and I opened this up and dug in.

There were a great many Above-Top-Secret American Navy papers in that box file and I leafed through them all, reading as I did so.

All concerned something called THE PHILADELPHIA EXPERIMENT, which appeared to be a project based upon Albert Einstein's unified field theory, employing the use of electromagnetic radiation in order to make an American warship radar-invisible.

Apparently an experiment had been conducted on 28 October 1943, at sea upon a vessel called the USS *Eldridge*. But things had not gone as intended. The electromagnetic radiation had rendered the entire ship *absolutely invisible*, leaving nothing to signal its presence but for a hull-shaped indentation in the sea.

Then things became a little confused. There were reports that the *Eldridge* had teleported accidentally to a naval yard in Norfolk, Virginia.

Rumours also abounded that dire things had befallen the crew of the invisibilised ship and that the entire project had later been abandoned as being far too dangerous to continue with.

There were photographs of 'portable field generators' and there were pages and pages of mathematical calculations and equations included in the collection of papers. Also there was much in the way of memos and telegrams, which proved that the knowledge and approval of this experiment went all the way up to the President of the United States himself. And it crossed my mind that I was probably holding in my hands a 'box of fireworks' as it were. Or maybe that should be a 'smoking pistol'. But certainly it was sensitive information. But could any of it actually be true?

Hugo Rune entered his study, wiping his chops with a napkin and belching mightily.

'Pardon myself,' he said to me. 'Have you perused the papers?'

'I have indeed,' I said to him. 'But as to whether I actually believe any of that – well, it is pretty far-fetched, is it not?'

'On the contrary,' said Hugo Rune. 'But not in the way you think. I certainly find it surprising. But only in the fact that anything that unprincipled scoundrel Einstein conceived of has actually worked.'

'You are not a fan of Mr Einstein, then?' I asked.

'I taught the man everything he knows. And then he cribs my notes and wins himself the Nobel Prize.'

'Ah,' I said. 'I see how that could tick you off.'

'Indeed.' And Hugo Rune made a very grumpy face. 'But friend Einstein is not truly behind this project. The real genius behind it all was Nikola Tesla, who sadly died last year. *Giving friend Einstein the opportunity to once more claim the credit!*' Mr Rune's voice rose to a rant that I found most uncomfortable.

'But you think it *did* work?' I said. 'A warship was actually turned invisible and possibly even teleported?'

'I have studied the equations and calculations; the maths seem sound enough.'

'So why, do you suppose, did your other self post it all to you?'

'Interesting question, Rizla. But the question should perhaps be, how did my other self come into the possession of this sensitive information in the first place?'

'It is all rather exciting, is it not?' I said. 'Do you suppose that it has the makings of our next case?'

'Why not tug out those now-knackered tarot cards that inhabit your pocket with all the fluff and toffees, fling the entire wad up into the air and we'll see which one comes down face up.'

'Fair enough,' I said and I did just that. And out of the seven remaining cards only one came down facing up.

And this card was THE SUN.

'Does that mean anything to you?' I asked.

'Absolutely nothing, Rizla. All this is most puzzling indeed.'

'Should we take an ale at Fangio's,' I asked, 'and mull the matter over?'

'It is a weekday,' Hugo Rune informed me, 'and we generally only visit The Purple Princess on Sunday lunchtimes.'

'Radical solutions require radical actions?' I suggested.

Hugo Rune pulled back the curtains and viewed a beautiful day. 'Tell you what, young Rizla,' he said, 'as it is such a beautiful day and we are still at present in our jim-jams and dressing gowns, as befits such gentlemen as we, what say we doll up in our summer togs?'

'The pale linen suits and the panama hats?' I asked. 'I signed for the delivery of these the other day. Ignoring the request for payment, naturally.'

'Naturally,' said Hugo Rune, and with that patted my shoulder. 'Linen suits and panama hats, I baggsy first the bathroom.'

And what a fuss that fellow made with bathing. I have never known anyone so fastidious about dress and personal hygiene as Mr Rune. As well as always being immaculately dressed he was always scrupulously clean. *Clinically* clean. *Perfectly* clean. There was probably some deep down psychological screw-up in his personality to account for all this constant cleaning and preening and grooming. But whatever it was, it was none of my business. And I was more than happy to be the constant companion of a man who dressed well and smelled of civet, ambergris and musk.

But at last he was done and I had my turn and just a little later than that, the two of us, looking all spruced up and chipper and most debonair in our panama hats and white cotton shirts and pale linen suits with matching gas-mask cases swinging from our shoulders, stepped out onto the streets of Brentford.

And set off to Fangio's bar.

34

The saloon bar was empty of customers and we approached the counter, behind which stood no barlord to bid us a hearty hello.

'A deserted bar,' said Hugo Rune. 'Shinny over the counter, Rizla, and fetch us a bottle of whisky. Better make it that twelve-year-old triple malt that Fangio thinks to conceal from me behind those Spanish knick-knacks.'

And I might well have done what he asked had Fangio not suddenly jumped out from behind the bar counter and given me a fright.

I went, 'Waah!' and took a step back.

Hugo Rune did not.

'How about *that*?' said Fangio. 'Is that good jumping-out or what? I've been taking lessons from Norman at the corner shop and I think we're in with a chance, come tomorrow night.'

'I have no doubt that there is sense to be found in your words,' said Hugo Rune, 'but, as with a rotten tooth, the extraction of it might be painful.'

'Behold the poster,' I said and I pointed to this poster.

This poster read:

> **BRENTFORD INTER-PUB**
>
> ## JUMPING-OUT
> ## COMPETITION
>
> **Prizes Prizes Prizes**

And the date below this was tomorrow's date.

'All becomes clear,' said Hugo Rune. 'Two pints of your latest guest ale, Bell Centennial, please.'

'Good choice,' said Fange and went about his business. 'And so, Mr Rune, will you be entering the competition this year?'

'*You* have previously entered a jumping-out competition?' I asked the Perfect Master.

'Oh no,' said Fangio. 'It's a different sort of competition every year. Last year it was a "Distaining the Vulgar Classes" competition. Mr Rune won. He was *most* impressive. No one else came near.'

'I will leave it this year to those who have been in training!' said Hugo Rune and took to the tasting of the ale. 'With Norman on your team you will probably succeed.'

'I'm not too sure,' said Fangio, drawing himself a double Scotch. 'They have a new guv'nor at The Four Horsemen, and they say he's a regular jack-in-the-box of a chap. He can appear as if from nowhere. Some say he's an ex-stage magician. But I prefer to believe that he is in league with the Devil.'

'It is not unheard of amongst the licensed profession,' said Hugo Rune. 'Rizla and I will attend the competition to see that there is no jiggery-pokery, as it were.'

'Most kind. Consider those beers on the house.'

I rolled my eyes and we left the bar counter and took to our favourite seats.

'So,' I said to Hugo Rune, 'the Philadelphia Experiment. Have you had any more thoughts on the subject?'

'If my other self sent those papers to me, he must have done so for a purpose.'

'Perhaps you are supposed to hand them over to the Ministry of Serendipity. I wonder how Mr McMurdo is getting on.'

'He is no longer two-dimensional,' said Hugo Rune. 'I prepared a potion for him. To fill him out, as it were.'

'So he is back to normal?' I said.

Hugo Rune made a so-so gesture and sipped once more at his ale.

'Go on then,' I said. 'Tell me what you have done to him this time.'

'It was his own fault,' said Himself. 'I told him, only a drop or two, but he gulped down the bottle. And now he weighs in at fifty-one stone and has to be moved about by forklift truck.'

I tried very hard not to laugh, but I did not succeed in the attempt.

'But tell me this,' I said to Hugo Rune. 'How *did* they make an American warship invisible?'

'With the aid of two field generators mounted on the decks of two separate ships projecting a stream of ionized protons, which cause a cross-polarisation of beta particles, resulting in the transperambulation of pseudo-cosmic anti-matter and invisibility.'

'Oh,' I said. 'That lad again. But surely I see a flaw here. The two ships doing the projecting would be clearly visible, would they not? It would only be the ship between that turned invisible. So what would actually be the point?'

'I suspect the idea was to project the proton streams across a considerable distance. A distance of many miles, perhaps.'

'Ye Gods!' I said, for a bit of a change. 'Then if the Germans got hold of the data, they might be able to invisibilise an invading army and send it across the Channel on invisible boats. To land. Invisibly.'

'The prospect holds little charm,' said Hugo Rune. 'But, and I hate to admit this, I am at a loss to know what to do. Or what I am *supposed* to do. About *what*.'

'We could have lunch,' I suggested. 'It is more than an hour since we had breakfast.'

'No wonder my belly is starting to grumble. How can I cut through Gordian knots and unravel inextricable conundra upon an empty stomach?'

'Dish of the day?' I asked.

'With a double helping of pudding.'

Old Pete had now entered the saloon bar, and also Norman from the corner shop. But happily he was sitting still and not doing jumping-out. The two sat side by side upon stools at the bar counter and Norman was complaining, bitterly.

'It's just not fair,' he complained. 'A man tries to make a living, yet there is always some blighter prepared to skim off the cream which is my bread and butter.'

Old Pete mumbled in assent. 'And he's flogging rhubarb,' he added. 'And that's out of season.'

Fangio took my order for two dishes of the day and then put in his three-pennyworth. 'And have you seen the beers he has on draught?' he said. 'Haettenschweiler and Trebuchet and Akzidenz Grotesk.'

'Foreign muck.' And Old Pete spat. And pinged a nearby spittoon.

'He's a penny a pint cheaper than me,' said Fangio.

'Really?' said Old Pete, finishing his beer and making to make good his leave.

'Don't you even think about it,' said Fangio. 'But I say it's a diabolical liberty and something should be done about it.'

'I agree,' I said to Fange. 'I think it is a dirty rotten swizz. But tell me, what are you talking about?'

'The new guv'nor at The Four Horsemen.'

'The one that is good at jumping-out?'

'What?' went Norman. 'This is the first I've heard of it.'

'He's apparently rather good,' said Fangio. 'A rumour going around is that he was trained by a Zen master in Tibet.'

'Apart from his skills at jumping-out,' I said, 'just what else has he done?'

'He's selling stuff,' said Fangio. 'Black-marketeering. Outrageous!'

'Something about a pot calling a kettle black?' I suggested.

'But at least I'm honest about what I do. Everything that I sell fell off the back of something. Or perhaps was pushed off, or quietly unloaded. But, after all, there is a war on.' And Fangio made a surly face.

'And so this new guv'nor is not playing by the unwritten rules?' I said.

'He's selling fresh produce,' said Old Pete. 'But out-of-season stuff and stuff that I've never even heard of. What in the name of Demeter, Goddess of allotmenteers, is a Sierra Leone bologi?'

I shrugged and Norman shrugged and Fangio shrugged too.

'And he's selling stuff that even *I* can't get hold of,' said Fangio. 'Television sets and transistor radios and something called a Game Boy™.'

'Well, *that* cannot be right,' I said.

'And *imported* cask beer!' Fangio fumed. 'How can anyone get hold of *that*?'

'Perhaps he really *is* in league with the Devil.' And I did crossings of myself and so did Norman, Fangio and Old Pete too.

And I returned to my table.

The dish of the day was baby clams in a young parsnip jelly. Spring chicken, with a touch of the tar-brush. Boyish aubergines served in a youthful Spam-jam ragout. And spotted dick for pudding.

It took bravery and determination in equal parts to pack it under our belts. Mr Rune dabbed at his chin with an oversized red gingham napkin and remarked that it was 'adequate'.

As I wore no waistcoat to slacken, I undid two lower shirt buttons and loosened the strap on my gas-mask case. Hugo Rune now yawned somewhat loudly and settled down for a nap.

'Oh, come on,' I said to him. 'There is something urgent that needs doing. And just because you do not know what it is, that does not mean you should just settle down for a nap.'

'How beautifully put, young Rizla. But I'll tell you what. You have ached so long to take a little wander about the borough, haven't you?'

'I have,' I said. 'And I have been a good boy and not slipped off for a wander when you were not looking.'

'This of course I know. So why not now go take a little wander? You never know what might occur.'

'You are sure it will be safe?' I said. 'And that I will not cause some cosmic catastrophe by eating the wrong gobstopper or letting slip about The Beatles, or something?'

'The time is right. The time is *now*,' said Hugo Rune. 'Awaken me when it is time for tea. Depart now, Rizla, do.'

Well, I was very pleased at this and I waited patiently until Fangio had slipped away from the bar counter to use the toilet before I quietly did slippings away of my own.

Because I had no intention of getting caught for the cost of our lunches.

And so I stepped out all alone onto the streets of Brentford. And I took in all that surrounded me, just me, alone with my thoughts.

The criss-cross tape upon the windows and the tram cables running overhead. The creaking of a trade bike passing by.

The smell of horse dung from the coalman's cart. And there a sailor home on leave, a soldier on his furlough. And I felt suddenly frightened and almost returned to the bar. Without Mr Rune I was truly alone in this time. I did not belong here and although much was familiar, so much more was alien. Overhead, in the sky above Ealing, barrage balloons bobbed amongst veils of smoke that drifted from the half-dowsed fires of last night's bombings. A pigeon circled in the sky. A dull grey London pigeon.

Yet there was something good and solid and safe about that pigeon. Amidst all the horror and burning and ruination and death, a London pigeon flew. Perhaps the many-times great-grandaddy of some pigeon that I might see fly by on such a day as this in nineteen sixty-seven. It was comforting. It was safe.

And would not you know it, or would not you not, that pigeon pooed on me. And then having pooed it fluttered a bit and then simply vanished away above Uncle Ted's Greengrocer's Shop.*

'Good grief,' I said, taking off my panama hat and wiping its sorry brim on a privet hedge. 'Pooped on by a pigeon. And a stealth-pigeon at that. Nothing is right in this horrible time. I really really hate it.'

And with that said, in a very grumpy voice, I slouched off down the road. I passed by the row of very pretty cottages that had always caught my fancy each time Mr Rune and I had passed them. And realised now quite why they had taken my fancy. *They* were not there in nineteen sixty-seven. I recalled my Aunt Edna saying that there had once been a row of lovely cottages there, but that they had all been flattened in the war with many dead.

And so now I viewed these cottages with sadness and put more slouch in my stride.

And presently I reached the door of The Four Horsemen, and wondered whether I might pop in and sample some of the new guv'nor's exotic beer. It could not hurt and nobody need know.

And so, with all the misplaced confidence of the underage drinker, I pushed upon the saloon bar door of The Four Horsemen.

All upon a whim it was.

It is funny how things go.

Because if I had had the faintest idea of what I was about to get myself into, I might well have walked right past that door and slouched on down to the High Street.

But probably not.

And so I entered into that bar.

And changed my life for ever.

---

* 'Uncle Ted' was not *my* Uncle Ted. Uncle Ted's Greengrocer's Shop was simply the name of the shop. Although it was run by a man named Ted, who was possibly someone's uncle.

35

There was a regular fog in that pub, though the technical term is fug. A wholesome, healthsome, fragrant fug, as of the Wild Woodbine. I stepped into this nebulosity and felt my way to the counter, encountering as I did so a regular rabble of folk. An aged piano was cranking out a popular dance-hall medley and there was much laughter and general joviality.

As I proceeded upon my tortuous route through this jocular throng, I recognised many faces coming towards me out of the swirling tobacco-flavoured mist. And all that I recognised were regular drinkers from The Purple Princess. As I saw them and they saw me they turned their shamed faces away.

'Traitorous bunch,' I said to myself. 'I of course am only here in the spirit of research.'

The polished mahogany bar top was before me as I squeezed between merrymakers and attempted to make myself heard above the all-encompassing hubbub. At last I caught the brand-new guv'nor's eye.

It was a steely blue eye that I caught. One of a pair housed above finely chiselled cheekbones and lying to either side of an aquiline nose, beneath which grew a delicate blond moustache. The hair of the barlord's head was blond and there was much of it. And there was a certain vitality about the carriage of this fellow. A certain athleticism about his physique that would surely have pegged him as a gymnast or sportsman rather than a publican.

'What is it, boy?' said he. Which I did not consider to be a good start. 'Have you come to collect the case of Kahana?'

Now there is a thing that folk who went through the Second World War will tell you. It is a thing to do with rationing and how there was never enough of anything. And this thing *is* that if you saw a queue, you got onto the end of it. In the hope that there might be something you needed waiting for you at the other end. And also, that if you were offered anything at all, you took it without question, whether you actually needed it or not. And as this new guv'nor clearly had me down as a delivery boy, come to collect a case of Kahana – well, I was not going to disillusion him. I mean, a case of Kahana! There was no telling just how much I might really need *that*. Whatever it was.

I nodded to the new guv'nor that I had *indeed* come to collect that case of Kahana. And he said that I would have to wait until it was packed, but would I care for a drink while I was waiting, on the house, of course.

So, as this all seemed to be working out so terribly well, I ordered a pint of the Haettenschweiler that I saw flagged up on the nearest pump handle.

And the new guv'nor laughed and said no to this. And poured me a lemonade.

And so I stood amidst the noisy throng, drinking lemonade and passive smoking and listening in to others' conversations.

A tall spare chap in a seaman's cap, with a rugged sweater and a whiskered chin, held forth to a crowd of smoking folk, who shared a joke and listened to him. He was clearly a sailor home from the sea and I cocked an ear to his talk.

'That there,' he said. 'Above the bar. Now *that* can tell a tale.' Above the bar hung a swordfish saw of almost a yard in length. 'I had signed aboard a merchant packet,' said the tall spare chap, 'in Tobago, hoping to make it back to Blighty before Christmas. We had a cargo of ivory, apes and peacocks, sandalwood, cedar wood and sweet white wine. But we got no further than the coast of Trinidad, when out of the blue an aeroplane fell from the sky. It struck the packet and for all I know I was the only survivor. I found myself in an open rowing boat, without oars to row with, or hope of rescue, drifting all alone and out at sea.'

The company 'ooohed' and 'oh'd' at this and so the seaman continued. 'And that night a mighty storm blew up, with breakers as high as a house, and being, as you know, a pious man, I prayed to the Lord to offer me salvation. There was a flash of lightning and that swordfish saw you see above the bar there burst up through the bottom of the boat.

'Using the skills I had acquired whilst once working as a circus strongman, I snapped off that saw, put my foot in the hole and used that saw to row the boat ashore.'

There was much cheering and I shook my head – that was quite a tale. And then the company took to the singing of that famous sea shanty 'Orange Claw Hammer' and I joined in wherever I could. Especially during the verse about 'I'll buy you a Cherry Phosphate'. And when that was done the tall spare seaman patted me roundly about the shoulder regions and ordered in a round of drinks for all the singers, including myself.

And I took this opportunity to acquire a pint of Haettenschweiler.

Which did not taste nearly as good as it sounded, which was a bit of a shame.

'Tell us another of your adventures, Jim,' called out a tweedy cleric, and the tall spare sailor man thumbed his grizzled chin and said, 'Well, I've many more.'

And then he went on to spin a marvellous yarn about how he had been torpedoed off yet another merchant packet in tropical waters, had been once more the sole survivor and found himself washed up upon a beautiful island where he was captured by cannibals, who later adopted him and later still made him their chief.

And I thought to myself what a very interesting fellow this was and what amazing adventures he had had and how very lucky he had been with the sinking of each boat. And I also thought that if I ever felt the desire to sign on for a voyage upon a merchant packet, I would check the crew list carefully to make sure that *his* name did *not* appear on it.

And while I listened I finished my drink and then felt a tap on my shoulder. 'The case of Kahana is ready,' said the new guv'nor. 'Come around behind the bar here and you can take it out through the back door.'

I squeezed between jolly folk, moved behind the bar counter and followed the muscular barlord. And in doing so now found myself in a rear parlour whose contents put Fangio to shame. Here were stacks of boxes labelled as containing electrical appliances. TVs and food mixers, irons and Teasmades and toasters and hi-fis and Hoovers. And there were crates of exotic fruit and veg and casks of ale from foreign parts and something that looked like a treasure chest.

So whistle I did between my teeth because I was very impressed. I have always had this thing about pirates and I actually met some during my adventures with Hugo Rune that are chronicled in

The Brightonomicon. And if ever there was a pirate hoard or ever a smugglers' den, then this was it.

'Don't just stand there with your jaw on your navel, boy,' quoth the brand-new guv'nor. 'There's the case of Kahana, with its address on the side. It's all paid for, so there'll be no money to collect. And don't go asking for a tip or I'll clip your ear if I hear of it. Deliver at the hurry-up, then come straight back for more.'

'Right,' I said and I gave a salute, then picked up the case of Kahana. Which looked to be twelve bottles of a tropical liqueur. I struggled under their weight.

The brand-new guv'nor opened the back door then propelled me through the opening upon the toe of his boot. I staggered and floundered but I did not fall. Not while carrying a case of Kahana.

The address on the case was that of a house on the Butts Estate. Which was a bit of a coincidence really, because I just happened to be going that way myself.

To deliver the case of Kahana.

To the house of Mr Hugo Rune.

Because after all, this *was* black-market contraband. And there *was* a war on. And that blighter *had* kicked me quite hard in the bottom.

And so I had *won* the case of Kahana.

I dropped it off at Mr Rune's manse and wandered back for more.

And so for the rest of the afternoon I went backwards and forwards from The Four Horseman to the house of Hugo Rune, with more and more contraband and an ever-growing smile on my face.

As it was now approaching teatime I thought that I had better return to The Purple Princess and wake up the snoozing Magus. But, I thought, I would pop into The Four Horsemen just the one more time before I did so. In the hope of picking up some wages.

Which I felt was fair as I had worked so hard all afternoon.

I re-entered the saloon bar and waded into the fug. The old piano tinkled and the jocularity and merriment were unabated. This really was a rather good fun sort of an establishment, but I suspected that I would probably not become a regular there myself.

The tall spare seaman seemed now rather drunk and was still holding forth, though the number of listeners had dropped off and more folk seemed interested in the antics of a dwarf who was dancing on top of the piano.

At the bar counter I found not the guv'nor, but rather the guv'nor's blondie-headed wife. She looked kindly upon me though, then told me to get out.

'I am the delivery boy,' I explained. 'I have been delivering for the new guv'nor for the entire afternoon and now I have come for my wages.'

'My husband never said anything about this to me,' she said to me.

I shrugged and smiled as I did so. 'He said I was to take two pounds out of the cash register,' I told her.

The lady of the bar room shook her blondie head and then fetched me two crisp oncers from the till.

It was at moments like this, although not that there ever had been any other moments quite like this, but say at *a* moment *such as this*, that I really quite wished that I kept a diary. Because then I could have circled the date and written 'LUCKY DAY'.

I smiled at the blondie lady then I turned away.

And then I heard her say, 'Oh no you don't!'

It was not a phrase that I wished to hear and I would have run when I heard it, but the bar was so damn crowded that I had got penned in.

'You are not going anywhere, young man,' said the blondie lady and she reached across the bar counter and spun me around. Strong lady.

'It has all been a terrible mistake,' I said. 'A misunderstanding. I am sorry I do not know what came over me.'

'I don't know what you are blabbering about,' said the blondie lady. 'But my husband *did* leave a message for you.'

'Yes?' I said. And I flinched as I said it.

'He said you were to deliver one more thing. It is only a small thing, but very important, and the person who needs it awaits it *now*. He will pay you a pound when you place it into his hands. Do you think you can manage that all right?'

'Ah,' I said. And, 'Yes I can.'

And she reached beneath the bar counter and pulled out a small cardboard box. It had those numbers and symbols that say 'military' and something about it that also said 'component'.

'It's a valve,' she said. 'And fragile, so don't drop it. Take it at once.' And she whispered the name and address where I should take it.

'And he will give me a pound?' I said.

'He will give you a pound.'

And I left The Four Horsemen with a spring in my step and a cardboard box tucked underneath my arm.

Only moments away now from that moment which would change my life.

And still quite blissfully unaware.

36

I had not gone but a hundred yards when a voice called out, 'Hold hard.' I wondered whether I should run, but did not for I recognised the voice.

I turned to see the tall spare sailor man ambling up, a tall spare sailor man who now looked all chipper and not drunk at all.

'Hold on there, lad,' he said.

I held my ground and he joined me there and beamed down smiles at me. 'I'll have to ask you to part with that box,' he said.

'Sorry,' I said, 'but I have to deliver it. It would be more than my job is worth to do otherwise.'

'I will pay you the pound for it.'

'It is yours.'

He dug into his seaman's trews and fished about for coins.

'It is only a valve,' I said. 'Nothing of value or interest.'

'On the contrary. That valve is of major importance.' He rooted out the coins he had and pressed them into my hand.

'I do not think that is a full pound,' I said.

'I will owe you the rest.'

'I have never met you before,' I said. 'I do not even know your name.'

'Everybody knows me around here,' said the tall spare seaman of a fellow. 'My name is Jimmy. Jimmy Pooley.'

And my heart skipped and my throat grew dry.

And I looked up at my father.

37

His hand had touched my own. My father's hand. The hand I had never felt as a child. That had never been there to wipe away a tear or give me a loving pat. And here he was, here in this time, years before I would be born.

And yes, as I looked up at him and he looked down at me, I could see it. The resemblance. Perhaps the way I would look when I grew up. I rather hoped so, because he had a rugged, handsome look.

'Are you all right?' my father asked. 'Your eyes are a-pop and your face has grown pale. Are you ill? Would you like to sit down?'

'I am fine,' I said. 'I just had a bit of a shock. But I am all right now. Here, take the valve, I do not want any more money. It does not matter.'

'Good boy,' said my dad. *My dad!* And he patted my head. And tousled my hair. 'This is very important. A matter of national security.'

'Are you a spy, then, or something?' I asked.

And my tall spare dad just laughed. 'Not a spy as such,' he replied. 'Although in a way. You might say I'm a secret agent.'

'Really?' I said and my eyes grew wide. Because how cool was *this*? My dad! A secret agent!

'I can't tell you why I need this,' he said, taking the box from beneath my arm. 'It's top secret. Where were you supposed to deliver it to?'

'Mr Betjamen at the electrical shop in the High Street.'

'The electrical shop! Of course, I should have realised.' My dad nodded thoughtfully and then said, 'You'd better run along now.'

'Run along?' I said. 'Oh no. If there is an adventure to be had in this, indeed a *case* to be had in this, then I want to be part of it.'

'Oh yes?' said my dad. And he laughed.

'I am *not just* a delivery boy,' I said. 'I too am a secret agent.'

And my dad laughed and laughed some more.

'I am!' I told him. 'I work for a top-secret organisation.' And now my dad looked as if he was coming near to wetting himself through all his laughter.

'I work for the Ministry of Serendipity,' I said.

Which stopped his laughter *dead* and he stared at me.

'It is true,' I said. 'I am the assistant of Mr Hugo Rune, guru's guru and self-styled Most Amazing Man Who Ever Lived.'

'*The* Hugo Rune?'

'There can never be another.'

'Then our paths have crossed through fate.' And my dad put his arm about my shoulders and led me off down the road. We walked to the High Street and evening was approaching, the shops were closed up and blinds were being pulled. My father steered me down an alleyway that ran parallel to the High Street, along behind the shops on the right-hand side.

'This valve is surely the breakthrough we have been waiting for,' said my father in a whispered tone. 'We have a twenty-four-hour surveillance running on The Four Horsemen. The contraband comes in by the ton, but we have no idea how. We have never seen it being unloaded.'

'Perhaps there is a secret tunnel,' I said. 'From Brentford Docks.'

My father shook his head. 'It is something more complicated than that. Every twenty-four hours, at precisely eight p.m., something sucks up half the borough's power.'

'Oh yes,' I said. 'I have noticed that, the lights all dim at eight o'clock. As regular as clockwork, so to speak. So what causes *that*, do you think?'

'I have no idea. But through spying, as it were, I have peeped into the back room at The Four Horsemen. At three minutes to eight it is empty, at five past eight it is once more full again.'

'It must be magic, then,' I said. 'There were some suggestions made that the new guv'nor might be in league with the Devil.'

'In league with *a* devil, I suspect. And one that wears a swastika upon its armband.'

'Well!' I said. 'So he *is* a spy. And his contraband comes from Germany?'

'The electrical appliances are years ahead of anything we have here. Their technical superiority is awesome.'

'Oh dear,' I said. 'Oh dear, oh dear, oh dear. But why are we now crouching in this alley?'

'To see what happens here at eight p.m.'

'And what do you expect to happen here?'

My father threw his hands up. 'Who can say? Perhaps a spaceship will drop down from the stars. Perhaps the Earth itself will open up and subterranean warriors in league with the Nazis will pour forth. Perhaps—'

'You have a rather lively imagination, do you not?' I said. 'Were those tales you told in the pub actually true?'

'We should be quiet now,' said my father. And he put his finger to his lips.

And so we crouched together in that alleyway, my dad and I, and I must confess that I did have a little sniff at my dad. Because I knew, because I had been told, that your own dad has a special smell that no other dads quite have.

And my dad smelled of pipe smoke. And of jersey wool.

And I really wanted to bury my face in his woolly jumper and have a good cuddle. But there was no way that I could ever have persuaded my dad as to who I really was. And it would probably have been very wrong to do so. And might have brought about some cosmic cataclysm or suchlike.

And so we crouched until it was nearly eight. And then my dad said, 'Damn!'

'Why did you say "damn"?' I asked him.

'Because I have messed this up,' he said. 'If there is some kind of electrical jiggery-pokery going on each night at eight within this shop that is connected to the mysterious arrival of goods at The Four Horsemen, it is *not* going to happen *tonight*.'

'Why not?' I asked.

'Because you did not deliver the vital valve,' said my dad. 'I have it here.'

'Oh dear.' And then I said, 'Hold on, no problem. I will take it around to the front door, knock, tell him I am sorry for the delay. No problem.'

'Are you sure?'

'I am sure.' And so I took the boxed valve and legged it as fast as I could around to the front of the shop.

And I bashed upon the front door and I did not have to bash for long before that door was thrown open and Mr Betjamen looked out at me all white-faced, a-sweat and in a lather.

'Sorry I got delayed,' I said. 'I have your valve.'

'You foolish boy! You foolish boy! Give it to me now! Give it here.'

'There is a pound delivery charge,' I said.

'There is no time for that now. You'll have to come back.'

'I am sorry,' I said, 'but I cannot.'

'Then come in. Come in. *Gott in Himmel!*'

'What did you say?'

'Just come inside.'

And I was ushered into the shop and the shop door was bolted behind us. And then I was led through to a back room where there was a great deal of very futuristic-looking electrical apparatus, the likes of which I had only seen once before. And that time only in passing.

'I will take the money in coins,' I said.

'You'll have to wait. I am on a tight schedule and this apparatus must be carefully attended to. Timing and accurate calibration are everything. Without it the consequences could be dire.' And Mr Betjamen snatched the box from my hand, tore the valve from it and slotted same into a hi-tech valve bank. Then he threw one of those big Frankenstein we-belong-dead power switches on a wall and all manner of strange things lit up, buzzed and flashed and hummed and made a lot of noise generally. And that bumper-car electrical smell, which I had come to recognise as one that rarely, if ever, presaged good fortune, began to fill the air.

'What does this thing do?' I shouted over the growing racket.

'None of your business. I'll fetch your money.'

'I am not in any hurry. I should like to watch.'

And Mr Betjamen turned away and rummaged in a drawer. And when this rummaging was done he turned once more to face me and would not you know it, or would not you not, he was now holding the inevitable Luger pistol. And this he pointed at me.

'Stupid nosy slovenly boy!' he shouted, above the roar of the electrical gubbinery. 'You could have delivered that valve on time, but no, you idled about and now that idling will cost you your life.'

'That is a bit drastic and unnecessary,' I said. 'Whatever is going on here is nothing to do with me. I will get off now, forget about the money. I will let myself out, you just carry on as if I had never been here.'

'No, you'll go nowhere, this is your end.'

And the shopkeeper pulled the trigger.

38

And I would certainly have died. As that gun was pointing right at my head. Most certainly would have died, if it had not been for my dad, who had entered quietly by the back door and who now struck Mr Betjamen a blow to the skull with what seemed to be half a brick.

'Thanks a lot,' I said. And I really meant it. 'Thank you oh so much.'

My dad was now tinkering with controls, and the noise was growing and growing.

'Do you know how this thing works?' I shouted.

'I don't even know what this thing *is*,' he shouted back.

'Then perhaps you should not tinker with the controls.'

But tinker he did, eliciting now a terrible whine, which grew to a terrible pitch.

'I think it is going to blow up!' I shouted as loud as I could shout. 'I think we had better run before it does.'

Smoke was now starting to fill the air and a terrible vibration was running through the very ground itself. The entire building was starting to shake. The dire consequences that Mr Betjamen had suggested would come, if the apparatus was not correctly attended to, seemed very near to coming. My father and I took flight.

We had not got far before it went up. The explosion was spectacular, all coloured firework flares and rainbow hues. The force of the blast sent dustbins hurtling after us down the alleyway, but we ducked-and-covered and survived intact.

My father rose and dusted me down. 'Are you sound of wind and limb?' he asked.

'I am,' I said. 'Although shaken.'

'You were very brave in there. You did very well.'

'You saved my life,' I said. 'He would have shot me in the head.'

'Well, he's gone to where all Nazis go. And we should be grateful for that.'

I shivered and my dad took off his jumper and wrapped it about me like a blanket.

And I looked up at that kindly man.

And I confess I wept.

THE FOOL

39

THE FOOL

I thanked my dad and said farewell and returned to Hugo Rune.

Himself was in a slightly truculent mood, having had to awaken Himself for tea and later too for dinner, as I had been out adventuring.

But when I told him the details of my adventuring (neglecting to mention that I had met my father) he perked up considerably and said, 'You just did *what?*'

And I explained again about the futuristic electrical contraption that I had seen in the back parlour of Mr Betjamen's electrical shop in the High Street. And how it had been the dead spit of a field generator that I had seen a photograph of amongst the papers in the Above-Top-Secret PROJECT RAINBOW/Philadelphia Experiment box file, that very morning.

And how the contraband goods at The Four Horsemen were being delivered there invisibly, through the use of said field generator.

And so was I not a pretty nifty secret agent to have been involved in the blowing up of the field generator, and everything?

But did Hugo Rune come over all smiles and pat me heartily upon the back in the spirit of congratulation?

No, he *did not*.

In fact he did nothing of the kind. Rather he called out to Fangio to supply him in haste with a map of the borough. Took pens and protractors from his pockets, made prolonged and complex calculations, cried, 'Yes and I shall have it!' Returned the map to Fangio, told me that he would meet me right here at eight-thirty tomorrow evening and then rushed from the saloon bar most speedily.

Leaving me to pay the bill for his luncheon, tea and dinner!

★

I sank several pints of Stone Informal, then wandered back to the manse and bed.

And I slept well upon that night, because I had met my father and had a brief adventure with him and that had made me very happy indeed.

And I mooched around during the following day, opening up boxes of contraband goods that I had liberated from The Four Horsemen, tinkering with their contents and missing Mr Rune.

At a little after eight of the evening clock, I took myself off to The Purple Princess, which proved upon this particular evening to be rather crowded as it was

BRENTFORD INTER-PUB

JUMPING-OUT COMPETITION

Prizes Prizes Prizes

I had hoped that perhaps my dad might turn up, but he did not. Nor indeed did the new guv'nor of The Four Horsemen, who had apparently been arrested the previous evening as an enemy agent and carted off to prison.

I do have to say that for the most part I was singularly unimpressed with the quality of the jumping-out in the inter-pub competition. Some of it was just plain silly, with folk bringing on large cardboard boxes, climbing into them and then springing out and going, 'Boo!'

And as for the technique of Mr Gardner the air-raid warden, who shouted, 'Zulus, thousands of them,' then pointed, and when folk had turned their heads in the direction of his pointing, left the bar – I think, perhaps, he had failed to actually read the poster, in order to see what the competition was all about.

But some were good, some were bad and some were utter rubbish. Mr Hartnel was superb and many spilled their beer and soiled their trousers when he came jumping out.

So it did look as if Mr Hartnel was going to be the outright winner and had it not been for the sudden arrival of an unannounced contestant, whose jumping-out outclassed the all and sundry, he no doubt would have been.

With a flash and a bang and a kind of a *whoomph*, Hugo Rune jumped out of nowhere, shocked all present and justly claimed the prize.

Well, I say, *justly* . . .

'You cheated,' I said to Hugo Rune. Once the evening was over and we had returned to the manse. 'You cheated and I know how you did it.'

'Of course you know, Rizla. But as to cheating, I recall no rules precluding the use of artificial aids.' The prize was a silver cup and Hugo Rune now placed this on the mantel shelf.

'A Philadelphia Experiment field generator! *That* is how you did it,' I said. 'But as to where you acquired it and by what means, I have no idea. I thought it had got blown up.'

Hugo Rune poured brandies and I took one graciously. 'They come in pairs,' he said. 'Although, as you saw this evening, they can be used singly, if they are carefully calibrated.'

'So where was the one that you used?' I asked.

Hugo Rune sipped brandy. 'When you told me the location of the one that was destroyed, you will recall that I called for a map. This was in order to work out the triangulation. The objective was, on the face of it, to sneak contraband into The Four Horsemen. But bear in mind, Rizla, these were simply test runs for horrors to come, in the shape of invisible invading troops. I had the location of one of the field generators; I had therefore to discover the location of the other.'

'Uncle Ted's Greengrocer's Shop,' I said. Suddenly.

'You are correct!' said Hugo Rune. 'But how?'

'The electrical shop would be about three hundred yards south of The Four Horsemen,' I said. 'Uncle Ted's would be about three hundred north. And yesterday, as I passed it, a pigeon pooed on my hat. Then simply vanished, right above Uncle Ted's shop. I will just bet Uncle Ted was tinkering with his field generator at the time.'

'Bravo, Rizla, Bravo. I had him arrested, shortly after I had the new guv'nor of The Four Horsemen arrested. And then I availed myself of the second and surviving field generator. It is presently housed in the conservatory.'

'Impressive,' I said. 'I did not even know this manse had a conservatory. And impressive also, how you recalibrated the field generator to project you into The Purple Princess so you could win the jumping-out competition. Impressive, if a little silly.'

'There is nothing silly about winning, Rizla. Losing can make you look rather silly. But winning? Never.'

'But I am a tad confused,' I said. 'This device actually projected you? Teleported you? Like the report said that the USS *Eldridge* was teleported to a shipyard in Norfolk, Virginia?'

'More than that, Rizla, it projected me into the future. I walked into the electronic field yesterday evening and it projected me into The Purple Princess at eight-thirty *this* evening.'

'This was a *very* dangerous weapon in the hands of the Third Reich,' I said. 'I think that, like the Chronovision, I should smash it up.'

'And I think not. We will hold on to it for now. As far as I am aware, the one in the conservatory is the only remaining prototype. It is the *original* prototype built here in Brentford by Nikola Tesla. And this contraband, Rizla—' Mr Rune made encompassing wavings at all the liberated contraband that was stacked against every wall.

And yes, I confess it, I did buffings of my fingernails.

'Pretty nifty, eh?' I said. 'We will be in pop-up toasters for life. Or we can sell the entire job lot to Fangio, if you wish.'

'Sadly, no.' And Hugo Rune did shakings of his head. 'All must be consigned to the flames, young Rizla.'

And this I too did shakings of the head.

'It must be,' said Himself. 'These goods are stolen goods. But *that* is not the problem. They were stolen from the future. Look at this. What do you make of *this*?'

He displayed a box with the words SONY MP3 PLAYER printed upon it.

'Now, I confess that I am baffled by that one,' I said. 'I think it might be an electric razor, or possibly a hearing aid.'

'It will not be invented until the turn of the twenty-first century,' said the Magus, gravely. 'Future technology, Rizla. This might well explain how the Reich gained the atomic bomb before the Allies, might it not?'

'Indeed it might,' I said. 'So must we really burn the lot?'

'I regret that we must. But do not lose heart. You did very well. We have a powerful weapon now, sitting there in my conservatory. And when the time comes for us to use it, we will use it wisely. Well done.'

'Why, thank you, Mr Rune,' I said. 'Thank you very much.'

And we clinked our brandy balloons together and Hugo Rune toasted me.

'There is only one thing that still puzzles me,' said the guru's guru, 'and that is the matter of the tarot card.'

'THE SUN?' I said.

'THE SUN, indeed. I am still at a loss to understand its significance. You did tell me everything about your adventure, didn't you, young Rizla?'

'Ahem,' went I. 'Pretty much so,' I said. And my fingers were crossed as I said this.

'Really?' said Hugo Rune. Smiling. 'Well, isn't that odd, then? Because I see two possible interpretations of the card. But if you have told me all, then I must discount them.'

'As a matter of interest,' I said, 'what might these two inter-pretations have been?'

'Well,' said the Magus, and he peeped at me through his brandy balloon. 'The Sun was, in ancient times, worshipped because it was considered to be the *father* of the Earth. And then, of course, you have the word *Sun* itself. How easily might such a word be misspelled, or misused? As in *son*, perhaps.

'Which would leave us with *father* and *son* – would *that* mean anything to you?'

And Hugo Rune did lookings at me.

And I did lookings at him.

And he winked and I smiled.

And no further words needed saying.

40

I wondered a lot about all that had happened. And I knew that all was significant. That field generator stood there in Mr Rune's conservatory and I certainly wondered about *that*.

Had it, I wondered, somehow been the means by which Mr Rune had transported himself and myself into this age? He had used the word *Retromancer* to describe himself,* hinting that it was through his magic that we had travelled back in time. But that field generator did not look like the product of the nineteen forties. Even though it bristled with valves and copper coils, there was still too much of the future about it. Had it, perhaps, been invented in the future and then found its way into the past?

And I was certainly not comfortable about it just sitting there, amongst the potted aspidistras and late-flowering triffids. Surely the underground network of German spies would soon locate it. Surely Mr Rune's life would be in danger.

And *mine* also.

'Dismantle it,' I said to Mr Rune. Upon a Bank Holiday Monday in the August of the year. 'Pack up the pieces and ship them away to various bank vaults, under assumed names, and—'

'Rizla,' said Hugo Rune. 'Do you want that egg?'

'I certainly do,' I said, moving my plate beyond his range and shielding it with my fork. 'But please leave my breakfast out of this. I am very worried about that machine just standing there in the conservatory. What if the manse were attacked? What if the Germans snatched it away? They must be furious about losing it.'

'Hopping mad,' said Hugo Rune. 'My overseas sources inform me

---

* Although I could not recall exactly when he did. But I assume that he must have done as it *is* the title of the book.

that Count Otto Black has had to return one of his Iron Crosses to the Führer.'

'Was Count Otto in charge of the project, then?'

'He is their man in Brentford, so to speak.'

'Perhaps we should just smash it up,' I said.

'No, Rizla, no. Its moment will come. Please do believe me on this. Some things are inevitable. Some things will surely happen. For example, if I draw your attention to the barrage balloon that hovers up there—' And he pointed towards the window.

I followed the direction of his pointing. Observed *no* such barrage balloon and returned my gaze to my breakfast.

Which now lacked for an egg.

'You thieving swine,' I said.

'Some things are *inevitable*,' said Hugo Rune. 'I was only seeking to prove a point.' And he dabbed at his mouth with an oversized red gingham napkin.

'So,' I said, 'if today we are to have a special word and that special word is to be "inevitable", I suppose you are about to read an article in the newspaper that will be the inspiration for a new case. Which in turn will involve a visit to Fangio's, where we will engage in a conversation that, although appearing irrelevant at the time, will later prove to be of great significance. And also we will revisit Mr McMurdo, who has probably now been relieved of his weight problem, but to such a degree that he floats at ceiling level. Then—'

'Stop that, Rizla, please. Are you suggesting that there is some kind of formula involved in the way we do business?'

I shrugged and said, 'Well—'

And Hugo Rune struck me with a sausage. 'Beastly boy,' he said. 'We have but two more cases to deal with here, before we move on.'

'We have *six* more cases,' I corrected him.

'Six more cases,' said Mr Rune, 'but only two more of them here. After they are dealt with, Rizla, we will be leaving this country.'

'Oh,' I said. 'And where will we be going?'

'To America,' said Hugo Rune. 'Aboard a great big liner.'

'Really?' I said. For this seemed most exciting.

Hugo Rune counted on his fingers.

'Why are you doing *that*?' I asked.

'I'd like to know how many seconds.'

'How many seconds until . . . ? No, hold on, *America*?'

'Sixteen seconds,' said Himself.

'*America?*' I said once more. 'We cannot go there, Mr Rune. America is going to get blown up by an atomic bomb.'

'It is our job to see that it doesn't.'

'Yes, I know, but what—'

'What if we do not? Then that will be the end for us.'

'Oh dear, oh dear,' I said. And my hands began to flap and I began to turn around and around in small circles.

'And stop that foolish behaviour. The bomb will not fall upon New York for months yet. We have plenty of time. And think of that nice ocean voyage.'

'I can think of the enemy submarines,' I said. 'We will not be travelling on the *Lusitania*, will we? I am not a very strong swimmer.'

'Wrong war, Rizla.' Hugo Rune shook his head and picked up the daily paper. 'Well, well, well,' he said. 'Now here's a thing.'

'An *inevitable* thing?' I asked.

41

What drew the eye of Hugo Rune now drew mine as well.

'Should I read aloud?' I asked.

The Magus nodded. 'Go on.'

HIGH SPIRITS – BARMAN CALLS
TIME ON PRANK-PLAYING POLT

The landlord of The Purple Princess, Brentford, has engaged the services of an exorcist to free him from the torments of a ghost known locally as Gusset—

I ceased my reading at this point. 'What is *this* old toot?' I asked. 'There is no haunting at The Purple Princess. Fangio is surely up to something.'

Hugo Rune did thoughtful noddings. 'The rest of the article does seem to consist of praise for his beer and high recommendations of his bar food and flavoured crisps.'

'Well, this *is not* a case, then,' I said. 'There is nothing to investigate.'

'Possibly so,' agreed Mr Rune. 'But as it is myself whom Fangio has engaged as exorcist, I do not think we should let that stand in the way of a free lunch.'

'I was once informed that there is no such thing as a free lunch,' I said, in a wistful manner.

'Then you were *mis*informed,' said Mr Hugo Rune. 'And now I must request that you produce a tarot card from what remains of the pack.'

I dug into my jacket pocket and removed a single card. 'THE FOOL,' I said. And Hugo Rune nodded and then began to pack.

I watched Mr Rune as he packed numerous items into a heavy pigskin valise.

'These would be instruments of exorcism, I suppose?' I said, as I did this watching.

'The full dog and pony show, Rizla. It is always best to go at such a venture with all of the trappings. It lends a professional look. Sets the tone. Creates a certain atmosphere and things of that nature, generally.'

'Shameful,' I said. 'And what is *that* for? I just saw you pop a toy ray gun into that valise.'

'The Zo Zo gun,' said Hugo Rune, drawing same from the pigskin valise and twirling it on his finger. 'Ideal for focusing a blast of psychic energy against a wayward creature of the dark side.'

'Are you being *paid* for performing this exorcism?' I enquired.

'The satisfaction of a job well done can be its own reward,' said the Magus. *And* without laughing. I was impressed.

'I am not impressed,' I said to him. 'I am getting the distinct feeling that you and Fangio are in this together. You are both up to something.'

Hugo Rune slipped a ball of string, a bicycle pump, a copy of *Old Moore's Almanac* and a pair of gardening gloves into the pigskin valise. 'So you will have no wish to accompany me and act as my assistant,' he said.

'Now I never said *that*,' I said.

'Then fetch me a small watering can from the garage.'

'We have a garage?' I said.

'And my robes, Rizla. From the wardrobe in my bedroom. The red papal number, I think. With the matching mitre.'

It was quite a struggle that day to get to Fangio's.

For while Hugo Rune made great strides ahead, swinging his stout stick and whistling, I laboured under the weight of a pigskin valise and it was quite a struggle.

The bar was crowded when we arrived and there was a certain carnival atmosphere. Garlic bunches were draped all around and about and Union Jack bunting adorned the bar counter. The air was a healthy blue with the smoke of Wild Woodbine. And the distinctive, if historically incorrect, tones of a steel pan flowed from a far corner, where a lady in a straw hat, from an as yet unbuilt town called Milton Keynes, played The Rolling Stones' 'Paint It Black'. I decided to turn a blind eye to that lot, simply drink beer and join in what fun there was to be had. I started first with the beer.

Amongst today's guest ales I found Saucy McFoodlefist. Which Old Pete informed me was also the name of a wraith that drifted at midnight across the allotments, wringing its transparent hands and calling out for sprouts.

I raised my eyebrows and shook my head and wondered where all this was leading.

'Ah, Mr Rune,' cried Fangio, sighting Himself towering amongst the revellers. 'Thank Saint Amand you're here. Would you care for a pint of something? Before you free this establishment from the curse that has befallen it and dispatch the unclean denizens of the world beyond to where they should rightfully be.'

Hugo Rune ordered a pint of Franklin Gothic for himself and a McFoodlefist shandy for me.

'You will want to keep a clear head for the exorcism,' he told me.

I ground my teeth, accepted my shandy and followed Hugo Rune.

'*And* bring the valise,' he said.

So I returned to the bar counter and, grumbling in a manner that was perhaps unprofessional for an exorcist's assistant, dragged the heavy bag of nonsense across the bar room floor.

We settled into our specially reserved chairs at our specially reserved table.

'There is not really a ghost here, is there?' I asked, as I supped my shandy and hated it.

'Did you know that the dead outnumber the living by eighteen to one?' asked Hugo Rune.

'No,' I said. 'But then I do not particularly care.'

'I feel a presence,' said the Magus and fluttered his fingers about.

'Perhaps it is the shade of P. T. Barnum,' I suggested. 'The King of Humbugs drawn to a kindred spirit, as it were.'

'Rizla,' said Hugo Rune, 'do try to get into *the spirit* of the thing. *As it were.* If you are not prepared mentally you will find that when a manifestation occurs, you will have egg on your face.'

'But not *my* egg,' I said. 'You stole *my* egg at breakfast.'

'Drink your shandy and say some prayers, or sing a hymn, or something.'

'Oh come on,' I said. 'This is absurd. You cannot expect me to take it seriously. It is all nonsense. And I will tell you why it is all nonsense, if you would care to listen.'

'I am all ears,' said Hugo Rune. 'Pray do enlighten me.'

'This is an alehouse,' I said. 'And also it is an inn, correct?'

'Fangio takes in the occasional traveller,' Hugo Rune agreed.

'Poor choice of phrase, but probably apt. So what I am saying is this. A haunted inn is a tourist attraction. People will come and stay at a haunted inn, in the hope of having a supernatural experience. I hate to use the expression "bite the hand that feeds you" – well, actually I do not, as it is wholly appropriate – but no barlord of a haunted inn would ever bite the hand that fed him by having his haunted inn exorcised.'

'Sound thinking, Rizla,' said Hugo Rune.

'And . . . and . . .' I said, because I had now thought of something else. 'Ghosts do not just pop up out of nowhere and start haunting places. Ghosts are established, they have a history. There was not even the tiniest hint last week that this bar had ever been haunted. I rest my case and I detest this shandy. Order a beer for me, please.'

And frankly I did not feel that there was anything else that needed saying. But that this entire fiasco would be better brought at once to a speedy end. With a confession from Fangio that he and Mr Rune were simply playing a harmless prank and no more should be thought, or said, about the matter.

'And that is what you think?' said Hugo Rune.

To which I nodded. Because it *was* what I thought. Although I had *not* actually said the last bit out loud.

'Then how do you account for *that*?'

And I looked.

And I saw.

And I could not.

'Eeek!' I shouted. 'It is a ghost!' Which was not too professional.

42

But then I shouted, 'Hold on a minute. That is not a ghost but a *clown!*'

For a clown stood there, as large as life, larger regarding the footwear.

He was your standard-issue clown as it happened. Slightly below average height. Burly and redolent of somewhere in central Europe. He wore the red nose and ginger wig that separate clown from accountant. The humorous trousers, whose humour is lost upon anyone over ten years of age. The garishly checked jacket with comedy squirting flower. Unique facial painting work of the type that has to be painted upon an egg and registered with Clown Central Office. Somewhere in Funland.

'Clown,' I said. '*Not* ghost.'

'Ghostly clown,' said Hugo Rune. 'See how his big shoes scarcely reach the floor.'

And sadly this was true. The big shoes were just scraping the floor. The clown grinned wickedly.

I became aware that the patrons of The Purple Princess did not appear to be cognisant of the ghost clown's presence. They were carrying on as ever they had, with the clown right there in their midst.

I shrank back behind my shandy. 'Can no one see him but us?' I asked Hugo Rune.

'This would appear to be the case. And what do you say to *that?*'

Old Pete, whose bladder was not what it had once been, having once been punctured through by a Jezail bullet in the Afghan Campaign of eighteen ninety-four, was plodding off to the Gents. And Mr Rune and I watched as he plodded right through the clown.

'That is oh so wrong,' I said to Mr Rune. 'There is something somehow altogether indecent about walking through a clown.'

The clown now waved at me, pulled out an item which proved to be a balloon, inflated this and tied the end and then proceeded to do one of those terrible things that clowns do. Create a balloon animal.

'There should be a law against clowns,' I said, shrinking low now in my chair. 'Especially ghostly ones. Please deal with it, Mr Rune.'

'Ah,' said the Magus. 'You have changed your tune.'

'Yes, well, call me a doubting Thomas but I can see him there in all his circus horror and I would like to be rid of him. Shall I fish out the Zo Zo gun so you can blast him in his silly red nose with it?'

'Let us not run before we can walk, Rizla. Nor skip before we have learned to perambulate upon a unicycle. The darling buds of May won't yodel up the canyon, if God is in His Heaven and there isn't an R in the month.'

'Not one of your best,' I told the Perfect Master. 'But I really would like you to get rid of that clown now. I do not fancy having to squeeze through him myself to get to the Gents. And the way things are going for me, I will need the Gents sooner rather than later.'

'Okey-dokey then.' Hugo Rune rose from his specially reserved chair and drew himself to his full impressive height. 'Robes, Rizla,' he said. And I hastened to oblige.

I fished Mr Rune's papal robes and matching mitre from the pigskin valise and helped with his togging-up. This togging-up now drew the attention of a punter or two. Who passed on this attention to others through the medium of elbow-rib-nudgings and into-ear-whisperings.

All these finally reached the landlord, who cried out for order.

'Are you about to perform the exorcism, Mr Rune?' called Fangio.

'I am,' said the guru's guru.

'Then get your drinks in quick, gentlemen, if you please.'

And there was a rush at the bar.

Hugo Rune fussed at his trappings. Adjusting a glittering amulet of the Doctor Strange persuasion at his throat. And, whilst I held up a hand mirror for him, slanting his mitre to the ever-popular 'rakish angle'.

The clown, for all this while, perused Himself and wore an unreadable expression beneath his painted smile. I observed that the balloon animal he had fashioned was not so much a balloon animal, but rather something crudely obscene. And this he waggled at me.

Mr Rune began to pull seemingly random items from the pigskin valise. A plastic plate, a bamboo cane. A set of Indian clubs. The patrons, now served to their satisfaction, had formed themselves into a half-circle behind the ethereal clown. And although it still appeared that only Mr Rune and I could actually see this apparition, the patrons made encouraging faces and toasted Mr Rune.

'What exactly is going to happen?' I whispered over my shandy.

'Queer things, Rizla,' said Hugo Rune. 'And I will require your assistance. So do you need to go to the toilet before we get started?'

'Actually I do.'

'Then do so.'

'Not if I have to squeeze through the clown.'

'Oh me, oh my.' And Hugo Rune called out to the clown. 'Friend Gusset,' he called, for that was the name as mentioned in the newspaper. 'Friend Gusset, kindly step aside and allow my servant to visit the gentlemen's excuse me.'

The clown held up his obscene balloon thing as one might hold an umbrella. And then he rose into the air and hovered near the ceiling.

'I am now getting *very* scared,' I said. 'And I truly, madly, deeply need the toilet.'

And with that made clear, I scurried away, slamming the door behind me. And I took myself into the nearest cubicle, slamming that door also.

And locking it.

I would have taken great steadying breaths, but that is not wise in a toilet. Instead I just got on with my business. Which was *pressing* now. And if I had not actually been doing my business when what happened next happened, I would certainly have done my business when it did. So to speak.

'Rizla,' came a voice from somewhere. Somewhere near at hand.

'Oh,' I went. And, 'Oooh.' And, 'Who?' And I got all in a lather.

'It is me, my boy. You know me as The Hermit.'

'The Hermit?' I said. Finishing my business and buttoning myself back into respectability. 'The vision I had on the tram, when Mr Rune and I were engaged upon our first case? That Hermit?'

'How many hermits a day do you generally meet on average?'

'Sorry,' I said. 'I am somewhat upset. There is a clown ghost out there and although I have been involved in some pretty terrifying adventures with Mr Rune, I am still most afeared of ghosts.'

'And not without good cause, Rizla. The one out there is a bad'n.

More demon than ghost. A foul and foetid fiend. And I, Diogenes, know fiends.'

'Are you really my guardian angel?' I asked.

'You might say I'm a friend indeed. As you are in need.'

'So are you here to help me?'

'That is what I do. Although up until now I haven't really had cause to. You seem to be getting on fine without my help.'

'If you have any help to offer now I will gladly take it,' I said.

'Then put your ear against the door of your cubicle and let me whisper to you.'

And so I did and he whispered to me and I was thankful for that.

I never heard him leave the Gents. I left the cubicle, washed and dried my hands and returned to the saloon bar, where the horrible clown still hovered up near the ceiling and Mr Rune greeted my reappearance with words to the effect that I had taken far too long and that he dreaded to think what I had been getting up to in there.

Which I did not think was funny.

But then he addressed the assembled throng, so what I thought was neither here, nor there.

'Ladies and gentlemen,' Hugo Rune addressed this throng. 'We are gathered today to drive from our midst an evil presence.' And he looked up at the hovering clown and the hovering clown dropped floorwards. 'Can any but myself and my highly trained second in command see this vision of nastiness?'

'Second in command' and 'highly trained' – I almost buffed my fingernails, while all about the bar there were shakings of heads.

'I haven't actually seen him,' called Fangio, 'but he's been playing havoc with my crisps and cellar stock. And I can't have that. He's not what I ordered, I want him removed.'

Hugo Rune did clearings of his throat. 'Not what you ordered?' he queried. 'Speak to me of this.'

'Ah,' went Fangio. 'Well, it's a private matter really. Walls have ears and all that. And there *is* a war on.'

The clown began to do a foolish dance. And Hugo Rune rose slightly on his toes. 'Spit it out now, Fangio,' he demanded. 'The more information I have at this time, the more effective will be my dispelling of this entity.'

The entity in question seemed to be squaring up. But just for what I had no way of knowing.

'I bought him,' said Fangio.

The crowd went, 'Ooooooh.'

'I'm sorry,' said the barlord, 'but it seemed like a good idea at the time. Haunted inns draw in punters. And you lot—' he gestured around and about at his patrons '—tend to be somewhat fickle. You all slunk off to The Four Horsemen not so long ago, when the new guv'nor undercut me with his beer prices.'

Which was true, but the patrons shrugged it off.

'And then this travelling mendicant turned up last week. An evil-looking beggar he was. And I told him how trade was coming and going and how it was ever the lot of the poor barlord that he should go without while others prospered.'

The patrons now did mumblings at this. And some of these mumblings concerned finding a beam to throw a hangman's rope over.

'Give me a break,' cried Fangio. 'I'm only trying to make a living here.'

'Continue with your tale,' said Hugo Rune.

The clown now took a step in his direction.

'This travelling mendicant told me that he was a dealer in ghosts. That he travelled the country, removing ghosts from premises where they were unwanted, then relocating them to places where other people wished for their installation. Places such as inns. Where having a ghost draws in the punters. Like I said, okay?'

'And so you purchased a ghost from this mendicant?' asked Mr Rune.

'We bartered,' said Fangio. 'And fair exchange is no robbery.'

'And now you are saddled with Gusset?'

Hugo Rune eyed Gusset the Clown.

Gusset the Clown eyed the Magus.

'I was done,' said Fangio. 'I asked for a nice grey lady who would waft about in a see-through nightgown. But instead I got an annoying invisible pain-in-the-bottom that troubles my beer and my crisps.'

'Then I must deal with it,' said Hugo Rune.

The ghost clown glared him daggers.

And then something happened. Something so unexpected and so utterly terrible that all those who witnessed it happen now speak of it only in whispers and cross themselves when they do.

A custard pie materialised in the right hand of the ghostly clown. A custard pie that materialised so all might behold it. And this custard pie was hurled with a horrible force.

And struck home in the face of Hugo Rune.

43

I had never seen such outrage on the face of Hugo Rune.

What face that could be seen beneath the pie.

He rose to an improbable height and as the crowd pressed back and collectively ducked, all painfully aware of the atrocity that had just been committed and fearing to be caught in the crossfire from the retribution that must surely follow, he threw his great arms wide then clapped his hands together.

A bolt of blue fire blazed out from these hands towards the grinning clown. And surely this bolt would have hit its mark, had it not been for the clown's inhuman reactions.

The phantom flan-flinger (for such was this pie) stepped nimbly aside. Big shoes and all, but light on his feet, he neatly dodged that bolt.

Not so, however, the lady in the straw hat, who had been playing the steel pan as we entered the bar. She dissolved, along with her pan, and vanished into the ether.

'Ooooh!' went the crowd and cowered even lower and some now sought likewise to vanish.

Hugo Rune spoke secret words and the flung flan vanished away.

'So,' said he to the nimble clown, 'a fight is what you want.'

The ethereal funster cocked his painted head upon one side, reached to his left ear and seemingly removed from it a tiny megaphone. This he put to his smiley mouth and whispered through the small end.

The words he whispered appeared through the big end of this tiny megaphone. They literally appeared in the air before him, there to be read by all. Except perhaps those who were cowering behind the otherwise invisible clown, for to them the words would have been back to front and therefore somewhat difficult to read. So to speak.

Or to explain. Clearly.

I read the words as they duly appeared and these were the words that I read:

Mr Hugo Rune, Magus, Grand Wazoo of the Hermetic Order of the Golden Sprout, Twelfth Dan Master in the Deadly Art of Dim Mak, reinventor of the ocarina, Best-Dressed Man of Nineteen Thirty-Three, explorer, swordsman, big-game hunter, this year's winner of the Brentford Inter-Pub Jumping-Out Competition, guru unto gurus, Lord of the Dance and King of the Wild Frontier. I salute you. I apologise and worship you as the God-like being you are.

'How exactly did he do *that?*' I asked Hugo Rune.

'The megaphone did it, not he,' replied the mage, 'and not as he might have wished it.'

For the ghost clown was now beating at his megaphone and shaking it all about.

'I felt he must make some verbal amends for the outrage he visited upon my person,' Mr Rune continued. 'Verbal for now, physical for the future.'

The ghost clown now shouted into the megaphone. He was definitely shouting, although his words could not be heard. But only seen, as they appeared in written form.

I didn't say those things, you knave, you pompous ape.

'Enough,' said Hugo Rune. 'Will you depart these premises of your own accord? Or must I be forced to punish you horribly before I hoik you out upon your greasy ear?'

You sham mountebank. I'll have your liver and lights.

'The hoiking it is, then. Hand me the Zo Zo gun, Rizla.'

Hold hard there, came forth the words and hovered in the air. Hold hard there and parley a while.

'What have we to speak of?' asked the Magus.

You clearly possess some small skills in the Magickal Artes. Perhaps you might wish to become my acolyte that I might train you further.

I flinched at this, but Mr Rune remained calm. So cool indeed was he that had he been a fridge, he would surely have been in need of defrosting, because the icebox unit at the top would have got all frozen up with great big lumps and—

'Calm your thoughts, my dear Rizla,' said Hugo Rune. 'This fellow interests me, *slightly*. Tell me, Mr Gusset, how did you come to be here?'

The clown did scratchings at his toupeed topknot, his squirty flower revolved.

I was deceived, were the words that appeared. Deceived and conveyed to this hovel.

'I'll have you know I keep a clean and tidy house,' complained Fangio. Who now appeared to be the only living person present in the bar, besides myself and Mr Rune. 'And I bartered fairly. Although what exactly that MP3 Player I bartered with actually does, I have no idea.'

I looked at Mr Rune.

And he looked back at me.

'Not good,' I said. 'A loose end there, I think.'

And Mr Rune nodded. 'But another must be tied here first,' said he. And addressing the clownish bogeyman he asked, 'Deceived by whom?'

One of your kind, came words in the air. But he is a greater wizard than you. One who can command such as myself. And such as me fear no man living, but I have fear of him.

'Intriguing,' said Hugo Rune. 'And would you care, or indeed dare, to speak the name of this mighty wizard?'

You'll know it soon enough.

'Then so mote it be.' And Hugo Rune interlaced his fingers and did knuckle-crackings. 'And so it is time for us to say farewell. My companion and myself have a free lunch that needs taking. And as for you, there is always something roasting *down below*.' And he spoke these final two words with heavy emphasis. Then flung forth his force.

The clown did duckings and divings too and Fangio lost his dartboard.

And now the clown flung more than just flans, and beams of mystical energy criss-crossed the saloon bar like searchlights in the Blitz. And many explosions flared around and about and I ducked down for cover.

Fangio howled and 'rued the day' and called for an end to

hostilities. But the Magus and the manky clown were fiercely battling it out. I peeped from beneath our specially reserved table, where I had taken to hiding, and watched in awe as this item and that levitated from the pigskin valise and bombarded the unwholesome prankster.

The unwholesome prankster retaliated with further flans, which hissed and bubbled as they struck walls, as if they were of noxious acid.

Then suddenly things went white all around and I became confused. There seemed to be white and whirlingness to every side of me. And then I became aware that this white and whirlingness was the ball of string that I had seen Mr Rune deposit into the heavy pigskin valise. And Mr Rune was now wearing the gardening gloves and the ball of string had extended itself and was wrapped all about the horrible clown, from throat to great big shoes, much in the way that a mummy might be, if wrapped not in linen but string.

The clown was struggling, but to no avail, and Mr Rune was smiling.

'And so, my fine fellow,' I heard him say, 'even the most heinous clown of Satan is no match for a ball of ACME garden twine that has been thrice blessed by Ava, the Goddess of Gardeners.'

Ava Gardner? I thought, but I did not say a word.

'So it is time for you to take your leave.' And Mr Rune approached the clown.

And I now rose to cheer my friend, thinking all was won.

But Hugo Rune had stepped too close and horrible horrors occurred.

The clown, though bound from neck to ankle, opened his mouth and out shot a terrible tongue. Like an evil black snake it curled into the bar and swept about Hugo Rune. The Magus was pinned by the atramentous coils that fixed him in a hideous embrace.

And words now flowed from the vile clown's ears, words that spelled out ill.

Your end is nigh, thou bumbling oaf. I crush your bloated body—

Then I heard the sounds of crackling bones as the black coils crushed my friend. It was surely the end and a horrible end and I felt sick to my soul.

So I leaped onto the table, threw wide my arms and shouted words of power. Words that I knew not the meaning of, but shouted all the same.

And there was a dreadful rushing roaring sound, as of a steam train bursting from a tunnel. A flash and a bang and a wallop and a whoosh and the bad clown vanished away.

Mr Rune lay prone upon the floor and I hastened to him to help. He raised himself upon his elbows and stared me full in the face.

'How?' he asked of me. 'How, Rizla, did you know those words? I sought to speak those very words myself, but the creature had me in its coils. How did you know what to call?'

I helped the Magus to his feet and dusted down his robes. Picked up his mitre, dusted this and handed it to him.

'In the toilet,' I said, 'I met The Hermit again. Diogenes, my guardian angel. He told me that I might find the need for words that I knew not the meaning of. And that when I did I must call them out as they entered my head or all would be lost to me. I just opened my mouth and the words you needed to speak came out of it.'

'You have the makings of a magician, young Rizla,' said Hugo Rune. 'And you have certainly earned yourself a free lunch.'

THE MAGICIAN

44

But, as I had said to Hugo Rune previously, I *had* been informed that there was no such thing as a free lunch and this day proved the point.

We had ordered, certainly, and Fangio, even viewing the ruination of his softly smoking bar, had indeed taken our order, when the saloon bar door opened and in strode Lord Jason Lark-Rising, fighter ace and all-round hero.

'Mr Rune,' he called to the Magus. 'I thought I'd find you here.'

'One more lunch for the boy in blue,' said Mr Hugo Rune.

'Sadly, no time for luncheon,' said His Lordship. 'Come with bad tidings, I regret. A break-in at your manse. I called by to say my hellos and found the front door off the hinge. The neighbours told me that they'd seen some workmen chappies earlier removing some complicated piece of futuristic-looking apparatus from there into a lorry. The neighbours said that these workmen chappies were being chivvied along by a tall thin chap with a great black beard. Ring any bells with you?'

'Count Otto Black,' I said, in a whisper. 'He has stolen the field generator.'

'And it is all my fault,' said Hugo Rune. 'I walked right into a trap. The great wizard, whom the clown feared? The mendicant who sold the ghost to Fangio? None other than Count Otto Black – who else could it possibly have been? And I allowed myself to fall into his trap, leaving the manse unattended to perform an exorcism here. He played upon my weak point, Rizla, and that is my vanity.'

'I am very sorry,' I said. 'This is all very bad.'

'It was *inevitable*,' said Hugo Rune. 'The word of the day. The word was *inevitable*. *I* am THE FOOL.'

45

THE MAGICIAN

I had never seen Himself look quite so down before. On the following morn he hardly touched my breakfast.

'Perk up,' I said, in that well-meaning yet totally inappropriate manner that some folk use when speaking to manic depressives. 'We might have lost the battle, but I am sure we will win the war.'

'Are you, young Rizla? Are you?' The Magus sank lower into his chair and seemed to be shrinking away.

'Count Otto snatched the Chronovision* but you still beat him and won it back.'

'Indeed, indeed.' The Magus now sank lower.

'You can steal my sausage if you want. I will look the other way.' But even this enticement failed to rouse him.

'I fear, Rizla,' he said at length, 'that I have become nothing more than an anachronism. A portly gent in out-of-date tweeds who dabbles in magic and never pays his bills.'

'Oh no,' I said. 'That is hardly fair. Well, some of it is, but, no.'

'There is no room for a magician in this age. It is all machines and technology.'

'You beat that evil clown through magic,' I said.

'You spoke the words, Rizla, not I.'

'Then I am a sorcerer's apprentice and I do not feel out of date.'

'You fail to grasp my point, Rizla. To quote my disciple Brian Eno: "Energy fools the magician." '†

'*Brian who?*' But I did not follow that up.

---

* See *The Brightonomicon*, if for some inexplicable reason you have not yet purchased a copy.
† A track from the *Before and After Science* album, 1977. One of his best, according to popular opinion.

'Think about it, Rizla. The reason why we are here. Technology, advanced technology. Atomic weapons, robots and computers. It is all to do with technology.'

'Are you saying that the technology is evil?' I asked.

'Not the technology itself, but those who wield it. Although I wonder at times . . .'

'You do? About what?'

'There is a hand at work behind all the cases that we have dealt with so far. A hand far greater than the unwashed mitt of Count Otto Black. Some huge dark force. I feel it, Rizla, I do.'

'It is Hitler,' I said. 'And many believe that he sold his soul to the Devil and that he himself is a black magician. Mr McMurdo said that his power comes from the dark arts. That he worships Wotan.'

'Hitler is a buffoon,' snarled the Magus. 'His only gift is for oratory. He is no military strategist − brute force is all he knows. And if he really *is* a black magician, then I do not consider him to be much of one. Shall we say that I went along with McMurdo's theories for reasons of my own. There is much more going on here. There is more at work than Herr Hitler. There is some vast inhuman force influencing events that I have yet to identify.'

'And I am sure that you will,' I said. 'In fact, I know that you will.'

Hugo Rune smiled and rose in his chair.

And somehow was eating my sausage.

'I need you to pick a card,' he said, when breakfasting was done. 'This will be our very last case here, because soon we must cross the Atlantic.'

'I am having some doubts about that,' I said, seating myself fireside and taking up the paper. 'I believe I expressed them to you. I would like once more to reiterate them.'

'Repetition does not enforce a point, Rizla, it merely belabours it. Our time is running out. Within days my other self will return here from Switzerland. I cannot come face to face with my other self—'

'Because it might create a quantum paradox that could trigger the transperambulation of pseudo-cosmic anti-matter and bring about the collapse of the universe?' I said.

'That and the fact that I owe him money, which he will be eager to collect.'

I made whistling sounds through my teeth. 'You even owe money to *yourself*,' I said. 'You are a first-class act.'

'Why, thank you, Rizla.' And Hugo Rune bowed. 'But also I know the date when the atomic blast will devastate New York and trigger a chain reaction that will decimate the entire United States of America. And thus, allowing for our travelling time, we will need to make haste.'

'Are you absolutely certain that repetition does not enforce a point?' I asked. 'Only—'

'Cease, young Rizla,' said Hugo Rune, 'and pick a card, if you will.'

I chose a card that I felt appropriate, but in hindsight it was perhaps not the best choice.

The card I chose was THE MAGICIAN.

It did not make Hugo Rune smile.

As the local newspaper failed to yield anything remotely resembling Cosmic Conundrum material, we donned our linen suits and panama hats and took ourselves off for a stroll.

This stroll led at length to The Purple Princess, which I found less than surprising.

We entered the bar, placed our stylishly cased gas masks upon the bar counter and beheld the barlord, Fangio.

'Now what in the name of all the unholies do *you* think you look like?' I asked.

And Fangio did a little twirl. 'What do you think?' he asked. 'Will I do?'

The barlord's face was made up in that style that is forever known and loved as 'Pantomime Dame'. And the costume that he wore was greatly in keeping with this look.

A blond wig covered his manly skull and a flowery frock his less than comely frame. I leaned over the bar counter, wondering if, perhaps, I might catch sight of a pair of Ruby slippers. But then could not quite remember which year *The Wizard of Oz* had actually come out.

'Let me guess,' I said. 'Christmas has come unexpectedly early and you are playing an ugly sister, possibly in an all-gay panto called *Cinderfella*.'

'Guess again,' said Fangio.

'No thank you,' I said. 'We will take two pints of Stone Informal and *not* in cocktail glasses.'

'Mr Rune,' said Fangio. 'Tell this foolish boy who I am.'

Hugo Rune cocked his head on one side and said, 'You are Vera Lynn.'

'Precisely,' said Fangio. 'The Forces' Sweetheart. An uncanny resemblance, don't you think?'

'Well, now that you mention it,' I said, 'I do not.'

'Well, there better had be,' said the barlord, pulling pints with fingers that were heavy on the nail varnish with some even on the nails. 'Firstly because—' And he nodded to a poster.

BRENTFORD INTER-PUB
LOOKALIKE COMPETITION

'Just our luck,' I said to Hugo Rune. 'These posters have all the potential for a half-decent running gag and we have to run off and leave them.'

'And that also,' said the barlord. 'You will note perhaps the scarcity of any cardboard boxes hereabouts.'

I nodded that indeed this was the case and asked just why it was.

'I've had the rozzers in,' said Fangio, presenting us with our pints. 'It seems that someone grassed me up for selling hokey goods.'

'In the King's English, Rizla,' said Hugo Rune, 'our noble barlord has been reported to the police for selling contraband. And so he intends to evade capture by cross-dressing, in the hope that no one will see through his cunning disguise.'

'Ah,' I said. 'But I do see a flaw in this. Surely if you enter the lookalike competition you will give the game away that you are not the *real* Vera Lynn.'

'Hm.' Fangio stroked at his stubbled chin. 'That is food for thought,' he said. 'And while we're on the subject—'

'It is a bit early for luncheon,' said Hugo Rune, 'in that we have only just finished breakfast.'

'Ah,' said Fangio. 'This is not so much about you eating your lunch here. It is more of a pecuniary matter.'

Himself raised an eyebrow to this. His stout stick tapped at his leg. 'Pecuniary?' he asked politely. 'What mean you by this?'

'I will, I regret, have to ask you to settle your *account*, Mr Rune,' said Fangio, taking a brisk step backwards beyond the range of the stout stick.

'My . . . ? My . . . ?' The word did not come easily to the mouth of Hugo Rune.

'Your *account*, sir, yes. I hadn't troubled you about it before because I felt that you'd probably settle up in your own time. I've kept an accurate tally of all that you and your companion have drunk and consumed here over the last six months. You'd be surprised just how much it has all added up to.'

'I would not,' I said.

'So if perhaps you would care to take out your chequebook.'

And *I* now took a step back. It was of course possible that Hugo Rune *did* possess a chequebook. All gentlemen possessed chequebooks. But I had certainly never actually witnessed such a chequebook and felt it unlikely that I would do so now.

Violence, yes.

Chequebook, no.

'I'll go and fetch the bill,' said Fangio. 'You can have those two pints on the house, as it were.'

And with that said he left the bar, returning moments later with the bill. Well, I assume that he probably did return in such fashion. Mr Rune and I, however, were not there to meet this return. Our two now-empty glasses stood upon the otherwise empty counter and silence echoed all throughout the otherwise empty bar.

46

'Outrageous,' said Himself, a-striding and a-swinging of his stick. I sought hard to keep up with this striding and already was growing quite weary.

'Please slow down,' I puffed and panted. 'I am sure we can deal with the matter.'

'Deal with the matter? *Deal with the matter?*' Hugo Rune turned fiercely upon me. 'How many times have I told you, Rizla? I offer the world my genius. All I expect in return is that the world cover my expenses.'

'You have told me more than once,' I said. 'I, however, unlike Fangio, have not been keeping a record.'

'I shall never again grace those premises with my august personage,' quoth the Magus. And I for one had no reason to doubt the sincerity of his words.

'Where to now then?' I asked. 'No telegrams. Nothing in the newspapers. No seemingly irrelevant something that later proves most pertinent to be found at The Purple Princess. It looks like we are stuffed for a case. As it were.'

'There is always the Ministry,' said Hugo Rune, gloomily.

'But *they* always contact *you*.'

'A change is as good as a rest. Let us hail up a cab.'

Recalling Hugo Rune's wanton excesses in the field of violence towards cab drivers, I was not altogether keen. And I only agreed to accompany him by cab if he crossed his heart and saw-this-wet-and-saw-this-dry and swore upon a stack of imaginary Bibles that under no circumstances would I see him visiting physical hurt upon the driver of our cab.

Grudgingly he conceded to this and I hailed up a cab.

★

Cabs were so much better in wartime days. They were huge inside, with great high ceilings, so that a gentleman had no need to take off his topper, nor a lady her bird-bedecked bonnet. And each cab had a built-in cocktail cabinet, plush leather seats and, even though this cab was motorised, a bale of hay in the boot to feed the horse.*

"Op in, your lordships,' said the cabby, his cockney tones at odds with his dapper livery. 'I expect you swells will want taking to the h'opera, or the 'ouses of Parleyament.'

I watched the guru's guru's knuckles whiten around his stick. I grinned and whispered, 'Do not forget what you promised.'

Hugo Rune contained himself and named our destination.

'Mornington Crescent, is it?' said the cabby, smiling back at us over his shoulder. 'Now there's a place and no mistake. 'It by a bomb last night, it were. Blew a great terrible 'ole.'

I looked up at Hugo Rune.

And he looked down at me.

'Drive at your swiftest and there is a silver sovereign in it for you,' said Mr Rune, in a manner that, to a stranger or casual listener-in (because all walls had ears), would certainly have passed for convincing.

'Drive then I will, your 'onour,' said the cabby and off we jolly well went.

We jolly well went at a fearsome pace, much to the amusement of Mr Rune, who cheered loudly and clapped his hands together when our driver had a passing cleric off his bicycle near Tottenham Court Road.

'You know what, your worshipfulness,' called the cabby, 'they do say as what there is a secret underground horganisation down below Mornington Crescent Tube. The Ministry of Dipperdy-do-dah, or some such. And 'ow there's elves and goblins and bugaboos from the middle of the Earth does work with them. And 'ow a gigantic fat troll called Hugo R—'

'Stop the cab here, please,' said Hugo Rune.

'Soon as you like then, your nobleness.'

The cabby slammed on the brakes and I shot forwards to land in an untidy heap upon the elegantly carpeted floor. Mr Rune, however,

* Cabbies still carry this today. It is a tradition, or an old charter, or something.

was made of sterner stuff and never even spilled the cocktail I had mixed for him.

He politely excused himself from my presence and left the cab. I climbed shakily to my feet and saw Mr Rune escorting our driver into a nearby alleyway.

The Magus returned most swiftly, wiping down the pommel of his stick. He opened the passenger door and I shook my head.

'You promised,' I said. 'On a stack of imaginary Bibles and everything.'

'You should have worded your directive a little more carefully, Rizla. I distinctly recall you saying that you did not want to *see* me visiting physical hurt upon the driver of the cab. Now kindly please take to the front seat and drive.'

I shook my head once more. Sadly. But did as Mr Rune bade me to do and I must say rather enjoyed it. Certainly I did do some basic graunchings of the gears and did shunt into a brewer's dray, but essentially I soon had the knack and there were no fatalities.

And, in truth, Mr Rune knocking the cabby about gave me a warm feeling inside. A warm and cosy feeling. Because as nothing so far this day had gone the way it should have gone, falling back on a tried and tested, if slightly clichéd, old favourite such as Mr Rune walloping a cab driver was not without its share of comfort and joy.

Presently this joy died away when we beheld Mornington Crescent. The station had taken a direct hit from a V2 flying bomb. I had seen one of those missiles in the Science Museum when I was a child and had been amazed by its size. I now stood and viewed the full horror of its capabilities.

Hugo Rune leaned over the chasm that yawned where the station had been. He kicked a stone into it and listened for a distant report. A policeman then chivvied us away and I asked Mr Rune what he thought we should do now.

'Regrettably, Rizla, we will be forced to use the tradesmen's entrance. Kindly follow me.'

His leadings led to a nearby and unscathed Lyons Corner House. Which was a wonderful art deco masterpiece of a café, all polished chrome and black enamel panelling. Mr Rune had a word or two with the head waiter and we were escorted backstage, as it were, to another one of those glorious brass-cage lifts. Mr Rune gave the head waiter a certain handshake, applied his special key to the lift and down we went at a big hurry-up.

The Ministry of Serendipity was deep deep down and safe from even the V2's excesses. We sauntered along the curious corridors and Mr Rune rapped with his cane onto the office door of Mr McMurdo.

I felt a certain dread attendant to that knocking. What, I wondered, would be the condition of Mr McMurdo this time? What horridness had Mr Rune 'accidentally' wrought upon him?

The knocking was answered by a bright and breezy, 'Come,' and we two entered the office.

Mr McMurdo was seated at this desk and all looked natural enough. He was *not* the size of a small country. Nor had his fingers grown in the manner of bamboo plants come summer. He smiled at us as we entered.

And then he rose to his feet.

And my eyes widened, as I beheld . . .

That he *was* perfectly normal.

'How good to see you, Mr Rune,' he said. 'And you too, Rizla. Would you care for a humbug?'

'Not for me, sir, thank you,' I said, trying hard not to stare.

'You would appear to be all present and correct,' said Hugo Rune. And he said this with a degree of puzzlement in his voice.

'New doctor,' said Mr McMurdo. 'Harley Street chap. All the latest gizmos. You'd be surprised what they have in their surgeries today, extraordinary apparatus.'

'And so you are now fully restored,' said Hugo Rune. 'And,' and he sighed most slightly, 'all through the aid of technology.'

'As right as ninepence,' said Mr McMurdo, 'and bright as a new pin. And trim and chipper as a pony girl's harness too, as it happens. I've never felt better than this.'

'I am so very pleased for you.' And Hugo Rune put out his hand, but the chipper chap did not shake it.

'And I will let bygones be bygones, no hard feelings, old fellow,' he said.

I could swear I heard Mr Rune's teeth grind at this, but he remained most calm.

'Care for a cocktail?' asked Mr McMurdo. 'I can knock us up a rather nifty Tokio Express. I have purchased one of these new electric cocktail shakers. Japanese built, perhaps a tad unpatriotic, but it certainly gets the job jobbed. Double for you with a little umbrella?'

But Hugo Rune shook his head.

'No?' said Mr McMurdo.

'No?' said I. Amazed.

'Given it up,' said Hugo Rune. 'Strictly teetotal from now on.'

And I held my breath.

'Well, never mind, never mind, sit yourself down, do.'

Mr McMurdo returned to his desk and sat himself behind it. We dropped into the visitors' chairs and Mr Rune cradled his stick.

'Been meaning to give you a call, actually,' said Mr McMurdo.

'A case?' said Hugo Rune.

'Not as such, dear fellow. In fact quite the opposite.'

Hugo Rune went, 'Mmmm?'

'Change in the air,' said Mr McMurdo. 'The wind of change, you might say. The Ministry is going through changes. Words from above regarding efficiency and suchlike. Bigwigs upstairs and all that kind of carry on.'

I wondered where this was leading. I did not have to wonder for long.

'Retirement,' said Mr McMurdo.

'You are going to retire?' said Hugo Rune. 'How splendid.'

'No, not me, my goodness no. So much paperwork, although less *actual* paperwork, what with all these new computers going "on line" as the boffins will have it.'

'I fail to understand,' said Hugo Rune. 'If not you—'

'*You*, dear fellow, retirement for *you*.'

'*For me!*' And Hugo Rune rose to his feet.

'Lucky old you, eh?' said Mr McMurdo, fiddling with papers on his desk. 'Time to put up those old feet of yours and let younger men do the hard work.'

I wondered perhaps whether I should excuse myself and slip quietly from the room. I dreaded to think as to where and to what this conversation would inevitably lead.

'Don't think of it so much as being put out to pasture,' said Mr McMurdo brightly. 'See it more as a just reward for services rendered.'

Mr Rune's face momentarily brightened. 'Ah,' said he. 'I see, a retirement, but on a pension equal to my present retainer, of course.'

'Ah, no,' said Mr McMurdo. 'Regrettably not. I tried to push that through with the bigwigs upstairs, but they said, sorry, no can do. All belts have to be tightened with a war on, you see. Your retainer constituted a considerable amount of our yearly budget. Had to stop your latest cheque to the bank, I regret to say.'

'I really think I should be leaving now,' I said.

'Please wait outside,' said Mr Hugo Rune.

I waved goodbye to Mr McMurdo and fled the room. And paced up and down outside. I did not wish to press my ear to the brassy door, for fear of what I might hear. Instead I whistled loudly as I paced and la-la-la'd and fol-de-roll'd and made a lot of noise.

Presently the door to Mr McMurdo's office opened and Hugo Rune emerged, wiping down the pommel of his stick. Under his arm he carried a briefcase.

'You did not—' I said. 'Please tell me you did not. Please.'

'I did not, Rizla, truthfully. We, how shall I put this? *Haggled*. And came to an agreement regarding a financial settlement. A golden handshake, I believe is the term.'

'Is that briefcase full of money?' I asked.

'Regrettably, no, Rizla. I have agreed to perform one final service for Mr McMurdo, in return for which he will furnish me with a sum of money sufficient to cover two first-class tickets aboard a luxury liner to America.'

'There is a certain symmetry to that,' I said. 'You seem to be taking this ever so well.'

'All good things must come to an end, Rizla. Even as the plumed peacock paradiddles plaintive parodies, the cackling crow doth hold no hallowed noodle. North *nor* South!'

'I cannot argue with *that*,' I said. 'So what is in the briefcase, if not money?'

'Secrets, dear Rizla, secrets. Which must be placed into the hands of the prime minister, by myself, at precisely three o' clock this afternoon.'

'Winston Churchill?' I said. 'Can I meet him, please?'

'I have told you that you will not like him.'

'Yes, but he *is* Winston Churchill. But *why* at precisely three o' clock this afternoon?'

'He is to make an important speech at three-fifteen on the wireless. *This* is that very speech.'

'Oh,' I said. 'How exciting. Can we have a read of it now?'

'Absolutely not! I have given my word to Mr McMurdo that I will not open the briefcase. He swore me to it, in fact. Upon a stack of actual Bibles.'

'All very hush-hush and top secret,' I said. 'It must be very important.'

'Naturally, Rizla. Or else the delivery would not have been entrusted to me.'

If I had any remarks to make about that, I kept them to myself.

'And so,' said Hugo Rune, 'might I suggest that we repair to an upper-class eatery and take a light lunch?'

'A *light* one?' I said. 'Now *that* I *would* like to see.'

47

The meal went far beyond my expectations. Which, I must say, *were* great. We dined at the Savoy Grill, but my initial difficulty was actually in gaining admittance.

We arrived in our commandeered cab and I held wide the door for Hugo Rune. But when I tried to enter the restaurant, I was informed it was *not for my kind*.

'You just wait until the nineteen sixties,' I told the commissionaire, who had me by the collar of my nice pale linen suit and was hauling me back down towards the cab.

Mr Rune set matters straight, explaining that I was his son, an eccentric millionaire in my own right who had taken to the driving of a cab as part of the War Effort, me being too sickly and weak to uniform-up and stick bayonets in the enemy.

The Savoy Grill quite took my fancy and, as I was certain that it survived the war, I thought that when (or perhaps *if*) I returned to my own time, I would visit it again to see how much it had changed.

On stage was a band called Liam Proven's Lords-a-Leaping Jazz Cats. The band leader Liam was an imposing figure in white tie, tailcoat and khaki shorts. There seemed to be a novelty element to the performance, with constant humorous interjections of the, 'I say, I say, I say, my wife once went to Hartlepool on a charabanc.'

'Zulus?'

'Yes, thousands of them.'

Followed by a drum-roll and a cymbal-crash.

'It is hard to believe, I know,' said Hugo Rune, taking out a pre-lunch cigar and slotting it into his mouth, 'but fifty years from now no one will remember Liam Proven.'

'*I* will remember him,' I said to Hugo Rune. And I do remember him well.

The band launched into a number called 'When Common Sense

Walks on a Single Leg, I'll Wear My Viable Trousers', and we launched into our soup.

'I do have to say,' I said, between polite spoonings, 'that I do not really think that delivering a speech to Winston Churchill qualifies as a case.'

'It's a *brief* case,' said Hugo Rune, tapping at the very one that rested in his lap. 'And there *is* a war on, you know.'

'I remain unconvinced,' I said. 'Although perhaps a real case has yet to present itself in some subtle furtive fashion.'

And then there came an explosion that drowned out everything else.

And then there came that commissionaire, who hurried to Hugo Rune. Urgent words entered Himself's ear; Himself nodded to these. The commissionaire departed and Hugo Rune pressed on with his soup.

'Well go on, then,' I said to him. 'Tell me what he whispered.'

'Oh, it was nothing, Rizla,' said the Magus. 'Our taxi was hit by a bomb, nothing more.'

Which caused me to choke on my soup. 'Hit by a bomb?' I said when I could. 'We were in that cab only minutes ago. We could have been blown up.'

'Such is the way with wars, young Rizla. But come now, calm yourself. Getting all hot under the collar plays havoc with the digestion.'

'I quite liked that cab,' I said, making a grumpy face.

'I'll let you choose another. There's a row of them outside.'

Liam Proven's Lords-a-Leaping Jazz Cats struck up the lively refrain 'My Love for You Is as Inappropriate as a Grocer's Apostrophe, Yet Sweeter than a Butcher's Turn-Up'.

Which was so damned catchy that I knew I would be whistling it for months.

Hugo Rune perused his pocket watch. 'I suggest we do keep this luncheon light, as I previously suggested. We will have time for no more than four courses, so choose with care. My appointment with Winnie must be kept, to the minute and the second of the hour.'

I was back to feeling all uncomfortable once more. The thought of Hugo Rune actually arriving on time for something, other than a restaurant opening, was, to me, unheard of.

'Cometh the hour, cometh the man, young Rizla.'

I shrugged and said that I agreed. Although I did wonder why we had not ordered all our other courses at the same time as we had ordered our soup. But fathoming the hows and whys of Hugo Rune had never proved a satisfying pastime. 'I will have the steak,' I said to the well-dressed waiter.

'And for sir's other three courses?'

'Three more steaks.'

Which tickled Hugo Rune.

And so we dined upon wondrous food and consumed wondrous wines. Smoked wondrous Wild Woodbines (for these were apparently quite the rage amongst the bright young things who thronged the Savoy Grill). And downed most wondrous brandies.

And although I did not know it then, this would be the very last five-star belly-buster that I would take with Hugo Rune in England. Which is why now, thinking back upon it, I treasure the memory.

Even that of our rapid and somewhat undignified departure.

It had seemed such a trifling matter, really. Hugo Rune had scribbled a request onto one of his calling cards and had it passed to Mr Proven. The tune in question that he wished to hear being that ever-popular standard 'It's Always Raining Dumplings When You're on the Gravy Train'. Mr Proven bowed to this request, announced it through the microphone and then turned with his baton to the band. But then a question of tempo arose which somewhat spoiled the mood.

'It's Always Raining Dumplings' is always played as 'swing'. And as everyone knows, swing is basically a four-four shuffle. As opposed to rock 'n' roll, which is all straight eights with a back beat, or waltz, which is three-four with an anticipated second beat. Swing is rarely, if ever, in fact never never, presented in five-four. An unnatural rhythm, which although finding favour in the nineteen sixties with such luminaries as Don Van Vliet, brought gratings to the nerves of the bright young things who thronged to the Savoy Grill.

It was the drummer who started the trouble, but is that not always the way?

Liam Proven had prefaced the requested tune with a most amusing jape which ran in this fashion:

Liam: I say, I say, I say, what do you call a fellow who hangs around with musicians?

Guitarist: A drummer.

Somewhat ancient that gag is now, but bright and new back then. The drummer failed to respond with the drum-roll and cymbal-crash and when the song began took to a five-four time signature that threw all his jovial comrades out of tempo. I thought this most amusing and clapped my hands to the beat as best I could. Mr Proven, however, drew his baton across his throat and demanded that the band begin again with the drummer called to order. The band began again, but this time the drummer put down his sticks and took to reading a book.

At this point Mr Rune rose unexpectedly from his chair, took himself over to the bandstand, mounted same, struck the drummer from his stool with a single swing of his stout stick, took up the tools of the drummer's trade and hammered out a solo that would have done credit to Keith Moon. The crowd stared, boggle-eyed and droopy-jawed, and when Mr Rune had completed his solo there was that certain silence which is generally known as the calm before the storm.

I remain to this day uncertain as to who threw the first punch. I think that it might have been me. The musicians certainly attacked Mr Rune, wielding their instruments as weapons in a manner that would one day find favour with Keith Richards. But Mr Rune was trained in the arts of Dim Mak. So it was probably his bringing down most of the band, including Mr Proven, that began the riot proper. And as some bright young thing was trying to climb onto the bandstand and have a go at Mr Rune, I felt it quite right to punch him.

I think it was an ARP man who fired the first shot. They were apparently allowed (in fact encouraged) to carry firearms and discharge them at whoever they pleased if they felt that it was necessary. He possibly shot the American serviceman by accident, as I think he was aiming at Mr Rune. But the American serviceman's companions-at-arms, who were all fairly armed to the teeth, returned fire.

But who threw the Molotov cocktail?

And why, I had to ask myself, had anyone brought a Molotov cocktail into the Savoy Grill in the first place?

I felt now that I probably would not be revisiting the Savoy Grill in the nineteen sixties, but it had made for a most memorable luncheon.

We felt it prudent to make a most rapid (if somewhat undignified) departure at this time and I snatched up the briefcase and we took our leave at speed.

We discovered outside, parked beside a hole in the ground where our conveyance had been, a number of unoccupied taxicabs. Their drivers, being cockneys, who only love jellied eels more than a good punch-up, had hastened inside, drawn by the sounds of gunfire and mayhem and were presently warring with waiters and bellboys and others *of their kind*.

'We'll take this one,' said Hugo Rune, a-dusting of his tweeds. 'The key is in the ignition. Broadcasting House if you will, please, Rizla.'

48

Now I really took to Broadcasting House, oh what a wonderful place. I parked the cab and stepped from it to view that famous façade.

Designed by the renowned architect Sir Thomas Dalberty, in the *zucker näse* style, as a lasting and poignant tribute to his wife Doris, opera singer and nasal pianist.

The flanged nostril atrium with its double-bow fronting and great use made of natural light conveys no hint of what is to come when one enters the perhaps *infamous* network of corridors. Constructed, it is to be believed, to resemble the pattern of neural pathways within the cerebellum of a snail.

Not for nothing did Captain Beefheart pen the words: 'This is recorded through a fly's ear and you have to have a fly's eye to see it.' And although the connection might seem at first superficial, if not downright tenuous, as Mr Rune so aptly put it, 'not on a wing and a prayer flies the wasp, but all on the toss of a coin'.

'Do you think it will be all right just to leave the cab here?' I asked Hugo Rune, who appeared to be applying make-up. 'And what are you doing to yourself?'

'Lock the cab and bring the key and I am applying make-up.'

'Why?'

'Because this is Broadcasting House.'

'Are you hoping to be taken for Vera Lynn? I think Fange has that covered.'

' 'I must look my best for the studio, Rizla. The lights do age one terribly.'

'I thought Mr Churchill's speech was going out on the wireless,' I said.

'It *is*,' said Hugo Rune. 'Lock the cab and follow me.'

And that is what I did.

★

There is something almost magical about the atrium of Broadcasting House. Perhaps because so many famous people have moved through it, loitered around and about it, swanned within and posed throughout it, been there and sat there and stood.

'I hope we see someone famous,' I said as we entered.

'We are bound to, Rizla,' replied Mr Rune. 'But please remember who you are with and try to remain dignified.'

'Oh look,' I said, pointing. 'Is that not Valentine Dyle?'

'Where? Where?' went Hugo Rune. 'Let me get his autograph.'

I looked at Mr Rune.

He looked at me.

Oh how we laughed together.

'I will have to ask you gentlemen to keep the laughter down,' said an official-looking body with a BBC-issue gas-mask case and a hint of the Lochs and Glens. 'I am the groundskeeper here and *this* is the BBC.'

'I have an appointment,' said Hugo Rune, 'at fifteen-hundred hours with the PM. You will find my name in the book if you look. That name is Hugo Rune.'

'Hoots mon,' said the official-looking body. 'Can ye hear that wee scratchin' sound? I ken that there's a moose loose aboot this Broad-casting Hoose.'

And I looked once more at Hugo Rune.

But he was looking elsewhere.

Elsewhere, as it happened, happened to be towards Miss Elsa Lancaster. I recognised her immediately, as *The Bride of Frankenstein* was one of my favourite movies. But who was that with her, I wondered. It was *not* Boris Karloff.

'That is Winston Churchill,' said Hugo Rune. And he waved to this fellow, who waved back at him. 'Just in case you were wondering.'

'That is never Winnie,' I said to Hugo Rune. 'Winnie was short and fat and looked like a bulldog with a big cigar in its chops.'

'I told you you wouldn't like him.'

'But *that* is not him. That is a tall skinny man with an eye-pencil moustache. That looks more like George Cole than Winston Churchill.'

'That,' said Hugo Rune, in a whisper and behind his hand, 'is because it *is* George Cole. He plays the part of Winston Churchill. And very well he does it too, when he's all done up in prosthetics.'

'No no no,' I said and shook my head to my no-ings. 'Winston Churchill is Winston Churchill, no one ever played him.'

'Lots of actors have played him over the years, young Rizla.'

'Yes, but that was in films and on TV—'

'And on the wireless?'

'Yes, on the wireless too.'

'I rest my case,' said Hugo Rune. 'Point made QED.'

'No. No. No,' I said once more. 'That is not what I mean and you know it.'

'Rizla.' And Hugo Rune now drew me to a quiet corner and whispered into my ear. 'George Cole does the voice. Other actors, stunt-doubles if you will, do the morale-boosting walkabouts of the East End, or go off to peace talks and war talks and whatnots. But there is no specific Winston Churchill. He is a construct. An idea. An ideal. Cometh the hour, cometh the man, and things of that nature generally.'

'And—' And Mr Rune raised his finger to staunch the flow of my protests. 'Even if there were a real Winston Churchill, he would *not* be running the English side of this war. The speech within this briefcase originated at the Ministry of Serendipity. And, as you know full well, the tactics employed in the military campaign against the Reich are put together by the computer Colossus at Bletchley Park.'

'So there is no real Winston Churchill? I find this most disappointing.'

'We'd be lost without George Cole,' said Hugo Rune. 'No one can do the voice as good as George.' And Mr Rune perused his watch. 'Ten minutes to go,' he said.

The official-looking body who had vanished from our sight now reappeared with a clipboard held tightly between official-looking fingers. 'Och braw the noo,' he intoned. 'If ye'll sign this piece of paper, I'll have—'

But he did not finish.

An explosion roared outside in the street and our latest cab went skywards.

Having done the instinctive duckings, Mr Rune and I returned to our feet and viewed the devastation without.

'Do I see some kind of pattern emerging here?' I asked. 'Has God got it in for taxis, or is some basic engine design fault bringing itself to the fore?'

Hugo Rune once more perused his watch. 'That one was a little too close for comfort,' he said. 'You will pardon me, Rizla, whilst I take myself off to the Gents.'

And with that he did so, leaving me to stand around and wait. But I really did not mind too much about the waiting, as it did give me an opportunity to see if I could spy out any more stars of the wireless set.

And would not you know it, or would not you not, I spied out the great Harry 'put on your plimsolls, Mother, I've got a dose of the runs' MacKentyre. Charlie 'if it looks like a ferret and smells like a ferret, it shouldn't be stirring my tea' MacAlistair. And Jimmy 'boil up the orange sauce, Uncle, I've just been bowled out for a duck' MacMackMack. And—

'Cease, Rizla,' said Hugo Rune, returning. 'It is neither big, nor clever. But, say, isn't that Leslie "if God is dog spelled backwards, then what the kcuf is taht?" Tomlinson?'

'No,' I said. 'Though it does look like him. Are you all better now?'

'Better now?' said Hugo Rune. 'Ah, I see what you mean. The taking myself off to the Gents. Just needed to highlight my cheek-bones – what do you think?'

'I think we have become caseless and plotless and lost,' I said. 'And now I know that Winnie is not Winnie, I think I would just like to go home and have a good sulk.'

'And miss all the excitement?'

I did head-bobbings to signify 'weighing-up'. 'We nearly got beaten to pulp at the Savoy Grill and the two cabs we requisitioned have exploded. Let us say that I have had sufficient excitement for today and perhaps a case will present itself tomorrow.'

'It has already presented itself,' said Hugo Rune. 'You have failed to put two and two together. I, however, have done that very thing. Come, Rizla, destiny awaits.'

At precisely three of the afternoon clock, myself and Mr Rune, George Cole, a radio producer called Neil and a number of probably nameless secret service fellows in morning suits and bowler hats gathered in a green room on the second floor of Broadcasting House. With a gravity that was little less than ludicrous, Hugo Rune clicked open the briefcase and passed a sheet of paper to the pretend prime minister.

George Cole examined this, turned the sheet over and looked at the back and then turned it front-wise again. 'And is this all there is?' he asked, in the voice of Winston Churchill. 'Nothing about fighting them on the beaches and in the fields and over the cricket greens and up the back passages or whatnot?'

Hugo Rune shook his head. 'Only what you see, I'm afraid.'

'I could perhaps put in something about "some chicken, some neck", or how this was "their finest hour". What exactly *is* my motivation? Should I pad it out with a bit of *King Lear*?'

'Best to stick to what it says on the paper,' said Hugo Rune. 'But there is one thing you *could* do.'

After we had left Broadcasting House, I thanked Hugo Rune.

'That was very decent of you,' I said, 'asking him to sign his autograph for me.'

'For *you*?' said the Perfect Master. 'For *me*, if you please.'

But he was only joking.

'So,' I said, 'should we listen to a wireless set and hear what this highly important message to the nation might be?'

But Hugo Rune shook his head. 'We should be getting on with the exciting stuff,' he said. 'And to do this we must return to the Ministry of Serendipity.'

'I really have lost the plot,' I said. 'Would you care to explain?'

'All in good time, young Rizla. But see – an unattended cab. I think you will find that your key fits the lock. Mornington Crescent, please. And as fast as you can.'

I halted the cab outside the Lyons Corner House, wherein lay the lift to the underground Ministry. I made to leave the cab, but Mr Rune said no.

'Stay here, Rizla, and keep the engine running. And be prepared to drive at speed the moment I return.'

And with that said Hugo Rune left the cab and vanished into the Lyons Corner House. I sat idly *brumming* the engine and tinkering about with things that did not belong to me. This tinkering led to me opening the glove compartment and finding to my joy not only *gloves*, but a service revolver as well. I twirled this dangerously on my finger and did aimings and the mouthings of phrases such as, 'Take a roadside rest, Fritz,' and, 'Cop this, Adolf, kapow kapow kapow.'

And then suddenly Hugo Rune returned, jumped into the rear seat and shouted, 'The cab up ahead, the one just leaving the corner, after it!'

'You would not care to explain?' I asked.

'After it, Rizla!' cried Mr Hugo Rune.

And so I gave chase. And clearly I *was* giving chase, because the cab across the street took off at speed and, with ne'er a care for a passing cleric on a bike, did swervings and acceleratings too.

'Faster, Rizla, faster. We can't let this blighter escape.'

'I would really like it if you told me what is going on,' I said. But Hugo Rune cried, 'Faster!' so I put the hammer down. Well, pressed my foot to the elegantly designed accelerator pedal anyway.

We passed around Piccadilly Circus, through Leicester Square, Trafalgar Square and up the Royal Mall towards the palace.

'Faster, Rizla, faster and run him off the road.'

'What?' I said. 'I cannot,' I said.

'Just do it!' shouted Hugo Rune.

And I put my foot down as far as it would go and my cab drew level with the other cab. And would not you know it, or would not you not, that other cab was being driven by Hugo Rune's arch-enemy, the ever evil bad Count Otto Black.

And in the back of that cab sat Mr McMurdo, wearing a fearsome expression.

'Off the road with them, Rizla,' shouted Mr Rune. 'Grind them into a tree.'

So I took a deep breath and swung the wheel and our cab struck their cab a devastating blow. There were showerings of sparks and grindings of metal and the cabs' running boards and wheel arches got sort of locked together, which caused them to leave the road and hurtle towards a very large tree indeed.

And yes, things really do seem to happen in slow motion in situations such as this. And what I saw surprised me all the more because it happened as if so slowly.

The entire front part of the other taxicab detached itself from the rest of the vehicle and rose into the sky.

It was the count upon his flying motorcycle. The rear section of his now driverless cab continued on at speed and ploughed into the tree. A terrible explosion occurred that freed the cab that Mr Rune and I were travelling in and allowed it to grind to a halt some hundred yards beyond. With both of us mostly unscathed.

And when I felt myself able to speak again, I raised my head from between my legs and managed to blurt out a, 'What was *that* all about?'

'Infamy and trickery,' said Hugo Rune.

'And Mr McMurdo,' I said. 'Oh dear. Was Count Otto kidnapping him? He was still in the cab, he must surely be—'

'Put completely out of service,' said Hugo Rune.

'I was going to say "killed",' I said.

'You cannot kill what has never lived,' said Mr Hugo Rune.

'And that is a statement I would really like explained.'

'And so it shall be, Rizla. You performed sterling work today and you will have the nation's thanks for it.'

'I could do with a beer,' I said. 'And a great deal of explanation.'

'Then let us return to Brentford and I will buy you a beer. But not I think in The Purple Princess. Brentford, please, Rizla, and don't spare the horsepower.'

THE MOON

49

THE MOON

'You really will have to explain,' I said, 'for I am most confused.'

'Energy fools the magician,' said Hugo Rune.

'As an explanation, that fails on so many levels,' I told the magician, but raised my glass to him all the same as I did so.

We were in the saloon bar of The Four Horsemen, which was under new new management. Jack Lane, former Brentford team captain and centre forward, and the man who hammered in three goals when Brentford won the FA Cup in nineteen twenty-seven, now stood behind the bar. Bald and bandy-legged, he had hardly changed at all since that famous day of glory.

'My suspicions were originally aroused by the healthsome state of the ghastly Mr McMurdo,' said Hugo Rune. 'Believe me, Rizla, it would take more than any Harley Street quack has to offer to set that fellow to rights. And then all that nonsense about putting *me* out to pasture. *Me* out to pasture? *Me?*'

'Quite so,' I said. 'Go on,' I also said.

'The second exploding cab confirmed my suspicions that something untoward was occurring. One cab, fair enough, Spontaneous Cab Combustion does happen once in a while. But *two*, I think not. You will note that I repaired to the Gents. Did you not think that was strange?'

'Well, I thought— Well, never mind,' I said.

'I felt that I needed to check the contents of the briefcase and so I slit the bottom and took a little peep inside.'

'Oh yes?' I said, intrigued.

'A bomb, Rizla. Small and of advanced design and timed to go off precisely at three.'

'To kill you and George Cole, oh no!'

'Oh yes.' And Hugo Rune drank ale. 'It is not altogether unpleasing, this,' he said. 'What did you say it was called?'

'Apple Chancery,' I said. 'But as a running gag, having all the beers named after typefaces never really gained its legs at all, did it?'

'There may be a bit of life left in it. But, as I was saying, a bomb of advanced design. I disarmed it, of course.'

'Of course,' I said. 'So what about the speech for the prime minister to read out?'

'I will get to that,' said the Magus. 'I had you drive me at speed to Mornington Crescent. There I found what I expected to find: dead and dying, precious files destroyed, computers wrecked, all lost. The Ministry had been infiltrated. My worst fears were founded.'

'Oh dear,' I said. 'Oh dear, oh dear, oh dear.'

'Quite so.'

'And then you had me chase after that cab because Count Otto was kidnapping Mr McMurdo.'

'Count Otto was *not* kidnapping him. Because that was *not* McMurdo. I found McMurdo's body at the Ministry – by the looks of him he had been dead for several days.'

'You did an awful lot of looking around down there in a very few minutes,' I said. 'But tell me please, for I do not understand – the McMurdo who tried to blow you up with a bomb in a briefcase was not the real McMurdo? So was he an actor like the one who plays Winston Churchill?'

'He was not a man, Rizla. Which was why he would not shake my hand. He was a robot, a construct, a mandroid, call it whatever you like.'

'Oh come on,' I said to Hugo Rune. 'I saw the robot at Bletchley Park, a proper nineteen-forties robot, all rivets and eye slits and clockwork. Nothing like what we saw in that office – a robot that can look and sound so convincingly like a human being – is likely to exist for hundreds of years yet, surely.'

'It is as I said,' said Hugo Rune. 'A great inhuman force is at work here, Rizla. A force far greater than Hitler or the horrible Count Otto Black. And now at last I know what it is. And it is a thing to fear.'

'Oh come on now,' I said. ' "You ain't afraid of no man." '

' "There's something out there," ' said Hugo Rune, ' "and it ain't no man." '*

'A robot?' I said. 'A great big robot, just like our Colossus?'

'A computer,' said Hugo Rune. 'And one possessed by the spirit of a God.'

I whistled and said, 'You mean Wotan.'

'That is entirely correct.'

'Pardon me for saying this—' and I took sup at my ale '—but this is a very big leap of logic. Do you have any definite proof? Is this not just a theory?'

'*Just a theory?*' Hugo Rune did risings in his seat. 'When Rune has a theory, it *is* a *theory proven*. Am I not Rune, whose eye is in the triangle? Whose nose cleaves the etheric continuum? Whose ears take in the Music of the Spheres?'

'You are indeed,' I said and I raised my glass to him. 'And it is a joy to see you once more on top form. For indeed you are THE MAGICIAN.'

We did not take too many beers. In fact we were quite restrained. I drove the taxi back to the manse, picking up fish and chips on the way that we might enjoy for some dinner.

And fish and chips in the paper, on your knee in a cosy chair, by the wireless set, is as English as English can be. And I switched on the wireless set to listen to the news. And perhaps catch some popular dance band music of the day. But probably not one led by Liam Proven.

'This is the voice of Free Radio Brentford,' came a crackling voice. And that voice seemed to me to be the voice of my friend Lad Nicholson.

'I did not know that Free Radio Brentford was about during the Second World War,' I said to Hugo Rune. The Magus leaned over and filched away one of my chips.

'And on the world stage today,' continued the voice that seemed to be that of Lad Nicholson, 'the long-awaited three-fifteen speech from the prime minister turned out to be something of a surprise. It stated, and I quote: "That for his services to the British Nation, Hugo Rune

---

* These classic lines of movie dialogue have been included to add that little bit of extra class to an otherwise pretty classy scene.

be awarded its highest honour and a state pension. And that from this day forth he must be addressed as either 'sir' or 'your lordship' by all and sundry and—" '

'And?' I said. And I turned to Mr Rune.

The Magus continued to munch on his dinner. 'It was all I had time to write on that piece of toilet paper in the Gents at Broadcasting House,' he explained. 'After I had disabled the bomb that was meant to kill myself and the mighty George Cole. I expect it is what the real Mr McMurdo would have wanted, don't you?'

And I just nodded my head.

Having dined, we then got down to work. We packed our clothes into steamer trunks and loaded them into the cab.

Then Mr Rune put out the rubbish, switched off the lights and closed up the manse.

'I really liked living there,' I told him. 'I think I will quite miss it. Along with the mysterious unnamed and unmentioned cook who always provided our breakfasts.'

'We have more adventures lying ahead,' said the Perfect Master. 'Now drive us to the allotments – I have items to collect from my workshop.'

At Mr Rune's behest I loaded all manner of interesting things into more steamer trunks, swung each aboard the Gravitite disc and nudged them into the lift. Once topside, all went into the cab and then we upped and left.

'I wonder how far we can get in this cab before it runs out of fuel,' I said to Hugo Rune. 'Because neither of us has a ration book, so I do not see how we will buy petrol.'

'Fear not for that, young Rizla,' called Hugo Rune, as he mixed himself a cocktail. 'London cabs never *have* and never *will* run on petrol. They run on tap water, taking advantage of the MacGreggor Mather's Water Car Patent, which is otherwise kept secret from the public and the motor industry.'

'There are so many legitimate reasons for hating cabbies, are there not?' I said. And I saw Mr Rune's head nod in the driving mirror.

★

I drove for many hours. Because we were driving to Liverpool and Liverpool is a goodly drive from Brentford, especially in a taxi with a top speed of sixty-five miles per hour.

'Tell me about the liner we are travelling on,' I said. 'Will it be luxurious?'

'Extremely,' said Hugo Rune. 'It is the RMS *Olympic*.'

'Hold on there,' I said in return. 'The *Olympic* was a sister ship to the *Titanic* and it ceased to ply the waters back in the nineteen thirties.'

'Well, you know best, young Rizla.'

'So it is still in service?' I said.

'It is a luxury liner, top class in all departments. And it is neutral. Like Switzerland.'

'You cannot have a neutral ship, can you?' I asked.

'You have to have at least one. Otherwise how are the rich supposed to take their cruises during wartime?'

'That is surely outrageous.'

'You won't say that when you are aboard.'

But I *did* say that when I was aboard. I was somewhat appalled. There were folk of every nation on board that magical liner. Rich folk all and all as friendly as can be. And there were military folk also. Those of the highest ranks. SS officers were clinking glasses with martial toffs from Eton. All around and about the world was in the grip of a terrible war that would leave millions homeless, wounded or dead, and here the swells were having it large and dancing the night away.

A seaman chappy in an immaculate white uniform showed us to our staterooms. And yes, they were POSH – port out, starboard home, Posh with a capital P.

I entered the suite of Hugo Rune, who was bouncing on his double bunk.

'Now *this*, young Rizla,' he said to me, 'really *is* the life.'

'This is shameful,' I said. 'Awful. With all the misery of this hideous war, the rich and privileged live like kings aboard this floating palace and have not a care in the world.'

'Oh, they have their cares,' said Hugo Rune. 'Which tie to wear for dinner. The jewelled coronet or the diamond pendant.'

'It is disgusting,' I said. 'And you should be ashamed of yourself.'

'*Me?*' said Hugo Rune, with outrage in his voice.

'You condone it. You revel in it—'

'Rizla.' And Hugo Rune ceased all his bouncing. 'You and I are on a mission to alter the course of this war. To save millions from nuclear death. Do you not feel that we deserve three square meals a day and a decent nest to curl up in come nightfall, whilst journeying forth on this noble quest?'

'Well,' I said. 'If you put it like that. But the rest of these people—'

'Their lives are not ours. Their morals are not ours. Do you not think that I hold them in contempt? Do you think that I lack all morality and sensibility?'

'Sorry,' I said. 'Of course not.'

'In that case, Rizla, I suggest we don our dinner suits and make our way to the bar. The *Olympic* sails at sunrise and I would recommend that you view this event from the top deck, with a gin and tonic in your hand. What say you to this matter?'

And I said *Yes* to it.

50

A regular pair of toffs we looked, as we sauntered down to the bar. This was the first time I had actually worn my dinner suit. Mr Rune had had it made to measure for me at a fashionable tailor shop in Piccadilly. Regarding the payment of the bill?

I had no regard for that.

The sheer scale of the RMS *Olympic* was daunting. The decks dwindled with perspective seemingly to infinity and the bar was nearly the size of a football pitch. It was all early neon, chrome and black, with elegant statuary of the art deco persuasion. All topless sylphlike females with slender bums and breasts.

Behind the bar counter were more colourful drinks than I had ever imagined existed. They covered the spectrum and went beyond and I looked on in awe. Behind the counter, before these bottles, stood a noble barman. A modish figure in a rapscallion jacket and feta-cheese-style pantaloons, he wore a jaunty little sailor's cap and a flower in his buttonhole. And he greeted our approach to his counter with a, 'Welcome aboard.'

'Pleased to be here,' I said with a smile. And then I said, 'Hold on.' And I gazed hard at that barman and I said, 'Fangio?'

'None other,' said he. 'But we'll keep that just between the three of us, if you don't mind. Or four, if you want to count my pet monkey Clarence here in his natty waistcoat and fez.'

I tipped a wink at Clarence and he raised his fez to me.

'What a joy to see you both here,' said Fangio. 'I had to, how shall I put this, make myself scarce, as it were. The customs men and the rozzers were hard at my heels. And although I hated like Satan's saucepan-full of collywobbles to have to run off before entering the Inter-Pub Lookalike Competition, I felt it best to sign on for a one-way passage to the home of the brave and the land of the free rather than stay behind and face the music. As it were.'

'Well, that makes everything clear,' I said. 'Except for Satan's saucepan.'

'Ah,' said Fangio. 'I'm experimenting with new terms of expression. Lord Cardigan welt me with a kipper if I'm telling you a lie.'

'I think it might need working on,' I said. 'But there is running-gag potential for sure, so work at it.'

'And what are you and Mr Rune doing here?' said Fangio. 'Having a bit of a holiday, is it now?'

'On the contrary,' said Hugo Rune, pointing to this bottle and that in the hope that Fangio might combine their contents into an interesting cocktail. 'We are here strictly on business. Undercover, as it were.'

'Well, it's my good fortune to run into you again. I have your bill for your outstanding account at The Purple Princess in my cabin.'

Mr Rune pointed with greater urgency and the matter of the outstanding account was never mentioned again.

'Tell you what though,' said Fangio in a confidential kind of a way, 'they're an odd old bunch, aren't they, the rich?'

He shook Hugo Rune's concoction and then poured it into a glass. The Magus downed this in one and swiftly ordered another.

And then he said, 'Odd? In what way?'

'They just look odd,' said Fangio. 'Especially the old ones – and there are some *really* old ones on board. Ancient dowagers and countesses. Eastern European nannas with unpronounceable names.'

'I fail to see what is so odd about that,' said Hugo Rune. 'And while you're at it, please pop in two of those olives and a squirt of mescaline.'

'Well, perhaps it's just me, then,' said Fangio. 'I can be all step-and-fetch-it-Barney-on-me-way-to-the-local-zoo at times, and don't go flattering me by telling me otherwise.'

'Forget what I said earlier,' I said. 'And how about serving *me* a drink?'

We spent the time until dawn in cocktail experimentation and succeeded in creating a number of drinks of such extreme unlikeliness as to baffle even ourselves. But then the dawn came up like thunder, as it sometimes does from Rangoon across the bay, and Mr Rune and I tottered topside to enjoy the leaving of port.

And it was a sight to remember, the lowering of the gangways, the belaying in and heaving to, some late and complicated pipings aboard, followed by lines being slipped and forecastles trimmed and things of that nature nautically.

And off slid the liner out into the sea and we were off on our way.

And I did yawnings and Hugo Rune did too and then we went off to our bunks.

I arose at three the following afternoon, bathed, dressed and went for a stroll on the promenade deck. It was late September now* and the sun was low in the sky, throwing long shadows and making the grandeur seem somehow even more grand. I tipped the brim of my panama to passing ladies and wished that I had a dandy cane to twirl between my fingers. This *was* the life, there was no mistake about it. And though it was all so terribly wrong, it still felt marvellous.

I had wandered about a half a mile along the portside deck when I spied the first of them. And with this spying I realised why Fangio had used the word *odd* to describe them. The first of the Eastern European nannas.

She was a tiny wrinkled thing with a face like a pickled prune and she was all swaddled up in numerous furs and seated in an old-fashioned wicker bath chair. A gentleman of military appearance with spectacular mustachios steered this chair along. Several children fussed about the prunish nanna, offering her sweeties and dabbing at her mouth with dainty handkerchiefs. Their costumes put me in mind of a photograph I had seen of the Czar and his family, shortly before they came to their terrible end in that cellar at Yekaterinburg in nineteen eighteen.

I offered that nanna a brim-tip and smile, but she returned this pleasantry with such a bitter-eyed look of pure loathing that it quite put the wind up me.

I decided to cease my stroll and find myself some breakfast.

There was seating in the First Class Diner for eighteen hundred people. The tablecloths were of Irish linen, the knives and forks of silver. The head waiter asked for my stateroom number and then led me to my table. Where, sitting squarely, his napkin tucked beneath his

---

* Although it might well be argued that it was still July, it was not, as it was September. It is unlikely that poor continuity plays a part in this, more likely that it is a product of the Chevalier Effect.

chin, Himself was already tucking in to kedgeree and pickled peacock eggs* and lapsang souchong tea.

'Good afternoon to you, Rizla,' he called. 'The same again for my young companion, if you will,' he said to the head waiter, who departed after clickings of the heels.

I sat myself in a comfy chair and accepted a cup of tea.

'How goes it, Rizla?' asked Hugo Rune. 'No seasickness setting in? All shipshape and Bristol fashion?'

'Never better,' I said, sipping tea. 'Although I saw one of those odd old women that Fangio mentioned. And I can confirm that they are *very* odd and really rather scary.'

'I think Bavarian beldames are the least of our concerns. But there are certainly some notable personages about this vessel. From the vantage point of this dining chair alone, I can see six high-ranking SS officers, who hopefully will be gracing Mr Pierrepoint's noose at Nuremberg come the war's conclusion. Two spies, two of America's Most Wanteds, three Mafia dons, a defrocked bishop and a shady lady with a crazy baby and a taste for tights and chicken bites and stalactites and troglodytes.'

'Right,' I said, nodding. 'And you must point out the last one to me.'

So Mr Rune pointed.

And I said, 'Oh yes.'

And presently my breakfast arrived.

Because one of the joys of being rich, and there are many, is that you can take your breakfast at any time of the day or night. And no one will call you a slob.

I got involved with my pickled eggs and said nothing more for a while.

'We will fall into a torpor on this voyage,' said Mr Rune, with a sudden sadness. 'We will need something to occupy our minds or we shall surely succumb to boredom and ennui.'

'I think we can afford to give it a couple of days,' I said, dipping a toast soldier into some kind of dip. 'There are many more combinations of cocktails that need trying and I have yet to know the joys of dinnertime.'

'Nevertheless, you have the remaining tarot cards?'

---

* Although technically these would be pea*hen* eggs.

'There's only four left now,' I said. And I named them: 'THE MOON, THE WHEEL OF FORTUNE, THE TOWER and DEATH itself.'

'Ah yes, DEATH,' said the Magus. 'That would be the card onto which you pasted a bit of sticking plaster, so as to distinguish it from the rest when I ask you to pick one out face down at random.'

'Can you blame me?' I said. 'Who would want to pick *that* card?'

'More tea?' asked Hugo Rune, and he poured it. 'Pick us another then, do.'

And so I chose THE MOON. 'It looks harmless,' I explained. 'And there was a lovely moon last night. THE MOON shall be our talisman, as it were.'

'Have a care, Rizla,' said the guru's guru. 'You are beginning to think in the manner of a magician. And little good ever came from that!' And then he popped one of my pickled eggs into his mouth and challenged me to a game of leapfrog on the poop deck.

When done with that, we dabbled in deck quoits, a chukka of cabin-boy polo, kept our hands in at korfball and waterskied a while behind the liner. And as the sun sank slowly in the west, we returned to our staterooms and dolled ourselves up for dinner.

My suit was laid out on my bunk before me, neatly pressed and made fragrant with what I supposed to be an expensive cologne. My shirt too was laundered and luxuriated within a cellophane sleeve. I unfolded this shirt and gave it a sniff and it too smelled most sweetly.

'I could *really* get used to this,' I said, for such treatment merits such clichés. And so I bathed and dried and gave myself a good all-over spraying with the complimentary bottle that held a prominent position on my toiletry table.

I then togged up in my finery and, growing just a tad dizzy from all the stuff I had sprayed on myself and others had sprayed on my clothes, I tottered out of my stateroom and went in search of dinner.

As Hugo Rune had yet to arrive, I seated myself in my reserved and comfy dining chair, ordered something preposterous from the drinks menu and wondered how many master forgers or post-modernist mistresses I could spy out amongst the gorgeously attired and moneyed classes.

They came and went before me, a cavalcade of opulence, the *jeunesse dorée* and the nouveau riche rubbing padded shoulders with nabobs and Plutocrats, patricians, princes and panjandrums. And would not you know it, or would not you not, they turned up their noses to me. In fact those that drew near to myself became decidedly sniffy. They dabbed at their upraised nostrils with initialled hand-kerchiefs and nosegays, made haughty disapproving sounds and hurried on their way.

I took a tentative sniff at myself, which caused my eyes to smart. 'Note to self,' I noted to myself. 'Do not go so heavy on the free smelly stuff in future.'

My drink arrived and I sipped at it and wondered where Mr Rune was. The last thing he had said to me before we went our separate ways was, 'Dinner promptly at eight, young Rizla.'

So what had become of him? I glanced down at my wristlet watch, and it was eight twenty-five.

At eight twenty-eight a bellboy appeared clasping a note in gloved fingers.

I unfolded this note and read the words on it. And at these my blood ran cold.

> *Please come at once*
> *to the Stateroom Suite of*
> *Lord Hugo Rune*

read this note,

> *for he has been taken gravely ill*
> *and may not survive until morning.*

51

I ran to the double-bunk side of the ailing Mr Rune, my hands a-flap and both my knees a-knocking.

Doctors and various medics of that well-spoken order that attend to the needs of the rich, and will always sign them off with a sick note even if they do not really need one, stood about looking concerned and eager to apply all manner of brand-new medical equipment, much of it involving valves and wires and electrodes.

I pushed in amongst them and stared at my sickly friend. He did not look *that* sickly, as it happened. It looked more as if he was just having a little nap before getting stuck into his dinner.

'What is wrong with him?' I asked. 'The message said that he was on his last legs.'

'Exhaustion,' said a medic with one of those circular mirror-things strapped upon his forehead. 'Brought on by too much waterskiing this afternoon, I suspect.'

'Then why did the message imply that he was dying?'

'I don't know what message you mean,' said the medical type. 'I never sent any message – did any of you send any message?'

His colleagues did shruggings of shoulders and shakings of heads.

'Well, someone sent it,' I said. 'I have it here.' But I did not have it there. 'I must have dropped it on the way,' I said.

'And *just who* are you?' asked a nurse, a shapely nurse with a pinched-in waist and large protruding bosoms.

'I am Mr Rune's closest friend. His aide and confidant. He is my mentor, my—'

But I did not finish what I had to say, which might have taken so much time to say if I had, because suddenly I was being pushed from the room.

'He is in capable hands,' said another medically inclined fellow, this one with an electric stethoscope about his neck. 'You go off and enjoy your dinner – it is grilled coelacanth tonight, I understand, prepared with Oyster Fall in Ponze dressing, topped carefully with grounded mouille and spring onions. Served with garden salad.'

'Is it?' I said. 'That sounds tasty. But I had better stay here with my friend. I really do think it would be for the best.'

But the medical personnel were having absolutely none of it whatsoever. Mr Rune was now under their professional care, he would be fussed over and looked after as befitted an exalted traveller in this floating palace and I was not to trouble myself, but rather go and enjoy my dinner.

And it had not escaped my notice that during the course of this conversation the medical team had been slapping surgical masks over their noses and turning their faces away.

It was that damned cologne that was doing for me once more.

'All right,' I said. 'I will leave. But I will be straight back here after dinner, so do not even think about locking the door and keeping me out.'

'Enjoy your dinner,' said one of these medics, although his voice was muffled by his mask.

As it happened I did *not* enjoy my dinner. I know what it was that I ordered, but what I ordered did not turn up on my plate. I ordered the soup, but I got fat bread rolls, all buttered. The steak, but I got a great big pie instead. The posh cheese and biscuits I wanted for afters, but I was served huge rolly pud. And so by the time I had finished, I was well and truly bloated and I had to loosen my cummerbund a couple of notches and engage the emergency gusset to the rear of my fitted trews.

And I do confess that I let out a terrible belch. Which did not increase my standing with the gentry. The waiter then brought me a milkshake and told me to drink it all up, because it was full of vitamins.

So it was with considerable effort that I attempted to rise and steer my patent-leather shoes towards my friend's sick-bunk. I would have made it, though, if it had not been for the unexpected arrival of a very pretty girl, who seated herself down in Mr Rune's chair and smiled most sweetly at me.

'You are not going just yet, are you?' she asked, and her eyelashes fluttered and she did pursings of the lips.

'I have to go and see my friend,' I said. 'He has been taken ill.'

'I'm sure he will be in good hands. The world's finest medical experts are aboard this ship. Doctors from all over the globe, the cream of the catheter crop, as it were.'

'I have no doubt of that,' I said, sipping my milkshake. 'Everything here is top notch.'

'Including yourself,' said this beautiful girl. Though I could not believe that she had.

'We have not been introduced,' I said, putting out my hand in the hope of touching hers. 'My name is Rizla. What is yours?'

But the angel giggled prettily. 'Rizla?' she said. 'What a wonderful name. I won't tell you mine, it's too dull.'

'You have a most exotic accent,' I said, for she did. 'Is it Eastern European?'

'Nowhere of consequence,' she replied, daintily diddling digits in her lap. 'I am the nursemaid of an old and distinguished lady. I was brought up in a small village, but later found work in the capital. My employer and I have been aboard this liner since the outbreak of the war.'

'That is a long time,' I said. 'But there are certainly worse jobs to be had. And far worse places to have them.'

'Few lives can be worse than mine,' she said, in a whispered voice. But did not want to elaborate.

'It would be lovely,' she said, 'if you and I were to take a little stroll upon the promenade deck. The full moon is out tonight and the sea looks so beautiful.'

'I really should return to my friend,' I said. 'Although your offer is certainly tempting.'

'There is no telling where a little stroll might lead to.' The beautiful young woman smiled at me.

Which left all sorts of potential erotic possibilities hanging in the air. As it were.

'Well,' I said. 'As *you* said, I am sure he is in good hands. What possible harm could a short stroll do? Although I do have to say that it probably will have to be a very short one, as I have rather too freely indulged in my dinner.'

'We can stroll slowly,' said the marvellous being and she rose elegantly to her feet and put out her arm to me. And I rose and took it and, smiling quite smugly, escorted her off to the deck.

The moon looked so achingly beautiful, the sea like a mirror reflecting its glory, the ship seemed to glide as on ice and the weather was warm. No more perfect night than this could I possibly imagine and I sought to add it to my store of remembered moments. In the hope that one day, many years from now, when I was old and wretched and done for, I would be able to look back with clarity and say, '*That* was a moment.'

'You seem thoughtful,' said the lovely girl. 'Are you a poet, perhaps, or a concert pianist, or maybe an artist?'

'I am none of those things,' I replied. 'I am like you, in employ to another. Although *he is* a great man.'

And we strolled a little further and I pulled a little on her arm and sought to draw her closer to my side. Because she did seem to be keeping herself somewhat at arm's length and I was now really keen to perhaps have a little snog with her and see where it led to.

But this nameless beauty maintained her distance, which I had to put down not to my lack of grace and manly charm, but more to the cologne I had doused myself with. Which, rather than dissipating as one might naturally have expected it to do, seemed, if anything, even more pungent than ever.

'Do you know what?' I said. 'I am thinking that I might repair to my accommodation, change my clothes and have a quick though *extremely thorough* shower. I would not be more than ten minutes at most – would you wait for me here?'

'Please don't leave me,' said the exquisite young woman. And tears welled in her wonderful eyes and her wonderful mouth grew crinkly.

'Oh sorry, sorry, sorry,' I said. 'I will do as you ask. It is just that I know how I smell.'

'We could talk, couldn't we?' she said. 'Sit here, perhaps?' And she gestured to a pair of steamer chairs that faced out towards the moon and the magical sea.

'Oh yes,' I said. 'I would like that very much.'

So down we sat and gazed at the moon, though I gazed mostly at her.

'Please tell me your name,' I said. 'I will bet that it is a romantic name, as might befit a faerie queen.'

'My name is Esmerelle,' said Esmerelle.

'And that is a beautiful name.' I reached out now to touch her hand, but this she pulled away.

'Might I tell you a story?' she asked. 'Of my homeland.'

'Might it lead to anything, how might I put this delicately, *interesting*?' I enquired.

'Oh yes, I can most certainly promise you *that*.'

'Does it involve pirates?' I asked, for I still harboured a great affection for pirates.

'No pirates,' she said. 'But there is a monster involved.'

'That is fair enough then,' I said. 'A monster *and* pirates might be asking a lot.'

'Would you like me to begin now?' asked my fabulous companion with but a hint of annoyance in her voice.

'Yes please,' I said. 'Carry on.' And I settled back in the moonlight and listened to the tale.

'More than a century ago in my village, there lived twin sisters. Young and gay and beautiful were they and as the village prospered, for the land was rich and lush, these sisters were carefree and joyous. But then one day a showman's waggon was driven into the village. A curious hunchbacked fellow in multicoloured garments drove this waggon and with him a dwarf of terrible aspect. Many of the villagers were afeared at the arrival of these unsavoury characters, but the twin sisters, who knew only happiness and frivolity, dallied near the waggon when it stopped for the watering of its horses and that its driver and diminutive companion might take a jug of mead at the alehouse. And while the horses and the travellers drank, the two sisters sneaked around to the rear of the waggon, which was as a gypsies' waggon with bowed canvas all about and a tiny door to the back. And they peeped in at a tiny window in this tiny door and there saw something wonderful within.'

'Was it a monkey?' I asked. For in my way I did like monkeys almost as much as I liked pirates. I was, in fact, very taken with Fangio's monkey Clarence. 'A golden monkey, perhaps?'

But Esmerelle shook her beautiful head, raven-haired tresses and all. 'Are you a complete stone-bonker?' she asked.

'Sorry,' I said. 'But I have always dreamed of seeing a golden monkey. Please carry on. I should not have butted in.'

'It was a golden mermaid,' said Esmerelle.

'How close was *that*?' I asked.

And Esmerelle sighed, which made me feel very guilty about behaving in such a foolish manner.

'I am so very sorry,' I said. 'Please carry on with your tale, I promise not to make any more stupid remarks.'

Esmerelle's eyes sparkled with reflected moonlight and she continued with her tale.

'Golden, she was, and alive. This was no showman's gaff. No stuffed chimera of ape and fish, but a living, breathing mermaid, who sat in a gilded cage. The two sisters were entranced by this mythical being made flesh. And they felt that they must free it from its prison and release it back into the sea. And so they entered the showman's waggon and were never seen again.' And Esmerelle sighed gently and diddled her fingers on the arms of her steamer chair.

'Hold on,' I said. 'That is not much of an end to the story. Surely there is more to it than that.'

'There is more,' said Esmerelle, 'but you might not wish to hear it.'

'You said there was a monster involved,' I replied. 'Get to that bit at least.'

'So be it. The two sisters tried to free the golden mermaid, but they could not open the cage. And then suddenly they heard the door of the waggon lock upon them and the waggoner whipped up the horses and drove away from the village. Although the sisters cried out for help, their cries went unheard and the waggon drove on and on for several days. Soon the sisters were starving and driven half-mad by this hunger. And they could hardly cry out any more because they were growing so weak. There was no food at all in that locked wagon and so, upon the third day of their awful confinement, they made a terrible decision. That if they were to survive they must eat the golden mermaid.'

I almost said, '*Alive?*' but held my tongue.

'They stabbed it,' said Esmerelle. 'The golden mermaid still flourished, you see, as if it had never the need for food. And they had begun to hate it and to envy it for watching their torment whilst remaining beautiful and unmoved. Oh yes, they *really* hated that mermaid. And so they killed it. They stabbed it through the bars of the cage and chopped it into pieces right there. And then they thrust those pieces into their mouths and never had they known such pleasure. That anything could taste so sweet.

'But mere moments later the waggon stopped and the door was unlocked and the waggoner looked into the back of his waggon. And there he saw the two sisters, dirty and dishevelled, with blood all about their faces and all over their hands. And the waggoner gave forth a terrible wail and wept for the loss of his treasure.

'And there and then he cursed those sisters for eating the sacred flesh of a merperson. And he cursed them with an everlasting hunger that should never be satisfied but by eating one of their own kind. The waggon had stopped high in the mountains and as the waggoner vented his curse a lone wolf howled on the mountainside.

'And so that curse came to be, that the sisters would live for evermore, tormented always by a hunger that they could only slake once every month. When, with the coming of the full moon, they would take on the awful aspects of that lone wolf and consume human flesh. And so must they do this for ever.'

'That is quite a story,' I said. 'And it has two monsters rather than one. Would you like me to tell you a story about how Mr Rune and I once travelled upon a subterranean ark and also visited the sunken city of Atlantis?'

'No,' said Esmerelle. 'You fail to understand. My story is not just a story. My story is real. Those events really happened.'

'I suppose it is possible that they might have done,' I said. 'I have experienced some very weird occurrences, so I would be prepared to believe such a tale. At a stretch.'

'It is a true story,' said Esmerelle. 'And there is a little more to it than that. The curse was even more horrible in that only one sister is able to eat at each full moon. And the sister who is unable to eat ages overnight to become a wizened, wretched creature. So each sister must nurture the other, if both are to survive. And so the strong one, who remains young, selects a victim for the one who has become old to feast upon. This victim is always a young, fit boy of teenage years and he is dowsed with a pungent unguent to tenderise his flesh and mask his human smell, which makes him easier to eat. And he is fed a last supper of fat bread rolls, well-buttered, great big pie and huge rolly pud. For stuffing, you see. As one might stuff a Christmas turkey. And washed down with a milkshake to add extra vitamins.'

A certain chill had now entered my bones and a certain squeaking sound came also to my ears. Along the deck trundled the wicker bath chair containing the ancient prune-like nanna, still being pushed by the striking gentleman with the amazing mustachios.

272

The bath chair was drawn level and the nanna stared at me.

'Meet my twin sister,' said Esmerelle.

And the nanna's eyes glowed in the moonlight.

52

I would have run like the wind at this point. Or, if not at this point, then definitely at the point where the ancient, wrinkled, prune-like nanna rose from her bath chair and metamorphosed right there and then into a terrible wolf. And it was a proper full-scale animatronic-style metamorphosis at that, with pruney skin shredding and big wolfy bits bursting out all over the place.

I would have run, I really would. But I did not. I could not. I was all weighed down by that special last supper, which was clearly designed for such effect. So I sort of staggered to my feet and lurched forwards like some B-movie zombie. The werewolf monster was clawing through blankets and old-lady trappings, its jaws all salivaed, its growlings most awful to hear.

And although I could not move too fast upon my wobbling legs, I was still able to lash out with justified and considerable fury and I managed to welt the fellow with the fine moustaches a blistering blow to the hooter, which sent him sprawling over the monster that was scrabbling up to eat me.

Which did not give me very much time, but gave me just enough. There was one of those things that I have never really understood rising from the deck near at hand. One of those things that look a bit like a grossly oversized ear trumpet and are constructed of polished-up brass on period liners like this. And although I did not know just what I might be getting into, anything was preferable to being eaten alive by a monstrous wolf, so I flung myself into this polished brass item and fell into darkness below.

The next thing I knew a couple of stoker-type sailors were yanking me into the light and telling me that I should not have been in there because that was a very dangerous place to be. And I was thanking them very much for this, but emphasising the fact that there were many more dangerous things in this world, when a lot of growling and clawing and scrabbling announced the imminent arrival of wolfish wickedness.

'I would run if I were you,' I told the stoker-types. 'It is what I intend to do and you would both do well to emulate my example.' Which was quite nicely put, although I think they failed to grasp the full import of its meaning.

I ran at a belly-sagging stagger as fast as I possibly could.

Behind me I heard growls and screams but I just lumbered on. Through a hatchway I went, but there was no lock, nor nothing to bar it behind me. And on and on I went, down a narrow corridor, until I reached a door with a sign that said CARGO HOLD.

Behind me rose growls and horrible sounds, and so I entered the cargo hold.

It was dimly lit and there were many steamer trunks and packing cases and crates of stuff and this, that and the other. I edged this way, that and the other trying to shrink through confined spaces and do my best to make myself invisible. But I was aware of one thing and that one thing was how members of the dog family are so noted for their sense of smell. And the way I smelled, I knew I must be leaving a trail that a half-nosed pup could follow.

But I kept right on squeezing and held my breath as I heard the door to the cargo hold smash and the growlings grow louder and louder.

'What would Hugo do?' I wondered to myself. 'Perhaps he would cast a mystic lightning bolt or simply pull a derringer from his shirt cuff and dispatch the beast in an instant. And then probably have some tailor in Knightsbridge run up a nice wolf-skin jacket for him from the pelt.

I heard the beast do sniffings, then heard it growl once more. And I fumbled along, as quietly as I could in the dim light, hoping desperately that some solution to my dire predicament would hastily reveal itself.

And then something nearly took off my hand.

And I say *nearly* because I felt it coming at me rather than saw it and I tore back my hand in a rush.

I had got myself a bit wedged against something that looked like a mighty steel coffin. It was all metal plates and rivets and seemed the sort of thing that would be likely to house something really dangerous.

And on this occasion first impressions were not incorrect, because

as my hand had brushed past a little barred air-hole kind of arrangement in the bolted lid, whatever lurked within had gone for it.

I flapped my hand. I was trembling now and I had had enough of
this business. I stared down at the metal coffin affair and read the label
that was pasted upon it:

PROPERTY OF BARON VON BACON.
DO NOT FEED.
DO NOT TOUCH.
AND CERTAINLY DO NOT OPEN.

Baron von Bacon, I knew that name. Creator of the Hell Hound
with the human brain that had feasted on dead bodies back at Mons.
Was the evil baron aboard this ship? It seemed that if he was not, then
his Hell Hound *was*.

And now there was growling in stereo, Hell Hound to the left of
me, werewolf to the right, here I was, stuck in the middle with . . .
just me.

And then an idea dawned that was little less than inspired. Had I had
longer to weigh up the disastrous potential attendant to the execution
of this idea, I might well have thought twice about translating thought
into action. But I was still young and foolish in my way and it did
seem such a good idea at the time.

And so I dragged open the bolts on the steely coffin, swung wide
the steely lid and cried, 'Kill, boy! British soldier dressed as a dog! Kill,
boy! Good boy! Kill!'

Well, there was always the chance that it understood English and I
must say that considering the speed with which it left its metallic
prison, it was certainly eager for freedom.

I now did duckings of my head as the fiends fell to hideous conflict.

The Hellish Hound and the Werewolf Monster tore at each other
in fury. From what I could see of the maelstrom of violence, they
appeared to be quite evenly matched.

I had never been a betting man. It was just one of those things that
never had come into my life. And anyway I was too young to enter a
bookies and really did not understand quite what went on within
them. But if I had had to place a bet upon which monster was going to

survive the fur-flying holocaust, I would have been really hard put to it to choose.

So I just slunk away, white-faced and trembling, and left them to sort it out for themselves. And I was halfway back along that narrow corridor when they came bucketing after me, bloody claws and teeth a-snapping and a-tearing. And I found some vigour in my legs now and so I took to my heels.

I made it up to a deck that I had not visited before. Perhaps it was one of those decks frequented by the lower classes, who like to dance jigs upon them, or sing Irish songs about sorrow and spuds. Or sorrow for lack of such spuds. But whatever the case, it was presently deserted and I burst onto it followed by two flailing monsters.

I tried hard to run, but tripped on my face and prepared to meet my maker. Howls and horror, growls and screams and moans and so much more.

Then nothing.

Then a kind of double splash.

And I raised my eyes and crawled to the side and peered down into the water. But the moonlight shone serenely upon the mirrored surface and all was once more calm and peaceful, pale and tranquil.

'Well,' I said, rising and dusting down my dining duds, 'I think that went rather well. We can chalk that one up as a success, I think.'

Which of course was *not* the thing to say, because whenever you do get a bit smug and make a remark like that, something will always pop up, spoil the moment and smack you back down to the ground.

This of course was just such an occasion, and the voice that I heard chilled my heart.

'You have murdered my sister,' cried Esmerelle, and then she was upon me. She hauled me to my feet and swung me around and as I stared into her beautiful face it transformed right there before my very eyes.

'Only me now!' she cried and she howled like a wolf. 'And so I must have revenge for the death of my sister. I'll tear your throat but let you live, and you shall be like me.' And so there was a terrible ripping and tearing of clothing and the beast rose up to gnaw at my throat and transform me into a werewolf.

And I prepared once more to meet my maker. *Hopefully* to meet my maker, for death would be better than *the werewolf alternative*.

And the terrible jaws with their terrible teeth came closer and closer and cl—

But then I saw that wolf face seem to fold, the jaws gaped wide but then dropped slack and I heard a *swish* and a *swish* and a *swish* and the monstrous beast fell past me.

It plunged over the rail and down and down and into the ocean below.

And I stared boggle-eyed into the face of my deliverer.

For Hugo Rune was wiping down the swordstick blade of his stout stick cane.

'Well, Rizla,' he said. 'This is a sorry business. You look, I must say, just a little pale, caught there in the light of THE MOON.'

THE WHEEL OF FORTUNE

53

THE WHEEL OF FORTUNE

We sat at the bar upon chromium stools and I had an all-over shiver. Hugo Rune ordered me something strong and Fangio served it to me.

'It was horrible,' I told the Magus, as I poured out the details. 'They were going to eat me. Horrible it was, just horrible. And Baron von Bacon's Hell Hound was on board too. And that was really horrible and—'

Hugo Rune nodded in a manner suggestive of the fact that he knew just how horrible it all was. And then he did sniffings at me. 'Pooh,' he said. 'You really pong. First it was of horses from the Tower of London, and now—' and he sniffed and did noddings of the head '—a perfume created from the gonads of the white wolf. Such a scent would surely attract any wolf, were or otherwise.'

I drank some more and grew sulky. 'And *they* all knew,' I grumped. 'These rich swine, when they sniffed me and turned away their heads, they knew I was marked for death.'

'If this has, as I suspect, been going on for some time, then it would be a case of "rather him than me".'

'It has been going on since the start of the war,' I said. 'Those monsters have been living aboard this ship since then.'

'Fascinating,' said Hugo Rune. 'I have not encountered one of their kind for more than fifty years. My blade, thrice-blessed for such business, has happily not lost its edge.'

'And you have saved my life once more,' said I, brightening. 'And I am very grateful for that. Thank you so much, Mr Rune.'

'I could not let my acolyte come to harm. Even if he *did* ignore my plea and swan off to dinner instead.'

'Your plea?' I said.

'The message you received in the dining salon.'

'So it was *you* who wrote the message. But—'

'You fail to understand. Yes, I see. She slipped me a sleeping draught, Rizla, this Esmerelle of yours. A Mickey Finn, as it were. She arrived at my suite with a cocktail that I had not ordered and then waited while I drank it. I was tricked once more, Rizla. I really do feel that I am losing *my* edge.'

'But the message?'

'I felt the drug taking hold and I feigned unconsciousness. She left my quarters, then I hastily scribbled the note and rang for room service.'

'It said you were dying,' I said.

'I might well have been.'

'You just looked like you were sleeping peacefully when I saw you.'

'A sleeping draught *will* create such an effect, Rizla. They wanted me out of the way while they dined upon you. They were no doubt thinking to reserve me for the next full moon. Had you taken my message at face value you would have sat with me in my bedchamber, and possibly remained safe until I regained consciousness. However, you—'

'Yes,' I said. 'All right. You just looked so peaceful and all those medics were there.'

'In on the conspiracy,' said Hugo Rune. 'I can assure you, Rizla, they felt the wrath of my stout stick when I awoke.'

Fangio served us further drinks and these we downed in silence. Presently Fangio tired of this silence and took once more to the toot.

'I was chatting,' said he, 'with the first mate. And the first mate says that this is the worst trip he's ever been on. And he's travelled on some stinkers – he was aboard the *Sloop John B*, you know.'

'Really?' I said. And I yawned.

'And there's three waiters working here who survived the *Titanic*.'

'Really?' I said. And I yawned while I said it.

'And the captain fell overboard on our first night out and was drowned.'

'Nobody mentioned *that*,' said Hugo Rune.

'The first mate said that they didn't want to panic the passengers. Lots of posh Eastern European nannas and suchlike.'

'Hm,' I said, without a yawn. And then said, 'Hm,' again.

'So, being a democratic crew, they drew lots to see who should captain the ship.'

'Oh dear,' I said. 'I think I know what is coming. Break out the lifeboats, Mr Rune – Captain Fangio is steering us into an iceberg.'

'Oh, don't be so silly,' said Fangio. 'They only drew lots amongst the long-standing seaman types. And a worthy fellow now steers the ship.'

'Well, thank whatever for *that*,' I said.

'And funnily enough,' Fangio continued, 'he's a Brentford man. I wonder if you ever ran into him. His name is Pooley, Jimmy Pooley.'

There was a moment of silence there.

Just before I screamed.

'Hold on, hold on, hold on, please,' said Fangio. 'No screaming in the posh bar. Not until tomorrow night anyway. I have been elected games and entertainment officer and put in charge of bar fun generally. I thought I'd start off with a Weeping and Wailing Competition tomorrow night.'

'No!' I protested. 'You do not understand. We are all doomed, doomed, I say.'

'You'd be in with a chance with that kind of wailing. But please keep it down now, you are frightening my monkey.'

'Sorry, Clarence,' I said to the creature, 'but we really are all doomed.'

Mr Rune said, 'Please speak clearly.'

So speak clearly I did.

'James Pooley,' I said, 'Brentford's James Pooley is now captaining the ship. And this would be – how should I put this? – well, how about James *Jonah* Pooley, sole survivor of many a shipwreck, scourge of the seven seas. A man, if ever there was one, who was born to wear an albatross around his neck.'

'I agree that he does have something of a reputation for that kind of thing,' said Fangio. 'But you shouldn't go tarnishing someone with a sticky brush just because they ate the parson's nose. Or is it the other way round?'

'It does not work for me either way,' I said. 'But trust me on this: if James "Down-with-all-hands-but-me" Pooley is at the helm, I am wearing my lifebelt for the remainder of the voyage.'

'I've been wearing *mine* since we left port,' said Fangio, lifting the hem of his blouse to expose said item, 'although not by choice. I was trying it on for size in my cabin and sort of got stuck in it. Funny thing that, really. Once I was vacuuming the house and it was a hot day and I was vacuuming naked and I fell forwards and you'll never guess what happened—'

'Correct,' said Hugo Rune, 'because we will certainly never attempt to. Let us take another cocktail, Rizla, then let us take to our beds.'

I have to admit that I did not sleep well. My dreams were haunted by snapping wolves on sinking ships and all was not right with the world. But then all was *not* right with the world and I was seriously beginning to wonder whether Hugo Rune and I really would be able to put the world to right. To my reckoning there were three tarot cards left. THE WHEEL OF FORTUNE, THE TOWER and the one with the sticking plaster on it, the terrible card known as DEATH. Just the three. And how near were we to putting the world to right? To stopping America being blown into nuclear fragments? Not too near, in my opinion. In fact just about as distant as we could possibly be. And so I did *not* sleep well and I did not have pleasant dreams.

Mr Rune woke me early and he looked bright enough. 'I have been thinking, Rizla,' he said, 'and thinking all of the night. We have but three cards left to be dealt and time is running out. If von Bacon's Hell Hound was aboard this ship, I am wondering what else might be down in the cargo hold. I feel that after we have fortified ourselves with a suitably heroic breakfast we might acquire the ship's manifest and take a little look around downstairs.'

'Splendid,' I said, 'because I was dreaming—'

'Rizla, I know what you dreamed.'

We breakfasted in the forward salon. It was all white Lloyd Loom chairs and tables, potted palms and posh folk. And I grew grumpy at the sight of these.

'Look at them,' I whispered to Hugo Rune, 'pointing at me and muttering behind their manicured hands. They know I was marked for death. The horrid rotten bunch.'

'I think it more likely,' said Himself, 'that they are commenting on the fact that you are wearing your lifebelt. It quite ruins the cut of your jacket.'

'This stays on,' I said. 'Even when I am using the toilet. And *that* is a challenge, believe you me.'

'I am prepared to believe you, Rizla. Now what shall we take for our brekkie?'

I had made the suggestion to Mr Rune that we should employ the services of Fangio's monkey as a food taster, just in case there were those aboard who might now seek to poison us. More werewolves perhaps, for they are known to exist in packs. Or SS officers mourning the loss of their Hell Hound. But Hugo Rune sniffed at each course as it came and pronounced that each passed muster.

And he was clearly confident in his talents (if belatedly demonstrated) as food sniffer, because he wolfed down his breakfast and goose-stepped many cups of tea.

'A stroll now, Rizla,' he said, when we were done, 'and let us see what we shall see.'

We wandered topside and mooched about the decks. Ignoring the sporting opportunities of deck javelins, tossing the grimble, side-stepping and that evergreen favourite 'pluck one out on a bended knee'. Although I never really saw the point of *that* game. Too many balls involved.

We gazed at the sea, which was flat as turquoise glass with no visible join to the sky. Mr Rune smoked a post-breakfast cheroot and I had another go at a Wild Woodbine but still was not making a lot of progress on the smoking front.

'I think,' said Hugo Rune, 'that we should now evade the eyes of our watchers and slip away to the cargo hold.'

'Our watchers?' I whispered. 'Now *this* is new.'

'Two gentlemen, wearing trenchcoats and snap-brimmed fedoras, have been following us since we left the forward salon. Clearly our cards are now marked, as they say, and we must be on our guard.'

I glanced back over my shoulder and noticed two fellows in trench-coats. As my eyes caught theirs they turned away, confirming Mr Rune's thoughts.

'Assassins, do you think?' I whispered.

'They have the look of Americans, Rizla. And there's no telling with *them*.'

Hugo Rune now performed a number of classic manoeuvres to

avoid surveillance without giving the impression of doing so. He employed the 'double-footed swan-dive', the 'partly-taken-aback' and the 'there-goes-ninepence-again' stratagems to splendid effect and soon we were at the cargo hold unfollowed.

The heavy padlocks now barring our entry were dealt with by Mr Rune and he and I slipped into the hold to see what we might see.

'There are many steamer trunks,' I said. 'Did you manage to acquire the cargo manifest?'

'Sadly, no, Rizla, it is locked in the captain's safe. The new captain would happily have allowed me to peruse it, but apparently he has mislaid the combination.'

'Oh dear,' I said, but quietly. But thought many more 'oh dears'.

'So employ your intuition, Rizla, and let us see what we can find.'

And so we searched. And there really did seem to be some most extraordinary things stored in that hold. A London taxicab, for instance, under a tarpaulin. And a number of coffins that I really did not want to open. But then, after much nosing about into other people's private possessions, I discovered what must surely be the mother lode.

'Mr Rune,' I called out. 'Mr Rune, you will never believe what I have just found here.'

And Mr Rune was soon at my side and Mr Rune asked, 'What?'

'See for yourself,' I said and I pointed. And Himself saw for himself.

'Oh, Rizla,' he said. 'Oh, well done indeed.'

And he read the label aloud.

HANDLE WITH EXTREME CARE
MARK ONE TESLA
IONIC FIELD GENERATOR

'It is the field generator that was stolen from your conservatory,' I said. 'But what is it doing here?'

'Heading for America,' said Hugo Rune. 'Everything falls neatly into place.'

'It does?' I said. 'Then please explain it to me.'

And I am sure that he would have done just that.
Had it not been for the interruption.
Which came as if a bolt from the blue.
As our ship struck something—

HARD

54

We headed to the topmost deck, for that would be the last to go underwater. By the time we reached it chaos reigned, with rich folk screaming and beating each other and fighting over the lifeboats.

'Would I be right in assuming,' I shouted to Hugo Rune, 'that this ship owns to a deficit in the lifeboat department, as did its sister ship the *Titanic*?'

'I rather suspect this to be the case,' yelled the Magus. And then he laid a hand upon a well-dressed seaman in a rather superior lifejacket, who was seeking to sneak on board the nearest lifeboat. Hugo Rune hauled this fellow from his feet and spoke to his dangling person.

'Speak to me, please,' said the guru's guru. 'And with precise phraseology, lest an ambiguity or inconsistency result in severe skull damage upon your part.' And he waggled his stout stick meaningfully. 'What *exactly* has happened?'

The dangling fellow squirmed about, but spoke as best he could. 'The ship has wandered slightly off course,' he cried, 'and has entered the Sargasso Sea.'

'*Slightly* off course!' roared Mr Rune. 'One thousand miles or more. And what was the nature of the obstacle we struck?'

'An ancient galleon, sir.'

Mr Rune let the fellow fall into the crowd. 'Come, Rizla,' he called unto me. 'It is to the bridge with us, to see how affairs might be righted.'

And so I got to go onto the bridge of the RMS *Olympic*. Which was a very exciting place to be. There was the big ship's steering wheel. And it was a really big one, nearly as high as a man. And there were those things with the levers on that the captain orders to be pulled for FULL STEAM AHEAD and suchlike. And big red buttons to press for foghorns and emergency sirens and so on. And a chart table and a framed picture of Queen Victoria.

And there was also my father. Dressed as the captain.

With a rather guilty look upon his face.

'Captain Pooley?' asked Hugo Rune, pushing onto the bridge.

'It is private up here,' said Captain Pooley. 'Please go back the way you came.' And then Captain Pooley caught sight of me and said, 'This *is* a surprise.'

'Do you know each other?' asked Hugo Rune.

And I looked hard at the Magus.

Surely he knew that this was my father. All that business with the tarot card and the SUN being father to the Earth and everything. And so on. And so forth. And suchlike.

'This is my—' And I looked up at my father. 'My casual acquaintance,' I continued. 'I met him in Brentford a while back.'

'I had no idea you were of wealthy stock,' said my father. 'Are you enjoying the voyage?'

'Well,' I said. And I did sort of noddings over my shoulder to where all that chaos reigned below and where rich folk were now leaping into the murky waters.

And indeed those waters were truly murky. Because from the lofty prominence of the wheelhouse you could get a really decent overview of the Sargasso Sea.

I had read about this sinister area when I was a child. The Ocean's Graveyard, it was called, amongst many other uncomplimentary things. It was a portion of the North Atlantic Ocean bogged with a surface-growing seaweed called *Sargassum*. It dwelt within the notorious horse latitudes, in an area known as the doldrums. When sailing ships found themselves windless and caught in this mire, they rarely if ever made home port again.

And legend had it that there were many ghost ships to be found there, barnacled up and choked with seaweed. With naught aboard but skeletons and the wraiths of long-dead sailors.

And yes, looking out from that wheelhouse you could see the wrecks. And there were many of them too, from ancient Romanesque sailing barques to twentieth-century shipping.

'Have you tried putting the engines into reverse?' asked Hugo Rune of the captain.

'You are Mr Hugo Rune,' said Captain Pooley, all of a suddenly sudden. 'I recognise you from your photograph in *John Bull*. Being congratulated by the King, after your famous four-way Channel swim.'

'A bet with George Formby,' Hugo Rune explained to me and he shook my father by the hand.

And that really meant quite a lot to me, though I would not perhaps wish to put into words just why.

'I would be grateful for any advice you might have to offer, Mr Rune,' said Captain Pooley. 'I did try reversing the engines, but it seemed to make matters worse. Both screws are now jammed and there appears to be imminent danger of the boilers blowing up.'

Himself gazed over the mayhem below. 'I think I see the stokers fighting their way into one of the lifeboats,' he said, 'so the boilers will probably be safe for now. Do you have any rum about yourself?'

'The special captain's bottle,' said the special captain.

'Then let's crack it open and discuss matters,' suggested Mr Rune, 'until all the foolish people have left the ship and there is some peace and quiet.'

And so that is what we did. We drank rum up there in the wheelhouse and watched the rich people bashing each other up, falling over the side, crowding the lifeboats and generally carrying on in a manner which, I have to confess, I found most amusing indeed.

Schadenfreude I know it is called. Or epicaricacy, as the English will have it. From the original Greek.

But they *would* have let me be eaten.

It was nightfall before it began to grow quiet. There came a few distant cries for help as foolish people went down on the overcrowded lifeboats. A number of piercing screams which, I was given to understand, might have something to do with the shark-infested waters. But then mostly calm.

And we had the great ship to ourselves.

We had left the wheelhouse by this time and, as the special captain's rum had all gone, adjourned to the bar to take advantage of the easy access to the counter.

And behind this counter stood Fangio.

And next to him sat his monkey.

'Jolly good to see you, Fange,' said I. 'Decided against fighting your way aboard a lifeboat, then? Wise.'

'Lifeboat?' said Fangio. 'I've been having a sleep and have only just come on shift. It's very quiet in here this evening. What is all this about lifeboats?'

'Nothing you should worry yourself about,' I told him. 'But this is the captain and the drinks are on him.'

'Are they?' asked my father. 'Well, I suppose they are. Or on the house, at least. I'll have a pint of Cooper Black, please, barman.'

'I think the running gag about typeface beer names has run its course,' I said.

'Pint of Cooper Black coming up,' said Fangio.

'Then make that *two*,' I said.

And, 'Three,' said Hugo Rune.

'So,' I said to my father, 'the ship is not actually in imminent danger of sinking?'

'Not in the least,' he replied. 'It's just a bit stuck, that's all.'

'I find this encouraging,' I said.

'I *did* miss something, didn't I?' said Fangio. Presenting us with our ales.

'I never saw you pull those,' I said.

'Because I never pulled them, it was my monkey. Did you know that if you sat an infinite number of monkeys down before an infinite number of typewriters, one of them would accidentally type out a book called *Retromancer*? So what *did* I miss?' implored Fangio. 'And why do you smell of white-wolf gonads, Rizla? I *did* miss something, didn't I?'

'The captain sort of bumped this ship a bit,' said Hugo Rune, taking his beer glass to his mouth. 'But it did lead to a lot of upper-class rats fleeing a non-sinking ship. So I think we must chalk it up as a success.'

'Except that we are in a hurry to reach New York,' I said.

'Precisely,' said Hugo Rune. 'So regrettably we cannot enjoy the peace and quiet and perhaps upgrade to better accommodation. We must make haste to extricate the ship from the Sargasso and head for the USA.'

'The Sargasso Sea?' wailed Fangio. 'Then all is lost. We are doomed, we are doomed.'

'Ah,' I said. 'I had forgotten about the Weeping and Wailing Competition. What time does it start? I would like to enter it too.'

'Eight o' clock,' said Fangio. 'We are doomed, we are doomed, oh mercy, mercy me.'

'Enough,' cried Hugo Rune and he raised his stick. 'Someone will have to don a diving suit and go down and cut free the screws. As originator of this idea that will save all of our lives, I nominate the captain to carry out the mission.'

'And as captain,' said the captain, 'I nominate this barman here.'

'And I nominate Clarence, my monkey,' said Fangio.

Fangio's monkey shook its head and pointed a finger at me.

'Oh no,' I said. 'I am not doing *that*. I know all about the shark-infested waters *and* I would get claustrophobic in a diving suit. *And* I am not a very strong swimmer.'

'Then *I* shall do it,' said Hugo Rune.

'*You?*' I said. 'Surely not.'

'It will have to be done, Rizla. And someone will have to do it.'

'We could perhaps draw lots for it,' I said. 'Or spin a bottle, or something. It does not seem fair that you should do it, you are rather—'

'Old?' said Hugo Rune. 'Portly?' he said also.

'Too dignified,' I said. 'But it *is* a job for a younger man. Either Fangio, or the captain, or myself.'

'Or the monkey,' said Fangio.

And the monkey bit him.

We had it all planned. Well, we almost did. We would have a few drinks then take ourselves off to the ship's casino. And there we would play cards, or throw dice, or otherwise gamble, but let fate decide by one means or another which of us should dive.

And I think we had at least come to the agreement that it would all rest upon a spin of the roulette wheel, upon THE WHEEL OF FORTUNE, as it were.

But then we heard the sounds.

That round of cannon shot.

And the blowing of many whistles.

And a kind of atavistic howling.

Which heralded the boarding party . . .

. . . of pirates.

55

Now I make no bones about it, in fact neither skull nor crossed bones, but I have always had this thing for pirates. How well I recall the dealings Mr Rune and I had with Captain Bartholomew Moulse-coomb, the Bog Troll Buccaneer* and his crew of scurvy pirate types. I really took to those fellows, I did. I do not know *exactly* what it is about pirates that I like so much. It might be one of so many things. The tricornes or cutlasses, peg legs or hand-hooks, frock coats or eyepatches, parrots or treasure chests. One of them, or maybe all. But I *do* like pirates. Monkeys I also like. But I like pirates the bestest.

And even as Fangio, my dad and myself were discussing THE WHEEL OF FORTUNE and I was telling them that I had chosen the tarot card of THE WHEEL OF FORTUNE, so we *must* be doing the right thing, grappling hooks were being thrown up onto the passenger decks and pirates, many lacking for bits and bobs of themselves, were swarming up ropes, with knives between their teeth, *arr'ing* and *arr-harr'ing* and belching rum-tainted breaths.

A pause in our conversation was occasioned by the bursting in of the posh saloon bar door and the bursting through the opening of this by a group of the most wretched, hideous, horrible, scabrous, foul and filthy scum of the sea as should ever end their evil days doing a dance for Jack Ketch.

An overwhelming rankness, the very foetor of the damned, engulfed us in a healthless miasma. I coughed, my father coughed, Mr Rune and Fangio coughed, but Fangio's monkey just grinned and chattered.

If they smelled bad, and they did, these malodorous blackguards, the looks of them were sufficient to strike fear into the bravest of hearts.

---

* For further details check your now-treasured copy of *The Brightonomicon*.

It was clear that any brief flirtations any of them ever had with hygiene had not led to a lasting relationship. They were filthy. They were bedraggled. Unkempt, unrinsed, soiled and begrimed. They were turbid, they were dreggy. Matted, caked and nauseatingly slimed.

And though I *did* have a thing about pirates, I did not take to this ghastly bunch.

'Who be cap'n here?' roared one of this putrid crew. One bigger and more repulsive than the rest. He wore a rotting tricorne titfer on his hideous head, a feculent frock coat, once of grey but now of gangrenous green. A pair of squalid seaman's boots and a threadbare fusty necktie.

I noticed that this necktie was that of the Queen's Own Electric Fusiliers. It is strange what catches your eye in moments of extreme terror.

'Who be cap'n here?' roared this malcontent once more.

Fangio now pointed at my father. As did his monkey and also Mr Rune.

My father began now to flap his hands and turn around in small circles. Which explained to me how I must have come by this undignified habit.

'We be takin' this ship,' quoth the large ungarnished pirate to my father. 'What say ye to this?'

'I say such is the law of the sea,' said my father. 'If you would be so kind as to put me in a longboat with a few weeks' supply of food and send me on my way, I'll be happy to even let you have my cap, if you fancy it.'

''Tis the cap of a nancy-boy,' now quoth the pulverulent pirate. 'But I might take it with your head still inside, if such takes my fancy.'

'Now hold on there,' I said, as I did not fancy any insalubrious malfeasant parting my daddy's head from his body. 'He said you can have the ship – there is no cause to go chopping his head off.'

'And who be you, my girly boy?' asked the besmutted buccaneer. 'We'll find a use for your botty parts as we might for a Portobello harlot.'

'Is he suggesting what I think he is suggesting?' asked Fangio of Hugo Rune.

'Silence!' roared the rank and rotten ruffian.

'If I might just crave a moment of your time, O lord of the sea,' said

Hugo Rune, stepping forwards and bowing low before our tainted tormentor. 'There is much treasure aboard this vessel and I can lead you to its whereabouts.'

'Such you will do indeed,' went the unwashed one and then took to *arr'ing* and *arr-harr'ing*, after the manner of his kind. Although even this did not endear him to me.

'But first,' continued Hugo Rune, 'why not slake your thirsts here? There is much fine liquor to be had and it would be our honour to serve you.'

'Arrr!' and, 'Arrr-harrr!' And the putrid pirates cheered at this.

'Take yourself to the rear of the bar counter,' said Hugo Rune to me, 'and serve our guests. Hurry now.'

And he gave me a look.

And I understood this look.

And I took to the rear of the counter.

The mildewed multitude called out for liquor, wine and ale and whisky. Fangio shook cocktails, his monkey pulled the pints and I handed out bags of crisps.

'Do you have any Kryptonite-flavoured crisps?' asked a septic seaman who knew nothing of continuity.

I was by now becoming able to deal with the extreme taint foisted onto the goodly air of the posh saloon bar by the scrofulous scoundrels. By the simple expedient of dipping two cocktail umbrellas in Angostura bitters and ramming them up my nostrils. Fangio's monkey was still looking happy enough.

Hugo Rune engaged the pirate captain in conversation. Whilst plying him with a mixture of drinks that could surely have brought down a rhino.

'And,' I heard him say, 'this floating city could serve you as a luxurious headquarters, whilst in it you scour the seas for further wealth. All that would be needed would be for half a dozen of your men to dive down and free the propellers that drive the ship.'

And I gathered from the pirate chieftain's reply to this that the notion of leaving the Sargasso Sea, where his forefathers had become trapped and where he and his father before him had lived since birth, preying upon the contents and crews of unhappy ships that fell victim to the *Sargassum* weed, found great favour with him.

'And so,' Mr Rune continued, 'myself and my companions would be honoured to throw in our lots with you and offer the highly specialised skills, which take years of training, to manage the actual movement of this great ship. You will find us a valuable asset.'

The scummy ruffian nodded his mouldy tricorne to this and then asked Mr Rune what progress had been made in the world beyond during the last two hundred years and whether the iPod had been invented yet. Which certainly had me baffled. But I did think that we were all starting to get along quite well. And I was joining in with some of the shanty singing. And my father was telling a tale about how he had been aboard a cross-Channel ferry that had gone down with all hands but himself and how he had been washed up on the beach at Hartlepool. Where the locals would have hanged him as a French spy, had he not been able to convince them that he was in fact a monkey. And Fangio had even encouraged several of the pirates to enter the Weeping and Wailing Competition. And Clarence was dancing a jig and rattling a tin cup for money.

When things suddenly went the shape of a pear in an unexpected fashion.

The door to the posh saloon bar, which had been burst in by the arriving pirates, and which had been eased back into its frame by my father, whom it appeared to me for the first time had a thing about tidiness and was perhaps just a tad obsessive-compulsive, burst open again, this time to admit the entrance of something more foul and unwholesome than all of the pocky pirates put together.

'Ahoy there to you, bonny lads!' cried out Count Otto Black.

There was a moment of silence then. Followed by mighty cheerings. The squalid leader of the bog-rotten bunch did evil toothless grinnings towards Mr Rune. 'I have enjoyed our conversation,' said he, 'whilst you tried to inveigle me with talk of your knowledge and the value of your fellows. But we need none of you, as we can move this mighty ship by other means. I only spared you my blade because I was ordered to do so by my master here, who predicted who would be found aboard this ship after she struck the Sargasso.'

Hugo Rune looked towards his arch-enemy. 'Why, if it isn't Count Rotto,' said he. 'We meet again. And how fitting that it should be amongst your own people. Those who share your fear of the bathroom.'

'Shall I cut him down by a foot or two?' asked the pongy pirate chief.

'All in good time.' Count Otto Black grinned. 'For now I will have words with my fat friend. And then you may cast them all over the side.'

'But we can jolly roger the little one?' asked the pirate captain.

'Be my guest,' said Count Otto. And he produced from his pocket a Luger pistol and pointed this at Hugo Rune. The pirates resumed their carousing and the count had words to say.

'This, I feel,' said Count Otto, smiling with evil upon Hugo Rune, 'will be our last time together. You are fighting out of your weight, my plump fellow, and that says much, does it not?'

I saw Mr Rune's knuckles whiten on the hand with which he held his stout stick. But he retained his dignity and regarded his enemy with a look which combined nonchalance and contempt to a winning effect.

'Poor old magician,' crowed Count Otto Black. 'Out of his time and out of his league. The world has changed, Hugo, changed for ever. The old Gods are reborn, but not within the frail bodies of men. Rather within mighty machines. Great engines of power. Do you understand anything of what I speak?'

'I understand all,' said Hugo Rune. 'I understand that the enemies of Goodness and Peace are possessed of a great computer, which is itself possessed by the spirit of Wotan.'

'Indeed, indeed.' And the count clapped his hands together. 'And Colossus was possessed by the spirit of Arthur, which you sent on its way.' And the count laughed cruelly. 'A bit of an error there on your part, I am thinking. An own goal.'

'We shall see,' said Hugo Rune. 'Matters will adjust themselves, of this I have no doubt.'

'Indeed they will, but you will not be here to see this occur. You will be deep at the bottom of the sea where you can cause no further annoyance.'

'And as this is to be the case,' said the Magus, 'then there would be no harm in you revealing to me your plans for world domination. Such is the way of the supervillain, is it not?'

'Indeed, indeed, indeed,' said Count Otto Black, thrice more. 'As you might well be aware, two days from now, at precisely twelve noon, an atomic bomb will fall upon New York. The Americans have been carrying out many experiments with atomic weaponry and they have a number of bombs in various stages of completion currently being transported hither and thus across North America. These will be triggered in a chain reaction by *my* bomb. America will cease to be, the Allies will capitulate before the nuclear might of the Third Reich and Germany will win the war.'

'And what will that make you?'

'I rather favour a position of power,' said the count, preening at himself with grubby fingers. 'Ultimate power! High Priest in the World Temple of Wotan rather suits me. For with the fall of the Allies, an ancient God will once more be restored to his rightful place and the beaten peoples of the world converted to his faith.'

'All well and good,' said Hugo Rune, in a voice that lacked not for irony. 'But how do you intend to deliver an atomic bomb to New York unnoticed?'

'It is on its way even now,' said the count. 'Germany is all but done for in terms of resources and cannot survive another year of war. A means of transporting the bomb, using what remains in the armament factories of the Reich, has been created. A Zeppelin, Hugo. The biggest ever built, powered by jets. And aboard this craft, along with the bomb itself, the computer possessed by Mankind's new God. Such will direct the dropping of the bomb, unseen from on high.'

'Such a mighty craft will surely be seen and shot down,' said Hugo Rune. 'This plan will never succeed.'

'Oh, I think it will,' said the count. 'Because no one will see the Zeppelin approaching New York. Because it will be invisible. Caught within the ionic beam of the Tesla field generator that I removed from your conservatory and which is even now down in the cargo hold. What think you of *that*?'

'I think we shall see what we shall see,' said Hugo Rune. 'I thank you for supplying me with this valuable information. I shall of course use it to confound your evil scheme.'

'No no no,' said Count Otto Black, taking then to the laughter so beloved of supervillains. 'Now you die, Hugo Rune. Hey, Captain,' he called to the pestiferous pirate. 'Weight this big one heavily and cast him over the side.'

56

And with that several loathsome swabs laid hands on Hugo Rune. They tore his stout stick from his grip and marched him from our sight.

I would have pleaded with Count Otto Black if I had thought that there would have been any point in doing so. But I knew better, so I kicked him in the ankle bone instead.

The count took to comedy hopping about, followed by calls for my death.

'Might we engage in jolly rogering first?' asked a stinking salt. Which made the count grin as he rubbed at his leg, and that fair put the willies up me.

So to speak.

But now another unexpected arrival caught the attention of one and all. Through the burst-beyond-all-repair doorway marched a number of German soldiers. Smartly turned out special troops were these, all shiny helmets with death's head motifs and lots of buckled leather. It had to be said that they seemed to me more fearsome than any bad pirate.

One who held rank amongst them stepped forwards, clicked heels and Heil-Hitlered Count Otto. The count did Heilings in reply and asked for a report.

'The field generator has been located in the cargo hold, *mein Herr*,' said the high-ranker. 'It is now being loaded onto the motor torpedo boat, as were your orders.' And this was followed by more heel-clicks and a little bit more Heil-Hitlering.

'Good,' said the count. 'And keep a steady eye upon the torpedo boat's propeller – I do not want it fouled up with *Sargassum*. Make ready to leave when fully loaded.' And yet more heel-clicks followed these words.

The excrementitious pirates who still remained in the posh saloon bar eyeballed these finely dressed soldiers. And perhaps little ill-oiled and poorly maintained cogs were starting to mesh together within their scruffious heads. They exchanged bitter glances and one, no fouler than the rest, being of leprous aspect and dunghill disposition, was caused to offer up words to the effect that, 'All don't seem right hereabouts.' And also, 'I smells a rat.'

Which *did* give me the opportunity to stick in my three-pennyworth. Because I had to save Hugo Rune somehow and the best way I could think of doing *that* was to cause a big diversion here, during which I could quietly slip away.

'He means to trick all of you,' I shouted and I pointed to the count. 'He was only using you to capture this ship. Now that he has what he wants he will desert you. Or probably have you all killed.'

'Shoot this outspoken turd!' cried the count and a soldier took aim at my person.

'Belay that,' called a pirate.

And I saw my father hurl the bottle that bounced off Count Otto's head.

Now there is one thing in particular that pirates and soldiers have in common and that is their love for a good old fight. Sailors particularly love fighting in a dancehall (oh, man, look at those cavemen go). Soldiers prefer a bar, and pirates will basically have-at-you wherever and whenever the opportunity arises.

There were half a dozen pirates and quite as many soldiers, so it made for even sides and a rather decent fight.

I ducked down behind the bar counter where I found Fangio, cowering with his monkey. I think my father stepped back from the actual fighting, but then it would have been hard for him to either throw a punch or defend himself as he was so engaged in flapping his hands and turning around in small circles.

Bottles flew and smashed above my head, showering glass flecks upon Fangio, monkey and me. Great war cries welled from pirate throats, and warrior calls were returned against these by the Führer's bully boys.

There was such a lovely row of etched-glass windows that looked out from that posh saloon bar towards a posh deck beyond and, even though I was *not* a betting man, I would have been prepared to put my money, if I had had any, upon these windows soon getting broken as fighting men crashed through them.

'There goes that lovely row of etched-glass windows,' wailed Fangio. With no one to hear him and offer a prize but me, and, it had to be faced, the Weeping and Wailing Competition was now unlikely to take place at all. Pirates and solders spilled out onto the posh deck beyond in a violent, horrid maelstrom.

And there they really got into the violence proper.

And then came strange and terrible sounds that chilled me to the marrow. I was rising from behind the bar counter, hoping that now would be my opportunity to flee from the bar and somehow save the life of Hugo Rune, when I saw the awful shapes and heard the awful cries. Great monstrous somethings were dropping down from above and wreaking a hideous havoc. In the darkness on deck, when all the light there was came only from this bar, flashes of twinkling scales were to be seen and glimpses of men being snatched up from the deck. And now the men on deck no longer fought each other. Now guns blazed into the sky and cutlasses swung above heads.

'Whatever are those creatures?' I asked.

But Fangio cowered below me.

Flashes of gun barrels, flashes of coloured scales, flashes of violence, flashes of death, all as in a strobe light of horror. I looked on and felt sick.

And then as suddenly as it had all begun, there was nothing. Silence only, darkness without, my father curled in a tight ball upon one side of the bar, Fangio likewise on the other and me standing there, shaking violently and peeping through my fingers.

But then a figure appeared beyond the shattered windows and waved to me and smiled, stepped into the bar and retrieved his stout stick.

For it was Hugo Rune.

57

The Magus entered the devastated bar and he was not alone. He was accompanied by warriors, beings of noble aspect with flowing locks of golden hair and romantic fairy-tale armour. They carried spears and antique weaponry and amongst their number was a beautiful young woman in silver trappings, a broadsword in her hand and a smile of triumph on her face.

'Princess Roellen of Purple Fane,' I said, recognising at once the gorgeous creature whose realm extended from the mountains of Ffafiod to the Sea of Garmillion, encompassing the forests of Cae-comphap and Pemanythnod. And to whom I had played a part in returning the Ring of Power™, which was also known as Isildur's Bane™.

'Fair night to you, Rizla,' called Princess Roellen. 'My men and I will take wine, if you will kindly offer it.'

'Oh,' I said. 'I will. I will. And hello, Mr Rune.'

The Magus picked his way between broken tables and shattered glassware and joined me at the bar.

'Are you all right?' he asked of me. 'No damage done at all?'

'I am fine.' I said. 'But you? They were going to weight you down and throw you into the sea.'

'And so they might well have done, had it not been for the chance but timely arrival of the beautiful Princess Roellen.'

This wonderful lady now joined us at the bar. 'Purple Fane is but a few leagues from here,' she said. 'But this Magus seeks to disillusion you. I came here not by chance, but at his silent calling. He spoke a message into my dreams asking that I fly to your assistance, because his own life might already have been taken and there would be no one to save yours. He is a great magician and he clearly cares deeply for you.'

'Well,' said Hugo Rune. And I saw him blush. A most extraordinary sight to see and just for this one time only.

'Drinks all round, then,' said Fangio, fishing out unbroken glasses from beneath the bar counter and searching for unbroken bottles from which to fill them.

'Those monsters,' I said, 'dropping down from the sky.'

'Did you *really* see such things?' asked Hugo Rune.

'Yes,' I said. 'I know I did – what were they?'

'Do you believe in dragons?' asked Princess Roellen.

'*Dragons?*' I said. And I made a certain face.

'Perhaps in the darkness, with all the chaos and confusion,' said Hugo Rune. 'There's just no telling really, is there?'

And he raised a glass to me.

And oh what a party we had. There was some concern because Count Otto had escaped along with the field generator. But Hugo Rune said not to worry about this because he now had a plan to thwart the evil count, so we partied until dawn and all had a really good time.

Princess Roellen ordered a number of her noble warriors to dive down and free the liner's propellers of *Sargassum* and others to stoke up the boilers and help get the ship back on course. And my father took himself back to the wheelhouse and stood proudly behind the wheel and vowed that the ship would wander nowhere whatsoever off course but only strike port in New York.

And so it came to be.

I removed myself to a drunken bed and did not awake until late the following afternoon. I think I would probably have slept even longer than that if I had not been awoken by the terrible noise and the very sudden shock.

I raced from my cabin up onto the deck and there met Hugo Rune.

'Have we struck an iceberg?' I begged to be told. 'Are we doomed? Are we sinking? What has happened?'

'We have arrived safely in New York, young Rizla,' said the Magus, lighting a cigar.

'But that noise and that shock, oh my God!'

And now we were joined by my father the captain, who had *that* look on his face.

'I am sure it can be fixed,' he said. 'I only took my eyes off the water for a moment. I just popped to the toilet.'

'You crashed the ship,' I said to him.

'Only a bit crashed, but yes.'

'Into the Statue of Liberty.'

I had been rather looking forward to seeing the Statue of Liberty. And so I was just a little disappointed that all I ever got to see of her was her feet. As the rest of her now lay at the bottom of New York Harbour.

I said farewell then to my father, who seemed rather keen to make a speedy departure. What with, it seemed, much of the American Navy now heading in our direction.

And that was the last that I ever saw of him.

But he went out with a bang and not a whimper.

Which was something!

I looked up at Hugo Rune.

And he looked down at me.

And, 'Welcome to America,' he said.

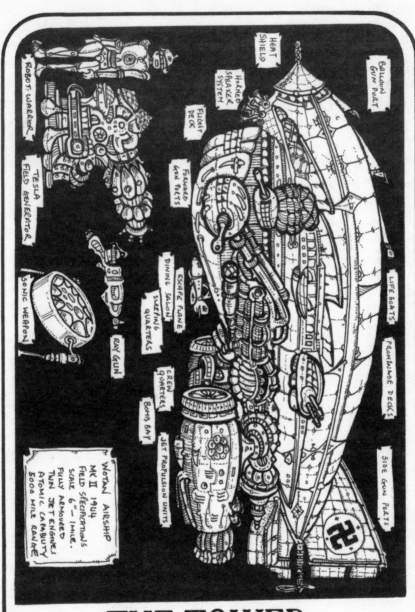

ROBOT WARRIOR

HEAT SHIELD

HORNED SPEAKER SYSTEM

BALLOON GUN PORT

FLIGHT DECK

TESLA FIELD GENERATOR

FORWARD GUN PORTS

LIFE BOATS

PROMENADE DECKS

DINING SALOON

ESCAPE PLANE

SLEEPING QUARTERS

SONIC WEAPON

RAY GUN

SIDE GUN PORTS

CREW QUARTERS

BOMB BAY

JET PROPULSION UNITS

WOTAN AIRSHIP
MK II 1944
FIELD SPECIFICATIONS
SCALE 6" = 1 MILE.
FULLY ARMOURED
TWIN JET ENGINES
ATOMIC CAPABILITY
5000 MILE RANGE

THE TOWER

58

THE TOWER

There was some unpleasantness. As the pirates had done so recently, American Marines came swarming onto the decks. My father was nowhere to be seen, and as there was no one else aboard the stricken liner but for Fangio, myself and Hugo Rune, we were taken into custody and not in the kindest of manners.

Because these fellows were less than pleased that the RMS *Olympic* had destroyed one of their national monuments. I might have enjoyed the motorboat journey over to the mainland, had I not been handcuffed. And being thrown into the cell did little to please me.

Also matters certainly were not helped by the fact that neither Mr Rune nor myself owned a passport. The word 'spies' came into play and there was talk about marching us outside and putting us up against a wall. If my hands had not been handcuffed they would surely have flapped.

Hugo Rune, however, took it all in good spirit and told me not to worry as he would soon have matters set to rights and we would be on our way.

As indeed we were.

I have never ceased to be not-surprised-at-all by the power of that 'certain handshake'. Mr Rune employed it first upon our interrogator, an evil-breathed brute who laid out instruments of torment for us to inspect prior to the commencement of questioning. From the shaking of this hand, Mr Rune's moved on to shake many more. Gradually rising up the chain of command until we were whisked away from the dismal cell and taken off to a comfy hotel.

Our steamer trunks and bits and bobs were brought to us, and I do take my hat off to Mr Rune, for he even arranged for Fangio to be released. There were some negotiations involved and these I understood involved the question of who was going to pay for the restoration of the Statue of Liberty. Mr Rune suggested, and this suggestion was gratefully accepted, that, as the RMS *Olympic* now stood completely empty of passengers and crew, the American Government should claim 'salvage' and sell it back to the White Star Line for more than a decent profit.

'And so all things adjust themselves to our satisfaction,' said the Magus to me, as we sat in the bar of Hotel Jericho.

'Not *all* things, surely,' I said. 'Tomorrow at noon an atom bomb will fall upon New York. This does *not* satisfy *me*.'

'Quietly, Rizla, quietly,' said Himself. 'Walls have ears even here and we would not wish to alarm the general population.'

Now I must say that I certainly took to the general population and I certainly took to New York. Many on arrival find its scale so daunting and the fear that they will be immediately robbed or murdered when they step out onto the street so great that they spend the first day in New York cowering in their hotel rooms. But not so I. I loved it. It was just so *big* and the people were just so amazing. The women were gorgeous and wonderfully dressed and the men all seemed tall and handsome and attired in the most fashionable couture.

'They *do know* there is a war on, do they not?' I whispered to Mr Rune. 'Only apart from the fact that there are a lot of well-dressed GIs escorting pretty ladies about, there does not seem to be much evidence.'

'There will be evidence enough tomorrow at noon if we don't act, young Rizla.'

I raised a glass of something delicious to my lips. 'And about that,' I said. 'Surely the best thing to do would be to inform the top bods of the American Army, Navy and Air Force and let them deal with the deadly Zeppelin.'

'Gosh!' said Hugo Rune. 'I wish I'd thought of that.'

And I really was about to revive that nail-buffing thing when he added the word, '*Buffoon!*'

'You have already done it, then?' I said.

'I made certain telephone calls,' said Mr Rune, 'whilst you were in the bathroom doing whatever you were doing for such a protracted period.'

'*Washing*,' I said. 'To remove the taint of wolf gonads and pongy pirates.'

'And you now smell delightful,' said the Magus. 'But inform the bigwigs of the military establishment I did.'

'And so they will be literally throwing a cage of steel about New York.'

'No, Rizla, they will not. They didn't believe me. They actually pooh-poohed the concept of a jet-powered invisible Zeppelin driven by a computer possessed by the spirit of Wotan, intent on nuking the country out of existence.'

'Well,' I said. And I made a certain face. 'When you speak it all out loud like that I can see why—'

'Plah!' said Hugo Rune. 'That *Americans* should doubt *me*? Preposterous!'

'Could you not employ your secret handshake? Perhaps with the president, or something?'

'No, Rizla. And think about this, if you will. When you were a child you read about the Second World War, didn't you?'

'All the time,' I said, 'in books and comics. And I played with toy soldiers and toy tanks and cannons.'

'And did you ever read about any invisible Zeppelins?'

'Definitely not,' I said.

'Precisely,' said Hugo Rune. 'Because this must never become part of history. We must foil the count's plan, but none must know of it. Thus will we restore order to history. We must do it anonymously, if it is to be done at all.'

'Wow,' I said. 'How exciting. But something of a responsibility. What if we fail?'

'Fail?' said the Magus. 'Outrageous also. Tell me what cards you have left.'

'You know what cards I have left,' I said. 'I am assuming that THE WHEEL OF FORTUNE is now used up. That leaves us with THE TOWER and DEATH.'

'And if I ask you to choose?'

'THE TOWER it is, then,' I said to Hugo Rune.

And he took to smiling and said, 'Yes, it is,' as if he knew something I did not.

'So what *is* this something that you know?' I asked him. 'You seem very happy with this card.'

'Oh, indeed I am, Rizla. There has been a purpose to these cards throughout all our cases. They have led us from one place to another and finally to here. I did not know the meaning of THE TOWER until now. Would you care for me to elucidate?'

'I certainly would,' I said.

And so, indeed, he did.

'The intention of Wotan,' said Hugo Rune, 'is to fly over New York invisibly and dispatch an atomic bomb. To fly invisibly will require the services of the Tesla field generator projecting an ionised particle beam at the great airship, as those boats bombarded the USS *Eldridge* with such beams during the Philadelphia Experiment, rendering her invisible. So, the Tesla field generator will have to be set up at some suitable location where it can project such a beam. Somewhere unhampered by all these high buildings. Are you following me?'

'I certainly am,' I said. 'They will need to mount it upon a tower. THE TOWER. I see.'

'Not just any tower,' said Hugo Rune, 'but the highest tower in New York. And that is?'

'The Empire State Building,' I said.

'Precisely,' said Hugo Rune.

'But hold on there,' I said. 'Someone is going to have to operate the field generator, make sure the ionisation field remains upon the Zeppelin. Surely that is a suicide mission. The operator will get blown to atoms once the bomb is dropped.'

'Unless that operator has a means of escape. A flying motorcycle combination, for instance.'

'Count Otto Black,' I said. 'Of course.'

Hugo Rune nodded and smiled.

'So tell me what your plan is,' I said. 'You have a plan, of course?'

'Hugo Rune *always* has a plan. Would you prefer that I whisper it to you? Or should I be enigmatic, tap my nose and say that I'll tell you tomorrow?'

'Let us break with tradition upon this occasion,' I said. 'Tell me out loud exactly what your plan is.'

'It is really a rather dull plan,' said the guru's guru. 'We make our way to the top of the Empire State Building and destroy the field generator. The Zeppelin will come drifting in, Wotan unaware that his craft is not invisible, and be shot down by the American anti-aircraft emplacements that are all about the harbour.'

'And *that* is it?' I asked. 'The big climax to all of these cases? That is all there is to it?'

'I expect the count will put up a fight,' said Hugo Rune. 'But, in the shell of a nut, that is all there is to it. We have the edge this time, Rizla. Because we know the meaning of the tarot card.'

I smiled and shrugged and finished my drink. 'Then I will take another of these,' I said. 'To toast our success.'

Hugo Rune ordered two more drinks so we might get into the toasting.

'What exactly *are* we drinking?' I asked the hotel barman.

'The cocktail-that-dare-not-speak-its-name,' said Fangio. For it indeed was he.

'It indeed is *you!*' I said. And quite surprised was I.

'And it indeed *is* me,' said Fangio. 'I took the liberty of following you to this hotel and saw a sign advertising for bar staff.'

'It is all so simple when it is explained,' I said.

'And isn't this a wonderful city?' said Fangio. 'So good they named it twice. I accidentally overheard your conversation with Mr Rune and I would like to offer my best wishes for the success of your endeavour.'

'Well, thank you very much, Fangio.' I raised my glass, which now contained the cocktail-that-dared-not-speak-its-name, and peered at it closely. It was of a colour that had no name and smelled like nothing on Earth. 'So do you think you will settle down in New York, or head to the West Coast, where all the sunshine is?'

'Definitely here,' said Fangio, and he brought out a bowl of chewing fat and placed it on the bar counter. 'It is my intention to open a little bar on the Lower East Side in the Genre Detective District. Fangio's Bar, I think I'll call it. And then I'll buddy up with the local colour – I believe a character named Lazlo Woodbine has an office around there. And you never know, one day I might find my way into a best-selling detective novel.' And he gulped down a piece of chewing fat and I noticed he was putting on weight.

'Well,' I said to Hugo Rune, 'this is all a bit odd, somehow. It is as if the end has already come and we are just tying up a few loose ends. I cannot help thinking that things never really happen quite as easily as that.'

Hugo Rune took out a cigar, placed it between his lips, raised the pommel of his stout stick to it and drew breath. A flame appeared as from nowhere and Mr Rune lit his cigar.

'Now *that* is just showing off,' I said. 'No good will come of *that*.'

'Rizla,' said Hugo Rune, 'for once we are ahead of the game. Savour the moment. Taste of its bitter-sweetness and things of that nature generally. Perk up, now.'

And I might well have perked up at this, but sadly I did not. Because I knew how these things have a tendency to work and all this happy-ever-aftering and everything-is-sorted nonsense never ever worked. And as if in proof of this, I spied, out of the corner of my eye, a small commotion. It was as if a number of fireflies were buzzing around in a circle near the far wall of the hotel bar. This whirling and buzzing grew slightly, then greatly, and then there was something of a flash.

And out of this flash walked two men in trenchcoats.

For out of that flash they *had* come. They certainly did not enter the bar through any doorway. But rather they simply appeared.

My mouth opened wide and I pointed at them. And Hugo Rune turned his head.

And suddenly these trenchcoat men had Lugers in their hands. And Mr Rune and I were in big trouble.

59

I could deal with the trenchcoats and even the Lugers, because I had become quite used to villains pointing them at me. What I could not really deal with was the way that these fellows appeared, in a flash and out of nowhere – *that* was *not* good.

I recognised them, of course, as the two suspicious characters who had followed us on board the liner. Although I *had* supposed that like all those posh passengers, they had gone into the Sargasso Sea to be eaten by sharks.

'Hands above your heads,' said the bigger of the two fellows, although there was not much in it when it came to height. 'Slowly and with care,' he added, but I did not take at all to the way he said it. I could not identify his accent and there was something altogether wrong about his manner of speech. His lips were out of sync with his words. It created a most disquieting effect.

'Is this a mirage?' asked Fangio. 'Or am I seeing things?'

And even though the old ones *are* always the best, now did not seem the time for merriment, what with the Lugers and all.

'Stand back,' the fellow with the dubbed-on-badly voice said to Fangio. 'You have seen nothing of this. Do you understand?'

'Well—' said Fangio.

'Best not,' I told him.

'I understand,' said the barman. 'I have seen nothing.'

'You two join us now.' And the fellow gestured with his Luger that we should go where he wished. Which appeared to be towards the blank wall from whence he had—

—There was a kind of a *whoomph* and there were some twinkling lights. And then Mr Rune and I and the two enigmatic trenchcoat wearers were no longer in the bar of the Jericho Hotel, but some-where else entirely. And somewhere altogether odd that made me feel very uneasy.

I had seen Fritz Lang's masterpiece *Metropolis* and in fact it remains to this day one of my very favourite movies. It seemed now to me that we had materialised on the set of this movie classic. In the laboratory of Rotwang the scientist/magician. There was a definite art deco feel to all the scientific paraphernalia and there were tall glass tubes, up and down through which ran crackles of electricity. So perhaps there was also a smidgen of Victor Frankenstein's laboratory also.

'Where are we?' I asked Mr Rune, in a whispery kind of a voice.

'I think,' the Magus replied, 'that the question might be better framed as *when* are we?'

'Shut up, the two of you,' went one or other of the trenchcoated weirdos, 'and bend your knees before the Nifty One.'

I shrugged and Hugo Rune shrugged, but the two fellows held their Lugers upon us, and so we bent our knees. I heard the sound of a great gong being struck and then the word 'depart'. The two fellows backed their way from the room, leaving us kneeling and baffled.

'Up you get now,' came a kindly voice. 'We can't have you kneeling there on the cold marble floor. You might get all kinds of aches and pains. Up now, if you will.' And a hand reached down and helped me up and I climbed to my feet.

'There, that's better now,' said the kindly voice.

And I looked into a kindly face. It was an old and grizzled face, but it had kindly ways about it, and although the mouth lacked for a vital tooth or two, its corners were turned up into a smile. And it was a kindly smile.

'It is you,' I said to this kindly personage. 'Diogenes, THE HERMIT. My holy guardian angel.'

'I have been called many things in my time,' said he of the kindly visage, 'but rarely anything quite so touching as that. By the by, I should have mentioned when last we met, in the Gents of the Purple Princess, that you did very well in taking my heed regarding the matter of the number twenty-seven.'

'A bus,' I said. 'With a bomb on board.'

'Yes, of course, and the bomb placed upon it by Count Otto Black.' Diogenes, or whomever he was, was helping up Hugo Rune. 'I get glimpses, you know. Sometimes they are very odd. I have one in my head at present about a gigantic rugby ball floating in the sky, making a terrible screaming noise and pouring down fire on the world.'

'Ah,' I said. 'That must mean—'

But Hugo Rune *sssshed* me to silence. 'Sir,' said he to the kindly one. 'We have not been introduced. I am Rune, whose senses keen to the vibrations of the cosmos. Whose third eye perceives the ethereality beyond aesthesia. Whose midnight growler—'

'Yes, yes, oh my, to be sure. Of course I know who you are, Mr Rune – you might say that I am your greatest fan. I have all the books of your exploits.' And now this kindly personage took himself over to a cluttered bookcase and ran a long and wrinkled finger along the leathern spines of a row of books. '*The Brightonomicon, Retromancer, The Most Amazing Man Who Ever Lived* – or perhaps that last one is for the future. But I am a fan. Do you think that I might have your autograph?' He plucked a book from the bookshelf and offered it to Hugo Rune.

'*The Book of Ultimate Truths*,' said the Magus, and approvingly. 'Bound in the skin of a scallywag, I see. Surely that is the forearm tattoo of Count Otto Black.'

'Oh my God,' I said and turned my face away.

'I thought it might amuse you.' The kindly fellow handed the Magus a silver fountain pen.

'Who shall I make it out to?' asked Himself.

'Oh, I think just a simple dedication. "To Hugo from Hugo" would suffice.'

And then I saw something that I had scarcely seen before. I saw the hand of Hugo Rune go suddenly all of a-quiver. And I saw him raise his eyes and stare into the eyes of our curious host. And I saw his mouth open and utter the words:

'*You* are *me*.'

I recall next that we sat at a table upon a balcony that overlooked a most wonderful city. It was everything that a proper city of the future should be. There were flying taxicabs and glassy tubes connecting cloud-piercing buildings one to another. And far overhead flew spaceships, and far below was the ground.

The future Hugo Rune, for so this fellow would have us believe that he was, poured drinks for us. And it occurred to me then, as perhaps it had done upon previous occasions, that no matter how weird and wonderful were my adventures with Hugo Rune, I never went thirsty.

'You are me?' said the Magus again, raising a futuristic drinking glass of the Tupperware persuasion to his lips and taking a sip from its electric-blue contents. 'You resemble me hardly at all.'

'I am one possible you, I suppose. One who turned his back upon the finer things of life. One who dedicated himself to science, rather than magic.'

Hugo Rune sighed and I sensed a great tiredness and a great sorrow as well.

'What year is this?' he asked his elder self.

'Nineteen ninety-nine,' said the other. 'Is it how you would have expected it to be?'

Hugo Rune shook his shaven head. But I nodded my hairy one.

'It is certainly what *I* had hoped for,' I said. 'I will be getting on towards fifty in nineteen ninety-nine. And it is exactly what I would have hoped for. There are jet packs and robot butlers, are there not?'

'Of course there are,' said the ancient Mr Rune. 'And first contact has been made with alien races and folk can teleport to other planets and—'

'Why have you brought us here?' asked my Hugo Rune.

'It is a delicate matter. Perhaps your acolyte here might wish to leave us whilst we talk. Go and watch some 3-D television, or something.'

'3-D television?' I said. 'Oh yes please.'

'I think *not*,' said my Mr Rune. 'What you have to say to me, you can say to him. I have no secrets from Rizla.'

Now this I did not believe to be altogether true, but I sat and listened to what was said and so never got to see *Futurama* in 3-D.

'All this,' said the ancient and slender Mr Rune, 'all that you see, this future – all of this hinges upon *your* decision, on what choices *you* make.'

The Magus looked out at the futuristic cityscape. It glinted and gleamed in the noonday sun. The air was pure as crystal. This was surely utopia.

'All of this depends upon the outcome of the Second World War,' the old one continued. 'And you have a most powerful part to play in this outcome.'

'I am on a mission,' said my Mr Rune. 'And I will set matters to right.'

'That is what I am afraid of.'

'Afraid of? I do not understand.' My Mr Rune raised a hairless eyebrow.

'It is complex, yet it is simple. All of this can only come to pass if the Allies *lose* the war. That is why I have brought you here to show you this future.'

'All of this?' And Hugo Rune shook his head. 'But there are scientific wonders here beyond what might ever reasonably be imagined. Are you telling me that such things can only occur if Germany wins the war?'

'Precisely. As you are already aware, the Tesla field generator can be calibrated to project matter through time. The one in Brentford brought back goods from the future that were to be sold across the counter of The Four Horsemen. You wisely destroyed these goods. A bonfire, I recall, in our back garden.'

I recalled that bonfire also. Mr Rune *had* made me destroy all that wonderful stuff that I had humped to his house from The Four Horsemen on the afternoon when I first met my father.

'When America is destroyed and the Allies capitulate, there will be a meeting of minds across the scientific community. The sharing of technology. Technology that will include the Tesla field generator. And with the aid of further technology acquired from the future, *this* future will come to be. And the you that I speak to now will become the me that you speak to now.'

'But only if the Allies lose?'

'If the Allies lose, a man will walk upon the Moon by nineteen fifty-five.'

'And plant there a swastika flag?'

'A new world, Hugo. A brave new world. You know that you are a man out of time. That the day of the magician is over. The future is forged from steel and glass and silicone, not from nostrums and incantations. And your name is known here, in this time. *The Book of Ultimate Truths* is as near to a Bible as there is.'

'And what of Wotan and the worship of Him?'

'A computer possessed by the spirit of a God? Did you *really* believe that to be true? But of course you did, for I am you now, as I was you then, and I remember. Magical thinking, Hugo Rune. Attributing the fantastic with the power to influence the mundane. Does Man really hear the voices of angels? Or are these voices simply the symptoms of mental illness that might be wafted away by carefully prescribed medication? You will find no Gods or magic here, my young self. We have moved beyond that now. Mankind is free of the shackles of religion and faith in the fantastic. This is a world of scientific reality. And you can play your part in bringing this world into being.'

The ancient Hugo Rune leaned back in his futuristic chair, which hovered as such a chair should, several inches above the balcony floor. And he regarded his younger self with a quizzical expression.

His younger self gazed back at him and there was a leaden silence.

'The choice is yours,' said the ancient one at length. 'Embrace the future, or continue to live in the past. You are the Retromancer. The choice is yours to make.'

And then there was a whoosh and a flash and a crash–tinkle–tinkle and the city of the future faded and was gone and we were back in the bar of Hotel Jericho.

60

'What just happened?' asked Fangio. 'I'm sure I just missed something.'

I looked up at Hugo Rune. The Magus seemed to stare, but not to see.

'Are you all right, Mr Rune?' I asked him. 'Was that *really you* that we met?'

'A possible me in a possible future.' Hugo Rune shook his head.

'But a real future, surely?' I said. 'Because that was the you who appeared to me during our first case and warned me to beware of the number twenty-seven.'

'And that is what concerns me,' said Himself. 'Without that future *me* warning *you*, we would surely be dead. But for that future me to exist, we must abandon our mission and let Germany win the war.'

'And you abandon magic and embrace modern science?'

'A paradox,' said Hugo Rune. 'But as my old pupil Wittgenstein was so fond of saying, "the laws of nature are not subject to the laws of nature".'

'I am not quite sure how that helps,' I said.

'I'll tell you what,' said Fangio. 'It's not déjà vu if it really *has* happened before.'

'And that does not help at all,' I said to Fangio. 'In fact, what was the point of you actually saying it?'

'Because you had that same conversation yesterday when you came in here. After those two blokes in trenchcoats appeared out of nowhere and spirited you away.'

'*Yesterday?*' I now said. 'That does not make any sense. We just came in here this afternoon.'

'*Yesterday* afternoon,' said Fangio. 'And you have just come in again and it's morning now.'

And I looked at Hugo Rune.

And he looked at me.

And then, as one we looked to the wall clock that hung above the bar.

'Eleven o' clock,' said Hugo Rune. 'Which means that we have but a single hour.'

'Would this be just an hour left to destroy that jet-powered invisible Zeppelin that is going to drop the atomic bomb on New York?' asked Fangio. 'Like you mentioned yesterday?'

And very loudly he asked this question. So loudly in fact that it silenced all conversation in the bar. And there had been *much* conversation and jolly conversation too, with GIs chatting to fashionable ladies and a ragtime jazz band pumping out a syncopated version of the ever popular 'I Took My Horse to Water But I Couldn't Get It Drunk'. In four-four time.

'What did you say, guy?' asked a GI of Fangio.

'My name isn't Guy,' replied the barman.

'Oh, a *wise* guy, is it?'

And Fangio looked puzzled.

And then the GI hit him with a hot pastrami on rye.

And then, for no reason that I could see, other than it appeared to be some fashionable motif of the day, the leader of the jazz band punched the drummer's lights out. And then the fists and fur began to fly.

'I think we should be making tracks,' I said to Hugo Rune. The Magus smote a sailor with his stout stick and then agreed that we should.

Now the taxi drivers in New York City are not as those in dear old London Town. Firstly you just cannot get at them. They cower behind (or rather in front of) a cage of steel, through a small slot in which you pass your payment for the trip. *In advance.*

'*In advance!*' cried Hugo Rune, raising his stout stick, before becoming painfully aware that he had no head to bring it down upon. '*IN ADVANCE?*'

'There's a war on, buddy,' the taxi driver replied. 'Even if you Limeys hadn't noticed. But don't worry yourselves about that, we'll dig you out of the ★★★★, just like we did in the sixteen-seventeen war.'

And I had never seen such whiteness on Mr Rune's knuckles before. Positively Arctic became those stick-gripping knucks.

'Money, Rizla!' cried the Magus. 'Pay this oaf and fast.'

'I do not have any money,' I said. 'And if I did have any money it would be English money and I do not think these colonials understand English currency.'

'Then give him your wristlet watch. Anything.'

'I will tell you what,' I said. 'Here, Mr Cabby, do you see this? Take us as fast as you can to the Empire State Building.'

And the cabby perused what I held in my hand. For I had poked it through the little money slot in the cage of steel. And he said, 'Yes, sir.' And he put his foot down. Hard.

Mr Rune smiled fondly upon me and said, 'Where did you get *that*?'

'Oh, *this*?' I said, glancing down at the revolver, whose snout I had poked through that little money slot and which I was now holding, trigger cocked, upon the cabby. 'I found this in the glovebox of the cab that we chased Count Otto Black down the Mall in. I have kept it on me ever since. But I have never had the opportunity to get it out and point it at somebody until now.'

Hugo Rune now did shakings of the head. 'But we were searched when we were captured by the US Marines. I do not recall them finding a pistol upon your person.'

'If you are going to be picky,' I said, 'then yes, there are many flaws in this, continuity-wise. But let us not be picky, because time is running out.'

'Excellent, Rizla, excellent.' Hugo Rune leaned back in his seat. And sighed. 'And no in-cab cocktail bar. A jolly poor show indeed.'

We raced across New York and I really did not have time to take in all of its wonder. And I know that I should have tried, because if Mr Rune failed in our mission, then within one short hour all of this would cease to be. And I *did* want to grab some moment in time, have something to cling to and remember, but my thoughts were whirling and my brain was all a-fog, because I just did not know what lay ahead.

For what *did* lie ahead?

Certainly we were heading for the Empire State Building. Where, if Mr Rune's theories were correct, the Tesla field generator would be positioned upon its uppermost pinnacle. But *then* what?

Did Mr Rune actually want now to halt the progress of the invisible Zeppelin? Knowing what potential the future held, should Germany win the war? And having met his elderly self, an elderly self who had saved our lives, who might not exist if Germany did *not* win the war. Had he actually reached a decision?

My head was *really* spinning. What *was* Mr Rune going to do? And what *would* be the result of his so doing?

'The Empire State Building, you ★★★★★★★★★★,' said the cabby, employing a term of profanity that was certainly new to me.

I thanked the cabby and in the company of Mr Rune I took my leave.

'*And no tip?*' The driver bawled after us. '★★★★★★★ ★★★★ and ★★★★★★!' But we let those pass and hurried onwards.

To be met by locked doors and a big CLOSED sign.

'Closed!' cried Hugo Rune. '*Closed!* The Empire State Building cannot be closed.'

A shabby type who was 'pushing broom' came mooching over to us. 'You can't go in there, fella,' he said. 'The bulls evacuated the building. There was a bomb warning, everybody had to leave.'

I looked at Hugo Rune.

And he in return looked at me.

'Count Otto Black,' we agreed.

'Who has the key to this building?' asked Hugo Rune.

'You'd have to ask at City Hall, fella.'

'Are there people inside this building? *Bomb-disposal people?*'

'But there's a bomb in there,' said the shabby type. 'If bomb-disposal people went in there, surely they'd get blown up if it went off.'

'He has a point there,' I said to Hugo Rune.

'*He has what!?*' And I turned away my face as the stout stick rose and fell. And then I had to do keeping-a-lookout whilst Hugo Rune applied this same stout stick to the beautiful etched glass doors of the Empire State Building, prior to us hurrying inside.

'I do not know what the point was of me keeping a lookout,' I said to Mr Rune, as we scurried across the concourse. 'Loads of people saw you breaking the glass.'

'Yes, but they are New Yorkers, they will pretend that nothing happened.'

'Then what was the point of me—' I threw up my hands as I scurried. 'Well,' I continued, 'I think that is a rather cynical view of New Yorkers. They would not like you very much if they heard you say that.'

'Perhaps they will take to me just a trifle if I save their city from nuclear destruction, then.'

'Yes, well . . . Where are we going? Should we not be going to the lift?'

'We have to pick up certain items of our baggage that I had dispatched here to be placed in a left-luggage locker.'

'I do not recall you doing *that*!' I said.

'I do not recall getting *too* picky regarding the matter of the unlikely revolver that you held upon the cabby. Best not get too picky over this, wouldn't you agree?'

And I agreed.

'You are planning to stop the bomb dropping?' I said. 'No matter what it does to the future?'

'I am perhaps risking my very existence in doing so,' replied the Magus, and, as we had reached the left-luggage lockers, fishing out a key from his waistcoat and applying it to a lock. 'But I must do what I know in my heart to be right. It is what I am, Rizla. What I might be is something else entirely.'

'So what do you have stored in the locker?' I asked.

'Let me whisper,' said Himself.

But his whispers were drowned by a terrible sound that came from the heavens above. A screaming sound as of millions of souls in horrible horrible torment. A great shadow darkened the concourse and a chill ran through my heart.

I cupped my hands over my ears and shouted, 'What is that? What is that?'

And Hugo Rune tore items from the locker and shouted that we must hurry.

'Time is running out for the world – the Zeppelin is upon us.'

61

It swung in the sky above New York, made visible to all. No larger craft was ever built by Man. It was surely nearly a mile in length and hundreds of feet in height. It shimmered, ghostly silver-grey, and uniformed figures were to be glimpsed at work upon its numerous decks. The great jet engines, mounted beneath the rear of this fantastic craft, throbbed and hummed. And upon the sides of this sky-borne warship, the swastikas, blood-red and fearsome, shone with a horrible clarity.

In the streets beneath there was panic. Fleeing, screaming people terrorised by what had materialised above. By this and by the ghastly sounds that issued from it. Rows of silver-horned loudspeakers poured down a sonic assault on the city below.

Mr Rune and I were in the lift now and that lift was moving up apace. 'They have certainly honed their skills in the martial arts of sound,' said Hugo Rune, 'since our encounter with Count Otto's daughter at Roberta Newman's Musical Academy. It is the frequency of fear, Rizla. They seek to terrorise the city before they utterly destroy it.'

'But why take the risk of making the Zeppelin visible? It clearly crept in stealthily under cover of the field generator's beam.' We were many storeys up, but with many yet to go.

'Do you think to understand the ego of a God?' asked Hugo Rune. 'We are dealing with forces here which might even, to some small degree, be beyond *my* understanding.'

By the time we reached the roof it seemed that all of New York was in chaos. The mighty Zeppelin loomed above, blotting out a third of the sky. And down from it showered balls of flame that drifted to the thoroughfares below to explode in hideous gouts of liquid fire.

'How can we stop *this*?' I shouted, as I tried to make myself heard above the horror-screams that roared from the airship's horned loud-speakers. 'It is too big, what can we do?'

'I must recalibrate the field generator, Rizla. *You* must cause a diversion.'

'Me?' And I clung to the guardrail where the tourists came to view the city beneath. A city now in a Hellish turmoil. The day itself was still and no wind blew to fling me from my perch. But it was oh so high that it was frightful. The world of Men so small below, and a Mad God hanging on high.

'A diversion?' I said. And then I said, 'Oh no!'

For I had spied out the field generator, manned by Count Otto Black.

'Rune!' he crowed from his lofty abode. 'Somewhat late for the party. But no matter. A big present will be heading your way, in precisely . . .' and he fished out a pocket watch and examined its face '. . . five minutes. Where is your God *now*, Hugo Rune?'

And Count Otto did that maniac laugh and raised his fists to the sky. I do have to say that he did look every bit the supervillain at that moment. Long and gaunt and all over horrid. Clad in a spiked Prussian helmet, with a German eagle emblem on the front. Flying goggles, a magnificent plumed coat, leather trousers, leather boots, that great black beard flying every which way. His gloved hands, clenched into thin fists, thrown above.

'It is all over for you now, Rune. And I must say farewell.' And he threw a switch, as such villains will, and the mighty airship vanished.

'Goodbye, you fools!' cried Count Otto Black, mounting his flying motorcycle.

'Rizla,' shouted Hugo Rune. 'I feel I need you to provide me with a little more than a diversion. I need the key to the field generator.'

'*Key?*' I shouted back. 'This is new.'

'The count has locked the controls. I need to recalibrate them if I am to save the day. And indeed win the war. He has the key, Rizla. You must take it from him.'

'Me?'

'Yes, you.' And Hugo Rune thrust in my direction the Gravitite disc, which was amongst various other items we had brought up from the left-luggage lockers oh so far below us now.

'And put these on,' said Hugo Rune. And he now flung goggles at me.

'Oh,' I said. 'I tried them on before. And all was wrong when I looked through them.'

'All was *right*, Rizla. Put them on – they will enable you to see the Zeppelin.'

And now we heard the roar of the count's motorcycle combination and he waved to us as he swept upwards upon it and into the 'clear' blue sky.

'I am frightened,' I cried to Mr Rune. 'We are too high. I am frightened.' And my hands began to flap and I began to turn around in small circles.

'And enough of *that*!' And Hugo Rune cuffed me across my chops and said, 'Be brave now, Rizla. All depends upon you.'

I took into myself the deepest of breaths and climbed onto the disc of Gravitite. And then I shouted, 'Up and away!' And in a state of fear above and beyond any previous states of fear that I had ever experienced, I was up and away.

The count on his motorcycle rose higher and higher and I on my disc gave chase. I tried very hard to focus my mind upon the fact that this was *really* happening, because I was seriously beginning to wonder whether I might just be dreaming the entire thing and be about to wake up at any moment in my cosy bed in Brentford, with the morning sun looking in at my window.

But then the count fired at me.

The bullet ricocheted off the Gravitite disc and I nearly fell to my doom.

'Oh no you do not, you blackguard,' I cried and I did nifty manoeuvrings. And I think I might well have swept around and knocked him right off his flying motorbike, had I not struck my head upon something I had not noticed and knocked *myself* almost into unconsciousness.

I managed an, 'Oh,' and also, 'That hurt,' and then I became aware. Through Mr Rune's goggles I saw things aright, and liked not all that I saw.

I was aboard the Zeppelin now. I had clouted my head upon an iron stanchion and fallen onto one of the many decks. And the Gravitite disc had—

'Oh no!' I could see the disc spinning off into the sky, getting further and further away.

Which was not good.

Far below me now I could see the roof of the Empire State Building and the field generator perched upon it, and Mr Rune frantically trying to do something or other to the controls. Although I did not know what he intended, and now, as I looked at my watch to see the final minutes ticking away, I realised that it no longer mattered. It was all too late. We had failed, the evil count had won. The atom bomb was about to drop and history about to change.

'Oh no,' I said. 'Oh no, oh no. Oh no. I cannot let this happen. I must do something.'

'You could jump,' said the voice of Count Otto Black. Who was climbing from his motorcycle combination, which was now parked nearby on the deck. 'Or I could fling you over the side. Or perhaps I know a better fate for you. One where you stand by helplessly and watch as your fat mentor and all that lies spread beneath him is annihilated.'

And a Luger pistol was trained on me once more and Count Otto Black urged me forwards.

If I had been in the mood to enjoy it I would oh so easily have fallen deeply in love with the Zeppelin. It was a thing of unutterable beauty and near faultless design. A thing, it must be said, that was not of the nineteen forties, but rather of some futuristic time.

Of the very time, perhaps, that Mr Rune and I had been transported to. Where we had met his future self.

'Forwards,' urged the count, and we entered the Zeppelin's flight deck. Sky-men dressed in elaborate uniforms, which were more of a Victorian style than of some possible future, worked at dials and stopcocks, pulling great levers and viewing shining consoles that ran with twinkling lights.

And at the very heart of this flight deck there was a raised golden dais, and upon this a throne of tubular glass, and upon this . . . *the robot*.

And this was a mighty fine robot. Far better than the one that I had viewed at Bletchley Park. This was a real vision-of-an-alternative-future sort of robot. All gold and finely muscled as a naked man. And there was something about it that was beyond any concept of 'Robot'. This was a mechanical being, but a *living* mechanical being. This was a thing of metal, possessed by the spirit of a God. And this construct of terrible power and wonder turned its head towards me. And if I had earlier known fear, it was as nothing before this.

'Black.' And its voice rang out and seemed to rattle my bones. The count threw me to the flight deck floor and placed his foot on my back.

'Heil, Wotan,' cried the count. And all the sky-men halted in their workings and joined him in this heil.

'Is all prepared, Black? Is all satisfactory?'

'All is prepared, O great one. The ionizing ray of the field generator is locked upon this craft. We can no longer be observed from below, and the moment the bomb falls from our bomb bay, we will be instantly teleported back to Berlin. There you may sit in glory, to await the Allies' surrender.'

And Count Otto Black almost did the mad laughings. But he restrained himself, for to do mad laughings in front of an ancient God reborn into the body of a robot was probably inappropriate.

I now struggled to get at my revolver, but it was all sort of bunched up in my jacket beneath me and the count's long foot was pressing down hard on my back.

'**Begin the countdown**,' came the terrible voice, rattling now my fillings and raising my hair on end.

I did not see who pressed the button, but one of the blighters did. Because now there came that pulled-emergency-cable-siren noise which signals that something somewhere is shortly to explode.

'**Ten**.' I struggled. But to no effect at all.

'**Nine**.' The count hauled me up.

'**Eight**.' He dragged me from the flight deck.

'**Seven**.' He took me to the rail.

'**Six**.' He lifted me high.

'**Five**.' He laughed in my face.

'**Four**.' Then I spat in his.

'**Three**.' Then he flung me.

Down

Two

And down

One

Zero

62

The great bomb fell with a rush and a scream and I fell down and down.

Then suddenly there came another rushing to my ears and something swept up and took me.

I found myself now in the arms of Hugo Rune, who smiled. and said, 'Perk up, Rizla.'

Which offered at least a moment of joy.

Before the bomb exploded.

63

And now I stood, though rather shakily, in the bar at Hotel Jericho. And Fangio was serving us cocktails that not even he knew the names of and I really really wanted to know just how he was there and I was there and Hugo Rune was there and all of New York was still standing.

'It was a dud,' I said to Hugo Rune. 'After everything, it failed to explode. You plucked me out of the sky by flying up to me on the Gravitite disc, I understand *that*, and please please please let me thank you for once more saving my life. But the bomb failed to explode. Thank all goodness for that.'

'But it *did* explode,' said Hugo Rune, 'and caused much devastation.'

'I think you will find that it did *not*,' I said, 'for we are both still here.'

'Ah yes, young Rizla. But then the atomic bomb did *not* explode *here*. Nor either did it explode *today*.'

'And it will be necessary,' I said, 'for you to explain to me just what you mean by that.'

'You did very well, Rizla,' said Himself. 'You did what I hoped you would do and kept their attention on you, rather than me. You see, I had a spare key for the field generator. A gentleman can never carry too many keys, I am sure that you agree.'

'Go on then,' I said. 'Carry on.'

'I recalibrated the field generator. We already knew that it was capable of transporting matter through time as well as space, did we not?'

'The count had set it to teleport the Zeppelin to Berlin the moment the bomb was dropped,' I said. 'Did it get there?'

'Not to Berlin, no.'

'I am intrigued,' I now said. 'You have me on the hook. Now reel me in, as it were.'

Hugo Rune smiled. 'I have had this little newspaper cutting in my wallet for several decades,' he said, 'and I never knew until today why I carried it. Here, have a read of it and tell me what you think.'

And the Perfect Master handed me a rather dog-eared and much-folded newspaper cutting and I read from it, aloud.

CURIOUS EVENT IN TUNGUSKA

Reports from our Russian correspondent state that at around 7.14 a.m. on the morning of 30 June 1908, a dreadful explosion occurred near Podkamennaya upon the Tunguska River. It is estimated that some eighty million trees have been knocked over and that an area of eight hundred square miles is affected.

The cause of this explosion is unknown, but many radical theories are being postulated. One report tells of a great shining craft seen in the morning sky moments prior to the explosion. We await further reports.

'The Tunguska Event,' I said. 'I have read of it and you—'

'With the aid of the field generator. I recalibrated it to transport the falling bomb to a time and a place where, even though it would explode, it would be so far out of the way as to cause little concern or danger to life and limb.'

'Incredible,' I said. 'Simply incredible.'

'Thank you, Rizla,' said Hugo Rune. 'I do my best to impress.'

'And that you certainly do.'

A faraway look appeared in the eyes of Hugo Rune. 'It isn't easy being a Perfect Master,' he said.

And I nodded thoughtfully.

'I only make it *look* easy,' he continued.

And I grinned somewhat at this. 'So what happened to Count Otto and to Wotan?' I asked.

'A shining craft seen in the morning sky? Caught too in the beam of the field generator. Gone, but not forgotten.'

'Incredible,' I said once more. 'I do not know what else to say.'

And so I did not really say very much more about anything. And Mr Rune and Fangio and I drank nameless cocktails until it was chucking-out time.

'I am going up to my room now,' I told Hugo Rune. 'I will see you in the morning.'

'Perhaps,' said Hugo Rune. 'Or perhaps not. But whatever the case, let me thank you, Rizla. Once more, together we have triumphed. It has been a good adventure and no more noble or worthy companion could I have had than yourself. Thank you, Rizla, thank you.'

And Hugo Rune gave me a manly hug.

And I gave him a hug too.

And then we shook hands and parted company and I took myself away to find my cosy bed.

DEATH

64

DEATH

I awoke to find myself once more in my cosy bed. The sun peeped in at my window and it was another day. And I yawned and stretched and then I became fully aware of my surroundings.

'Oh my,' I went. And, 'What?' I went. And things of that nature, confusedly. And I leaped from my bed and rushed to my window and flung the curtains wide.

Before me lay the town of Brentford, beautiful as ever.

But—

I turned back to my bed and turned on the wireless set.

'And hello all,' came the unsober tones of the Voice of Free Radio Brentford. 'Another day to say, "Stick it to the Man, I'm pulling a sickie,"' and Lad Nicholson could be heard taking a noisy toke of something illegal.

'So far, so very good,' I said.

But—

I hastily dressed and ran down to breakfast.

'Something special for you today, my hen,' said my Aunt Edna, smiling as she said it.

I made a face of suspicion and asked, 'Not Bratwurst?'

'Heavens no, who would eat such foreign muck? This is a *double* full English.' And my aunt placed before me the breakfast of the Gods and I fell to it with knife and fork and washed it down with tea.

'This is wonderful,' I told my aunt, even though it is rude to speak with your mouth full. 'Probably the bestest breakfast I have ever tasted. But can I ask you two questions – and please do not think that I am a mentalist regarding the first of these.'

My Aunty Edna worried at a sprout with a Woolworth's patent

sprout worrier. 'Go on then, ask,' she said. 'You teenagers will be the death of me every which way as it is.'

'The first question,' I said, 'and please do not laugh – but who won the Second World War?'

My aunt did not laugh.

But—

She paused.

'Now that,' she finally said, 'depends on what you mean by "won".'

'Did *we* win?' I said. 'Did the Allies win?'

'You could say that, I think, yes.'

And I went, 'Phew,' as one might do, and forked down further breakfast.

'You said you had two questions,' said my aunt. 'What is the second?'

I dabbed at my mouth with an oversized red gingham serviette. 'I was just wondering,' I said, 'as to why I have been given this treat of the double English breakfast?'

My aunt did smilings upon me. 'I think you know why,' she said.

I shook my head and said I did not.

'Such a modest boy,' said my aunt.

I stared at this lady and wondered. Did she know? Was she somehow aware of what had happened? That what had been had ceased to be? Or had never been?

But I did not want to think too much about that and though I would remember for ever my adventures with Mr Rune – who I was already missing quite badly – thinking too hard about what exactly they all meant and how they all worked was likely to bring on a collapse of the brain box. And I did not wish to live out the rest of my days as a hopeless loony.

'I do not know quite what to say,' I said to my aunt.

'Then say nothing. Just make me proud.'

'Just make you proud? All right.'

'Get that big breakfast inside you and make me proud, all right?'

'Absolutely all right,' I said. 'Everything is absolutely all right.'

'Well, it will be,' said my aunt, 'when you come back later from your visit to the labour exchange . . . WITH A JOB.'

But—

But there were no buts to be butted. And so I finished my breakfast, washed and brushed up and was ushered through the front door of our home at the end of my Aunt Edna's broom.

Work!

Well, it was going to have to come to that eventually and I knew it well enough. It was clear that Mr Rune had returned me to my own time on the exact same day as I had left it. Which once more made telling the tale of my adventures with him sound like the tallest of all tall tales or a work of Far-Fetched Fiction.

But—

And I looked all around and about me. The street signs were only in English. No brass band music issued from open windows and no swastika bunting sullied the skyline. All was as it should be and I was happy for that.

And it was that Monday morning again. But a good and free one this time. Although there was still that matter of finding a job, and that, it seemed, had to be faced.

But—

Perhaps, I thought to myself, now would be the time to get into the smoking of the Wild Woodbine, which so far I had failed to get to grips with. Having that ciggie protruding from my face would add that extra bit of professionalism. And if a job I had to find, then I would do so in the company of Wild Woodbine.

And it was Monday morning, so Norman Hartnel's dad (the fellow I had met during my wartime adventure who was so keen to mete out corporal punishment upon me) would be away, and his son, my friend, behind the counter to sell me these very Wild Woodbines.

So all would be well and a happy ever after.

I reached Norman's shop and I peeped in through the window. I looked at the names of the products. Not a German sweetie was there to be seen, but many an ad for Wild Woodbine.

I pushed on the door and the shop bell rang and I took a wander inside.

Norman was numbering papers. The paperboy had not turned in for work this morning, preferring to take the advice of Lad Nicholson, stick it to the Man and pull a sickie.

Norman looked up from his numberings and viewed me with evident distaste. 'I shouldn't really be talking to you,' he said. 'Getting us thrown out of the pub last night. You are a menace you are.'

'I apologise for all that,' I said. For *all that* now seemed oh so long ago. 'I know I behaved badly. Something to do with only being served German lager, was it not?'

'It was no such thing,' said Norman. 'Although . . .' And he made a curious face. 'When I come to think about it, I can't actually remember what it was about. But whatever it was, I do know that it was all your fault.'

'Fair enough,' I said. 'A packet of Wild Woodbine, please.'

'Don't be silly,' said Norman. 'You are underage.'

'I have to get a job today,' I said, 'and—'

But—

Norman now fell into laughter.

'Get a job?' he went, between mirthful outbursts. '*You* get a job? You lazy, shiftless—' And he ha-ha-hah'd.

'It is not funny,' I said. 'Well, I suppose it is quite funny—'

But—

The shop doorbell went *ping* at the entry of a customer.

'Come back later,' said Norman to me. 'I'm busy.' And he dabbed at his eyes with an undersized plain brown hankie that matched his shopkeeper's coat. 'And I have proper customers to serve. Oh dear!'

And I saw Norman's face literally cloud over and his mouth fall open and his eyes go all a-goggle in his head.

'What is the matter with you?' I asked. But he was staring past me. I turned to see what he was staring at.

And there stood Count Otto Black.

65

The count wore his spiked Prussian helmet, plumed leather greatcoat and fine riding boots. His beard looked all-over bristly and his eyes seemed lit from within.

In his hand he held a Luger pistol and this he pointed at me.

'Oh,' I said. And then, 'Oh dear. I really thought you were dead.'

'In Tunguska? With Wotan? With the dreams of a mighty tomorrow?'

'That tomorrow should never be. That tomorrow was wrong.'

'Is that *him*?' Norman's mouth was moving now. 'Is that the man you were talking about last night? Is that—'

'Shut up!' said Count Otto Black.

'Is it Hugo Rune?' asked Norman.

'Hugo Rune?' Count Otto aimed his Luger at the loquacious young shopkeeper. 'I will do for that bloated popinjay! But first I will do for you.' And the Luger swung once more in my direction. 'You helped to ruin the plans that would have changed the world. You destroyed my future and now I end yours.'

But—

The shop doorbell went *ping* once more and another person entered.

'Through to the back,' hissed Count Otto Black, 'or I will shoot everyone here.'

'All right,' I said. 'Please do not go shooting any innocent people, I am going, I am going.'

Norman lifted the counter flap and Count Otto Black urged me forwards.

I entered the grim and ill-lit kitchenette, with the count's Luger pressing most hard at the nape of my neck. The count closed the door behind us and we stood there in the all but darkness. And I could feel my heart beating loudly and horrid blood all pumping in my ears.

'You have no idea what you have done,' intoned the count. 'No idea how large the chaos you have wrought upon this world.' And he pushed me hard with his pistol.

I took a sort of leap in the dark. And turned to view through the gloom the horrid face of the man who would murder me. 'I did what was right and Mr Rune did what was right. That future was never meant to be. That future was evil, as you are evil.'

'Oh what a brave, outspoken boy.' And the count did evil *harr-harrings*. 'You understand nothing. Rune and I are linked together, our names on either side of the page slip cut from the book of Life and Death. He cannot kill me and I cannot kill him. But should one cease to be in this world, then so shall the other. And so he and I dance on through history. And he has his foolish acolyte boys such as you who do his bidding, but understand not the balance that exists between he and I. I have put paid to other Rizlas before you. And now I put paid to you.'

'You will have to speak up a bit,' I said. 'I cannot hear you properly.'

'What?' cried the count. 'Are you mad? I tell you that you are going to die and you ask me to speak up a bit?'

'Well, come forwards a bit, then,' I said. 'You might miss if you try to shoot me from there. It is so dark in here.'

'Insane. You are quite insane.' And Count Otto Black took a single step forwards—

But—

He did not take a second one.

I heard a kind of horrified gasp. And then I heard nothing more.

I stepped very carefully and switched on the light to the kitchen-ette. A fly-specked bulb illuminated boxes, bits and bobs and bobbins—

And the Bottomless Pit.

It yawned there where Norman had uncovered it, and I well remembered our former conversation regarding said uncovering. Dark and foreboding it was and endlessly down it went. And I leaned fearfully over its brink and peered into its endless depths.

'Count Otto,' I called. 'Can you hear me?'

But—

Answer came there none. Only the rank smell of brimstone, which I had, of course, noticed when I entered the shop. But had not bothered to comment upon, because, after all, I *did* know where it came from.

'Oh yes,' I said. And I made a fist with my right hand and punched at the air with it. 'You are gone. Down into the pit. Goodbye to you, oh yes!'

The kitchenette door opened and Norman's face peeped in.

'Oh thank goodness for that,' he said. 'I thought you'd both fallen in. It's the Bottomless Pit, you know, out of the Book of Revelation. I have got great plans for it. Plans that could change the world. Bring about a utopian future—'

But—

I edged my way around the pit and patted Norman's shoulder. 'I have to go and find a job now,' I said. 'See you later in The Purple Princess for a beer?'

'Lunchtime,' said Norman. 'The new barman turns a blind eye to underage drinking.'

'Goodbye, Norman,' I said to Norman.

'Goodbye,' he said to me.

66

I helped myself to Wild Woodbines and took my leave of the shop. Then I took myself to the Memorial Park and sat down on a bench. I *would* look for work, I really would, but perhaps this was not the day.

'I got him,' I said to myself. As I placed a Wild Woodbine into my mouth and lit up. 'I got him good, I did.'

And I heard the sound of cackling laughter, which nearly had me wetting myself.

'You *did* get him good,' said an ancient. Who somehow now sat at the far end of the bench. Though I had not seen him arrive.

'Oh dear,' I said. 'You startled me.' And then I looked hard at this ancient. He was an aged ancient ancient, but with a kindly face.

'You,' I said. 'It is you from the future. The future Hugo Rune.'

'It is now the Hugo Rune of the now,' said Hugo Rune of the now.

'But,' I said. '*My* Mr Rune. I do not understand. You are so old and—'

'Done?'

'Distinguished, I might have said.'

'But I *am* done,' said Hugo Rune. 'And I am happy for it. My time is past now, Rizla. And you have freed me from a future I had no care for. I am a magician. I have no time for a future which lacks for magic. It is your world now, Rizla. Make of it what you will.'

'Why are you suddenly old?' I asked.

'Because you have freed me from this world. You have destroyed Count Otto Black. He can never return from where you dispatched him to. He is gone for ever. And as my life is linked to his, when he is gone then so am I.'

'Oh no!' I cried and tears sprang to my eyes. 'Then I have killed you. I would have anything other than that. You have been to me the father I never had. I cannot have killed you. Please say that it is not so.'

'I thank you for it, Rizla. I am free now. Write of our adventures. Tell the world of Hugo Rune. Feel free to exaggerate. But write me as a kindly man. And if they ever dramatise your book, I would like David Warner to play my part.'

And before my eyes the Magus was fading.

'Goodbye, Rizla,' he said.

But I cried, 'No, please, please do not go.'

But—

And his hand touched mine for a moment.

And Hugo Rune was gone.

And I sat there on that bench and I had a good old cry. That wonderful figure was no more and I would never ever see him again. I felt guilty, I felt sad, but I knew that he was happy.

He had done what he had set out to do and I had helped him do it. All was as it should be now, but I felt a terrible loss. I wiped away a tear and sighed and sucked upon my Woodbine.

'And would you just be sitting there moping your life away and not sharing your fags?' asked a voice that I knew rather well.

I looked up into the smiling face of one John Vincent Omally.

'Would you look at yourself, Jim,' said he. 'My bestest friend draped over a park bench like a wino. What is that all about? I am asking myself.'

'I have had a bit of an emotional time, as it happens, John,' I said. And I offered my cigarette.

My bestest friend took it and sucked upon same. 'I was just in Norman's,' he said. 'The lad tells me that you are thinking to take to *The Work*.'

'Such is expected of me,' I said, taking back my cigarette and giving it a puff. 'Although I do have to confess that I am not altogether keen.'

Omally seated himself beside me and stared off into the distance. 'I am sure great days lie ahead for the both of us,' he said. 'Although I do not believe that these days will involve us getting too deeply involved in *The Work*.'

'You really think so?' I asked my bestest friend.

'Would I lie to you?' said John Omally.

'No, I do not think that you would.'

And we sat there together and shared another cigarette.

And we talked of this thing, that thing and the other. And if this had been a movie, rather than real life, the camera would have slowly pulled out from the two of us sitting there, moved back and upwards taking in the Memorial Park, the rows of Victorian terraced houses, the pubs and the shops and the flat blocks and all that is Brentford. And then, perhaps, by some FX cleverness pulled out further, from Brentford to all of London, to all of England and then to all of the world.

And then perhaps off into the darkness of space.

Then fade to the words

THE END.

THE ORDER
OF THE
GOLDEN SPROUT

— . —

The New Official
ROBERT RANKIN
Fan Club

— . —

12 Months Membership consists of . . .

Four Fantastic Full Colour Issues of the Club Magazine featuring:

Previously unpublished work by Robert Rankin
News
Reviews
Event details
Articles
And much more.

Club Events @ free or discounted rates

Access to members only website area

Membership is £16 worldwide and available through the club website:

www.thegoldensprout.com

The Order of the Golden Sprout exists thanks to the permission
and support of Robert Rankin and his publishers.